AF438752

THE ENCHANTED SWANS

CHRISTY NICHOLAS

GREEN DRAGON PUBLISHING

Second Edition 2023

Copyright © 2017 Christy Nicholas
Cover art © 2022 by GetCovers
Internal design © 2023 by Green Dragon Publishing

All rights reserved. No part of this book may be reproduced in any form or by any electronic or mechanical means including information storage and retrieval systems, except in the case of brief quotations embodied in critical articles or reviews, without permission in writing from its publisher, Green Dragon Publishing.

The characters and events portrayed in this book are fictitious or are used fictitiously. Any similarity to real persons, living or dead, is purely coincidental and not intended by the author.

All brand names and product names used in this book are trademarks, registered trademarks, or trade names of their respective holders. Green Dragon Publishing is not associated with any product or vendor in this book.

Published by Green Dragon Publishing
Beacon Falls, CT
www.GreenDragonArtist.com
All rights reserved.

MAP OF IRELAND

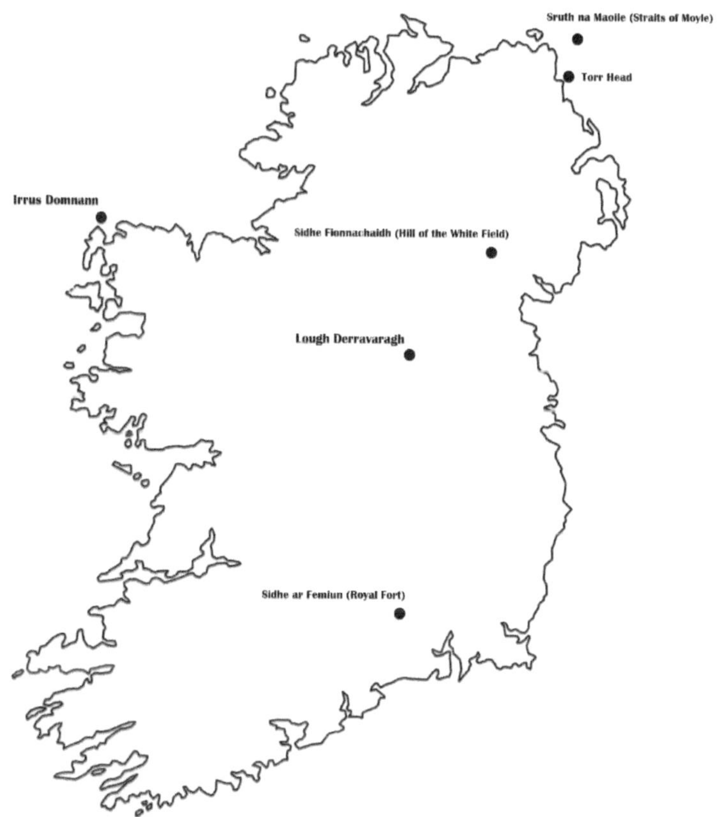

Pronunciation Guide

NAMES
Áedammair – AWD-uh-mare
Aed - Ayd
Aed Mór – Ayd Moor
Aillbha – AL-vuh
Aobh Bán – Eve Bawn
Aoife Rua – EE-fuh ROO-uh
Banbha – BAN-vuh
Bé Chuille – BAY Khuill-eh
Bilé – BI-lee
Bodb Dearg – BOH derg
Cailín – Kaw-LEEN
Caomhóg – KEEV-owg
Cliach – KLEE-ikh
Deoch – DEE-uhk
Dian Cécht – DEE-an Keckt
Donnchadh – DUN-chuh
Ériu – EYHR-ooh
Fiachra – FEE-kruh
Fionn MacCumhall – FINN Muh Cool
Fionnuala – Finn-OOL-uh
Fir Bolg – FEAR bol-uhg
Fomhóire – Fom-OR-eh
Illbreach – ILL-brehk
Lasairfhiona – LASS-ar-een-uh
Macha – MAHK-uh Midhir – MID-ear
Mochán – MUH-kawn
Niamh – NEEV Nuada
Parthalón – PAR-tho-lawn
Saoirse – SEER-shuh
Scáthach – SKAT-huk
Scuida – SKWEE-duh
Tadhg – Tyg
Tuatha Dé Dannan – TOO-ah day DAN-in (People of the Goddess Danu, The Fairy Folk)

PLACES

Carraig na Rón – CARE-ig na Rown (Rock of the Seals)
Dun Sgathaich – Doon Skath-ihg
Emhain Macha – EH-vin MAKH-uh (Navan Fort)
Uisneach – ISH-nuhk
Inis Gluaire—IN-ish GLOO-reh
Irrus Domnann – ERR-us DOW-an
Lough Derravaragh – Lock DAR-uh-ver-uh
Saol Eile – Sail ELL-eh (Otherlife/Afterlife)
Sídhe ar Femuin – Shee ar FEHM-ihn
Sídhe Fionnachaidh – Shee FINN-ahk-eethe (Hill of the White Field)
Sruth na Maoile – Srooth nah Mwayl
Tailltin – TALL-chin
Tír na nÓg – Tear nuh NOHG (An otherworld, or Land of the Young)

OTHER

Ard-Rí – Ard-ree (High King)
Banríon – Bahn-REE-ahn (Queen)
Bantiarna – Bahn-tee-AR-nah (Lady or princess)
Filíd – FEE-lee (The Order of the Filíd, plural. Filí is singular)
Geas – Gesh (A curse or compulsion)
Iunula – EE-noo-la (A solid gold mantle worn over the shoulders)
Léine/léinte – LEYN-yuh (A tunic/tunics down to the knee)
Ollamh – OLL-av (An advanced Filíd)
Samhain – SOW-ehn (End of the Harvest Festival/New Year)
Tiarna – tee-AR-nah (King)

Chapter One

"We would not give up our own country—Ireland—if we were to get the whole world as an estate, and the Country of the Young along with it."
-- **Isabella Augusta, Lady Gregory.**

In the 20th winter of Ard-Rí Bodb Dearg's reign (460 BCE)

I didn't want to set my mother's body on fire, but everyone was watching.

As Fionnuala, one of the People known as the Tuatha Dé, and the eldest child of *Tiarna* Lir, I knew my duty. That didn't mean I had to like it.

My throat burned with tears, but they weren't proper. I wanted to yell and scream, to pull Mother out of her bower and beg her to wake up, to stop this foolish sham. But it was no sham.

A curved horn blew, announcing the final procession. With a slow march, the guard carried the meadow-sweet bower with Mother's body on top. She was dressed in finery and painted in tribal markings. She carried a single white rose in her hand. The bearers also bore painted marks and wore traditional white garb. Their feet were bare upon the stony path.

After they'd placed her bower on the pyre, Cliach the bard handed me his torch. I must burn my beloved mother's body and send her off to Tir na nÓg, the Land of the Ever Young.

I swallowed down a lump in my throat and could barely breathe. After this, I could give in to the hammering tears, to cry and rage. When I was alone, I could punch the wooden wall until my hand bled. But now, I must do my duty.

Father stood as still as stone, his back rigid and his face blank. As the widower, his face was painted with more tribal symbols. He had no words to say, no gestures to make, which was just as well. If he moved, he might have broken into a thousand pieces.

I touched the flame to the closest corner of the meadow-sweet bower. One branch curled up in glowing, crackling embers. The burning brush was strangely mesmerizing, a beautiful pattern of magic and sorrow.

A stem popped with the heat and the flame grew. Soon, the heat drove me back to my father, Lir, and brother, Aed. Back to watch Mother's sparks fly into the darkened sky as her spirit went home.

Chief Druid Bé Chuille, tall and thin with her iron-gray hair and weathered face carved from ash, lifted her face to the night. She wore her formal cloak of office, made with a rainbow of bird feathers, and spoke the final ritual words. "I bless the eternal spirit of our much-loved daughter, Aobh Ban, to the Land of the Ever-Young. May she be forever beautiful in our memories."

Mother's hair crisped into sparks, flying into the twilight summer sky. They danced toward the stars and glowed brightly in the indigo gloom. The final fragments of my mother's life spiraled away from our world.

Tuatha Dé didn't die, not like humans did. We lived forever after in the Otherlife, amongst those who passed before us.

But those left behind feel the pain of their leaving. We miss them and cherish their memories as their abandoned body burns into the sky and their spirit travels to the stars.

I clutched Aed's hand, and he no longer fidgeted. It seemed like forever until the sparks faded.

Father's face crumpled and he turned away, breaking protocol. My aunt, Aoife Rua, stopped him with a hand on his arm, speaking into his ear. Father stared at her and scowled, but then shook his head and left.

The *ard-rí*, our high king, kept silent about Father's rude departure, so nobody else spoke. And while I ached to escape to my own tears, it fell to me to stay, to uphold family honor and play host. Somewhere in the back of my mind, I raged against my father escaping and leaving this duty to me.

Now, we shuffled back to the main hall for a great feast with much drinking, relating cherished memories of the deceased. It should be a joyful wake, a celebration of her life, but I had no heart to celebrate.

I touched the complex braids that made my head ache and wished I could comb them out. I wanted to run away from the crowds of well-wishing strangers. Run away to the forest, or to my room, anywhere but this great bustle of people and clamor. To climb up the flower-strewn hills to an empty stone circle and escape the crush of noise and bodies.

But if I shirked my duty, who would it fall to then? My little brother, all of eight winters old? The twin babies? Cliach, our bard who was already drunk? Maire Mór, our headwoman? No, I must take charge.

Maire's kitchen girls were passing around platters of flatbread, cheese, milk, honey, nuts, and fruit for the visitors.

My raven, Hawlen, fluttered in and perched on my shoulder, landing on the padded patch designed for that purpose. Most royal children did this on all their clothing to reduce the wear and tear their companions created.

She cawed and asked, "Is everything ready for after the feast?"

I gave a solemn nod. "Maire Mór has everything in hand. I made sure yesterday."

Each room would be filled with welcoming gifts and fragrant flowers. A cauldron of steaming rosewater would be set near the crackling hearth, ready for washing.

In the main hall, I slipped into my seat. My stomach roiled, and I waved away a platter of bread when my brother offered it.

The *ard-rí*, the leader of the People, Bodb Dearg, was a bear of a man with wild red hair and a forked beard. His wife, *Banríon* Dervla, was short with fair skin and dark hair.

When they'd arrived the day before, my father was nowhere to be found, so I'd approached our royal guests with my hands out, palms up in welcome. "I welcome you both, you and your kin. I welcome you into our homes. I welcome you to our flatbread and our ale. Be safe and sound within our walls."

After a nod of acknowledgement for the formal guest-offer, the *ard-rí* had offered a small basket. The flatbread and cheese within represented the guest's gift and it was my duty, as host, to return an equal gift.

I gave him two stone pots of honey-butter. The *ard-rí's* stern face broke into a wide grin as he took the pots. "Fionnuala! You look well, my dear girl. You are so like your fair mother. But where is Lir?"

With a bow, I said, "He's still unwell from his grief. Please, do excuse him. Would you care to follow me to your rooms?"

"Of course, my dear, show us the way!"

Our hillfort, *Sídhe Fionnachaidh*, the Hill of the White Field, wasn't as big as the royal one, but large enough to hold twenty roundhouses of various sizes plus the main feast hall, stables, and pens. A palisade of sharpened logs surrounded the whole hillfort as well as a glamor veil to keep the Milesians from finding us.

Once our visitors were settled in, I sought our bard, Cliach, who was still asleep in his room. I peeked inside, but after noting the empty meadskin in his hand, slammed the door shut to wake him. "Cliach! Wake up, Bard! You were supposed to be out at Mother's bower, performing the final rituals!"

With a groan, he held his head. He blinked through bloodshot eyes. "Aobh? Aobh, are you here with me, at last?"

A cold chill ran down my spine at the mention of my Mother. I shook the chill off and picked up one of his discarded *léine*, tossing it on his bed. "Cliach, it's Fionnuala, you silly man. Get up, you're late! The Ard-Rí has arrived!"

The Filíd, those who spoke to the Gods, would assist Mother's spirit to Tir na nÒg. Cliach was of the lowest priestly caste, but he was our bard, and therefore must attend such duties.

I glanced at him now, either drunk again or still drunk from the day before. I didn't know which and truly didn't care. Next to him sat Mother's younger sisters, Aoife Rua and Aillbhe. They both looked so much like my mother, yet just different enough to look like a cruel parody of her.

Aoife Rua, the eldest, came to me with a sad smile. "I am so very sorry for your mother's death. I will miss my sister dearly."

Accepting her hug, I was unable to breathe for the lump in my throat.

My aunt held my shoulders and searched my eyes. "You will be the woman of your hillfort now. That's a lot of responsibility for someone so young."

I nodded, still mute. I didn't want to think about the mountain of duties waiting for me just now.

Aoife Rua pursed her lips and glanced toward Father's empty chair. "She was the best of us, indeed. A delightful woman."

I spoke with the *ard-rí's* sister and brothers, as well as his other foster-children, but now all the names, which had been drilled into my memory by my raven, swam together like mud. I laughed at their awkward jokes and drank to their shallow toasts. Inside, my spirit died, bit by bit, with the trickery and false joy.

Finally, when my cheeks ached from smiling, the *Banríon* Dervla pulled me aside. "Come, walk with me outside for a spell, my dear."

I glanced at the feast table, but Aed was still there, playing his part, so I followed her outside.

Once we emerged into the garden, Dervla took my hand. "You can drop the smile now, sweetling. There is no one here but us."

With a glance of pure gratitude, I waggled my lips and massaged my aching cheeks. I must have looked silly, but Dervla had the grace not to laugh.

Instead, she took my arm as we strolled down the paths. The cool night air cleared my head and calmed my frayed nerves.

The *banríon* spoke in her quiet voice. "I loved your mother well, though she wasn't my daughter by blood."

My breath caught in my throat. "She's the daughter of your first husband, *Tiarna* Oillel, right?"

"Yes. His first wife had given him three children and I had but a winter wed to him before he died. Their care fell to me, and I love them."

She gave me a sweet smile, and for a moment, she reminded me of Mother. And in that moment, my heart warmed.

"Your father will need a new wife."

The words struck me in the chest, and I stared at her. "But my mother just died!"

She took my hands in hers and squeezed. "Yes, I know, my dear. To be fair, your father can remain a widower for a few seasons. But I want you to get used to the idea now."

"But why must he marry again?"

She patted my hand. "Men need women to temper their worst impulses. You father is too powerful a leader to stay unwed. And as eldest daughter, you should find him a bride you can live with."

My head spun with too many tasks, too much responsibility.

She drew me in for a fierce hug. "Later, Nuala. Think about that later. I just wanted to make sure you keep that in mind."

We stared at the stars, pinpoint lights which reminded me of the sparks from Mother's burning hair. One shot across the sky, then disappeared.

Dervla patted my hand. "There, you seem much less frantic. But I can't monopolize your company for long."

I appreciated her wisdom and her help. Both fortified me for another round at my mother's wake.

When we returned to the hall, Aoife Rua was speaking with Maire Mór. The headwoman didn't look pleased, and I wondered what my aunt was asking for.

But then Cliach interrupted drew my aunt away. Maire Mór heaved a sigh of relief, and when she saw me watching, we exchanged a grin.

Whatever Cliach said to Aoife Rua seemed to upset her, as she stalked away from the bard in a huff. I scowled at him for being rude to a royal guest and followed her into the gardens.

She was sitting on a stone bench, and I sat next to her. "Are you well, Aunt?"

Aoife Rua glared at me, her eyes glistening with unshed tears, and shrugged. "I'm well enough. But your ollamh is presumptuous."

I glanced back toward the hall, gritting my teeth. "He's only a bard. I apologize on his behalf. Is there anything I can do to make up for his insult?"

She waved her hand. "No, you need not apologize. He's his own man, after all. But I do have a question for you, Nuala." She turned to me, entreaty on her face.

"Of course, whatever I can do!"

"Will you show me around the ringfort? I've never been here before and want to see everything."

I wanted to say no, so I could go crawl into my bed and cry my eyes out, but instead, I drew her to her feet. "Come, I'll show you the kitchens first, and we can get something to drink."

As I brought her through the kitchens, the great hall, and past the guest rooms, my aunt studied odd things, like tapestry edges and tallow torches. Almost as if she were assessing our wealth, or our attention to detail.

I wanted to ask her why, but my mind was too numb to form a diplomatic question. Instead, I brought her from place to place, until we found ourselves in front of my parents' room, now empty of my mother. It was musty and close, and in need of a good cleaning.

Tears pushed against my eyes and I wanted to run into the cool night to sob in peace.

Aoife Rua walked right in and yanked the tapestry from in front of the window, letting in the sparkling starlight, so like my mother's ashes rising into the sky, and I lost my fight against sorrow.

The morning after the funeral, I woke raw, as if I'd run a hundred leagues the day before and then swam the same again. My muscles creaked and complained, and my eyes were crusted shut.

I washed at the basin, splashing away the worst of it, but I'd have to go for a swim later in the lough to get properly clean.

Later. Oh, sweet Danu, later. What would I be doing later? What should I be doing now? Everything had changed. Mother was dead, and I was lost. New tears streaked my cheeks. Would I ever stop crying?

My raven, Hawlen, flew in and landed on her perch. "None of that, young Fionnuala. You grieved well enough yesterday. Today you must get back to work."

I clenched my fists. "Enough? How is it ever enough, Hawlen? How can you grieve *enough* for your mother?" I shouted those last words.

She shifted back and forth on her perch and fluffed her wings. "*Caw!* Yes, well, I could have phrased that better. You may grieve every day, but as the eldest daughter of a *tiarna*, you should not show your grief publicly. It is indecorous."

I glared, but she was right. And since my raven was tasked with teaching me the proper forms of courtesy and magic, she was simply performing her duty.

I took a deep breath and calmed my heart, humming and willing the tune into magic. I visualized calm green earth energy flowing up through me on each indrawn breath, and the red rage flowing out of my fingertips.

My magic used both visual cues and singing to refine it into proper use. I was still learning how, but this was one of many techniques Hawlen had taught me.

I prepared for my day, dressing and plaiting my hair. It was redder than my mother's white-blond hair, but just as long and straight. Once that was done, I glanced at Hawlen with a deep sigh. "Very well. What must I do today?"

She cocked her head. "You must bid your guests farewell, for they will travel home today. You will need to arrange for anything your mother supervised. Many of those tasks may fall upon your shoulders. You should speak with Cliach about composing her legacy song. You must talk to Saoirse about a milk-nurse for the babes."

I nodded at each task and fixed them in my mind. "Can I bring Aed with me? He may never have to do this himself, but still, he should learn the process."

Hawlen fluttered her wings. "Yes, bring him. It may give you comfort as well to have him near."

When I knocked on Aed's door, he was sitting on his bed in a daze. Without looking up, he spoke in a monotone. "What do you want, Nuala?"

Taken aback, I sat next to him. "I was hoping you'd shadow me today, to learn how to manage a household."

He glared at me. "Is that all her death is to you, a learning opportunity? Sweet Danu, Nuala. I knew you were cold, but that's beyond icy."

I fought the urge to strangle my little brother. "That isn't what I meant. I just didn't want to do everything alone, and I thought you might like company today."

"Fine." He sulked as he rose, and I waited outside until he changed into his day clothing.

Our first task was the twins. We sought Nanny Saoirse in the nursery. She'd just put one of the babes into swaddling blankets when I poked my head in. "Nanny?"

"Ah, Nuala, Aed, my lovely children! Do come in, come in! Have you met your brothers yet? They're full of pink and health."

I wanted nothing to do with the children who had killed my mother. But I approached the closest crib and stared at the bundle of woolen blankets.

He looked so peaceful, asleep and wrinkled. As soon as the babe yawned, I had to smile. How could I even consider blaming this tiny, innocent thing for Mother's death?

When Nanny placed the other bundle into my arms, he felt warm and smelled milky and fresh. "What are their names?"

"Your sweet mother named this one Fiachra, but we don't have a name for the second child. She didn't know she'd have twins. Would you like to name the other?"

My eyes grew wide. "I'd never! No, it's not my place to do so, Nanny. I should ask Father."

Nanny Saoirse scowled. "Your father is in no shape for such things, and the child can't stay nameless. He'll lose his spirit if he doesn't have a name for too long."

While I stared at the babe still in my arms, my mind raced. He'd need strength without his mother. Strength and luck. *Conn* meant chief. Even though he was the youngest, he was the child of a *tiarna* and may very well grow to have his own chiefdom. "Name him Conn, Nanny. He must be strong, after all."

"Conn it is, Nuala. Go, now, I've plenty to do to take care of the wee ones."

I paused, remembering Hawlen's instructions. "They need a wet-nurse, don't they?"

She waved her hand. "Already arranged, child. I had one waiting, as your mother never had much milk."

I gazed at Conn and made a silent vow to the Goddess Danu to protect him and his brother from whatever life threw at them, just as I'd promised Mother as she died. "Thank you, Saoirse."

She didn't answer me, cooing at the babe in her arms. I stared at the other twin, Fiachra, and my heart broke. He'd never know Mother, the poor wee thing.

On our way to talk to Cliach, we found Maire Mór. The large headwoman was directing servants to clean the main hall from last night's festivities.

I touched her arm. "Maire, have you a moment? I need a word."

After giving a few last instructions to the workmen, she embraced us both in a warm, solid hug. Mother had been a slight, willowy woman and not given to many hugs. Maire Mór enveloped us like a field of yellow flowers on a warm summer day. I didn't want her to let go.

Then she held us at arm's length, searching both of our faces. "What can I help you with this morning? Have you eaten yet? You must eat. Tann! Fetch the children porridge! With plenty of sweetening and cream!" She yelled the last at a passing kitchen boy.

I gave her a sad smile. Maire Mór would, of course, make sure we had food and comfort. She ran the whole hillfort, and I couldn't monopolize her time for long. "We need to talk to you about managing the household. Things that Mother used to do. Then I have to find Cliach."

She blinked several times. "But of course! Why do you think I'm clearing the hall? I know my job, young *bantiarna*, never fear. I'll let you know what I can't assign elsewhere. But I wouldn't recommend talking to the bard just now."

I furrowed my brow. "Why not?"

She sniffed. "He's a bit worse for wear after yesterday."

I let out a bitter snort as my indignation rose, and I snapped my words. "Drunk, you mean. Maire, if I can get up this morning, the bard of the Court can do no less. He has duties, too."

Then I chided myself for taking my temper out on Maire Mór. "I'm sorry, Maire. I shouldn't have snapped at you."

The headwoman patted my shoulder. "Not to worry, Nuala. Today, of all days, no one would dream of taking you to task. You grab your brother and eat your breakfast over there and talk to the bard later, aye?"

Tann returned with two bowls of steaming porridge, thick with honey and cream. We took them with thanks.

The thick, gloopy porridge soothed my raw throat. Tann had mixed yellow raisins in and the bursts of sweet helped to soothe my frayed nerves.

Our next task was to bid farewell to our guests. They trooped out of the main hall, some holding their heads after too much celebration the night before. I exchanged a formal farewell with the *ard-rí,* the *banríon,* then each visitor.

Aoife Rua clasped me close. "You must come visit me soon. I'd like to get to know you better."

She wore my mother's smile. For some reason, that made my tears burn more than any other farewell.

Aillbhe, Mother's youngest sister, said nothing as she gave us a fierce hug. Tears in her eyes matched my own.

After the last guest left, I went in search of the bard. Everyone knew he'd worshipped my mother, but he owed a duty to his *ard-rí* and to his *túath.* I'd try to be gentle, but I couldn't let him get away with such behavior.

His room smelled sour, with clothing and furniture tossed everywhere. He wasn't in the great hall, which teemed with Maire Mór's bustle. When we finally found the bard, draped across a kitchen hearth bench, he stank of old ale and vomit.

I had skill at healing, but it would take me a great deal of effort to sober him, and he didn't deserve such effort.

I fought the urge to vomit as we filled a bucket with icy well water. With a smile of grim satisfaction, Aed upended it over the bard's head, much to the delight of the kitchen girls.

He awoke with a splutter, shot to his feet, and then held his head between his hands with a moan. When he opened his eyes, he blinked at us through narrowed slits.

Cliach then peered at Aed, who still held the bucket. "What'd you do that for, child? I wasn't hurting anyone here." His bedraggled hair dripped as he gazed up with sad, bloodshot eyes. For a moment, my sympathy overwhelmed my revulsion.

Then I took the bucket from Aed's hands and glared at the bard. "How dare you dishonor my mother with this disgusting, slovenly display? You're a reflection upon our household. I've a mind to send you back to the Oak Grove in disgrace!"

The bard cowered and prostrated himself before me. I had an incredible urge to kick him. Aed rolled his eyes and stifled a chuckle.

Cliach said, "Please, my *bantiarna*, please, I am but a weak man behind this shell of a bard. Please have mercy upon me."

The entire kitchen had fallen silent. I stared for several long moments. "I give you one chance to redeem yourself. Only one. What do you need for the legacy song for Mother?" I choked on the words.

His face crumbled and he sobbed into his hands. I sniffed back my own tears and raised the bucket again.

Cliach gave a slow nod, his lips set in a grim line as he pushed himself to his feet. His sodden clothes dripped and sucked with each movement, and they hadn't been fresh to begin with.

Cliach gathered himself with swaying dignity. "I shall create the legacy song, *bantiarna*. I know all I need to know of Aobh Ban."

He walked away with stiff deliberation.

Now that my tasks were done, I needed something else to occupy my mind. I usually had weapons training in the mornings and raven lessons in the afternoons, but today was a mad day.

Half the morning had already passed, but I needed to expend my frustrations on the training pell. "Aed, let's go find Weaponmistress Scuida. I need to fight something."

I dreamt of wandering through the forest, the mist so thick I couldn't see the trunks of the trees in front of me. Eerie light shone through the trees from above, but it wasn't sunlight. It was the light of the underworld, the place beneath the hills.

A high, ululating whistle pierced the air, just barely audible. Mists distorted the sound and I couldn't figure out where it came from.

Footsteps crunched on summer leaves as a figure formed in the mists. Light radiated from the form, and the fog glowed in pale yellow light.

The figure walked closer, and my heart raced with each step, until I saw white-blonde hair flowing to the waist. It billowed around her head in a halo of light, though there was no wind. She was dressed in white, a long flowing gown.

Mother.

I tried to breathe, but it came out a sob and I fought the urge to rush into her arms, to hug her, to demand she come back to us.

But I knew better. If a fetch reached out from Tír na nÒg, one should never touch them, and certainly never invite them into your home.

Her hand reached out, palm up in supplication.

I swallowed against my fear and my love. "Mother, is it truly you?"

"It is, my dear, my special child, my Fionnuala. Oh, how I've missed you!"

My last memory of her face had been in a rictus of pain from childbirth, drawn and strained with grief. She'd strained against all her agony to make me promise to take good care of my brothers, the same brothers she'd died giving birth to. Now, she looked peaceful.

"Mother, I've missed you so much."

She dropped her hand and her brow furrowed. "You must take warning, Fionnuala. Dark times come."

"Dark times? Is it Father? Will something happen to Father?"

Her glow pulsed. "In a way, yes. The darkness will seem like a blessing, but a curse will fall upon you and those you love. A curse you cannot fully escape."

My mind whirled with possibilities. "Who casts this curse upon us?"

She shook her head. "I cannot tell you that. I can help, I can warn, but I cannot stop it."

Frustrated, I threw up my hands. "How can a warning help if I can't escape the curse?"

Mother pressed her lips together. "You can prepare. There are tasks you must complete and choices to make. You must choose wisely."

"But how am I to know what the right choices are? I don't even know the questions!"

Then I remembered Dervla's insistence that Father must marry again, and that I must choose Mother's successor.

"You will know, my child. As for the curse, you might deflect it to another."

"To whom?"

"That is *not* your choice. You must learn all you can."

Why should someone else suffer a curse meant for me? Unless someone deserved the evil. But who was I to judge the punishment?

My mother started to fade. I took a step forward, my hand outstretched. "Wait, Mother! Don't go, not yet!"

"You must learn, Fionnuala. Ask the ravens."

The light grew brighter, and her image disappeared. All that remained was a brightness so strong, I couldn't keep my eyes open.

Then my vision faded until dim fog once again surrounded me. Not even a bird or forest creature broke the still silence.

I wept.

In the days that followed, I didn't want to think about anyone replacing Mother, so I pushed the vision to the back of my mind until I almost forgot it.

In the 24th winter of Ard-Rí Bodb Dearg's reign (456 BCE) 4 years later

I was standing on the ramparts, getting the overnight report from the head guard, when a group of twenty people approached the gate. We hadn't received any message about formal visitors, so I rushed down to fetch Father and Aed for a proper, formal greeting.

As we arrived breathless at the door, the leader approached, his arms wide. "Greetings, *Tiarna* Lir."

Father gave a guarded smile and spoke in a formal tone. "*Tiarna* Illbreach, I welcome you both, you and your kin."

He finished the formal greeting and placed his hands over his guest's. Then Illbreach turned to the stunning woman beside him, with midnight hair and dusky skin. "This is my eldest daughter, Maeve. And then my son, Tadhg." He gestured to a young man about my own age, all long legs and curly, brown hair.

Maeve's smile was like the sun coming out from behind storm clouds. I glanced at Father, remembering Banríon Dervla's task that I find him a new wife, but he paid her no attention. Instead, he was glancing up at the guards.

I cleared my throat, embarrassed for his rudeness. "Please, come inside. We're about to sit for a meal."

We weren't, actually, about to sit for a meal, but hospitality demanded that we offer our guests food, and so we did. As they settled at the feast table, I made sure Maire Mór had the staff she needed for surprise visitors, sent servants to get the guest rooms ready, and finally, sat beside Father.

The *tiarna's* son, Tadhg, gave me a saucy grin, and my cheeks grew warm. I glanced at Maeve, who placed a hand on Father's arm. "You have some delightful forests. What's the hunting like here?"

Father just shrugged and took a long swig from his mug.

If Banríon Dervla had sent this delegation to us with the intention of offering some options for my father's next wife, they needed time together.

I answered for Father. "We have great stags in the forest north of here and are planning a hunt next week. However, we can shift the hunt to tomorrow, if you'd like to join us."

Her eyes grew wide and she covered her mouth. "Oh, no, I don't hunt myself. But I know men enjoy such things."

I narrowed my eyes, but it was true that some women didn't enjoy hunting. Mother had always been excellent with a bow, as am I. But this frail flower didn't look like she had the arm strength for such exercise.

Clearing my throat, I asked, "Father, why don't you take Maeve to the stables after our meal? I'm sure she'd love to see the new horses."

He grunted, but I kept my smile plastered on. Then he shoved a chunk of bread in his mouth.

Tadhg gave me a grin. "I'd love to see the gardens, if you have the time to show me."

That made my cheeks burn again.

We finished the meal in awkward silence. I didn't know how to engage my father's interest in Maeve. I didn't exactly have experience in making matches.

After the sweets course, Tadhg rose and offered me his arm. With a final glance at Maeve, who scooted close to Father, and to Cliach, who was pulling out his harp, I left fate to itself.

At the very least, I needed some fresh air.

The sun was just touching the treetops as we emerged from the kitchen door. "These gardens were mostly herbs for flavor and healing, but outside the walls were food plots, with ornamental flowers growing on the outer walls."

"And do you use the healing herbs? I'd heard you had some skill."

I looked anywhere but his eyes. "I do, but most of my skill is in magic. I have learned herblore from our headwoman, though."

As we strolled along the path, Tadhg asked, "Which are your favorite flowers?"

We'd just came to my favorite, so I gestured toward them. "The primroses always struck me as delicate and sweet."

He bent to sniff one bloom and then rose. "Much like you, then. But not nearly as clever."

I'd always imagined that women in the tales who fell in love quickly had been short on character or perhaps silly. That was, perhaps, rather naive of me.

Over the course of the next few days, I spent a lot of time with our visitors, especially Tadhg. I looked forward to time with him, but made sure to speak with Maeve, as well. I wanted to gauge how she might be as a stepmother.

Despite all my efforts and Illbreach's urging, Father barely spoke to Maeve. I needed to get to know her better, to find ways in which she and

Father might enjoy each other's company. So, when I went to help Maire Mór by weeding the kitchen garden, I asked Maeve to help me.

She wrinkled her nose. "The garden? But isn't that horribly dirty?"

I stared at her, trying to decide if she was joking, but she seemed genuinely disgusted. "Yes, but it's also necessary work. My mother taught me that no noble is above the lowliest tasks."

She sniffed and I caught a glimpse of her haughty eyes. At that point, I knew I couldn't stand being in a home with her in charge, and I gave up trying to match her with Father. I was now relieved at his indifference.

After our guests left, I asked Father about Maeve, but he just shrugged. Perhaps she was too different from Mother, with her dark hair and skin. Maybe he'd be interested in someone who looked like the woman he'd fallen in love with.

Chapter Two

A month passed since *Tiarna* Illbreach's visit, and I kept thinking about Tadhg. As I stood on the ramparts, looking out into the woods, wind howled and lightning flashed. I delighted in the violent weather with visceral pleasure. Storms energized me, making me feel alive and vibrant.

When we moved below the hills, I'd miss wild weather like this. I'd visited the other realm once, a place we called *Saol Eile*. Not the Afterworld, but an Otherworld.

The weather underground was fair, but boring and bland. I wanted to stay above, to become a legendary huntress and stalk the hills for prey, only seen in brief glimpses and spoken of in whispered tales. I could terrorize groups of bandits and exact retribution for evils they visited upon others.

The clop of horse hooves caught my attention and peered down toward the gates. A line of torches approached, dancing fitfully in the wind. We had visitors.

I rushed down into the hall, where the guards had just finished their supper. Noise and clamor assaulted me, but I found Maire Mór. "Visitors, Maire, quick! We must prepare!"

"Oh, bother. Why didn't they send word? How rude." Despite her complaints, she burst into action, sending a crew of kitchen maids to clear the detritus of the meal from the hall and another to set new plates, platters and pitchers.

Hospitality required that we offer food and drink to any visitor, even if we'd just finished a three-day feast.

I went to search for Father, and found him in his room, drunk. *Wonderful.* "Father? Father, get up. You must dress. We have guests."

He struggled to sit up. "Guests? Who? Who comes at this hour? Who dares come without permission?"

"I don't know, Father. I saw their torches. Just get up, please?" I got him to his feet and pulled out a clean *léine*. The one he wore was stained with wine.

He waved his arms and staggered to his bed. "No, it's too late at night. Bar the gates!"

I propped him up and got his *léine* up over his head. Then I called to his raven, "Lawstern! Lawstern, can you fetch Donal? I need help!"

"*Caw!* I'm no white messenger, Fionnuala. You know that."

"Please, Lawstern, just this once? I can't do this on my own!"

"Very well. I shall seek him."

When he arrived, Donal got Father dressed, and his protests faded. He finally looked presentable, with a wide red belt over his *léine*, and we led him to the great hall just as the guests filed in.

A dozen warriors and a dozen more servants entered. They wore an unfamiliar fashion and one had a ginger cat sitting on his shoulder, like a bonded raven.

Father sullenly picked imaginary bits of dirt off his clean *léine*. With a sigh, I draped his five-colored brat over his shoulders and played hostess.

I held my hands out, palms up, to their leader. "I welcome you to *Sídhe Fionnachaidh*, the Hill of the White Field, you and your kin. I welcome you into our homes. I welcome you to our flatbread and our ale. Be safe and sound within our walls." Maire hastily placed a bottle of mead into my hand and I offered this as host-gift.

The leader bowed, his black warrior braids falling almost to the ground. "Thank you, kind Lady." He held out a wooden box no bigger than his hand as a guest-gift. When I lifted the lid and spied ocean salt, I smiled in genuine gratitude. We lived far from the sea and salt was a welcome gift.

As they sat, I had my first good look at the men and differences in their appearance fell into place. They weren't Tuatha Dé, the People, which meant they must be Milesians.

My blood ran cold and the hall grew silent as I glanced at Father. He *hated* Milesians. He blamed them for all that had gone wrong in the last twenty winters. The war for the land, his loss of the *ard-rí*, and our agreement to move below the hills. Probably the death of Mother, as well. But he didn't seem to have noticed yet.

When his men were all settled, the leader cocked his head at me.

I gave him a polite smile. "I am Fionnuala, daughter of *Tiarna* Lir. How may I serve you?"

"Greetings, lovely *Bantiarna* Fionnuala. I am Áedammair, *Tiarna* of the Manapii. You have my thanks for hosting us on this wild and raw night. We were traveling to Emhain Macha until the storm drove us to shelter. I've been upon this road many times, but have never before seen this fort. Is it recently built?"

A few people gasped, and I took a sip of my mead as glanced again at Father. "No, it's been here for many hundred winters. It's normally hidden by our glamor veil, and it's unusual for such a Milesian to find us, even in a storm."

He gave a solemn nod. "I've studied in an oak grove with one of your kind for many winters, my lady. I have talent in Filíd arts. Perhaps that's why we found ourselves here in our hour of need."

I hadn't heard that Milesians could work any sort of magic, and I had to make a shift in my opinions of them.

I was about to ask the Milesian who he'd studied with when Father pounded a large fist on the table, making mugs and platters jump. "How dare you come to my hillfort! You, who stole our land. You, who killed our *tiarnaí*. You, who cursed our children! Begone from my sight, Milesian scum! You're not welcome here!"

I rose, my hands out to calm him. "Father, please! I've already extended them guest-right! You can't curse them, you must—"

"I must do nothing! I must—" Lawstern flitted to his shoulder and whispered in his ear, halting his tirade. He threw a glare at Áedammair, narrowed his gaze at me, then stalked out, slamming the solid wooden door with a thump.

I took a deep breath. "I must apologize for my father's behavior. He's been overwrought since," I swallowed to keep my own tears away, "since my mother passed on. May I offer you mead?" I picked up the closest pitcher.

I thanked whichever gods watched over us that Áedammair accepted my thin excuse and held out his mug.

After more conversation and lots of mead, our guests relaxed. Cliach sang several tunes of love and joy, which further lightened the mood.

When Father returned to the hall, he seemed less sullen and grudgingly nodded to Áedammair. He didn't apologize, but he did share a mug of mead with them. I let out a breath of relief.

Lawstern left Father's shoulder and flew around the hall. When he came to the cat upon the Milesian's shoulder, the cat hissed and swiped, but then the raven wisely flew out of range and landed on his own perch. The cat sat back on his master's shoulder. They continued to glare at each other through the evening.

Could Milesians bond to cats like we did to ravens? Perhaps we underestimated their power and dismissed them too easily.

Then Cliach began a song of lost love, a sad tune of a woman who'd lost her betrothed to the sea. A tear fell down Father's cheek just before he burst into a howl.

I wanted to throttle the bard. Why would he choose a poignant love song? Had he no sense at all?

Father threw his half-full mug against the hearth. The honey wine sizzled in the fire. He lifted an empty bench and flung it against the wall, splintering it into jagged bits.

My heart leapt to my throat as he snatched up one of these shards and brandished it like a weapon against friend and foe alike. He growled and spun, searching for an enemy.

Nervously, I stepped in front of him, my hands out again. "Father, please, you must relax. There is no one here to hurt you."

He feinted to my right, trying to get past me to the Milesians. Áedammair placed himself between the maddened man and his own guard, while Cliach quickly changed his tune, literally.

A soft song, almost a lullaby, came from the bard's harp now. He played a gentle arpeggio with soothing words. I added my own voice and pushed a peaceful, sleepy magic through the words and the tune.

Father's eyelids drooped and he lost his grip on the wooden shard. The makeshift weapon dropped with a clatter to the floor, and he slumped on the flagstones. A few higher chirps came from the ravens.

The subtle magic in the song drifted across the crowd, a wave of peace and joy.

With Donal's help, we removed Father from the hall. Cliach's tune followed us into his room. He was snoring by the time we got him into bed.

I returned to the great hall, my face burning with embarrassment. As soon as I sat, Áedammair handed me one of the sweets the servants had brought. "You have much to manage with your father, it seems."

I spared a glance toward the hallway and nodded. "Ever since my mother passed, he's been difficult. But I can't fault his heart for hurting."

He laid a hand over mine, warm and calloused. "We all grieve in our lives, *Bantiarna*. And each person's grief has a different face."

My throat closed at his kind words, and I could only manage a wan smile.

Then our guest broke into a grin. "But I cannot be a good guest if I make my hostess weep. Instead, I shall make you laugh! Ruadhri, bring your creature here and make the lovely woman smile."

The man with the cat on his shoulder scooted down to our end of the table. His cat climbed on his head and started kneading his scalp. He grimaced in pain and tried to extract the feline, but she held on tight.

I had to admit, that did make me smile, despite my grief.

Áedammair clapped his hands and let out a bark of laughter. "There! I have succeeded. Now, may I tempt you with another sweet?"

When Áedammair and his Milesians left the next morning, I watched them leave with a sad heart.

Three moons later, I was knee-deep in the gardens when Father summoned us. I hastily changed into a clean *léine* and arrived in the main hall just as Aed did.

And I stopped dead in my tracks, staring at the young man standing beside him, Tadhg.

I glanced around for *Tiarna* Illbreach, but didn't see him anywhere. With confusion, I stood beside my brother, waiting for our father to explain.

He cleared his throat and clapped a hand on Tadhg's shoulder. The boy almost staggered from the weight of it. "I want you to welcome your new foster-brother! Tadhg will be staying with us for the next five cycles of the season, or until I deem him ready to leave. I will teach him how to be a leader, a warrior, and a hunter."

I swallowed my disappointment and looked at my feet. I had no wish to be a sister to Tadhg, not even a foster-sister. But at least we'd be able to get to know each other more. When I glanced up, he was staring straight at me.

That made my heart pound in my chest. Aed rescued me by stepping forward and taking Tadhg into a hug. "Welcome to our family!"

I did the same, and Father waved us away. "The first thing I'll do is to show you how to inspect the guards."

Later that evening, as I was retrieving arrows from target practice, someone cleared their throat behind me. I spun to find Tadhg wearing a sheepish expression. Despite my nerves, I raised my eyebrows.

He poked the dirt with his toe. "Would you like some help with that?"

Shaking my head, I said, "I'm about done. But I have to repair some tack. You can help me if you like."

He gave me a grin, and we spent a quiet evening in the armory, cutting and burnishing leather strips, repairing a bridle, and fletching new arrows.

Tadhg carved a knotwork design into one bit of leather, showing me how to mark out the pattern first. I showed him our technique for coloring the leather red.

By the time we were done, I no longer stuttered when talking to him, and was really looking forward to the next few seasons.

Now, if I could only find Father a new bride, I might even be able to start planning my own life.

Chapter Three

In the 25th winter of Ard-Rí Bodb Dearg's reign (455 BCE) 1 year later

When the messenger arrived, he came straight to me rather than Father. Everyone was learning that any issue would be resolved more quickly that way.

"*Banríon* Dervla sends her good wishes and would like to inform you that she's sending her cousin to visit."

At least this time, we got some warning of the visitors. I let Maire Mór know first, then went down to the hall to inform Father. I hoped the *banríon*'s own cousin would be a better option than Illbreach's daughter had been.

I glanced toward Aed and Tadhg, sitting further down the table, chatting with one of the guards. They both stared as I tapped Father on the arm.

Keeping my voice steady, I said, "We need to prepare for visitors. They should arrive tomorrow."

"What? I want no visitors! Tell them to stay away. Tell them all to stay away!"

In a fluid motion, he leapt to his feet and grabbed a bench, throwing it against the wall.

Father threw a bench against the wall. My heart raced as I dove under the table. Tadhg crawled down with me, giving my hand a squeeze.

When Father stomped from the hall, muttering under his breath, I ran. I needed to get away from Father, from his uncertain temper, from my endless duties, and everyone and everything.

Once clear of the hillfort, I rushed up the path through the woods. I grabbed a large branch and hit a sturdy pine tree. I hit it over and over again until the branch shattered into splinters and my hands were raw with scratches.

My temper momentarily spent, I walked into a part of the forest I hadn't explored in several moons. As I wandered, I found a new clearing with a roundhouse.

Curious, I flitted through the trees, silent as the wind, examining the structure from all sides. Smoke fought with the rain and drifted up through the straw. And someone was home.

How could this be here, on our veiled land? Or perhaps our veil hid our fort, so they believed they were on unclaimed land, as if any part of the island could be truly unclaimed.

This was something I must tell Father, despite his temper and his violence.

I backed away from the clearing and ran toward home. The rain chose that moment to become a deluge, and soon I couldn't see in front of me. I huddled under an uprooted tree, my teeth chattering.

Footsteps shuffling through leaves made me turn to see Tadhg, his dark hair plastered to his head. He'd brought an oiled skin tent and set it up as a lean-to without a word. Then we both huddled beneath the meager shelter. "Fionnuala?"

A sob escaped and he held me close. It felt good in his arms, and I cried on his shoulder as the rain fell.

Eventually, he held me at arms-length and searched my eyes. "Did he hurt you?"

"No, he'd never hurt me. It's just… how will I ever do it, Tadhg? How can I run a household like this? I can't even keep two kitchen maids from fighting. How can I run a feast, or mete out justice? Father won't do his duty and Mother isn't here—"

"Shh, shh. You have me, don't you? I've been learning a lot from your father. You never have to do it all alone. You have people who can help, like Scuida, Aed, Maire Mór, and Cliach…"

I let out a bitter laugh. "That one! Cliach can't help himself out of a bottle of mead."

"Well, fair enough on Cliach."

"And Aed would rather fight me than help. Besides, he's only thirteen. How much help could he be?"

"He'll grow into it. It takes time to learn confidence in our roles, but I've seen it. You've learned a lot in just the past few seasons. You're growing into a formidable person, mark my words. And I'll be honored to see you take wing as the woman you're destined to be."

I gazed up into his eyes. They were so kind and full of love that my heart broke. I gave him a shy smile, and he put a finger to my lips, returning mine with a mischievous grin.

Then he kissed me.

Tadhg's lips tasted soft and sweet, but the kiss warmed me right down my spine and to the soles of my feet. It lasted longer than any brotherly kiss and soon we hugged each other tightly. I no longer noticed the cold and chill of the rain.

After an eon, we broke our embrace, and I giggled. "That was—"

"That was delightful, my dearest Fionnuala."

He kissed me again and time slipped away.

A loud crack startled me, and I jumped out of his arms, searching frantically for the source.

He let out a low, liquid chuckle. "It's just a branch falling, dear heart. Nothing to worry about."

I settled back down with a nervous laugh, but my eyes still darted to the trees.

He put his arm around me again. I leaned my head against his shoulder as rain splattered on our bed of wet leaves.

This was peaceful and quiet, and I felt utterly comfortable with Tadhg. I trusted him, and lying in his arms felt like home. I shut my eyes and my breathing slowed.

For once, I had no duties, no responsibilities. Just comfort.

We'd just about fallen asleep to the *drip-drip-drip* of the rain when a raucous caw startled me, and I jerked out of Tadhg's embrace.

My face burned with embarrassment as Hawlen flew into our meager shelter and fluffed her wet feathers. "You're needed. Now."

Panic gripped my heart. Had Dervla's cousin arrived already? She must be early.

As the raven flew off into the misty rains, Tadhg gave me a sheepish look, though we'd done nothing but kiss. I struggled to my feet, brushing wet twigs and leaves from my clothing, then ran toward the hillfort.

Once inside the palisade, I heard an angry cry. I ran straight to Father's room, but he wasn't there. As I listened to the howling voice, I realized it wasn't Father, but a child's wail.

I hurried to the nursery roundhouse and flung open the door. Nanny Saoirse cradled one of the twins in her arms, an awkward bundle at five winters old. Whichever twin she held, he howled and fretted, his skin flushed and blotchy.

I tried to take him, but Nanny Saoirse resisted. We tugged for several moments before the ravens arrived. Hawlen, Totawg, and Lawstarn fluttered in, which made a racket enough to drown the child's sobs.

Hawlen cawed. "Saoirse! Release him to Fionnuala so she can heal him."

The Nanny scowled. "I won't! He's mine to care for."

Totawg flew at the woman, batting his wings in her eyes until she finally released the twin into my arms.

I held the burning child and sang my healing chant; a low, rhythmic charm of light and calm. The song grew louder as the ravens harmonized. We formed an ethereal chorus as Tadhg finally arrived, watching from the doorway.

As the chant grew louder, I drew the earth's healing power up through the ground. Magic flowed into my feet, my legs, my torso, out through my arms and hands. It was a cool stream, a sweet healing balm. The twin glowed with pale blue light and his cries eased. I pushed more of my will into the magic and the glow increased as his fever cooled.

I lost all track of time as I rocked my little brother and sang. My legs thrummed and grew tired, but still I sang.

When I finally opened my eyes, the rain had stopped, and the late afternoon sun peeked through the winter clouds. Pale mist still clung to the hills, and threaded tendrils reached through the window, but the child's fever had faded. His angry red blotches had receded to pink healthy cheeks, and I drew a tired sigh of relief.

I surrendered the now sleeping twin to Nanny Saoirse and collapsed on a bench. My legs felt like seaweed, and I ached to curl up and sleep right there, but Tadhg and Hawlen got me to my feet and herded me into my room.

As Tadhg tucked me in, I grabbed his arm. "Wait, there's something Father must know. I almost forgot."

He raised his eyebrows. "You're not going to tell him about our kissing, are you?"

"No, not that. The cottage. There's a roundhouse on the hill near where we met. Milesians."

His eyes grew wide. "That close? Our veils must be weakening."

Memory of the bench made my heart pound. Suddenly, I didn't want to see my Father or give him any bad news. "Will you tell him?"

He gave a nod and then kissed my forehead. "I will. You sleep."

"What about the visitors? They might be here soon."

"I promise, if they come tonight, I'll fetch you. Now sleep!"

I had one last thought before I fell into an exhausted slumber. I might have saved my little brother's life. Perhaps I had some purpose in this world, after all.

The next morning, Father summoned me to the hall as he broke his fast.

I waited respectfully while he ate his eggs and oats, occasionally glancing up at me. Finally, he cleared his throat. "Tell me what you found yesterday."

I stole a glance at the doorway, where Tadhg had just arrived. He gave me an encouraging nod. "I was walking up through the forest path, heading up the hill—"

He waved his hand. "I don't care what you were doing. I want to know what you saw."

I swallowed down both my temper and my tears. "I saw a roundhouse. It looked recently built. I don't think it was someone of the People. There were three cows in the field nearby, and someone had started plowing rows."

He grunted and took a long drink of his ale. Then he raised his hand with a gesture. One of the guards ran up. "Yes, my *tiarna*?"

"Take a group to check out this roundhouse. If the residents are one of the People, invite them to feast tonight."

I exchanged a glance with the guard, then he asked, "And if they aren't?"

My father leveled a glare at him, and I swallowed down my fear. "Father, you can't just kill them, even if they're just Milesians!"

He rolled his eyes. "Fine. Don't hurt them. But tell them to move. This is our land."

Over the next few hours, I waited with anxious worry until the guards returned. I was terrified that I'd be the reason these innocent people would be killed or hurt.

When they returned, the leader went to report to Father, but one of the others pulled me aside. "We found them."

I swallowed, giving him a nod to continue, afraid of what he'd say.

"Don't worry, bantiarna. They weren't hurt at all. In fact, they were already thinking of moving closer to their king."

"Who's their king?"

"Áedammair, one of those Milesians."

Remembering Banríon Dervla's message, I waited on the ramparts, watching for our visitors, but they didn't come that day. Perhaps the rain had kept them away, but that was just as well. Father was still in a foul mood about the roundhouse.

The next morning, I waited again. I hoped they'd arrive soon, as I had many things to take care of, and couldn't spend all day waiting on their arrival. If Dervla's cousin had manners, she would have sent a messenger with news of their delay.

I ran down to take care of my morning weeding, but climbed the ramparts again every moment I could, searching the path.

Later that afternoon, when I finally spied visitors approaching, I frowned at the size of the party. Just three people? They must not be of very high status to have such a small group.

I rushed down to fetch Father, but he was already up and ready, for a wonder. He stood waiting at the door with Cliach. Tadhg and Aed came rushing in out of breath just as we opened the gate.

The woman in the middle wore a thick veil, and her guards wore grim expressions. Father put out his hands, palms up, and began the formal greeting.

Instead of lifting her veil, the visitor said, "I am Grainne. I have come to see if you are worthy of me."

I suppressed a cough. She was direct and brave, I had to admit that. Father looked like he'd swallowed a squirrel. "Please, come and join us for our meal."

She still didn't lift her veil, and I began to wonder why. Was she ill-favored? Old? Father wouldn't need a young wife, after all. He had plenty of heirs already. His need for a wife was to keep his temper balanced, according to Dervla. An older wife might be exactly what he needed.

Maire Mór brought out fruit and cheese, along with ale and mead. Father raised his glass in honor of our visitors. Well, visitor and two guards. I still wondered why she traveled with such a small group.

Cliach came in and settled into the corner, uncovering his harp and getting ready for a song. Father asked Grainne a question, and she answered in a clipped tone.

The bard's head snapped up and he narrowed his gaze at the visitor. I glanced between them, certain that he recognized her.

He strummed the harp strings and played a quiet tune, nothing loud enough to interrupt Father's conversation. But then Grainne held up a hand. "You will stop playing, Bard."

Even if they did know each other, this seemed horribly rude. To silence anyone from the *druí* class was a huge breach of etiquette, especially from a guest.

Cliach ceased his strumming and rose, lifting his chin. "My tiarna, it seems my services are not required. If I may be excused?"

Father's gaze moved from Grainne to Cliach and back again and he glowered. "What's this? Why would you make such a command in my hall?"

Everyone grew silent as the three of them stared at each other. Finally, Grainne threw back her veil, revealing a worn, sun-lined face with sparkling gray eyes. "Your bard is known to me, *Tiarna* Lir. And if I am to be your wife, he will have to go."

Cliach straightened his spine. "If you take her as your wife, then I must return to the Oak Grove."

Father clenched his jaw and held up his hands. "Enough! Cliach, return to your room. Grainne, you have incredible nerve, coming to my home and giving orders. I think it best that you leave. Now."

Her expression barely changed as she gave a single nod. "I agree completely. This is not a household I wish to live in."

With that, she gathered her guards and left as dusk fell. Tadhg came up behind me and gave my shoulders a reassuring hug. I leaned into his embrace and let out a sigh of relief. I was never so glad to see a visitor leave.

Over the course of the next several moons, I dreamt of Mother almost every night. A few times, I even dreamt of Tadhg, but I welcomed those dreams. In between, I dreamt of being lost in the wilderness, weathering a fierce storm, stuck on a rocky island, or sailing on the sea.

I was always with others, but I never saw who. Whenever I turned, my companions drifted away into the mists. White feathers and phantasmal faces loomed in terrifying glimpses.

Each morning, I woke in a cold sweat, with breathless gasps and a raw throat.

When I asked Hawlen about my dreams, she clacked her beak and said, "You have little gift for prophecy. Your mother had that gift, but your talents are for healing."

"But these dreams *must* mean something. I have them almost every night. Something's going to happen, something Mother's trying to warn me about. Maybe she's lending me her gift for prophecy?"

The raven fluttered her wings but didn't answer.

I gave her a frustrated glare. "She said I needed to ask the ravens, so I'm asking. How can I prepare?"

Hawlen preened under her wing and let out a caw. "I don't know, but I can ask the Council of White Ravens. You said you saw white feathers several times? Perhaps that means them."

The Council of White Ravens worked as the ruling body of the ravens. Their young served as messengers around the land. I'd only once seen a white raven, at *Ard-Rí* Bodb Dearg's court. "White feathers, demonic faces, twisted and black, with scars. I didn't think they were ravens, though. Could they have been Fomorians?"

Hawlen shook her head. "The Fomorians weren't the monsters as the tales describe, black or twisted. They're only true crime was that they lived in this land before us. As the victors, your People painted them as evil. But they looked like the Tuatha Dé, though with darker hair. Sometimes their skin was brown, but never black. *Banríon* Dervla has Fomorian blood."

"I'd heard that rumor. But the tales always paint them as evil."

Hawlen cocked her head. "Not evil. They could be greedy and ambitious, but so can the Tuatha Dé or the Milesians. If your enemies are demonic, your own people are virtuous for having defeated them. Seldom is a loser painted in a kind light."

The Fomorians and the Fir Bolg before them were often the subject of cautionary tales, telling about the evils of greed and bestial rage. "But aren't the Filíd charged with true histories? How could they lie?"

"They are not lies, but exaggerations."

My pride in my race welled up and I yelled at Hawlen. "That can't be right! We're the honorable ones. Aren't we?"

Then I recalled the tales of the Battle of Tailltin. And the Milesians who'd guested with us, sharing their battle stories. They'd skewed the tales to favor the valor of the Milesians, the victors.

I tried not to believe we'd done the same thing with the Fomorians, but I couldn't escape the facts.

Chapter Four

In the 27th winter of Ard-Rí Bodb Dearg's reign (453 BCE) 2 years later

We were summoned to visit court, and it would be nice to see people who weren't constantly mad with grief, or clearing up after those who were mad with grief. I stared at the passing landscape as we rode to the royal hillfort.

I'd tried to heal Father's pain time and time again, but he blocked all my attempts. Hawlen was teaching me how to get around his resistance, but I still had a lot to learn. It was like unraveling a complex puzzle that changed each moment. By the time I untangled one strand with a new melody, he'd created a new weave with a mysterious tune. I ended up farther away from breaking the block than when I started.

Father excelled at misdirection magic, like the veils which guarded our hillfort from the Milesians, like the one who had built too close to us.

They lived such short lives, why bother to build homes at all? There would barely be time to enjoy a home before they withered and died, like mayflies in the dusk. As we passed one of their settlements, I remembered the Milesian king who visited us, Áedammair. Did he live nearby?

We circled around the back of the circular hillfort surrounded by tall, wooden defensive spikes, large enough to hold several hundred men and over fifty roundhouses.

Aed nudged my shoulder. "Do you think we'll get to eat right away, Nuala?"

I grimaced at him. "Just as soon as the formal greetings and Guest-Right declarations are done. You know that."

"I realize how it *should* go, but you know that isn't how it always works."

With a roll of my eyes, I said, "Stop grousing. We'll eat when we eat." The heavy aroma of a roast pig and freshly baked flatbread made my stomach rumble.

At fifteen winters, Aed was a bottomless pit. He ate more food than I thought could fit in his tall, lanky frame. He constantly thought of food. Well, almost constantly; sometimes he spared a thought for girls. Especially if they were carrying food.

I touched the twins' arms and pointed up. They were aged seven now, and needed distractions before they got bored and acted up. "Look, Conn, Fiachra. Do you see the banner in the ramparts? That's our welcome. They've raised Father's symbol, announcing that we're here."

Conn squinted in the bright spring sunlight. I could just make out the white hill on a green background, the symbol of our home.

Aed bounced with restless energy beside me. However, each guest must be welcomed properly and each host must be thanked down the line. I waited patiently for our turn until finally I faced *Banríon* Dervla and *Ard-Rí* Bodb Dearg.

The dark *banríon* put her hands out, palms up. "I welcome you Fionnuala, daughter of Lir and Aobh Bán, you and your kin."

As I finished the formal greeting, I covered her palms with mine and recited the response. "Thanks be unto you, *Banríon* Dervla. I am honored by your hospitality and welcome."

As we exchanged gifts, she winked and whispered, "Come see me later. I have a surprise for you."

I hid a smile, suddenly excited. Still, I had my duty, so I turned to the *ard-rí* and repeated the ritual while the *banríon* repeated hers with Aed.

When we finished, Aed bent close and whispered, "Can we eat yet? I smell something delicious."

"Patience, Aed!"

He frowned. "I don't want them to eat it all before I get some."

I pressed my lips together. "There'll be plenty of food, Aed, even for you!"

The hall had room for over two hundred guests, but our paltry forty still made a great din as we clambered for seats. Banners were hung along the rafters of the long hall, and great platters of food were already on the wooden tables.

Guards took their places on benches while my brothers and I, along with Cliach and Father, took the seats on the royal dais. The twins ate with Nanny Saoirse.

Sweet honey-butter on still-warm bread never tasted so good as it did that morning. It melted in my mouth and I closed my eyes in pure delight. I mopped up some that dripped down my chin as Aed laughed. I didn't care. It tasted wonderful.

After our meal, Dervla led me into her huge solar, her retreat from court life. She kept the solar full of plants and singing birds, some of which flew to Dervla's hand as she fed them. A bright blue bird hopped on her finger and made me grin in delight, despite my worries for Father.

"And how has your father been as of late, my dear?" Dervla asked with a concerned expression.

I blinked several times, surprised by tears of frustration. "He's not well, I'm afraid. He's still wracked with grief every day."

"I know you have not yet had luck finding him a new bride, but we might have a solution for that. Does he fulfill his duties as a *tiarna?*"

I could never admit his failings to the *ard-rí*, but perhaps to his *banríon*, in private, I could. I hung my head, unwilling to answer.

She narrowed her gaze and said, "I noticed that he was sullen at the welcome meal. He spoke to no one, yet consumed copious quantities of mead. Is he often so at home?"

Should I tell her of the violent outbursts of rage and despair? Of the broken furniture and damaged walls? I must tell her. "He gets upset sometimes. He howls or cries."

Her narrowed eyes glinted. "Has he struck you at all? Or anyone?"

"No, no, no, he's never hit any of us. He might throw a chair or a bench. Usually at a wall."

"And who is on hand to ease his rage?"

I stared at my feet. "Me, usually. We've even moved our beds into his room, in case he wakes in the night in a temper."

A black songbird landed on her shoulder and chirped several times until the *banríon* gave the wee thing a couple of grains from her hand. It pecked at them and then flew into the apple tree. "He needs a wife to calm him."

I bowed my head, ashamed that I hadn't helped my father more. I was the lady of the household now and ought to be able to manage things.

A strong, cool hand under my chin forced me to gaze into Dervla's black eyes. "This is not your fault, young lady. It's not up to you to heal everyone, no matter how great your talent."

I gave her a meek nod.

"Now, you need some fun. Would you care to go for a ride with me this afternoon? You can bring your foster-brother and Aed. We shall explore the high hill and the stones there. It's a powerful place. Do bring your ravens, for they'll not want to miss the chance. Oh! I almost forgot."

The *banríon* went to a table and brought back a package wrapped in pale blue fabric, handing it to me. "Well? Go ahead and unwrap it, child."

I peeled away the fabric to reveal a sparkling pale blue jewel on a fine silver chain. I held it up, gasping in wonder.

"I saw this and thought of your mother's eyes. Your eyes, too, as a matter of fact. Think of her when you look at it, so that she may be remembered."

Walking out with Dervla's party, we basked in the heat and gazed at the brilliant blue sky. I wanted to drink in all that I could of this world before I left it forever to live below the hills.

Dervla's foster-daughters, our aunts, joined us, Aoife Rua and Aillbhe, along with Aed, Tadhg, the twins, Nanny, and our ravens. Hawlen always taught me that nine was a sacred number.

Power buzzed as we approached the hilltop, like a thousand bees within my mind. My skin tingled and energy flowed through my blood.

The hill was crowned by a circle of nine ancient standing stones. Each one was weathered and beaten, covered in white and yellow lichen. One faced north and bore carved curving patterns in an elegant design. I wanted to trace the lines with my finger, but I knew it might call up magic.

After so long under the cloud of my father's misery, I gave in to the urge to spin, my arms outstretched, face turned to the sun and my eyes closed. I spun round and round, thrilled by the sheer power flowing through me.

Tadhg laughed and took my hands as we both twirled, and I delighted in dancing with my best, closest friend. His hands felt warm in mine and his laughter was like music.

I pulled in Aed to our group and eventually we all danced around the circle. In and out of the stones, we wove a pattern of joy and delight.

We were on top of the world. No worries, no duties, no anger, no screaming. Green grass under my bare feet felt soft and silky, with a trace of morning dew.

I lay on my back to soak in the earth's energy. It thrummed through my skin and bones, revitalizing my tired, achy muscles. When had I become so bone-tired?

As we giddily soaked in the enchanting power, Dervla opened her basket and brought out cheese, apples, nuts, bread, and chilled mead. We chatted and gossiped about nothing among ourselves for hours.

Aillbha was quiet and shy, and looked like a mix between Aoife and Mother. She was only four winters older than I was.

Aoife Rua turned to me with solemn black eyes, sparkling with curiosity. "I heard the hill near your hillfort is covered in white flowers in the spring and thus earned the name Hill of the White Field. Is that true?"

I gave a smile, thinking of my home. "Yes, it is. Right now, it's covered in white pignut flowers."

Tadhg took my hand. "It's a truly magical sight."

Dervla handed me an apple. "And your new home under the hills, have you seen it yet?"

About to bite into my apple, I shook my head. "Father took us to see the site, but nothing had been built yet."

Aed grabbed the apple from my hand. "Father took Tadhg and me, last moon. It's amazing."

I glanced at Tadhg, and he gave me a shrug. They must have kept the trip a secret from me. I set my jaw to keep from saying something out of jealousy.

The *banríon* gave me a smile. "The palace is stunning, full of high arches and breezy spaces. I asked them to build a solar like mine."

Why would she put in a solar? What good is a solar without a true sun, anyway?

None of this seemed fair, and the sparkling day turned sour. Why should she get to plan my future home? And why should Aed and Tadhg see it before me?

At the feast that evening, Father acted like his normal, morose self. He sat beside the *ard-rí* and *banríon* on the royal dais as a noble guest. Aed, Tadhg, and I sat at the lower tables, with Bodb Dearg's son, Aed Mòr.

Aed Mòr was a pretty lad, tall and fair, and two winters older than I. He'd glance my way and I'd pretend not to notice. I liked him well enough, but he wasn't Tadhg.

Father was on his fifth mug of mead when the *ard-rí* stood and held up his arms for silence. "Friends and subjects, I have a proposal and an announcement. Pray, attend!"

Father muttered and stared into his cup, but everyone else looked up from their meal.

Bodb Dearg gestured to Dervla, and she, in turn, held up her hand. Aoife Rua and Aillbha walked in, carrying themselves with formal dignity. Aoife wore a necklace of large blue stones flecked with gold and a shoulder cape of elaborately hammered gold that covered her shoulders over a deep blue gown. Aillbha wore green jewels in her hair and a slimmer gold mantle, over a pale green gown.

"It has come to my attention that one of my *tiarnaí* is in want of a good wife, someone to cleave unto him and run his *túath*. Someone to love him and honor him and bear him children. Someone to be his other part, to cherish him, and please him."

A murmur ran through the hall. Only one *tiarna* was unmarried at present. I glanced at Father, but he was still staring sullenly into his empty mug.

"I therefore offer to you, *Tiarna* Lir of *Sídhe Fionnachaidh*, the choice of your new bride. Will you do me the honor of choosing one of my foster-daughters? Aoife Rua, she of the red hair, or Aillbha, my little dark raven. Which of these fine ladies would please you most?"

Everyone stared at Father. He'd blinked blearily up from his mug. "What? Me?"

Someone giggled, and I willed Father to comport himself with dignity. A flare of anger flashed through me, and I wanted to speak for him, to spare us his drunken foolishness, but Father put his hands on the stone table, pushed up, and swayed.

He peered at the two young women, then spoke in measured tones. "Which is the oldest? That's how I chose my fair Aobh Bán, and I grew to love her more than life itself."

Aoife Rua gave a sweet smile and stepped forward. She gazed at Father from under lowered lashes, placing a hand on his chest. A sunbeam found her, making her skin and hair glow, and the golden *iunula* glittered. Motes of dust danced around her like sparkling stars.

Beside me, Aed stared at Aoife in a way he usually stared at the young kitchen maids. I rolled my eyes.

I saw a shadow of Mother's smile in Aoife's. Father's mouth hung open, and I wondered if he was lost in the memory of his dead love. A wave of sweet adoration swept through me, and I hugged myself. Everyone else in the hall stared at Aoife Rua.

She leaned closer to Father and took his hand in both of hers, so tiny against his callused skin. She lifted his hand against her cheek and shut her eyes. Father let out a half-moan, half-sob.

Dervla clapped her hands together and the staccato sound roused everyone from their enchantment.

Toasts were raised to the couple, and after several well-wishes, Bodb Dearg stood again. "I've also an announcement to make. Tadhg, son of Illbreach, foster-son of Lir, please step forward."

I glanced at my friend as his eyes darted between the *ard-rí* and me. He looked as confused as I was. Tadhg marched to the dais and stood beside the *ard-rí*.

Had Father made an arrangement for Tadhg and myself? But we were foster-siblings. Despite that, hope bloomed in my heart, and I gripped the table, waiting for the *ard-rí* to call me up to stand beside my dearest friend and future husband.

"Illbreach wanted to make this announcement himself, but a small accident during a stag hunt prevented his attendance today. However, he didn't wish to wait."

Murmurs flew around the hall as I looked at Tadhg. His gaze darted around the room as if searching for some hidden threat.

"Tadhg, you now have nineteen winters and it's time you were betrothed. To this end, your father has made an agreement."

I held my breath. Tadhg risked a quick glance toward me. Images of a joyful wedding flicked through my frantic thoughts.

A wide smile spread across the *ard-rí*'s face. "You are to be wed to young Aillbha, my little raven."

It felt like someone had punched me in the stomach. Tadhg and Aillbha? *No, please, no. It can't be.* Silently, I begged him to refuse.

Tadhg gazed at the *ard-rí*'s third foster-daughter. She was dark and lovely, with plump curves and a sweet disposition. She, too, gazed up under lowered lashes, her smile guileless.

If Tadhg refused this lovely young lady so publicly, he would insult her, the *ard-rí*, his own father, and would make Tadhg a virtual outcast among his kin.

He didn't answer at first but stared at Aillbha with a stiff smile. Then he searched the crowd, and our gazes locked. Desperate indecision danced in his eyes, and I wanted to cry out for him, for us, but I stood as frozen as if bound by magic.

I knew then that I loved Tadhg. He wasn't just my best friend and confidante, but my soul-friend, the one who completed me.

My thoughts must have shown on my face for he turned back to Aillbha. "I would be honored to wed such a fair flower."

The apple I'd been eating turned to sour ashes in my mouth.

The weddings would be in a fortnight. As preparations were made, we stayed at the fort. Father walked around with a dreamy smile on his face and, for once, didn't get drunk every night. And while Hawlen insisted I have afternoon lessons each day, I still couldn't believe Tadhg was to marry someone else.

Every day, I wanted to speak to Tadhg, to declare my deep love. A foster-bond was almost as strong as a blood-bond. Tadhg could inherit my father's lands or administer his estate. He might be a chief under Father and enjoy many other privileges a blood-son had.

And I was forbidden to marry him, unless the foster-bond was broken by a Filí.

But Aillbha was the foster-daughter of the *ard-rí*. As Aillbha's husband, Tadhg could be *ard-rí* himself one day.

Hawlen cawed. "Pay attention, Fionnuala! You must learn the ceremony before the wedding."

I pulled myself from the fog of desperation. "You've drilled me for days. I know what I must do. Can't you just leave me alone?"

The raven cocked her head and contemplated my pout. "You must stop dreaming, child. I know what you want. It cannot be, not without a great deal of heartache and trouble. To upset the order of things is against the greater good. Your father is, for once in many winters, happy again. Will you rob him of this brief joy for your own selfish desires?"

I clenched my jaw, but Hawlen was right. I couldn't change what was ordained. Once both weddings happened, Tadhg would be related by marriage as well as by foster-bond.

My stomach roiled in protest. It just wasn't fair. As a royal daughter, I knew full well that I had no say in my marriage, but it still wasn't fair.

I glanced out the window, where the gray clouds reflected my mood. I wanted to cry in frustration and pound my fists against the wooden walls.

"Fionnuala! Desist in your pouting."

"I'm not pouting. I'm angry. There's a difference."

"There is no difference when there's nothing to be done. Being angry without proposing a solution is mere self-punishment. If you have a solution, tell me, and we shall work to make it happen."

I sighed. "You know there's no solution."

"Then tend your lessons."

I didn't want to be any part of a wedding, even if it ruined Father's joy. I could only imagine Tadhg being wed to Aillbha and their wedding night. A night where she'd share what I deserved.

I sighed again but listened to my raven. It was my duty. I detested that word, *duty*.

I glanced at my dress, of deep forest greens and gold. The headdress was delicately silver filigree with leaves around the base, and branches topped in ruby berries rising two full hands above my brow.

Tadhg would see me in my finery. Perhaps he'd be mesmerized by my beauty and abandon his arranged bride, stealing me away in front of everyone. My stomach knotted and I told myself I shouldn't think of him. He was gone from me now.

Chapter Five

It took some work to speak with Tadhg alone, but he agreed to meet with me. As we sat along the riverbank in the late afternoon, I turned to him and gritted my teeth. "But do you *want* to marry her?"

He picked up a flat stone and threw it into the river. It skipped four times before sinking into the sparkling ripples. "She wouldn't be my first choice, no."

My heart leapt in my chest. Could I be his first choice?

Tadhg fiddled with a second stone and gazed at me. His eyes looked sad and my sudden glimmer of hope died. He dropped his stone and took my hands. "You. You've always been my first choice, Nuala. My lovely Nuala."

He stroked my hair, and I wanted to cry.

"But our duty is to marry where we're bid. Aillbha is to be my wife. I can't go against the *ard-rí's* decision. It's my duty."

"Duty! Always, duty. I hate that word. I hate it!" I snatched the stone he dropped and pelted it against a tree. It ricocheted back toward us and we ducked.

Tadhg let out a chuckle. "And it will be for naught if you kill us before the wedding, Nuala!"

I swallowed my angry answer. No amount of railing or ranting would change the facts, but I wouldn't be drawn into joking. I wasn't done yet. The only hope I had left lay in desperate measures.

I swallowed and then plunged in. "What if we lie together?"

He gaped at me, his eyes wide.

"If we were together, perhaps your *duty* wouldn't be so clear."

I wanted Tadhg more than anything I'd ever wanted, to lie beside him and feel his hands over my body, to kiss him and be one with him. If he had a lover, he wouldn't be suitable for marriage to the *ard-rí's* foster-daughter.

In my heart, I knew this was folly. Nobles took lovers all the time, from the common folk. As long as any heirs were properly acknowledged and cared for, no one cried foul. Children from such lovers were often raised alongside the heirs and sometimes became heirs in their own right. But I wasn't common folk. I was also a noble, and was therefore forbidden.

Tadhg shook his head. "I couldn't do that. I must have one love and one love only. I'd be too torn were I to take a lover. Besides, how would that be fair to you? I'd still have to marry Aillbha and you'd need to wed someone else."

Suddenly fed up with having no control over my fate, I jumped to my feet. "I won't! If I can't marry you, I will never marry anyone!"

Tadhg rose and tried to hug me, but I pounded my fists on his chest. He caught my elbows and drew me in tight. I had no wish to be coddled. I wanted to rage against my destiny, against my *duty*, against the strict rules of royal life.

"Shh, shh, my dear, dear friend, my best friend. You'll always be that, no matter what happens. But we can't be lovers."

I shoved him away and ran into the woods. He was just letting this happen. It was his fault. If he'd just stand up to his father, we could be together.

We could run away and be lovers, sleep in a new place every night, and greet the world each morning in our love and joy.

Eventually I slowed, panting and pressing against the stitch in my side. I wanted anger, or vengeance. I wanted something to hit. I wanted to relish my pain and the red, raw power rolling through me.

So I sought out the Royal Weaponmaster. He raised his eyebrows as he took me in, panting and wet with sweat.

I clenched my jaw. "I need to hit things."

He shrugged and pulled out two wooden swords. I attacked him with furious vigor, again and again. I swung hard and artlessly until the wooden practice sword cracked and shattered, sending splinters flying. He grunted and fetched another one.

Despite my ferocity, he contented himself with parrying each of my attacks until I could no longer lift the heavy weapon.

When sweat streamed down my cheeks and through my clothes, I thanked the patient man. He opened his mouth for a question, but then closed it, and collected the practice swords.

Seven days later, we were eating supper in the hall when every raven flew away in a sudden rustle of wings. All conversation stopped as the *ard-rí* and *banríon* exchanged a worried glance. Silence thundered until Bodb Dearg gestured to his bard to play.

The bard burst into a sprightly tune, a legend of the Dagda in one of his more comical endeavors.

Curious, I sent a tendril of will toward Hawlen. She'd taught me communication spells, and I wasn't sure it would work, but I wanted to try.

Through the night, I sent my magic, searching for my bond, my teacher, my friend. Out, out, farther I quested, over twilight-clad hills and dew-wet leaves. I searched until I heard her mind.

But she flew intent upon her purpose, whatever that might be, and didn't answer my magic. Instead, I rode along in her mind and became one with her senses. We beat our wings hard against the chilly wind and the moon distorted shadows upon the ground. We flapped harder and glided faster toward... what? I glimpsed an enormous earthen mound with a white chalk face before the link broke.

I gasped and opened my eyes, blinking from the sudden glare.

Aed cocked his head. "Nuala? Are you ill?"

As I shook my head, he handed me a cup of wine, but I didn't take it. My senses reeled, as if I was being turned upside down. I tried to pull up the link again, but the bond slithered away even as I recalled the details.

The ravens were called to that place. I'd seen hundreds, perhaps thousands of ravens landing on the mound in the moonlight. What was happening?

The twins should get their raven eggs soon. Maybe that's why the ravens held a conclave. But royal children were born all the time.

Aoife asked from across the feast table, "You look pale, child. Do you need some air? Perhaps a quiet walk in the gardens would clear your head?"

Her smile looked so much like my mother's and her suggestion sounded perfect. I took her arm, and we left the hall, strolling out into the cool night air.

My aunt glanced toward the sky. "It's such a brilliant night. The full moon dims the stars, but I prefer the moon, don't you?"

I gave her a shrug. "I don't know. I love the twinkling stars overhead. One can see a trail of them on clear nights as if the gods spilled white paint."

Aoife Rua stopped next to a white rose and breathed in its fragrance. "I shall ask for white roses at the wedding. Are you looking forward to the feast?"

Strangely enough, mention of the wedding didn't fill me with dread. Instead, a calm acceptance washed over me. "Please, you must call me Nuala."

"Nuala it is. And you must call me Mother."

Something fought against my calm. I'd never call someone else Mother. It was disrespectful to her spirit, but I didn't know how to say that. Hawlen would have advised me to say nothing, so I remained silent.

Aoife lifted my chin with one cool white finger and made me peer up into her eyes. "No, I suppose that won't do, will it? I suppose Aunt or Stepmother would be best."

I could call her aunt, and perhaps even stepmother. After all, she'd been my aunt all my life. I gave her a nod and she released my chin. I could still feel where her cold fingers had touched my skin and it tingled, like when I healed someone.

What would life be like with my aunt in charge of the *túath*? She seemed friendly and stern in flashes. Mother had been kind, though she had everyone's respect. She rarely yelled and left most discipline to our ravens or Father. However, she brooked no breaches of etiquette.

A season before Mother died, Aed and I had crafted a trap for Maire Mór. We'd rigged a bucket of flour over the kitchen door. When the flour billowed everywhere, Maire looked like a shade covered in white.

We'd rolled on the floor of my room in giggles when Mother marched into our rooms, pulled us up by the ear. "I don't have to figure out who's at fault for this, do I? I can tell by your guilty faces."

I'd never heard her sound so angry. My tears of laughter turned to tears of remorse.

She held up one hand. "No, I don't want to hear your apologies, though Maire Mór will take them and straight away. Then you will clean up the flour and give your victim a bath."

My eyes grew wide. "A *bantiarna* giving a housekeeper a bath? It should be the other way around!"

Mother gave me a fierce scowl. "When a *bantiarna* behaves like a common scullery maid, she shall be treated like one!"

I bowed my head in shame.

"After the bath, you shall both work in the mills and grind flour. You wasted a whole bucket. Therefore, you will grind *two* buckets."

Aed chose this moment to be contrary. "But we aren't millers! We're royal children. We're trained to rule and manage, not grind flour."

Mother glared, hands on her hips. "And what part of managing resources includes wasting them?"

We bowed our heads and went to our punishments.

I thought about relating this tale to my aunt, but thought better of it. No sense in giving her ideas.

"What are your rooms like at home, Nuala? Do you like them?"

"My room isn't far from Father's, with plenty of space for both Hawlen and me. It's my duty to clean up after her, but she isn't messy. What's the name of your raven?"

"Nawlet. She has a patch of white on her chest. Her grandfather was a Messenger." Pride shone in her voice.

I cocked my head. "I didn't think the Messenger caste bred with the others. Was there a great tale of love?"

Aoife laughed, her voice rippling in the quiet night. "Indeed and it is, to hear her tell of it. I shall let her tell the tale another day. She'd not forgive me if I ruined her opportunity for a new audience."

Ravens loved to tell stories, which was one reason they made such excellent teachers.

"And what of your brother's rooms? And your father's? It's been many moons since I visited the place where I shall spend my life."

"But you won't be there long! Remember, we're to move to the place under the hills within eight winters."

She furrowed her lovely brow. "Oh? I thought you'd already moved. That is interesting, indeed." She glanced up at the sky again. "You haven't been to the new fort, correct?"

"Only before anything was built. The site's lovely, with rolling hills and a surrounding forest."

"Well, we should plan an expedition, first thing after the wedding. We can't have the *banríon* and the *bantiarna* living in ignorance, can we?"

She offered her arm, and I placed my hand in it. "Indeed, we cannot!"

In that moment, I decided that Aoife Rua was the best choice for my father, after all.

The day of the wedding dawned bright, but by midday, clouds dimmed the sky. Decked out in my stiff finery, I did a turn as Hawlen and Aed inspected my outfit. I ached to ask her where she'd gone, but her glare kept me from inquiring.

Aed tweaked a branch from my crown that stuck out at a right angle. "This part looks funny. Why does it stick up so much?"

"Because I'm a clumsy girl and must have bent it." I grimaced and removed the silver crown to bend it back into place.

Hawlen pecked here and there and tucked a fold of cloth. Finally, she gave a nod. "Acceptable."

"Thank Danu! I'm starving!"

"Tsk. Here, have some nuts to tide you over." Hawlen pushed her own meal toward us. We exchanged a glance and split the bounty. The groundnuts were delicious and while I was still nervous, at least I wasn't nervous *and* hungry.

Aed, being a younger child, wore a simpler outfit. We both wore white robes with golden embroidery in complex spirals. We each wore sashes of purple to signify our royal birth and silver *iunula* over our shoulders, hammered with more spirals.

We descended the stairs carefully and climbed the processional path to the stone circle on the hill.

This wasn't the same circle Dervla had brought us to, but one on the other side of the hillfort. Twenty-seven stones stood stark against the morning sun. Swirls had been carved in many of them, but they covered the tall altar stone.

I followed the designs with my eyes, but got lost in the twists and turns of the amazing art. I'd seen them somewhere before. Then I recalled that brief glimpse of a white stone that night the ravens had disappeared. The designs were the same.

The *ard-rí* and *banríon*'s ravens perched upon the altar stone. Dark clouds blew across the blue sky.

The flat hill was crowded with wedding guests and servants. Voices barking orders, people giggling, and shuffled feet overwhelmed me. I took in a deep breath to quell my panic and fought the urge to flee.

Aed and I stood near the carved altar stone, and he fumbled to grab my hand, giving it a squeeze.

Bé Chuille was in the middle, her forest green robes stitched with gold. A mantle of iridescent black raven feather covered the high druid's shoulders, with an edge of incredibly rare white raven feathers. She held an oaken staff, grown in a twisted braid, with a glowing crystal of deep rose pink caged in the top.

A dozen ravens swooped in and landed around the edge of the stone circle as Father and Tadhg approached.

They were both resplendent in purple and blue. Father wore his cloak or brat of red, blue, green, and yellow, with checkers of white throughout. Tadhg's brat had fewer colors as he was lower ranked. Their brats whipped in sudden gusts of wind.

They each wore golden crowns, Father's with oak leaves and three black raven feathers, and Tadhg's with pinecones and one feather, as the son of a *tiarna*.

I'd managed to put Tadhg and his new bride out of my mind all morning with the stress of getting ready. But now, I caught my breath at the sight of him.

His blue-black curls shone in the late morning sunlight. He once claimed Fir Bolg ancestry, far back in his ancestry, and his brooding features today made that seem more likely. He didn't look happy, and I entertained the fancy he might refuse this match at the last minute.

I swallowed against a sob, forcing myself to swallow and peered down the aisle. The crowd grew silent as the brides arrived.

Aoife Rua dressed in purple as father had, and it complimented her bright red hair, which flowed loose and glittered in the light. A gold circlet rested on her brow, in perfect elegance and style. She held a bouquet of white roses and wore swirling gold jewelry around her upper arms.

Beside her, the dark-haired Aillbha had dressed in blue, her pale skin shining like alabaster. My heart caught in my throat. Why would Tadhg give up such a wife, a foster-daughter to the *ard-rí* himself?

Everyone stared as the two women marched to the altar.

As each couple made declarations of honor and respect, I concentrated on the dancing motes of dust in the sun until the light dimmed under gathering clouds.

The High Ollamh recited the long list of laws to which each party must adhere. Individual ownership of land and cattle, permissions for major decisions, rules of divorce, all the details of marital contracts.

Just as both pairs swore their final vows, hands laid flat upon the carved blessing stone, lightning flashed as a burst of thunder rumbled across the hill.

Everyone jumped and nervous muttering spread through the assembly. I shot a glance at Hawlen as she fluttered her wings, and then I stared into the sky. Roiling clouds darkened the world, an ill omen for a wedding. A part of me cheered at this censure from the gods to Tadhg's marriage.

Bé Chuille finished the last of the ceremony, but her face looked strained with forced optimism. She glanced at the surrounding ravens, as they fluttered their wings, and settled themselves after the latest boom of thunder.

Heavy drops of cool rain splattered on my head as everyone sprinted for shelter. I couldn't run, not downhill in the rain with this cumbersome formal dress and crown. I picked my way down the increasingly slippery slope.

By the time I got near the hillfort, I was a muddy mess. My hair was soaked and bedraggled, my gown disgusting with mud, and my spirit shattered.

As we approached the entrance, nine strangers stood near the door. Bé Chuille exchanged a glance with the *ard-rí* and approached them. With all the authority and dignity as a High Ollamh, she put out her hands, palms up. "Welcome, guests! Who has come calling?"

The two in front exchanged glances. I peered at their braided hair and leather armor, realizing they must be Milesians. The older one answered. "We have recently built homes nearby and wish to bring a gift for the wedding."

I swallowed and glanced toward the *ard-rí*, but the *banríon* was already approaching them with her hands up. "We welcome you both, you and your kin. I welcome you into our homes…"

As she completed the formal greeting, I ducked behind Aed. I *did* recognize one of the strangers. Áedammair, the Milesian *tiarna* who'd sheltered in our hillfort on a stormy night like this.

The *ard-rí* declared the feast open and the visitors joined us, though the celebration seemed muted.

I couldn't tell if the undercurrent was due to the thunderstorm on a wedding day, within moments of the final vows, or the uninvited guests. Neither were good omens.

Still, as mead and wine flowed, people relaxed their nervous energy and let loose with revelry. Soon there was singing, dancing, and laughter, like any wedding feast.

I escaped to my room and changed to cleaner and more practical attire. By the time I returned, the brides and grooms had retired to their own bridal suites to begin their consummation. Pressing my hands against my eyes, I tried not to think of what Tadhg and Aillbhe were doing at this very moment, and I took a long draft of mead.

Hawlen landed on my shoulder and whispered in my ear. "Something's brewing. Can you feel it?"

I took another drink of mead. "The storm, you mean?"

"Yes, the storm, but something caused it. Something dangerous."

I tried to crane my neck to look at her on my shoulder. "Does this have something to do with the raven conclave the other day?"

Hawlen cawed, "Perhaps. Well done on that ride, Fionnuala. I sensed your spirit, but I had to cut the connection. That conclave was private."

I swallowed, suddenly nervous about having been caught. "I understand."

"I will research further into this. I sensed magical working during the ceremony, even before the storm arrived. It may have been an accident, by someone working magic without a thought to consequences."

How many times had Hawlen taught me that all magic had a price? A shiver ran down my spine at the idea of someone working great magic without thought of the consequences.

My raven departed, taking my desire to celebrate with her.

Someone pretended to be in the throes of passion, and his friends laughed. They were making fun of Tadhg and Aillbhe, in their room, consummating their marriage.

I ran out to the garden, huddling on a bench beneath a bower. The rain raged just past my knees, matching the tears down my cheeks.

All the escapism in the world wasn't enough to hold back the images of Tadhg with his bride. His lovely dark curls fell upon her chest, as they rhythmically took each other in carnal pleasure.

In my mind, she caressed him as she stroked his chest, as I longed to do. I fancied I could even hear their cries of passion over the sound of raindrops.

Footsteps came toward me. I hastily wiped my tears and glanced up just as Áedammair, the Milesian *tiarna*, sat beside me. "You seem upset, my *bantiarna*. Is there anything I can do to make you happy once more?"

I gave him a half-smile. "Thank you for the kind offer. But I'm afraid sharing this misery won't help it. I'd rather be alone right now."

He took my hand, and it looked tiny in his. "Then perhaps I can help another day." Áedammair kissed my knuckles, then my forehead, and left.

The next morning dawned bright, and while I didn't have nightmares about my mother, images of Tadhg and his new bride had kept me from getting any rest. I yawned my way through my morning wash and stumbled down into the main hall to break my fast.

Only a few other guests were in attendance, so many must still be sleeping off their revelries. I spied one of Áedammair's Milesians, so he must still be in the hillfort. For some reason, this made the day seem brighter.

After eating an apple and some porridge, I wandered into the garden. I wanted to listen to bees and smell sweet flowers. Anything to keep my mind off Tadhg still being in his marriage bed.

I had just bent to sniff the scent of a pink rose when someone walked toward me, their footsteps crunching in the gravel. I smiled as Áedammair approached. "Are you an early riser, too, then?"

"I find that the dawn is too beautiful to waste. As are you." He took my hands in his and kissed them.

My cheeks burned and I couldn't speak.

He cleared his throat. "I must ask you a favor, *Bantiarna* Fionnuala."

"Only if you promise to call me Nuala."

He gave me a grin. "Very well, Nuala. I understand that your father has a new bride. And you have been running his household since your mother died."

He took a deep breath, as if collecting his thoughts, or perhaps trying to find words. "I would like to ask if you would consider being in charge of my household?"

I furrowed my brow. "As a headwoman? While I'm flattered at your confidence in my abilities, I'm afraid I couldn't do that. My father will want me to marry a *tiarna*."

He shook his head, looking troubled. "No, no, I must have used the wrong words." Áedammair cleared his throat again. "I'm asking you to be my wife, Nuala. To marry me and be in charge of my house. To be my *banríon*."

My mind was a jumble of thoughts, ideas rushing through with no order. My stomach dropped to my feet, and I couldn't meet his entreating eyes. I stared at the ground, the path, anywhere but at him.

I loved Tadhg. Áedammair was kind, and I enjoyed talking with him, but how could I marry him? He wasn't even of the People.

He bowed his head. "I understand it may take some time to think about my offer. I will leave you alone with your thoughts."

He turned to leave, but I caught his arm. "Wait! Yes, I do need time to think, but I must ask, why me? Surely you have women of your own people?"

Áedammair gave a wide grin. "Because the first time I saw you, your loveliness became my sun."

My cheeks burned hot as he left with a jaunty step.

Once he was out of sight, I sat on the garden bench and rubbed my temples. How could my entire life be so turned around in just a few days? I tried to make sense of things, but nothing fell into place.

Would Father approve this marriage? I doubted it. But he has a new wife himself, so why not grant me the freedom to marry where I wished? After all, even if he was a Milesian, Áedammair was a *tiarna*.

Besides, they'd taken Tadhg from me. They owed me.

I hurried back into the hall, searching for Father. He stumbled in, his face drawn with too much drink. I didn't see Aoife Rua and was glad to be able to confront him alone. I clutched his arm. "Father! I must ask you something."

He waved at me and sat heavily at the table. "Wait until I've eaten, child."

I waited with undisguised impatience while he ate and picked at a piece of buttered bread. When he finally wiped his mouth, I burst out with, "Father, I've gotten a marriage offer!"

He blinked as if trying to process my words. "Who asks for you?"

I swallowed, trying to make my voice work. "Áedammair." My mouth ached to say Tadhg.

He scowled and waved his hand. "I don't know who that is."

"He's the Milesian *tiarna* who's visiting. Remember? He came to our hillfort once, during a horrible storm."

Father's scowl deepened as he glanced around the table, but the only other people breaking their fast were too far away to hear. He placed his hands on the table and spoke in a low, implacable tone. "Absolutely not. No child of mine will marry one of *them*. I forbid it. Never, ever mention it again."

We traveled back home the next day. Though the sun shone bright, a cloud of sullen anger colored everything I saw.

Chapter Six

In the 29th winter of Ard-Rí Bodb Dearg's reign (451 BCE) 2 years later

Fiachra patted the pale blue egg, mottled with dark spots, with reverence. "How long before they hatch?"

Hawlen flapped her wings and dug at an itchy spot. "It could be any day now."

Conn gasped and caressed his own. "But what if we aren't here? Will we lose them?"

"No, they'll wait for you. But the bond will be stronger if you are the first person they see."

Fiachra's eyes grew wide. "How do we know? We might be sleeping, or eating, or fishing, or fighting, or—"

The raven let out a chuckle, which sounded more like a caw. "Calm, child. We will call you when the event is imminent."

Fiachra cocked his head. "What's imamamament?"

"Imminent means soon."

Fiachra narrowed his eyes. "Why don't you just say *soon* then?"

I covered my mouth before a laugh escaped.

Hawlen clacked her beak. "We'll make sure you are here in time, even if it should be in the darkest hour of the night."

The smile that lit Fiachra's face was so sweet, I wanted to cry. Such a dear child. I hugged him until he wriggled to get free.

Hawlen spread her wings, cocking her own head and peering at the eggs.

"Look alive, children. The event will be upon us soon. Fionnuala, Aed, run to the kitchens for meat. Maire Mór will know what we need."

Aed frowned. "Me? Why do I have to get the meat? I want to see the eggs hatch."

I rolled my eyes. "Oh, do come on, Aed. Let the twins have their moment and help me do the dirty work for once, huh?"

We returned with two bowls of minced raw beef, still steaming from the slaughter, pools of thick blood forming in the bottom.

Fiachra and Conn sat on either side as their eggs jumped and rocked. Every time an egg moved, so did a child. They were like puppets attached on a single string.

I elbowed Aed in the ribs and we exchanged a grin. Conn scowled, but Fiachra let out a joyful giggle.

Totawg, Aed's raven, came in while we fetched the meat, but now Lawstarn and Nawlet joined, Father and Aoife's bondmates.

The raw meat made me queasy, but I swallowed and concentrated on the eggs dancing in their straw nests.

Aed poked at the meat. "Well? I thought you said it would happen soon. Are the omniscient ravens wrong for once?"

I slapped his hand away. "Hush, Aed. Have patience."

A loud crack made both twins jump. Conn let out a whoop and scooted closer to his egg. He hastily covered his mouth and glanced around, as if waiting for a scolding. However, Aoife didn't appear, and he dropped his hand.

The crack grew larger. *Tip-tap* came from the inside as the tiny creature worked free from the constrictive shell. *Tip-tap, tip-tap.* Another crack appeared next to the first and a chunk of shell fell away to reveal a glistening black beak.

Conn inched closer and grabbed a bloody handful of meat. Then he leaned down until his face almost touched the still wobbly egg.

Crack! The egg split open and both sides fell away to reveal a shiny black ball of claws and beak. The hatchling let out a peep and Conn froze, blood dripping from his fingers.

I poked him in the shoulder. "Feed him, silly!"

Conn glanced up with wide eyes and then shoved the handful of raw meat at the bird. He didn't even flinch when its beak darted out to grab the nearest morsel. It gobbled that one down and reached for another. And another. Soon, nothing remained in Conn's hand but a bloody mess. The baby raven pecked at his skin.

He stroked the scrawny hatchling's still wet, scrawny head, and the bird peered up into his eyes. Their gazes locked for several moments before it peeped again, climbed into Conn's lap, and curled up. Conn's smile glowed as he touched the bird's head.

"Why won't mine crack? It's been jumping for just as long." Fiachra sounded panicked. "Does it need help? Is something wrong? Should I break it?"

Totawg clacked his beak. "Patience, child. It will hatch when it's ready, never fear. We'd know if something were wrong."

Little bits of Fiachra's egg fell off, but the inner membrane, thick and white, didn't split. Three quarters of the shell cracked before it opened to reveal its treasure. The hatchling shook off the remnants of the inner shell and stepped forward into the boy's waiting hands.

Encouraged by Conn, who now quietly cradled the tiny bird in the corner, crooning it to sleep, Fiachra calmly fed his hatchling the rest of the meat. Soon, all four young ones were asleep, piled in the corner.

I sighed and gathered the empty bowls. "Well, that was a sight to see, certainly!"

Hawlen nodded. "It's unusual to have twin royal children, so two hatchlings at once are a rare event, indeed. These will be a handful. I need no prophesy to see that."

Inside Aoife Rua's solar, I squinted at the small lump in the fine thread I spun. Peasants might get away with rough-spun thread, but as the daughter of a *tiarna*, I should have produced a beautiful, perfect thread.

My stepmother hulked over me with beetled brows and a stern mouth. "Fionnuala! Stop that daydreaming at once. You know quite well I tolerate no idleness in my home."

I should never have let her see me pause in my work. Once, such criticism would have set off my temper. My cheeks burned with both shame and rage, and I wanted to vent that frustration in angry words. But now, I knew better than to give my aunt any cause to berate me.

I once thought Aoife Rua was the best choice for my father's new wife. After two cycles of the seasons, I now knew that had been a foolish choice. She was imperious, fractious, and had a worse temper than Father.

I bent back to my spindle and after a few intense moments, Aoife Rua turned away to scrutinize the other ladies' work.

After she critiqued each piece, Aoife called for the bard to entertain them. Cliach arrived with his clothes stained and wrinkled and his hair in a tangle.

Aoife Rua looked him up and down, her lip curled. "It's well past midday. How dare you come in here looking like a wastrel! You're a court bard and should be properly presentable!"

Cliach peered with squinted eyes, as if he didn't quite recognize her. He must be drunk, perhaps still from the night before. One of the girls giggled.

Aoife darted a glance around to find which girl laughed but couldn't pick her out.

She turned back to the bard. "Get yourself cleaned and combed immediately. I expect you back in no more than a quarter hour. Go!"

Instead of scuttling off to do her bidding, he threw his head back and let out a long, loud laugh, his whole body shaking with mirth.

Aoife glared as if he'd gone mad.

And perhaps that's exactly what happened. Cliach had never recovered from my mother's death, and when Father brought his new wife home, giving orders and taking charge, he withdrew from life. Perhaps his mind had finally cracked under the strain.

Aoife's voice grew higher until it screeched. "Stop! Stop that this instant! Stop it, I say!"

Cliach just laughed louder. He dropped to the floor and lay on his side, clutching his stomach. What if he truly couldn't stop? Had someone laid a curse or *geas* upon him?

My aunt snapped, "Fionnuala! Get Maire Mór!"

I ran down the hall as fast as I could run. Dallying would earn me a cuff on the ear.

As I skidded into the kitchen, I clutched at the headwoman's sleeve.

Maire gave me a good-natured smile. "Nuala? What is it, my dear? Are the Milesians on your tail?"

I shook my head. "It's Cliach. He can't stop laughing. He's in the solar with Aoife."

Her expression sobered at once. She gathered several supplies. "Send your raven and whichever others are around up to meet me. By Brige's fire, I should have you as well, with your healing gifts, but I'll not subject you to Aoife's wrath without cause. Wait, I can take him to the nursery. Meet us there."

As she left the kitchen, I called for Hawlen in my mind. My control had improved over the last seasons, as my need for silent communications had grown. *Hawlen, Cliach needs healing. Maire will take him to the nursery. Can you gather the others?*

A brief acknowledgement came from my teacher and I grabbed some of my own supplies, rushing past three roundhouses to the nursery.

The twins were big enough to sleep in their own rooms now, sturdy children of nine winters, so the nursery had been turned into a sickroom.

A few guards brought the still-laughing bard in, and Maire Mór directed them to place him on the cot. Once they left, she tapped her chin with her lips pursed. Several slaps on the face had no effect on the now hysterical bard.

It wasn't a humorous laugh. It was a desperate, mad, sunk into delirium laugh that tried to draw me in to its madness. I fought against that with every heartbeat.

I had to leave. I rushed out of the room just as the ravens winged in through the windows. Once outside, I took several deep breaths to calm myself. I concentrated on building a mental wall against the sound, a technique Hawlen had taught me.

Was this how Mother had blocked my healing? Brick by brick, I made it thick and strong, humming to bolster the magic's purpose. It didn't stop the madness completely, but my barrier muted the laughter's power. Thus steeled, I reentered the room.

The wall worked well, and I had a flash of an idea. What if I crafted the bricks into something sharp? An offensive weapon rather than defensive? Not against poor Cliach, but something to consider for the future.

As Maire Mór worked on Cliach, I paced behind her. He'd curled into a ball, knees against his chest as he rocked back and forth. His throat sounded raw with the constant cackling, now more of a hacking cough. Maire rubbed his chest with some ointment she used when we had colds, something that opened the breath and cleared our minds.

It didn't seem to help Cliach.

Hawlen called, "Fionnuala! Come, put your hands on his head. I shall direct you."

I walked around the cot and touched Cliach's greasy hair. He must not have washed for weeks. Crawling creatures on his scalp skittered, and I resisted the urge to pull away.

Gather your will and visualize it as a pale blue light. Build it into a large, flaming ball within your heart.

I hummed to charge the magic. My fireball flickered and pulsed in my mind.

This is healing energy, energy to soothe the mad soul. It is calm, it is quiet, it is a still lough on a foggy morning. It is a blue sky on a lazy afternoon.

I infused my shining orb with these images. Then, I opened my mouth to turn my hum into a single, strong note.

Now, gently push tendrils of this energy through your hands and into his mind. Very little at first, so he doesn't notice the intrusion. This magic can be very dangerous if misused, mind you, so use caution.

Tiny threads of radiant light blue energy flowed down my arms, into my hands and through each finger before they caressed his skull, his mind, and hopefully swirled into his brain. My voice wavered, so I took a breath and sang again.

Tendrils danced like ice crystals on a frozen lough. They twisted and combined into mystical knots, like on the embroidered Filíd robes or carved into the standing stones. Cliach's maniacal laughter eased, lower in volume, not as desperate.

Good, good, now push a little more energy into the healing, just a bit at a time.

His laughter turned to giggles and finally ragged gasps. My song grew soft now, almost a lullaby. Maire Mór dribbled a sleeping potion into his mouth and finally, the mad bard slipped into sleep.

Every muscle in my body ached, but severing contact was dangerous. I had to pull the tendrils of power gently back into myself and release them into the sacred earth before I let go of my patient.

Once I finished, I crumpled to the ground, all strength gone. The cold flagstones felt comforting, and I clung to their immobile strength as my mind drifted into sleep.

Father's angry voice penetrated my exhausted fog. "What is going on here? What was that horrific sound? What have you done to my daughter?"

Aoife came in behind him and frowned. "Your bard has gone quite mad, Lir. He's calm now, and there's no need for you to yell to wake him."

"What? How dare you order me about! Woman, get back into your solar!"

I didn't need to open my eyes to see my stepmother straighten her spine. "I will not! I have a duty here, which I shall finish before I leave."

"Your duty! As if you knew aught of duty. Where has your sense of duty been these last nights, as I lie alone and cold? Where are the children you promised to bear me?"

Her voice grew sharper. "Cold as your heart, you mean? There's your answer."

I wanted to crawl away and hide. This wasn't their first fight, and I had no wish to be witness to another, but I had no strength to rise.

Aed must have had the same idea, for he lifted me to my feet and we stumbled from the sickroom.

Their argument followed us as we entered the main roundhouse. I could even hear their angry words in my room, through the window I always left open for Hawlen.

Aed sat beside me and gave me a sideways hug, but I shook him off. "If only they wouldn't argue so in front of everyone."

My brother's eyes lit up. "They'll get better, you'll see. I have a scheme to help them love each other. It'll work, I swear!"

With that, he rushed out of my room and shut the door.

I tried to snort, but I had no strength for even that. I prayed that Aed would at least seek his raven's advice. Love magic was prone to error and heartache.

As I drifted into an exhausted sleep, I dreamt again.

White feathers smothered me, and I couldn't escape them. I pushed through, trying to find my way out of the mass, but I swam in a sea of white, struggling against the tide. Wind blew me in several directions and I tumbled out to the endless frozen ocean.

I woke with a gasp and sat up, covered in sticky, cold sweat.

Hawlen waited on her perch, cocking her head at me. "You screamed, child. What happened in the dream land?"

I glanced at the dark window. I must have slept the entire day and well into the night. After taking a few moments to gather my thoughts, I related the dream to my raven.

She clacked her beak and asked, "How many times have you dreamt like this? For how long?"

"The first time was after Mother died. Since then, about once every moon? It's hard to keep track. They're not always this bad. Sometimes it's just a memory of the feathers, or the sensation I was flying forever."

"Hmm. You might be picking up someone else's fears in your dream. Create a block, so other thoughts don't intrude."

"Can you teach me?"

"Indeed. Not tonight, though. For now, I shall block for you. You need your rest."

The next day, determined never again to be caught without some protection, I practiced making an arrow of power.

I left early in the morning, before Aoife Rua woke, so I could have some time to myself, and strode up the path through the woods.

As I came across the spot where I'd spent that afternoon with Tadhg, the breath caught in my throat. I kept moving. I would never feel comfortable in that spot again.

Finally, I spotted a clearing and settled with my back to a solid oak tree. Dried leaves crackled under me as I closed my eyes and pulled power up through my body. Blue, glowing power, shaped by my hands into a ball. This much, I knew how to do.

Now, to form it into some sort of weapon. I knew how to shoot a bow, that was my favorite, so I molded the ball into a long, thin arrow, complete with head and fletching. It hovered before me, faintly glowing blue with sparks on either end.

I glanced around and chose a hillock across the clearing. Launching the arrow, I aimed it at the hillock.

The arrow disappeared immediately.

Patiently, I pulled the power up and tried again. This time, it got a third of the way there before disintegrating.

Again, I formed the arrow, this time concentrating so hard on the form, my nails bit into the palms of my hands. When I let it go, it reached the hillock but then shattered into a thousand blue sparks.

I was already exhausted and realized I needed a lot of practice with this. But at least I had a start.

As we broke our fast the next morning, no one spoke of Cliach's breakdown. However, the ravens called the Filíd to come fetch him. I had enough power to quell his immediate terror, but I couldn't make him whole again. He would need the council of healers for that, in the Oak Grove.

What would it be like in that sacred place? Unless I wished to dedicate myself to the Filíd, I would never know. The Sacred Oak Grove was where the Filíd lived and taught, where the acolytes learned, and was forbidden to all outsiders.

I stared at my cooling porridge and pushed the chunks around with my spoon. Heavy footsteps made me glance up as Father entered the hall.

His face was drawn and his eyes looked hollow. His hair appeared unkempt and tangled, almost as bad as Cliach's had been. *What's wrong with our household that everyone's gone mad?*

He sat beside me and gestured to the servant for food. "Are you well, daughter? Hawlen said you did good work on the bard yesterday."

"The strongest spell I ever performed, but I'm rested now, Father."

"Good, good, that's good. Rest is good." He patted me on the shoulder, absently. "Where are your brothers?"

"Aed's already out at fighter practice. Scuida will give him his final test for spear later this week. The twins were in the garden, last I saw."

"The garden? Why the garden?"

I smiled. "One of the kitchen maids noticed they loved plants, so she's teaching them the different herbs and flowers. They might have talent with the herb side of healing."

A smile settled on his face, the first I'd seen in a while. "Ah, that's a noble calling and practical, too. As much as I loved your mother, prophesy is for disaster, not daily life."

It's the first time he'd mentioned Mother in casual conversation since her death. His smile was full of forlorn loss.

I placed my hand on his arm. "Do you miss her so much, Father?"

Father let out a deep sigh, staring at the table. "I miss her like my arm was cut off. My heart aches every day." He turned to me and caressed my hair. "Then I see her smile in your own, and I realize there's still a bit of her in this world."

I swallowed down my tears.

"I didn't see you last night. Your brother came to bed, but I didn't see you. Did you sleep in your own room?"

Giving a nod, I swallowed. "I was so exhausted. Besides, I had bad dreams. I would have woken all of you."

He nodded, but he narrowed his eyes. "Bad dreams?"

"Nothing so bad, truly, just disturbed visions."

"What sort of visions?"

I waved my hand, wishing I'd never mentioned it. "Hawlen doesn't think they're prophesies, just someone else's fears bleeding into my mind. She promised to teach me how to block them."

"Ah, that's fine, then. Tonight, we'll all be back together again."

Was I channeling my aunt in my dreams? Somehow, her power felt familiar to me, and that might be a reason. I must remember to ask Hawlen.

But no, my nightmares had started long before she married Father. Perhaps Cliach's spirit was intruding on my dreams? I'd know once he left for the Oak Grove.

I thought again of morphing those mental bricks into something sharp but wasn't sure how to modulate the magic. Instead, I decided to channel my frustrations into something that might actually work, so I headed to the training grounds.

After a brutal session of archery with Scuida and a quick meal, I returned to my room for afternoon lessons.

Not only was Hawlen waiting, but two other ravens I didn't recognize. One was completely white. I halted in the doorway, my heart racing.

"Fionnuala, may I present the Messenger Bawleen the Bright and his assistant, Dawler."

I bowed to both with respect and awe. I'd never met a Messenger.

"Bawleen brings us disturbing news. Do you remember that conclave we had?"

I nodded, the white stone covered in spiral carvings flashing in my mind.

"We all agree that there is a great chaos stirring. We don't know who or why. They've done an excellent job of diverting and diffusing their power so we cannot track it. This denotes great skill and deviousness. Bawleen believes it might be channeled here."

My eyes grew wide. "Here? You mean, this is the target, or the source?"

Bawleen spoke, his voice deep and resonant. "We are not certain, child. We sense the nexus in the lines. I wished to warn you, as the lady of the house."

"Me? But my aunt, my stepmother, she's the lady of the house now."

Bawleen unfurled his wings. "Not in the eyes of the ravens, not until she gives your father a child. Once she has spawned, she will be part of this household, but not before. Also…"

The raven's pause made me glance up. He cocked his head as if listening. After several silent moments, he spoke. "There is something about her. I can't discern if she is the source or target of the magic, but she definitely has a connection. I must investigate." He flew away and Dawler gave an apologetic glance before following.

"What did he mean, that she's connected to the lines?"

"The lines of magic that run beneath the land. We tap into them when we work earth magic."

"Could she be the target of this magic?"

"We shall find out. In the meantime, let me teach you how to deflect."

"Deflect what?"

"Curses. If something evil comes to this household, you'll need to understand how to keep it from harming anyone, including your stepmother."

After five days of lessons in curse deflection, I wanted nothing to do with such things. Redirecting power was hard, even using the songs Hawlen taught me.

Not only did I need to choose the right way to deflect the magic, which depended on the sender, the flavor of the power, and the purpose of the curse, but I had to choose *where* to deflect it.

A deflection toward the nearest target might be disastrous. A push back to the creator might not be feasible as they would have their own defenses. To deflect it randomly might curse an innocent bystander or a loved one.

Just as today's lesson finished, the white raven returned. I sat on my bed, rubbing my arms.

The white raven clacked his beak several times before speaking. "We cannot tell yet if your stepmother is the target, but she is related to the power. It may be unconscious. We've discovered a *geas* upon her, a prohibition against her killing others."

That sounded odd. "Who would place such a *geas* upon her? And why?"

Bawleen exchanged a glance with his assistant and I caught the impression that I'd asked an impertinent question. I raised my chin, as I wanted an answer, and thought it was a relevant question.

"One of the lesser gods did so on a dare when she was a child. There was no malice, but it may be why she is attracting this magic. Any regard by a god will attract such things."

Just as the People enjoyed games, so did the gods. There were many tales of the Gods' play and silliness in the lore.

The white raven unfurled his wings. "We charge you to watch your stepmother. If something should go wrong, inform Hawlen and she shall pass on the word."

"Something wrong? Like what?"

The raven stretched his wings to full span and the memory of white feathers made me flinch. "Unexplained clumsiness. Unusual temper. Magic workings. Periods of sorrow. Anything out of the ordinary might prove someone is working through her or affected her mind."

A chill filled my blood at the thought of someone controlling anyone, even my stepmother. I didn't love her, but she'd married Father, whom I loved dearly.

Anything done to her would affect the entire household. I wished I had more offensive magic. It would help protect her from whatever tried to get in. I vowed to myself to figure out a way to turn that protective wall magic into a weapon, in case my stepmother needed guarding. "I shall keep vigilant, I promise."

With a nod, the ravens left again.

When I came to supper that day, I studied my stepmother with new eyes. She'd attracted a god's attention as a child. Why? Maybe she hadn't done anything, but her parents had. Or that she had a destiny. Gods were capricious with their attentions.

Aoife Rua prattled on about something Maire Mór wanted while Father ate his meal. He spoke no word to his bride, but had hearty greetings for me and my brothers.

The twins had just begun to sup in the great hall, with fresh manners and etiquette lessons from their ravens. They sat stiffly, eating with small bites and drinking in tiny sips, careful lest they spill a crumb.

I hid a grin and nudged Aed with a nod toward them.

My brother giggled under his breath. "How did your lessons go today, Nuala?"

"Well enough, but I'm exhausted. What about yours? I expected to see you at the archery range."

He shook his head. "No, I begged the morning off for a project I'm working on with Totawg."

"What sort of project?"

Aed's secretive smile made me narrow my eyes.

"Aed, what are you up to?"

"Nothing bad, I promise."

"And Totawg's helping you?" If his raven was complicit, this project shouldn't be all that destructive. Well, it could, as Totawg was a bit reckless.

My brother fiddled with his flatbread and his voice dropped to a whisper. "Well, he had been. Now, I'm working on my own."

I glanced around, but no one was paying attention to us. "Aed, you'd better tell me now. If I have to cover for you, I need the details."

He drew back. "Since when do you have to cover for me?"

I raised my eyebrows. "Since always?"

Aed gave me a half-smile. "It's just a little spell. Nothing big like your healing."

I narrowed my eyes. "What sort of spell?"

He pushed his stew around with his spoon and mumbled, "A love spell."

I muffled an exclamation and forced my voice into a fierce whisper. "A love spell? Aed, are you mad? You know those are dangerous, even for skilled ollamhs! What do you think you're doing, messing with such things? And on whom? Have you fallen for some kitchen girl that won't give you a glance?"

He waved his hand. "No, no, no, nothing for me, nothing so selfish. I wanted, well, I wanted something for Father and Aoife."

I snuck a glance at them, eating at the head of the table and studiously ignoring each other. We both watched while Father poured more wine, drank it, and grabbed a chunk of cheese. Aoife ate her stew, each bite precise and measured. She stared straight ahead into nothing.

"I don't think it worked, Aed."

His eyes fell to his own plate. "I guess not. Well, no harm done, right?"

A cold hand of dread gripped the back of my neck as a clatter at the head of the table caught our attention.

Aoife Rua righted her goblet. "Lir, the headmistress refuses to do as I say about the summer garden. She has no respect for my commands. You must speak to her about this, now!"

Father stared at her, but his gaze slipped away and back to his plate. He dipped his bread into the stew.

"Lir, pay attention! How am I to run your household without the respect of your servants?"

He took a long draught of his wine.

"Lir! I'm talking to you!"

Father pushed his chair back and stood. He towered over his wife. "Respect? Woman, respect must be earned. It's not given. Earn it and you won't need to run to me for help. A wife's duty is to order her husband's household. If you can't perform this duty, you're no proper wife. And if you pester me again about such pettiness, you'll suffer my wrath!"

In the thunderous silence, Father grabbed his wine goblet and stormed from the hall.

Father hadn't lost his temper in public in a whole moon. Since they got married, he only argued with Aoife Rua in their room. Now, in the great hall, before all their guards and servants, that was new.

Aed and I exchanged a guilty glance. We hadn't done anything to defuse the situation, but it really wasn't our place. Still, I felt like I'd failed, and Aed looked sheepish.

Aoife Rua marched out of the hall, her cheeks flaming as red as her hair.

Aed whispered, "Nuala, did I cause all that?"

"I don't know, Aed. Perhaps your spell stirred up something. Maybe it's just delayed. The strain between them was already there, so you didn't create *that*."

When we crept into bed that night, Father hadn't yet arrived. Aoife was in their bed, staring at the ceiling.

As I tucked in Fiachra, he whispered, "Is Father mad at us, Nuala?"

I kissed him on the forehead. "No, sweetling, he's not mad at you. He has a lot on his mind just now. Never you fear."

Conn sat up so abruptly he elbowed Fiachra in the ear. "I want a kiss, too!"

"Of course, my sweet child. One for you." They both giggled as I stroked their silky hair until they shut their eyes. I wished Mother had lived, so she could see what sweet boys she'd borne.

Aoife's voice sounded flat. "You spoil those children, Fionnuala. You're not their mother, and you will make them weak with your coddling."

When I glanced over, she was still staring at the ceiling. I straightened my spine. "This is how our mother treated both Aed and me. It did not make us weak."

Aoife sat up, her eyes flashing. "You *are* weak. Both of you. Look at you, still sleeping in your Father's room like babes, and you almost a woman grown yourself. I've never seen anything so disgusting in my life."

Father stalked into the room and struck Aoife across the face so hard she fell to the floor with a sickening thud.

I gasped and ran to her, but Father glowered. "Leave her. She shall learn the consequences of her vile tongue once and for all."

"But—"

"No, Nuala. You and Aed get in your beds. I shall deal with your stepmother."

Aed jumped up. "Father, please, let me help!"

"No! Get back in your bed."

Then he walked around the bed and lifted her. She moaned, but bright streaks of red flowed where her head had struck the flagstones. I sent a panicked cry of help to Hawlen and received a sleepy response.

Father carried Aoife down the hall.

Aed asked, "Nuala, what should we do?"

All three of my brothers watched me for instructions, but I had no idea. Father had *never* struck Mother. As far as I knew, he'd never struck another woman, except in battle.

Father's servant, Donal, might have stopped Father before he hit her, but Aoife Rua had dismissed him as soon as she married Father.

Hawlen flew in, landing on her perch. "I heard your panic, but not your words. What happened?"

"Father struck Aoife, hard. She hit her head on the floor. She was bleeding, and he took her away."

The raven nodded and cocked her head for several moments. "I've alerted the others. Lawstern will bring Maire Mór. She can tend the wound."

The look in Father's steely eyes had been so wild, so unnaturally feral, that he felt like another person. Then I remembered my duty and swallowed down my nervousness. "Is this something we should tell Bawleen?" I stroked Conn's hair. He looked as frightened as I felt.

Hawlen cocked her head to consider. "It may be. I shall mention it. It's well you called me this night. I have other news. We've gotten word from the Council."

I glanced back down the hallway, not wanting to hear anything more upsetting tonight, but knowing Father was in no state for such things. "What news? What's wrong?"

A hint of concern tinged Hawlen's voice. "What do you know of the Milesians and their relationship to the society of the ravens?"

I hadn't expected an examination in social policy. "I've only met one band of Milesians, when they came to our hillfort during a storm. *Tiarna* Áedammair. One had a cat on his shoulder. Do they bond with them, like we do with ravens? Do they speak with the ravens?"

The raven nodded. "So far, they have respected us. Their cats are only trained pets, though, without our intelligence. The Milesians don't have nearly as much magic as the *Tuatha Dé*, and therefore, their *tiarnaí* and *banríona* aren't bonded, but they have honored us and left us to be free. However, something has now changed."

My blood grew cold. "What happened?"

Hawlen bowed her head. "A member of the council has been murdered."

I couldn't breathe for a moment. How could they kill thinking creatures of magic and love? "Was it just one mad person? Someone who went insane and killed whatever came in sight?"

She shook her head. "Organized hunt parties are killing all the birds. Swans, ravens, even finches."

The slaughter of ravens was horrible enough. They were sacred creatures, projections of the gods upon this world. My gut roiled with disgust and horror. "What can be done?"

Hawlen fluttered her wings. "We've informed the *ard-rí* of this crime. He may call a council of his own. The only thing the ravens can do is to remove the bond teaching. Since they do not bond with us, that is no true punishment."

"Do their Filíd have any sway over the matter?"

She clacked her beak. "Perhaps we can reach an agreement between their Filíd, our council, and their *tiarnaí*."

That night, my dreams were white again, with more feathers. They were swan feathers, not white ravens. Someone hunted me as I dodged arrows and stones, and they dropped into the roiling sea below me. Would the Milesians hunt me?

Aoife fell into a deep sleep and did not emerge, despite all our efforts. Maire Mór did her best to help Aoife, and I came to help the next day at Father's request.

We moved her into her beloved solar, the bright sunlight warm upon her face each day. Aed and I took turns nursing her, with me sitting beside her each morning, and him each afternoon. Maire Mór took the evenings. But she didn't wake.

Days passed and we bathed and fed her. We dribbled broth in her mouth and wiped up the drops. She grew thin and frail. But she didn't wake.

Ten days after the incident, as I was giving her a drink of honey-water, she let out a haunted moan, a rising wail that cut through the walls like a winter wind. My skin prickled with goosebumps, and I stroked her lank hair.

Aoife Rua's eyes flew open and I drew back, startled. As her gaze darted around the room like a frightened rabbit, I took her hands. "Aunt? It's me, Nuala."

She turned her gaze to me, and her eyes were clouded with chilling madness, but not recognition.

With a shriek, she scratched at my eyes with her nails. Aoife Rua writhed and screeched as Aed and Maire Mór rushed in.

My brother grabbed her shoulders as I held down her feet. Maire tied several garments into ropes. With a great deal of effort, the headwoman tied my aunt's left arm to the bed frame. Then Aed tied the other arm. They held Aoife Rua's legs as I secured them to the bottom frame.

My stepmother had no sense left in her eyes. They darted about like a caged animal searching for an escape from her torment.

When I left her to Aed's care, I headed down to Maire's lair.

The headwoman took a long look at me. "You look horrible, child."

I'm certain I was a fright, and I hung my head.

"Aoife? Is she aught better?"

I swallowed against the grim news. "No. Should we call the Filíd? Would they be better able to heal her?"

Maire shook her head. "No, they won't take her. Cliach was one of their own, and so they took him into the Grove for healing, but she is no Drui. This is the best place for her to heal."

It had been a faint hope that I could shove my responsibility to someone else, and I hadn't really expected that to be an option.

"But you need to take care of yourself, child! Sit, sit, here. Have some stew, some bread and there's a nice sharp cheese to go with it. Sit, now, I tell you! We can go over house accounts later. You need food and rest, in that order. That is an order, mind you!"

Maire Mór understood me so well. I almost wished she was my stepmother instead.

The next morning, Hawlen flew in just as I finished dressing. I turned to her abruptly and asked, "How do I request an Ollamh for our court? Can I even do such a thing?"

She cocked her head and considered for a moment. "You can request it. Do you consider that a wise choice?"

"Why not? We've lost our bard. We must have one member of the priestly caste here for consultation and to maintain our status, apart from the need of a historian and advisor. With Aoife ill and Cliach gone…" Something in Hawlen's gaze made me stop.

She clacked her beak. "You realize if you were to bring in an Ollamh, your household would be required to move below ground immediately?"

My skin prickled and I rubbed my arms. "I didn't. But why?"

"Because all the Filíd have moved into the world below. To move one above, for anything more than a visit, would violate the treaty. You know the People cannot break their word without severe consequences."

Deflated, I sat on my bed. "But what should I do? Father needs help, and I can't run this place on my own."

"You have Aed's help and my own. Your Father is more coherent and reasonable than after your mother's death."

"But what if the Filíd sends someone anyhow?"

She ruffled her wings. "They will not. They can't send a new one uninvited."

Father had never had much use for Cliach as an advisor, so I had no big fear of that.

I straightened my back. "Very well, then. What should my tasks for the day be?"

Hawlen ticked off each one with a clack of her beak. "One, you must speak to Maire Mór to assign your stepmother's tasks. Two, you must arrange for a rota of nurses for Aoife Rua. Three, you must arrange for evening entertainment. Your father is more likely to ask for a new bard."

I nodded after each chore and then hurried to the kitchen. Dealing with Maire Mór would be the easiest task, and I had a great belief in doing the easy ones first.

Chapter Seven

In the 30th winter of Ard-Rí Bodb Dearg's reign (450 BCE) eight months later

The sun shone bright through the solar window that morning as I fed Aoife. I'd untied her so she could sit up and take each mouthful. I should have been learning lessons at the same time, but my mind kept wandering.

Hawlen cawed to drag me back into focus. "Name for me the gods and their family tree, Nuala."

I rolled my eyes as I brought the spoon to my stepmother's lips. "You know that I know this, Hawlen. Have you no new lessons for me?"

"Yes, you know this. You must understand this without conscious thought. You must feel the knowledge in your bones."

I shot her a scowl. "Why? Why is this so important? It's not as if I'll ever meet a god. They seldom visit the People any longer. Not for many, many winters."

"Indulge me, child. Name the Gods."

With a sigh, I spooned more honeyed porridge into Aoife's mouth and mopped up the dribble with a cloth. "Danú is the Mother Goddess and Bilé is her mate. Their children were Dian Cécht, The Dagda, and Nuada. Now, will you answer questions for me?"

Hawlen nodded.

"Fine. How did the Milesians defeat us?"

The raven clicked her beak. "You know that answer."

Waving a hand toward her, I dipped the spoon back into the porridge. "I learned all the guff about their superior weapons and cold iron. That nasty stuff burns right through our skin. But weapons aren't everything."

"They also have greater motivation for survival and greater numbers."

I turned to her, my brow furrowed. "Greater motivation? How so?"

"Their shorter lives make them more desperate to keep them. They fight more fiercely than we do. We rely upon magic, and they don't."

Then Hawlen asked, "Who were Dian Cécht's children?"

"Airmid, Miach, and Etan."

"And the Dagda's children?"

Even the twins knew this. "Brigit, Neit, Bodb Dearg, Cermait, Ogma, Midhir, and Angus Og. My turn. How do young ravens know what to teach young nobles?"

If Hawlen could have smiled, I swear she would have. "We have a collective knowledge we can access. If not, I'd never keep up with your questions!"

That made me laugh.

Hawlen rewarded my humor with a new question. "And Ogma's talent?"

I'd expected a question about Nuada's children. This question made me dig into my memory, and I paused in feeding Aoife Rua. "Ogma created the Ogham letters we use on grave markers."

"Why did you hesitate?"

I hung my head. "I incorrectly anticipated your question pattern."

"Do not presume. That is an error in both lessons and in battle. What would Scuida have done if you'd hesitated in spear practice?"

I let out a mirthless chuckle. "She would have thumped me on the head to drive the lesson home."

Hawlen flew over and pecked me on the scalp. I covered my head and shot her a glare. "Ow!"

"Now perhaps you will remember this lesson here, as well."

"That wasn't necessary!"

"I beg to differ." Hawlen settled on her perch again and preened under her wing. I rubbed the sore spot on my head, then returned to feeding Aoife Rua.

Aed entered with Totawg on his shoulder, and Hawlen scooted over to give his colleague room on the perch.

I turned to my brother and handed him the bowl. "I'm almost finished with her lunch. You get to bathe her today."

"Oh, come on, Nuala! I bathed her two days ago!"

"Yes and I bathed her yesterday. Your turn. Clean the bowl, will you? I'll get her shift off."

Aed grumbled as he sanded out the bowl and placed it on the sideboard.

Totawg fluttered down to stand on the sill beside the bed and peered down. "Is she improved? Something has changed about her. I can feel it in the lines of power."

I peered at my stepmother, but her face remained slack. "I can't tell. She barely says a thing, just small mutters now and then."

Aoife's hand shot out and grabbed Totawg. She ripped his black feathers out in an explosion of raucous cries. Hawlen cawed and Aed screamed as I tried to wrest her hands from the bird's delicate body.

She was stronger than she should have been, lying in her bed for so many moons. I struggled to pry her fingers open as she clawed and scrabbled against the bird's skin. Totawg spread his wings in a panicked attempt to take flight and the din of screeching ravens pounded in my head.

I got one finger pried away and then a second. Finally, I removed her entire hand from his body. She clutched at a wing, but Totawg fluttered off through the window.

Aed ran from the room still screaming. When Hawlen was hurt, I felt an echo of her pain, so I couldn't even imagine what Aed was feeling right now. Bits of black feathers floated in the air and descended on the now still room.

I tried to soothe my stepmother with a healing song, a lullaby sung in calm tones, but she fought against me and struggled toward Hawlen. My raven scooted to the far side of the perch, away from her grabbing hands.

She hummed tunelessly, a mocking grin on her face. Twisted power danced around her head and her hands. How had I not seen this magic before? Strong control power, to make us like her, to make us think of Mother.

Aoife Rua looked nothing like Mother now, but I still tasted that tingle of power, that urge to follow her commands. "Hawlen, get out! I don't want her to get hold of you, too!"

Though I threw up my protective wall, Aoife's will slid right through it. Hawlen squawked a protest and flitted out the window.

With the raven gone, Aoife eased her straining. I put calm will into my song and my hands, the white-blue healing light coating with comfort and quiet upon her raw nerves.

My power battled her control magic, which slid around each new barrier I erected. Strike and parry, block and thrust, like a melee on the battlefield, but with only our wills and our music.

Another wall up and then another. She slid her vicious attack over and around, through the mesh of the construct.

Finally, she must have tired. Her efforts flagged and my walls held her in. After almost an hour of constant battle, she fell into a fitful sleep.

I retied her restraints before she attacked a servant in the night.

I swallowed and glanced at the window. To kill a raven was abhorrent. Even the insult of trying to kill one might have grave consequences to Father's reputation.

Luckily, Totawg hadn't been hurt badly. The raven would have some sore muscles and patches where Aoife had torn his feathers away, but he'd recover. Hawlen promised she wouldn't report the incident to the Council. We didn't need a Council censure on top of everything else.

Aoife had definitely been using magic to manipulate us all. The raw power within her hands had burned as she attacked Totawg. Had she always used such power? Is this why she'd connected to the earth lines? She'd seemed so much like Mother when she first married Father. Was that part of her magic, as well?

I had felt so powerless against her. In the future, I must have some sort of defense against an attack, something that didn't rely upon me having weapons on hand. I would create a weapon of power, something I could use anytime. In the meantime, the ravens needed to know about Aoife Rua.

I sent a message to the white messenger raven, Bawleen, that night.

Aoife fell back into apathy for many days after the raven incident. Father peeked in each day, but never sat with her or spoke to her.

Then, for the first time since she fell, she began to speak small words. "No," when Aed fed her porridge. "Help," when she got tangled in her blankets.

Eventually, she even said "please," a word she'd never spoken before. Soon, she spoke almost normally.

But none of the ravens came close to her, except her own Nawlet.

"Is today the day, do you think?" Aoife asked in a quiet tone.

"Maybe." I replied. "Let's see how your legs work today."

My stepmother seemed so frail now. Her curvy softness had withered into sticks. We'd practiced walking every day this week. Today, we'd try to make it all the way to the main hall.

I helped her sit up on her bed. Then, I sat beside her with my shoulder under her arm and helped her stand.

She was unsteady, but I held on. "Don't be afraid to use me as a cane, Aunt. You're doing great. Try a step, now."

She pushed one foot forward and slid it on the flagstones. "My feet are cold."

"Would you like another layer of stockings? Sit back down, and I'll put some on you."

The spring day was warm, but mornings were chilly. Perhaps the cold sank into her bones, as she had no fat left to warm her.

Once I got the stockings on, we tried again. "One step first, that's good. Now another. Aed, can you get the door? A third one. Good."

Eventually, we made it all the way to the feast hall. When we arrived, the guards at the table, the servants and the twins all stared. A half-hearted cheer came from the guards and then some whooped and pounded their hands on the table.

Aoife gave a shy smile and concentrated on her feet as we moved her, step by step, to her place beside Father's chair.

He'd drunk heavily the night before, to celebrate a visiting bard. The bard was on a pilgrimage and had already left that morning.

I thought again of a bard or an Ollamh to replace Cliach. We'd never received word of his health or status after they took him to the Oak Grove. My enquiries after his health were met with platitudes. Not that I wanted his morose self back, but I missed his music.

Aed and I did our best to sing, but Father complained about our efforts. We started the twins on songs, but I had little talent as a teacher and the ravens were no help at all in matters of non-avian singing. We needed a true bard to teach them the nuances of their voice and the tales.

Aed was feeding Aoife her morning porridge when Father appeared in the doorway. He watched his son feed his wife, then he shut his eyes for several moments. Then he opened them and gripped his chair's back. "Is she well, Nuala? Is she healed?"

"Well enough, Father, as you can see. You can ask her yourself."

He scowled at my cheek and turned to Aoife. "How are you, wife?"

Aoife stared at him, swaying in her chair. She'd grown so thin that a stray breeze might knock her over.

I expected her to cower from him looming over her, yet her eyes looked like ice. "The first words you've spoken to me in several seasons and you cannot even say *my name*?" Her words turned into a hiss.

Father turned pale and the muscles of his jaw clenched, but he did not let fly the angry retort in his eyes.

My aunt snatched the spoon from Aed. "I am well enough, *husband*." She took her own bite of the porridge and glared at Father, as if daring him to say something.

With a grunt, Father yanked his chair out, making it noisy on purpose, and sat. He raised his hand for a servant to bring him a bowl of porridge. He dribbled honey into it, added a dollop of butter, and stirred it for several moments.

No one broke the silence with idle chatter.

Aoife Rua turned to Father, as if the intervening moons never happened. "I need to assess the garden. I'm certain it has been neglected while I rested."

I gave her a decisive nod. "I can take you when we're done here. We've added some new herbs the Milesians brought from their homeland. Some are rather tasty. One is a mustard and another is useful for some herbal remedies."

Aoife glanced around the hall, as if searching for evidence of visitors she hadn't noticed before. "Milesians? Are they here?"

Aed mopped some of his stew up with a chunk of bread. "They visited last season. A delegation appeared beyond our veil and asked for trade options. A Hellenic trader also came with olive oil and wine and tales of the southern seas."

Father grunted. "They wanted to get into our hall and rob us blind, that's what they wanted."

I pursed my lips. "Father, please. They were kind people and polite. They violated no guest laws and left in peace."

"And now they understand our defenses and our numbers. They might invade at any time."

I rolled my eyes. "And have they? They can't get past our veil without our help. We're safe here."

I fervently hoped that was true. No other mortals had pierced our veil since that one stormy night when Áedammair came, so many seasons past. But if one got through, so could others.

Father offered no argument. He finished the final bite of his meal and pushed back from the table. His chair made another horrible screech against the stones, then left without another word.

Aoife asked, "has he been like this since I fell ill?"

I nodded. "He's spoken more today than in the past week. Perhaps you're good for him."

She furrowed her brow. "I doubt that. I don't remember him even coming to see me."

While Aed and I had urged Father many times to sit with his wife, to help her heal, he refused, saying that he had no healing talent and had more important things to take care of as *tiarna*. But letting Aoife Rua know that wouldn't be kind.

Over the next few days, we helped Aoife regain her strength. We walked her to the feast hall, to the garden, and back to her room. Eventually, she walked without help, though she used a walking stick.

She spoke meekly to everyone, and acted kindly to me, Aed, and the twins.

And yet she snapped at Father constantly.

Father, on the other hand, ignored anything Aoife did. Nothing Aoife said seemed worthy of his notice.

Even her smiles, where I now saw the will of her magic, didn't make him react. The glow of my Mother's shade danced upon her lips. Still, he disregarded her.

Despite her attempts to use magic on us, I felt sorry for her. To be ignored was soul-destroying, especially by a loved one.

Did Aoife love Father? I didn't know and could never ask. State marriages were common for nobles, and the true love Mother and Father had found was rare.

Though I'd sent a dutiful message to Bawleen of Aoife Rua's magic, I heard nothing. I doubted if the Council considered such small magic a threat, but it would have been nice to get an acknowledgement.

One day, after fighter practice, Aed and I sat alone in the kitchen. Aed stuffed a piece of bread in his mouth and spoke around the crumbs. "Maybe we could lock them together in their room until they work things out?"

"That would never work. They're in their room every night and barely speak."

"Yes, but what if we were to return to our own rooms for a few nights? Give them some marriage time?"

I gave him a tired look. "Father had a fit the last time we suggested that. He couldn't bear to be parted from us. And he barely looks at her, much less touches her."

Aed pursed his lips. "Well, what if we left all together? We could run away for a week."

I waved off the suggestion. "He'd have the entire garrison scour the forest. He'd even recruit the Milesians in the next county to help search."

"Ha!"

Rolling my eyes, I gave a shrug. "Well, perhaps not the Milesians. He'd ask our neighbors, though."

"Nuala, we have no neighbors. Not any of the People, not anymore. All the nearby People have moved under the hills. We're the only ones left in this county."

We ate and tried to think of a solution. Then I had an idea. "I know! We could ask the *ard-rí* for an invitation to court, just us children! Father would never say no to a royal summons!"

Aed's eyes widened with hope. "That could work, Nuala! We'd stay for a moon and Aoife and Father would be all alone each night. That would give them plenty of time to make up!"

We both grinned and planned our adventure.

A royal messenger arrived a few days later, and we all gathered in the feast hall to hear the boy's news. After he delivered his message, I stared at him. "All of us? Father, Aoife Rua, *and* all the children?"

The boy nodded. "That's what the *ard-rí* said. You're all to visit. Nothing official, mind you, just a family outing."

That would ruin our plan. I'd have to think of something else. Perhaps if Father and Aoife didn't feel well?

I glanced toward the gardens. I had plenty of herbs that would make them not want to travel. But then they might cancel the entire trip.

Then I giggled to myself. I had one herb that would upset the bowels enough that no self-respecting man would admit the details.

While I had qualms at the idea of poisoning anyone, this wouldn't really hurt them. Just a bit of discomfort to keep them home. If I added a little to their stew the night before, they wouldn't risk traveling.

I'd insist that we couldn't ignore a summons from the *ard-rí*, and that I'd care for the children, with the ravens and guards. I could recruit Scuida to come with us, since her cousin lived at the royal hillfort.

I hummed to myself and went to the garden to pluck leaves from a senna plant. That Hellenic trader had cautioned me on its use, but I learned the herbal healing techniques as well as the magic ones. I'd put just enough to make them both cramp for a day or two.

That evening was frantic as everyone prepared for the trip. I was helping the twins pack. Fiachra had made a pile, but frowned at it. "Should I bring my bed?"

Conn rolled his eyes. "Idiot! The *ard-rí* has hundreds of beds."

"What about my practice sword? Scuida would be mad if I neglected practice for a whole week."

Conn's brow furrowed. "Then we should bring our bows, too."

"They'll have bows for you to practice with, never fear. Maybe we can convince Scuida to come with us. That way you won't miss any of your lessons. And the ravens will come."

Conn scowled. He didn't care for his raven lessons. Fiachra grinned. "Wonderful! Crawma is telling me the tale of the Fir Bolg and the Fomor invasions! I didn't want her to stop last night, but she insisted I had to go to bed." A flicker of a pout flashed across his face, but then he brightened. "She can tell more on the journey!"

"Maybe she can, sweetling. Now, finish your packing. I have to talk to Father."

When I reached the hall, Father looked slightly green. I hadn't realized the senna would work so quickly and glanced at Aoife. Our stepmother showed no distress.

He stood, excused himself, and hurried to the door. Aoife watched him leave with a curious smile on her face. Her expression suddenly sharpened, and she glanced toward me, then back toward Father. My stepmother then rose and followed him with a measured march.

By Danu, did she realize I gave them something?

The bustle and noise of the great hall closed in on me. What if she thought I meant to hurt her? I needed to flee. I ran down the hall, through the kitchens, the garden enclosure, and past the stables. I reached the outer palisade and clung to the gate, catching my breath.

The last shreds of daylight clung to the clouds above and painted them dark peach and purple in the velvet twilight. I breathed deep of the dusk air and pulled in the serene power of the earth.

Calmer now, I walked toward the woods to escape the confines of my home. Father's home. Did I just poison Father in a scheme to make him love my stepmother? That was stupider than Aed's love spell.

Hawlen had taught me many times of the follies of using magic for petty ends. The tales were full of such idiocy. What had I been thinking?

I just wanted Father to be happy. Was happiness such a terrible goal? Not even a selfish goal. I didn't want power or wealth, nor did I want to change the world. I just wanted my Father and stepmother to be happy.

The horrible reality was that, between me and my brother, we tried to force love. That wasn't a proper use of magic. I could almost hear Hawlen's voice chiding me for my idiocy.

Tears ran unbidden down my cheeks as I dashed up the hill to the sacred stones. Perhaps they'd give me comfort. Maybe I could reverse the folly of my meddling. I'd ask the gods for help.

The final glimmer of color left the last cloud on the horizon as I reached the crest. The stones were dark and threatening in the dim, cobalt light. Only a few stars glimmered above me and no moon. A waning moon was the best time for banishment magic.

I marched around the stones and concentrated on the earth, our land, our home, our power. I stroked each stone as I passed and traced the tops in a lazy caress while I hummed a tuneless note.

Power coursed into my feet with every step on consecrated ground. The resulting light didn't have the pale blue of healing energy, but the angry red of baneful magic.

I felt lightheaded and floated on air. My ears buzzed and my skin grew hot, like with fever. When I completed my circle, I fell on the ground before the altar stone.

I couldn't see the stone's curved carvings, but they throbbed with ambient light to my inner sight. They beat green and orange, red and yellow and played upon the ghost clouds in my mind. They pulsed to an inner music and something radiated within the earth. It synchronized to my heartbeat, to my blood.

I sang a song of sorrow, regret, and confession. I threw myself on the mercy of the gods, but offered no justification for my meddling. I asked forgiveness and pledged to do no more harm. I begged for a resolution to the problem.

No answer came.

The song of the earth subsided with a powerful boom and the magic faded. I don't know if anything heard me.

Drained, I struggled to my feet and brushed off the dirt and grass. I plodded back to the hall, where Fiachra and Conn still argued about what they should bring on the trip.

That night, my nightmares returned.

I'd kept them at bay for many nights with the shields Hawlen taught me, but they finally broke through and attacked with a vengeance, as if angry at having been held back for so long.

I was smothered in white feathers, whipped by cold, salty sea storms and drowned in a choppy lough, all while tangled in delicate silver chains. In desperation, I formed my magic into sharp, tiny points, but they fell flat against the feathers.

I screamed for someone to help and someone called my name. "Nuala! Wake up. You still have to pack."

I cracked an eye open to find Aoife Rua shaking me awake. Aed's bed lay empty and rumpled, as were the twins'. I pulled myself out of bed. "Pack?"

"Yes, girl, pack! You were the one to receive the messenger, weren't you? Your father won't join us, as he's feeling poorly. I shall come and play the mother to you all. Won't that be lovely?"

She smiled, and I didn't like the smile. The magic she used to resemble Mother was blatant, and no longer held any power for me.

Our plans to give Aoife Rua and Father time to be together lay in shambles.

I ran to my room and pulled down several dresses, the small circlet I wore to state occasions, and the blue jewel Dervla had gifted to me.

Would I need anything else? We'd only be gone for a fortnight. I moved my trunk outside my door for the servants to collect and ran to check on Father.

But when I got to his room, he wouldn't open the door. I knocked a second time. "Father, please. I want to say goodbye. Won't you let me in?"

Grudgingly, he complied.

He sat with pillows propped behind his back, looking pale and drawn, and the stench of vomit clung to the air. I breathed through my mouth, guilty at what I had done. "Father?"

"Come, Nuala. Come closer." He grasped both my hands. "Take care of your brothers, will you? You're in charge of them, not Aoife. Make sure they attend the *ard-rí* and comport themselves with dignity and grace to their station."

"I promise."

"And keep close watch on Aed. His eye and other parts are roving, and I'll have no scandals."

I gave him a grin. "I shall. And what will you do while we are away?"

"I shall get better, so we may go on a hunt when you return. Would you like that? I've neglected you all this last season. We need time together as a family."

"I'd like that. We'll be back soon, Father. You'll barely realize we left."

He managed a wan smile, and I left him in peace.

I passed Fiachra in the hall. He carried so many things, he couldn't see around the mass.

"Fiachra! No, you can't take all that. You can bring three things. Three."

"But Nuala! I wanted to show my new toys to the children in the royal hall!"

"They have toys as well, and it would be more polite to allow them to show off."

He pouted. "I don't want them to think I have nothing."

With my lips pursed, I said, "Which is why you can bring three. But only three."

"Fine." He stomped back into his room with a grumble.

Conn appeared with a small pack, just his clothes.

"Are you bringing nothing else, Conn?"

Fiachra's voice piped up, "Can I bring his three toys, too?"

I stifled a giggle. "No, Fiachra. Only three of your own things."

Conn reached into a bag tied to his belt and pulled out three shining objects, holding them out to me.

He held three stones. One with red and black veins, another with bright green with gold flecks and a third which shone vivid blue.

He put a finger to his lips and put them back into his pouch. I smiled and stroked his hair. Conn appreciated the smaller, more precious things. He had great potential as a shaper of events. Fiachra was more action than thought. A warrior, not a politician.

I called to the twins. "I'm off to speak to Maire Mór before we leave. I'll meet you at the stables!"

By the time I finished with the headmistress, everyone was waiting in the stable yard.

Father had recently commissioned an enormous chariot. It looked like a normal chariot, but much longer. A third wheel was near the front center where the yoke attached to the horses. Yes, horses, four of them. I'd never seen such a ridiculous thing.

It also had a cover, like a tent, but open on the sides to make travel in the rain more comfortable.

Wooden benches were built into the sides, so we could all sit while we traveled. The baggage had already been secured near the front.

No longer a chariot, this was some hybrid monstrosity. Would it even move?

Aed and I chose seats near the middle. Fiachra and Conn bounced around to find the best place to sit while still gazing out of the sides.

They made the chariot shake and I was getting a headache. "Settle down, boys. I don't want this thing to break."

Conn sat beside me and Fiachra chose a space near Aed. He only stayed still a moment before he tried a different spot and then a third. "Fiachra! Choose one seat."

"But I want to see everything on the way, and you can't see everything in one seat!"

"Then sit near the front, where you can see everything as we pass on either side."

With a grin, he jumped up on the luggage and perched in the middle. He proudly surveyed all before him like a *tiarna*.

I let out a chuckle. "Conn, do you want to join your brother?"

Conn shook his head. "No, I can see plenty from here. I'd rather see it well than see it all."

Aoife Rua climbed into the chariot with dignity. Once seated, she nodded to the driver and his wife to go. It creaked and groaned, but eventually, the huge contraption moved.

Aoife asked, "Have you eaten yet today, children?"

I glanced at the twins, but they shook their heads.

She pursed her lips. "Well, it's a grand thing I thought of that. Here, I brought bread and cheese." She passed out loaves of wheaten bread and goat's cheese. We each ate while watching the world pass by, our ravens curled up to nap next to us.

I couldn't see much out of the sides, as the morning mists shrouded the countryside and I could barely see the trees.

Soon, the novelty wore off and both twins curled up to sleep under a bench. I dozed off to the rhythmic beat of horse hooves.

Normally I would only dream of the white feathers at home, but they waited for me. This time they seemed gentle, nearly caressing me, but I was still frightened. They urged me to join them, to fly away forever into the night sky before it came. Before what came? What was coming? The move below the hills? The end of days?

I woke abruptly as the carriage came to a halt.

Mists hugged the lough beside us. Some ducks gathered to one side and ate chunks of bread. I didn't see our stepmother anywhere.

The twins were still sleeping and Aed let out a snore. My head felt groggy. I blinked my eyes and tried to focus, but fog pounded on my mind and worms wriggled in my skull.

Aoife's voice drifted somewhere in the mists. Angry words? To whom? To the chariot driver and his wife?

"No, my lady, we'd never do that. It's more than our lives are worth."

Aoife's tone was harsher than I'd heard since she fell ill. "I'll make it worth your lives and more. I've plenty of gold and silver for your troubles."

"Truly, we can't. We wouldn't, even if we could. The children are precious to us, as if they were our own."

Aoife spat a curse. Soon, her form appeared from the blanket of white, while fingers of mist embraced her curves like a lover.

She held a long, white branch. Gripping it tight, she walked to Aed. Then, she lifted the branch high over his slumbering head.

I cried out, but only managed a whimper, but it caught my stepmother's attention. She lowered the branch and glared at me. "Oh, so you're awake? Well, perhaps your magic is stronger than I thought. At least your ravens are still asleep. They *loved* the bread I gave them."

She wasn't making any sense, but my mind wasn't working well. I didn't see her own raven, Nawlet. Where was the carriage driver and his wife? I didn't see anyone around. Had they run away?

My stepmother lifted the club again, but something seemed to physically prevent her from swinging it. With a blistering curse, my stepmother threw it into the lough.

The splash woke Aed, Fiachra, and Conn, but they acted like I felt, fuzzy and weak.

I tried to make sense of Aoife's actions. "What are you doing, Aunt?"

She whirled back to face me. "Doing? What am I doing? You are a dim one, aren't you? You shouldn't have to ask such a stupid question. Now I see you *are* your father's daughter."

My aunt's gaze narrowed at my throat. I placed my hand over the blue pendant *Banríon* Dervla had given me, the one that she said reminded her of my mother's eyes. With a growl, Aoife Rua grabbed it, ripping the chain from my neck. "First, I need to get rid of this. I can smell Dervla's meddling magic all over it."

She tossed the gem into the lake, and I didn't have the wits or strength to stop her.

Then, my aunt lifted her arms and chanted. I didn't recognize the words, but a green light grew between her palms. Nawlet flew to her shoulder, but she brushed him away. He tried several more times until she struck him. He shook off the blow and went to the other ravens to rouse them.

Her chant rose in volume. *"Airearen bothereco, I agintzen duzun!"*

I couldn't make sense of the words. My mind wandered over the alien shape of the words, the odd accent, the harsh sounds. Then buzzing filled my ears.

The green light grew and morphed into an enormous bird with white feathers and a powerful, wicked beak.

I shrieked, strangled and pitiful, and the terror within me gibbered and screamed and made me scramble away from it. I tried again to cry for help, but my mouth wouldn't work.

"Etorri niregana, eta nire nahia egoztea!"

The bird locked gazes with me and my nightmare became real. This spirit, this air phantasm, had hounded me in the dreamlands. Despite my fear, I was determined to fight back. This time, I had my body and my magic.

Drawing upon my power, I formed a wall of protection, brick by brick, each glowing with blue light.

I pushed through the fog still shrouding my mind, and it hurt. I glanced at the ducks, sleeping by the loughside, then glanced down at Hawlen, and I grew angry. How dare she poison our ravens?

Now that I'd built my wall, I drew my power into a physical form, an arrow to direct into the heart of the creature. The blue light grew darker and pulsed.

When the arrow grew as strong as I could make it, I launched it at the bird's heart.

My target struck true and the bird screamed. Aoife screeched with an inhuman sound. Her voice cut through my mind-fog like scraping on raw nerves. I covered my ears as I fell to my knees.

And for all my efforts, I'd done very little. The bird still glowed green in the white mist.

I cried out, "Why, Aunt? Why are you doing this?"

Aoife Rua glared at me with hate in her eyes vying with the madness. She snarled in primal ferocity. "*You* ask that? You, who think to steal the *banrion*'s affection from me? You, who poisoned me? You, who cast spells to make my husband hate me? You're a petty, spoiled child, willful and meddling."

She paced, lifting her arms with each sentence. "Lir only loves his children. He doesn't care about getting more heirs. He leaves me cold in my marriage bed. Without you, he'll turn to me, his lawful wife. We will have scores of children and he'll love me until the end of our days!"

My heart raced as I struggled to my feet. "But we didn't try to hurt you! I swear by Danu herself!"

But hadn't I put those herbs in her stew? She stopped pacing and I thought my plea had reached her.

Then Aed gripped my hand and his eyes grew wide. "We were trying to help Father love you."

Our stepmother spoke with quiet determination, which terrified me more. "Your intent is not my concern. The result is all that counts, and now he cannot stand me. My *geas* prevents me from killing you, but I can make sure you never meddle in my affairs again."

As madness flamed within her eyes, I fortified our magic wall. Between our held hands, Aed's power melded into mine, a faint purple tint to my blue.

I threw up a second wall behind the first, then a third. Then I readied another arrow. Two more hands touched my back, Fiachra and Conn adding their strength.

My stepmother gathered her power and spoke another spell. This time, I understood the words, and they chilled my heart.

"For three hundred winters, you shall bide upon this *Lough Derravaragh*.

For three hundred winters, you shall bide upon the *Sruth na Maoile*.

For three hundred winters, you shall bide upon *Irrus Domnann*.

And when at last your time has done, the bells of the New God shall ring.

And when a *tiarna* of the north weds a *banrion* of the south,

Only then may you return to your true forms once again."

The curse burrowed into me, as if thousands of worms crawled inside my skull. I wanted to scream, to rip the creatures away.

My arrow flickered blue-purple to pinkish-orange and back. I drew back with my will, as if drawing a bow. I scoured my brain for Scuida's target lessons and launched it.

This time, I didn't target the bird. This time, I aimed at Aoife's own heart.

But I'd waited too long. The arrow flew just as she launched her bird. Time slowed as the bird attacked. Its wings grew until it blotted out the sky, the mists, the lough, and everything around us. My brothers screamed and clutched at my clothes.

I'd spent all my power in the second arrow. My voice wouldn't heed my will, but I ached to scream. Instead, I called Hawlen, Father, the gods themselves, anyone who might hear. Feathers came closer and closer. They smelled of rotten meat and scorched earth.

White wings enveloped us in my horrible nightmare. I fought against their suffocating mass until I could scream no more, my throat raw and tight.

Chapter Eight

Even as my voice died, mists enveloped us. My muscles ached and stretched, and my skin burned. I stared at my arm as the hairs thickened into bristles. Then my fingers melted into white feathers.

More white feathers covered my body. Instead of arms, I had wings. I flapped them, trying to rid myself of the feathers. I looked at my brothers, but in their place stood three huge swans.

I cried out, but only a strangled honk emerged. I prayed that this was only another nightmare, but I knew in my heart that wasn't true. Aoife Rua's curse crept into my ever-growing dread.

Aoife Rua had used her sorcery to transform us into creatures of the lough. And some time as we transformed, she'd disappeared. Even the monstrous chariot had gone, leaving nothing but tracks in the mud. And our ravens had been drugged asleep in the back of the chariot.

Aed shivered and I placed my wing around him, hugging tight. Fiachra cried out in confusion. I gathered my brothers and held them, wishing I had been stronger, more powerful, against Aoife Rua.

Without my voice, I couldn't even sing healing magic. How could I calm my brothers when my soul cried out in pain and betrayal?

My plaintive keen shot across the lough and echoed over the water. Not a human cry, but beautifully poignant. My brothers joined me and we wept for our fate.

My voice died with a scratchy squawk. In the sudden silence, Fiachra nudged me and entreated me with soulful swan's eyes. Sweet Danu, he must be hungry.

I kicked at the bread left by the still-sleeping ducks, drugged with Aoife's evil magic. Instead, I chewed tall reeds along the shore and found them delicious. I motioned to my brothers to taste the sweet grasses and we had our first meal as swans.

I tested my voice, but couldn't coax more than swan noises. That made me want to keen again, but I sensed Hawlen wake up, far away.

Hawlen, can you hear me?

A muffled query echoed in my mind. *Barely.*

Aoife has transformed us into swans. You must tell the ard-rí! She left us at the lough. Are you still in the chariot?

Her voice sounded as fuzzy as my head still was. *Fionnuala? What are you talking about? Yes, we're in the chariot. Where are you?*

Aoife cast an evil curse upon us and turned us into swans. You must tell the ard-rí!

Hawlen paused. *She's tied us in the chariot. I have told Machawna, the ard-rí's raven. I shall report what happens.*

I had little choice but to wait.

Aoife's spell was far beyond anything I'd ever seen. Would a prayer to the gods help? I had no standing stones for focus. I didn't know of any nearby, anyhow, and I dared not leave my brothers. Besides, the curse said we were bound to the lough.

Conn and Fiachra both wilted into sobs.

Hawlen's voice sounded weak. *The ard-rí has greeted Aoife. Her lies are smooth, but he does not believe them. She gives a tale of you running away into the forest and getting killed by a boar.*

Anger pricked my skin and my feathers ruffled.

The ard-rí accuses her as a liar and a sorceress. He is coming.

Coming? Coming here?

Yes, he comes with Bé Chuille. She will try to lift the curse.

A precious spark of hope sprang up in my heart. The High Ollamh could break the curse, or at least make Aoife break it herself. We might be freed after all! But Bé Chuille was a diviner. She didn't specialize in curses or transformation.

When the royal party finally arrived in a flurry of activity and noise, the muted silence of the misty lough gave way to shouts, commands, and the jingle of tack.

Aoife was pulled from a chariot bound in silver chains. She stood straight and tall, not one hair mussed and not one tear shed. Her red-gold hair shimmered, beautiful despite her evil. Bé Chuille's acolytes marched her toward us at the lough's edge.

I stared at my stepmother and she returned my gaze without a shred of regret in her eyes.

The *ard-rí* approached. "Are these the children, Aoife? The younglings you pledged to protect when you wed their father? The children you betrayed and transformed with your wicked spell?"

Her eyes flashed and she straightened her shoulders. "I didn't betray anyone! They worked magic upon my me and my husband. They're cruel brats and deserve their punishment. It's my right as their stepmother to mete out justice!"

Bé Chuille studied us, lifting my beak and gazing into my eyes. I held on to any hope the Ollamh might offer like a talisman against the creeping darkness of despair.

The High Ollamh pounded her braided oaken staff into the ground three times. Then she raised her hands and chanted, the rose crystal glowing.

Her power rushed through the ground and into her body, a rumble of the earth with a green and brown glow. The power she commanded was so much greater than my own feeble trickle.

She shut her eyes and her long, white hair rose, as if lifted by the wind. The air smelled of burnt trees and lightning. My feathers tingled and twitched and I knew she worked great magic.

The rose crystal shimmered and blew away the remnants of fog with a *crack*. The lough beyond the mists grew clear and the far shore was crowded with pine trees. More swans swam on the other side, alerted by the lovely music of the Ollamh's voice.

I tried to channel my magic into her spell, but it slipped away, like water from oiled leather.

The enchantment grew deeper, stronger and soon the whole glade was lit in a rose glow. Power washed over me like an ocean wave and pushed us to the ground with sheer force. My skin tingled and burned and a cry tore from my throat. That cry sounded inhuman, full of pain and pleasure. When I opened my eyes again, I glanced down full of hope and expectation, but I was still a swan.

Bé Chuille scowled, let out a curse, lifted her hands and restarted her chant. Again, the power glowed throughout the glade. Again, the air stunk of burning wood. I braced myself against the tingling of power.

After the second wave washed over us, I was unsurprised to see that we were still swans.

The Ollamh tried a third time, but in truth, I no longer had any expectations that it would work. That precious gem of hope I'd held shattered into a thousand crystalline shards and sparkled upon the loamy ground.

After the third spell failed, I let out a mournful keen and my brothers joined me. The haunted sound bounced around the glade and everyone but Aoife Rua sobbed.

Ard-rí Bodb Dearg, with fury in his voice, told his foster-daughter, "Break the curse, Aoife Rua. Break it now, and we will not punish you. I raised you, child, I took you in when your father died. I nurtured and cared for you, gave you everything your heart desired. You were a delightful daughter, full of fire and power, but also kindness. What happened to that daughter? Where has your compassion gone?"

No kindness flickered in her eyes as Aoife turned to him, only madness. "Gone, all gone, Father dearest. Gone when you sold me to a man still in love with my sister. Gone when he almost killed me for daring to come between him and his beloved children. Oh, those perfect children. They did nothing wrong, ever! And now they can never come between us again!"

The *ard-rí* was powerfully built and not easily intimidated. Yet he took several steps back from Aoife's anger.

Dervla pleaded, "At least allow them human voices. Give them their voices, and we can let you live."

Aoife Rua glared at her foster-mother, her lip curled with loathing. "Their voices, so they can whisper fresh betrayals? I will not."

Bé Chuille's eyes flashed and she strode to Aoife until they were but inches apart. "You *will*. Or would you prefer to die? Not to go to *Tír na nÓg*, to live among the Gods, no. Your treachery does not deserve such a reward. Instead, I will destroy you and your life-force will rot into salted ground. Is that what you prefer?"

Aoife Rua paled and stumbled back.

My stepmother let out a long sigh and bowed her head. "I shall give them their voices back." Her next words came out in a snarl. "May they have no joy of them!"

Her hands glowed green, and she pulled a well of power from below the earth. Not good, sweet earthen power, but something wicked, sickly, and spoiled. When it dissipated, a wave of nausea swept over me.

I tried my voice. It was rough and painful, but I said, "I can speak."

Then, I cried. I cried as myself and not as a swan. It broke my heart to hear my brothers crying beside me.

Dervla turned from us, tears in her own eyes, and faced Aoife. "And now, foster-daughter, since you will not break the curse, you must be punished. You must leave."

Aoife's eyes darted from me to the *banrion*. "Leave? And go where? Will you send me back to the man who can't stand the sight of me? The man who beat me almost to death?"

The *banríon* glanced at her husband. Bodb Dearg shook his head. "No, we won't send you back to Lir. The poor man has suffered enough grief and you would but add to it. But you must leave the People. You must leave this land. You may never again set foot on the island as long as you live, and that life will be long."

Dervla turned to me, placing a hand on my head. "You've cursed children I loved, the children of your sister, my dear Aobh Bán. Therefore, I curse you to become a phantasm of the air, forever to ride upon the ever-present winds. You will cast no more curses and cause no more harm."

She nodded to Bé Chuille and the High Ollamh pulled up power once again.

Aoife screamed and backed up until a pine tree halted her retreat. "Wait! May I at least have the same mercy I showed the children? May I keep my voice?"

The *ard-rí* scowled. "Will you transform the children back to their natural forms?"

Aoife Rua clenched her jaw. "I cannot. But they are still alive."

Bé Chuille exchanged a glance with Bodb Dearg and Dervla. The *banríon* said, "Since you granted the children their voices, you may keep your own."

Tears glittered in the corners of the *ard-rí's* eyes as the Ollamh cast her curse. Old, dark magic erupted from the earth and yanked at Aoife's body. Black, gold, and orange sparks snaked up her legs and her torso. It twisted at her body, and the earth groaned in a raucous clash.

Aoife stared at the cracks in her skin, alarm clear in her maddened eyes. She struggled, pushing the magic down and away, but it crept upward in a tangled knotwork until the earth power covered her.

My aunt's red silken hair burned into pale light and her body faded into a shred of cloud. Her mouth formed into a scream, but I only heard a whisper of terror. Her back arched in a rictus of fear and pain.

The wind blew the slight shadow of her former self into wisps of nothing. The echo of her last cry faded in the mournful breeze.

With a deep sigh and a sad face, the *ard-rí* turned to me. "I don't know how else we might help you, Fionnuala. I shall send word to your father. We will study how to transform you back."

He turned to Machawna and his raven took off, along with the others in the clearing. "The ravens will form a conclave and offer their help, as well."

Bé Chuille placed a comforting hand on my wing. "As will the Filíd, child. We have some with more transformational magic than me. It's possible there is still hope. In the meantime, you must come back to the court with us and we shall care for you there."

My voice still cracked, but I said, "Thank you, High Ollamh. But I believe we're bound to this lough by the curse for three hundred winters. Another six hundred in other places."

The *ard-rí's* face drained of all color. "Nine hundred winters?"

I didn't want to consider nine hundred winters. It wasn't a real number. I squared my shoulders. "I promised both Mother and Father that I'd take care of my brothers, and that's what I shall do. Whether that be as People among your court or as swans on this lough, that is my one duty."

Dervla gave me a tearful smile and clapped her hands. "Well, we shall do what we can to help with that duty. You shall have visitors and feasts, with songs to help you pass the time until we can transform you back."

I gave her a nod. "Your help is welcome. I—" my polished phrases stumbled, "I should like to see my father."

The *ard-rí* nodded. "Of course. I haven't given up hope that we can break this curse, so bide for a while as the magical folk sort this out."

That night was warm and clear, but full of bittersweet. When the *ard-rí*'s party left, he left several of his guards. They built a bonfire on the shore and prepared a meal while they chatted with us.

I wasn't interested in talk. If the Filíd couldn't break the curse, would we remain as we were, never aging, never dying? Would Father visit us, or will he be so horrified that he'll shunned our company?

I let out a sob and didn't care who heard it. One of the guards, an older woman with a lined face and short, dark hair, knelt beside me. "*Bantiarna* Fionnuala, is that you? Please, child, don't weep. We're here, and we won't leave you alone."

I pulled my sorrow within myself, but I couldn't stop my tears.

"Here, have some flatbread. I baked it fresh this morning with cheese and chives."

I remembered the bread that Aoife had fed us and backed away. Still, I must eat. I forced myself to try. First, I tried to take it with my hands, but my wingtip knocked the morsel to the ground. She picked it up and brushed a leaf away, holding it out again.

Finally, I pecked at it. At first, I bit the guard's fingers, but I managed to eat the chunk of flatbread. The salty, cheesy bread was delicious, and my stomach growled.

As my siblings took flatbread from the other guards, I asked the kind guard, "What's your name?"

"*Lasairfhiona*, but most people call me Las. Would you like to call me Las?" She gave me a smile, and she had a broken tooth. It gave her a rakish look.

I glanced at her well-muscled arms and imagined she was a formidable warrior. "Yes, please. I still have my voice, but some sounds are more difficult. You should call me Nuala."

"Have you tried to fly yet, Nuala?"

I shook my head. I didn't want to try to be a swan. What if I forgot I was one of the Tuatha Dé and flew into the sky, never to return?

As the sun dipped below the horizon, the lough turned dark and the mists rose again. I shook my head again. "Not now, not today. Perhaps tomorrow I shall try."

"If you do, I'd love to see your graceful flight. You were a lovely young woman, and you make a beautiful swan."

Her compliment made me feel like a girl again and I fought back more tears.

Fiachra spoke around a beak of bread, crumbs spraying everywhere. "I want to fly! Can I fly, Nuala?"

"Let's wait until tomorrow, when the sun is high. We can test our wings when everyone can see for miles."

"But what if it's foggy, like today?"

I rolled my eyes. "The air smells drier this evening."

"But we could still fly a little tonight, couldn't we?"

"No, not tonight. Are you full?"

Conn broke in. "I am, but I want a drink. My mouth is all gummy."

Las gave a chuckle. "The lough is right there, child. Drink to your heart's content."

The twins waddled to the water's edge. Fiachra dipped his head into the water and then came up, spluttering and shaking drops everywhere. Conn cocked his head, then just touched his beak to the surface, scooping the liquid up, then lifting his beak high, so the water trickled down his throat.

Aed's head drooped to the ground, "This is all my fault, isn't it?"

I stared at my brother. "What? How can you say that, Aed?"

"I put the love spell on Father and Aoife. I don't know what went wrong, but it messed everything up and it's my fault Father hit her and she got sick for so long and I made her go mad, Nuala! It's all my fault!" Aed's whole body heaved and shook as he wept through his words.

I put a wing around him. "No, no, Aed, it's not your fault. Aoife was working magic on us long before you tried. Do you remember her smile and how much it looked like Mother's? That was a charm. Even after

I realized that, I said nothing about it. If anyone's at fault, it's me for not mentioning her magic."

I held him tighter. "I wanted Father to be happy, so I kept quiet. Now look at us." I spread my wings to the lough, the pine-shrouded shore, and the guards. "We're here because Aoife is mad and selfish and no one was able to stop her. It's never your fault, Aed."

Aed still stared at his feet, but he gave a grudging nod. Then he glanced up, entreaty on his face. "But then it's not your fault, either!"

I pressed my beak together, but couldn't argue with his logic. "I'm exhausted, as I'm sure the boys are. Wouldn't you like to curl up and go to sleep?"

Las's voice was barely audible. "Would you like us to sing you to sleep, *bantiarna*?"

"That would be kind, Las, thank you."

The rough guards, full of strength and gruff as they were, nevertheless had sweet voices. These guards must have worked together on campaign many times, for they harmonized a sweet lullaby.

> *"A leanbh mo chléibh go n-eirí do chodhladh leat"*
> Child of my heart, sleep calmly,
> *"Séan is sonas gach oíche do choir"*
> And well all night and be happy.

In the 30th winter of Ard-Rí Bodb Dearg's reign, and the first winter of our curse (450 BCE)

The next morning dawned brightly and the sun sparkled on the lough in time to the music of the sunrise. Larks and sparrows added to the harmonies and lifted my heart. It made me want to sing, despite the horrible curse laid upon us.

I sang a song of the morning, a song of the sun. My voice came clearer and richer than it had ever been and soared into the sweet, high notes, then rolling gently into the low ones.

Without thinking, I spread my wings to fly, running to build up speed. And fell flat on my face. Someone giggled behind me, and I turned to glare at Aed, his head cocked. "Did you trip?"

"I did not. If you're so smart, why don't you try it?"

He lifted his wings, flapped, and then ran along the shore, picking up speed. His foot caught a root and he skidded flat on his belly in the mud. I let out a laugh, and the twins yawned.

Conn cocked his head and watched as Fiachra tried next. He got off the ground, but then smacked into a bush.

"Danu's right breast! That hurt!"

I couldn't hide my smile.

Finally, Conn studied the sky, then the shoreline. He ran in the other direction, where there were fewer obstacles along the waterline. Conn ran a good, long distance before flapping. A few moments later, he was soaring over the water.

After a few more tries, we were all in the sky, diving and wheeling. The joy of our success filled my heart and I sang out in wonder, my voice riding on the wind.

Aed's eyes grew wide with delight, and he sang along with me. Fiachra coughed, but Conn jumped right in. Fiachra found his stride in both flight and song just as we circled the lough and landed near the guards.

As we landed, Las clapped her hands. "Oh, what a delightful way to wake up! Thank you for such a lovely morning serenade."

The short, round guard pumped his hand into the air in triumph. "That deserves strong accolades. You must be starved after the long night. I know I am."

Just as we finished a meal of sausage and bread, the *ard-rí, banríon*, and their entourage returned.

Dervla gave me a fierce hug, holding on longer than ever before. "My raven spoke with your father's, and he's beside himself with worry. He should arrive this afternoon. Did you sleep well? Did you have nightmares?"

I shook my head. "No, the white feathers didn't return. What dream would be worse that my reality?"

Dervla gave me another hug. "We'll get this curse lifted soon, and you shall be back at *Sídhe Fionnachaidh,* where you belong."

I prayed to all the Gods that she was right.

A splash distracted me and I turned my long neck to find the twins playing in the shallow water of the shore. I wanted to smile, despite our plight. Trust them to find joy in a desperate strait.

Dervla sat next to me on a log. "I've word from the Council of Ravens. They haven't had much experience with reversing this sort of curse, but they haven't given up hope."

My heart sank at her words. Hope is all well and good, but if the ravens, the keepers of magical lore, didn't know how to break our curse, where else would we search?

"Now, no tears. Not yet." Dervla lifted my beak up as I fought against my despair. "My raven, Trawnag, had an idea, and he's passed it on to the White Council. I don't want to get your hopes too far on it, but it might just work, gods willing."

Despite myself, I glanced up. "What's his idea?"

Dervla's face lit up in a hopeful smile. "That we should ask the gods themselves."

My stomach flipped. What a bold idea! What a frightening idea. The gods had the power to kill us on a whim, or banish us to a fate worse than the curse.

But the old tales were full of transformation magic performed by the gods. The Morrigan transformed into a raven at will. Tuan, grandson of Parthalón, lived as a stag, a boar, and a salmon.

But none of those tales had swans. And we weren't gods.

"I realize it's a lot to take in, but it's our best course, and if they won't help, we're no worse off."

No worse off. I paced along the shoreline, my mind racing. No worse off. Except that the gods might crush us under their feet. I couldn't shake the sense of imminent disaster.

Dervla patted my shoulder and we sat in silence, each captive of our own thoughts.

I gazed out over the lough. My brothers were still diving, playing a game with made-up rules. Their giggles and shouts skipped across the water.

These were my brothers, my blood, and I swore to my mother on her death bed to keep them from harm. I had to do something, but I was powerless.

I detested being powerless. Having no power was a curse worse than being a swan. To remove my ability to shape my fate was a horrible thing.

Las and the other three guards were removing their armor. I didn't envy them, forced to baby-sit spoiled, cursed royal children. Perhaps it would be better for everyone if we flew away. But we couldn't even do that, as Aoife had bound us to this lough.

Maybe Father would have an idea. Maybe the Gods would answer the raven's plea. Maybe the Filíd would find a spell to break the curse. But that was a lot of maybes, and as my mother once said, *maybes seldom were.*

Instead of cleaning their armor, the guards waded into the water and joined my brothers' game.

I wished I could smile. Such things didn't work with a swan's bill, but my mood must have shown in my eyes, as Dervla patted me on the shoulder. "That's all good then, my sweet child. You bide here and enjoy the rest. I'll try to find you a bard for entertainment. We'll bring court here for a feast!"

Having people around might help keep my mind off the horrifying prospects, but somehow I doubted it.

While the *banríon* departed with her own guards, she left Las and one other guard, the short man who spoke to me earlier. He offered his palms in formal greeting. "I don't think we've properly met, *Bantiarna* Fionnuala. I'm Torr, Las's second-in-command."

"I'm pleased to meet you, Torr. I apologize for such boring duty as you've been assigned, though."

He let out a deep, low laugh that echoed across the glen. "This is the easiest post I've had in winters! Please, never apologize for such luxury. I'm honored to be part of this duty. What are your brothers' names?"

I turned to the other three swans. "The largest is my brother, Aed. He's eighteen winters old. The twins, Fiachra and Conn, are ten this season."

Torr bowed to all four of them. "I am pleased to guard you."

"And please, don't call me *bantiarna*. My name is Nuala."

Las gave me a bow. "As you wish, Nuala. Now that we've had a swim, we're going to work through some drills. Would you care to join us for fighter training?"

Fiachra held out his wings. "We have no hands. How would we hold a weapon?"

With a chuckle, Torr weaved his hands in a pattern. "We can teach you how to avoid being hit by a weapon, can't we?"

If we were to remain in this form for any length of time, learning defensive measures wasn't a horrible idea. Besides, I had years of bow training to help, even if I had to retrain my instincts. And doing something other than moping around all day sounded great. "Very well. Where do we start?"

When we were learning technique from Scuida, she'd attack us and let us figure out different ways to counter the attack, an effective but exhausting method.

Las, on the other hand, explained a technique first and then we practiced it slowly, pulling the nuances out of each variant and angle. She refined our balance, each muscle's placement, and how that affected our movements.

After just one hour, I was panting and aching. Even the twins wilted and they had an endless supply of energy. The slow work tired me much more than I would have believed.

When we took a break to eat, Aed asked, "Where did you learn that method, Las?"

"I trained for a time in *Dun Sgathaich*, far north and east of here, over the sea. There's a warrior woman named Scáthach who trains those she deems worthy. I was honored to be her student for many winters."

Torr turned. "Scáthach? She's a true legend."

"That she is and for good reason. I believe that woman could stand against a full army single-handed and win. And she's taught for at least three hundred winters, so she's no young thing."

I cocked my head. "Is she one of the People, then?"

Las nodded. "She moved there many winters ago, after a boasting argument about physical prowess with the Dagda."

The twins curled up and napped in the afternoon sun and Aed eyed them wistfully. I wanted a nap myself, after that morning's effort. But before I could sleep, the sound of hoof beats roused us.

Father rode in our old chariot, the one he'd had since I'd been a child. A pang of homesickness shot through me and a sob escaped.

"Nuala? What's hurt you?"

I heard Las' voice, but my mind made no sense of the words until she shook me and I opened my eyes. "I'm sorry, Las. It's nothing. I'm better now. Thank you."

She raised her eyebrows, but stepped away as my father's chariot came to a halt.

As he climbed out of the chariot, I realized my father was old. His hair, beard and even his eyebrows were gray. His face looked ashen, even worse than after Mother died.

How many winters did Father have? Surely, less than a hundred. He shouldn't look so wasted and frail.

Struggling to my feet, I bowed. "Father, I am so happy to see you."

He lifted me and squeezed. I squawked in surprise and he eased his grip, but still held me firm. "Oh, Nuala, my daughter! I didn't believe the *banríon*'s raven. I thought it had to be an elaborate jest, but it's true! Aed? Fiachra? Conn? These are all you?"

My brothers shouted out greetings and Father stood surrounded by four solid swans. We vied for his attention and hugs. The reunion descended into a half-mad, half-angry shouting match, as if each of us wanted to prove who we were.

After many tears and not a few fallen white feathers, Father sat in our midst. "How did this happen? I know Aoife cast a curse, but how did she get through your own defenses?"

I shook my head. "I'm not sure, Father. Aoife was so angry, saying we stole your affection from her. She must have been very lonely to come to such straits."

Aed fluttered his wings. "Say it, Nuala. She'd gone mad. Not just mad-angry, but mad-insane. Every imagined slight grew into something huge."

My head drooped. "We must have earned her anger, if not her reaction."

Aed squawked. "Stop apologizing! This is her fault, not yours! Didn't you just tell me that yesterday?"

"I know, but—"

Father patted my wing. "He's right. You mustn't blame yourself for her evil actions. She had many options, first and foremost to talk to me. Or to you. Or to the Filíd, or her raven. What did Nawlet do when she attacked?"

Fiachra fluttered his huge white wings. "She hit him, Father! Her own raven! She hit him and he fell to the ground. Then he went to help the other ravens she'd drugged."

Father shook his head and stared at his hands. The lapping of the waters of the lough filled the silence.

Conn asked, "Father?"

"Yes, son?"

"Can you fix us now? I'm tired of being a swan."

A plaintive plea of a child for his father's help. My helplessness made my eyes burn. At Conn's age, a parent could fix anything, change the world, make any injury better. But neither Father nor I could fix this.

"Oh, my dear Conn, I wish I could. I wish it more than anything I've wished for in my life, even more than wishing your mother alive again. But the *ard-rí* says there's hope, so we must keep hope in our hearts, aye?"

We gathered again for a hug and my throat closed. I swallowed, loath to show weakness before my brothers. I was the eldest, and I must stay strong.

Las approached with a cider skin and offered it to Father.

He smiled in thanks. "What's your name, guard? Are you taking good care of my children?"

"I'm Las and that's Torr back there. We're happy to keep your children company for as long as they need us."

Even if that's nine hundred winters?

Las poured cider into a shallow bowl and placed it on the ground. I dipped my bill in and scooped the sweet, delicious drink. The alcoholic burned my throat and made my head swim, but it was a welcome relief to the worry.

I drank more than normal and reveled in my wickedness.

Dervla returned with food, a bard and several musicians. With the amount of cider I drank, the feast and the music was nothing more than a blur of shattered images.

Eventually, the royal visitors returned home. We slept that night beside the trees, on the shore with Father, Las, and Torr.

Chapter Nine

The next morning, I woke to pouring rain. My wing muscles were stiff from our impromptu flight and fighter practice.

I stretched one wing out and moaned at the pain. Then I stretched the other and waddled to the lough. A good swim might get the kinks out.

No one else seemed awake yet, and I treasured the solitude. After I paddled around, stretching my aching muscles, I returned and fluffed out my feathers to dry them.

I stared at my brothers as they slept. Aed was the biggest, longer than me but not as solid. Conn and Fiachra were smaller, still fuzzy with the brownish-gray feathers of cygnets, young swans.

As the camp woke, Torr fried bread and cheese on a pan, filling the glade with delicious aromas.

As he bit into his slice, I asked Father, "Will you be returning home today?"

He sucked in cool air as he chewed the hot cheesebread. "I won't leave until we hear from the Filíd or the ravens."

"But what about *Sidhe Fionnachaidh*?"

He waved his hand as he took another bite, and mumbled around the food. "Maire Mór is perfectly capable of running the *túath* when we're not there."

While it might be true, a stab of guilt still spread in my heart.

So we waited. In the meantime, we practiced flying and swimming. Getting used to our new swan bodies took time, and even if we could break the curse quickly, I wanted to be comfortable in this body.

And if we must stay as swans for nine hundred years, we needed to start now. But I didn't want to think about that.

Instead, I thought about flying as I winged up over the lough and to the north end of the tree line. Aed flew behind me, but Fiachra and Conn had gone in another direction together.

As treetops rushed below me, I grew dizzy trying to focus on them. My flight faltered and I lost altitude.

Aed pulled up beside me. "What happened? You skipped a wing beat."

"I'm just getting used to this."

Just then, I spied a line of smoke beyond the trees, and I nodded to Aed for us to go investigate. As we flew closer, aching pain gripped our muscles. We must be getting too far from the lough, and the curse was drawing us back. But I wanted to know who was living so close to us.

Aed and I settled in a sturdy tree. Swans weren't good at perching on branches, but we braced against the trunk with our wings as I peered through the branches.

Smoke seeped through the center of the roundhouse, surrounded by animal pens for cows, pigs, and chickens.

A murder of crows settled into the field, where neat rows of crops grew. A few ravens joined them, and I thought of Hawlen, still recovering at the royal hillfort. These weren't the huge, magical birds that bonded with the People, but their smaller, mundane cousins. But still, they were ravens, and sacred to the People.

As we watched, two children ran outside, laughing and chasing each other. A woman emerged carrying a basket of clothing.

I exchanged a smile with Aed at this scene of domestic peace. Then someone inside the house shouted.

The woman put down her basket and hurried back inside. A moment later, she came out again with a man. He carried a bow and wore a scowl.

He knocked an arrow and aimed at a raven. I held my breath as he let loose, and in a flurry of feathers, the raven fell. The other birds scattered as the man stalked to the fallen one.

Aed let out an outraged squawk and I placed a wing on his beak. "Shh. We mustn't be found."

"But Nuala! That was a *raven!*"

My heart raced and I ached to attack the hunter, but we could do nothing for the poor bird. As the man picked up the corpse, its wings flopped to either side.

We flew back to the lough in silence, and I prayed to all the gods that Hawlen was safe.

Six days after we were cursed, Bé Chuille arrived with nine other Filíd, in a formal assembly. They approached as if at court, with a messenger sent to ask permission to enter our camp.

A chill crept up my spine. If they were giving me formal honors as a resident of the lough, then they hadn't found a counter-spell for the curse. Three hundred winters at this lough.

Father looked startled, but I nodded, as if I had been granted sovereignty.

I didn't hear the High Ollamh's ceremonial greeting, but a sharp nudge from Aed brought me back to the present. I made the welcome response and we exchanged gifts.

I didn't care about the greeting ritual. I just wanted to know what she'd discovered.

Finally, the High Ollamh spoke. "We have searched our records and our powers for anything that might help to alleviate your plight." She turned to a short man and placed a hand on his shoulder. "Porrig, here, is well-versed in transformational magic. I have brought him here so he may study you and formulate a counter-spell."

Porrig, a wiry old man with a wispy white beard, held his hands out, palm up in greeting. "*Bantiarna* Fionnuala, I'm honored to help. May I touch you? It will help me get a sense of the curse working."

I nodded and my brothers inched closer. Soon, we overwhelmed the tiny man with our swan bodies and I hissed them back.

My reaction startled me. I wasn't angry enough to have done such a thing, but it was instinctive when Porrig poked me.

My blood grew cold. What if we became swans in mind as well as body? How long would we retain our minds in this form? I prayed hard to the gods that Porrig could help.

The little Ollamh muttered under his breath as he examined me, making odd little sounds, grunts, and clicks, as he passed his hands over my wings and back, my tail, even my webbed feet and bill.

It felt odd, as no man had ever touched me this way before. There was nothing sensual about his attentions. His touch was clinical and detached. Still, the hum of power in his hands tingled and burned at points, and I let out a giggle.

"Hmm, yes, I see. Hmm." A spark jumped out from my wingtip and he stepped back in alarm. "Tsk, tsk, that wasn't very nice!"

"I didn't do that!"

"I know, my dear. It's the curse. The magic has cloaked you in several layers of protective web. Quite clever, really. I've never seen anything like this. Fascinating construction, it is. The inner layers shift and reproduce as I attack the outer layers."

He turned to Bé Chuille with a query in his eyes. "Are you sure I can't speak to the spellworker?"

"Quite sure. She was banished into an air phantasm."

"A phantasm? I should love to have seen that. But I do see your point. Pity. Pity. Hmm. Yes. That might have been hasty. Well, that can't be helped, can it? Come closer, boys. Let me touch your energy as well. Perhaps she didn't craft her curse as thoroughly with you."

Aed submitted to his odd assessment. Then Conn and Fiachra, though the latter fluttered his wings with annoyance at Porrig's explorations. "Yes, well, let me consider this. It may take time, but I've a few ideas. I need to work them out before I experiment, certainly. No good in making things worse. Eh?"

Once again, my spark of hope was squashed, but not dead entirely. Perhaps underneath this flighty personality lay great power and the ability we needed.

The little Ollamh left and Bé Chuille eyed me. "How are you coping, Fionnuala?"

I swallowed and glanced at Father. "Well enough, High Ollamh. Will our ravens be back soon, do you think?"

Her jaw clenched. "All the ravens have disappeared, every single one. I've never seen such a thing. It is most disconcerting."

The Ollamh put her hand on my head gave me one last smile before she gathered her entourage and left the glade.

After the Filíd departed, we hugged Father goodbye, which assuaged my guilt.

And then we were alone again, except for Las and Torr.

Mornings were dedicated to learning our new lives, such as practicing flying, swimming, and learning ways to defend ourselves. Early afternoons were for lessons, despite all of us arguing against the need. With the ravens still all missing, Las and Torr insisted. Then in the evenings, we made crafts, sang, talked, and socialized.

I missed Hawlen terribly, and I noticed Aed scanning the skies when he thought I wasn't looking. I couldn't chide him, as I did the same.

We were learning aspects of flying that could help us if we needed to fight. Aed discovered a particular talent at batting with his wings, while I was the fastest flyer. Fiachra had entirely too much enthusiasm and often wandered off from the lessons. Conn listened intently and tried any suggested techniques with quiet determination.

We'd just finished today's history lesson and were getting ready for our evening meal. The setting sun lit the surrounding tree line with orange fire, and mists rose from the lough, waking the evening insects. They rippled on the surface of the water and sparkled in the sunbeams.

A sudden cessation of noise and the beat of many wings made me glance behind us, to see four black ravens and one white one coming in for a landing.

I leapt to my feet and waddled to them, joy bursting in my heart. "Hawlen! Hawlen, you're back! Oh, I'm so happy to see you!"

I couldn't be proper and decorous. I'd missed my teacher, my confidante, my best friend, so much these trying days. It was awkward, as my large white wings encircled her smaller black body.

The other ravens greeted their own bondmates, while the white one stood to one side with dignity.

After my buffeting hug, Hawlen cocked her head at me. "Fionnuala, are you well?"

The question struck me as silly. "I'm a swan! How can I be well?"

She fluttered her wings. "That's fair, but you mustn't dwell on it too long. How are you faring?"

I gave a sullen shrug. "We've kept ourselves busy and waited for word from you and from the Filíd. Have you brought us good news?" My legs were weak with quivering anticipation as I glanced at the white raven.

Instead of answering, Hawlen turned to the newcomer. "May I present *Bantiarna* Fionnuala, daughter of Lir, *Tiarna* of *Sídhe Fionnachaidh*, child of the Tuatha Dé Dannan?"

The new raven inclined his head once. Hawlen continued, "*Bantiarna* Fionnuala, may I present High Councilor Stawn of the White Council of Ravens, our leader and wisest elder?"

I bowed awkwardly in my swan form. He approached me and examined me from all sides. Stawn poked and prodded, much as Porrig had. He opened my bill and sniffed at my breath, then lifted feathers in my wings and peered deep into my eyes.

He examined my brothers less thoroughly and then walked off, gestured for Hawlen to join him.

They chattered in raven-speak conference for a long time. At several points, their voices rose and fell in argument. I exchanged worried glances with my brothers, but none of us knew what was happening.

Then Stawn just flew away and my hopes flew with him.

Aed asked, "Does that mean he can't help, either?"

"I don't know, Aed. I don't know." I put my wing around his shoulders and he trembled, either with fear or tears.

"Then what was that all for? If he can't help, he shouldn't have come in the first place!"

I glanced in the direction the white raven had flown, grief and despair warring in my mind. "Aed, Aed, calm down. They're all doing as much as they can. You must have patience."

He pulled away from me, his wings unfurling. "I'm tired of patience. I'm tired of *let's wait and see.* If they can help us, then they should do so! I've had enough of conferences and speculation and inspections!"

And I'd had enough of his whining. "Aed! Don't you think they'd help us immediately, if they could? I'm just as sick of this as you are, but do you hear me complain?"

He glared at me. "You should! You should yell and scream about the unfairness of this, even more than me! Why aren't you angry, Nuala? Did she kill the fire in you as well as the girl?"

I couldn't think of anything to say to that, so I shoved him. He stared at me with anger and a bit of fear in his eyes. Then he shoved me harder.

I stumbled back and my face grew warm. I flew at Aed with my feet forward, intent on kicking him in the face.

Hawlen flew between us. "Stop it! Children, stop this now! This does not help. Now listen, all of you. Stawn believes he can build something, but he isn't certain. He will commune with the Morrigan to discover a way to heal the damage."

My temper cooling, I asked, "Healing? I thought he was learning transformation magic?"

"It is, but with any transformation, there's a change in the body. Healing might help fix the body to its natural form. Any transformation puts a strain on nature. Your natural form wants to come back, it strains to return, but the magic prevents it."

An idea burst into my head. "If it's healing, maybe I can do something! I can help, at least. I can lend my power to what Stawn has—"

Hawlen held up a wing. "No, child. The High Raven has so much more magic than you, it would be like a drop in the ocean. Especially if he convinces the Morrigan to help. To even try to combine your power with that of a goddess might kill you. You have no experience with this level of magic."

It stung to hear my own powers dismissed so easily. Anger and resentment bubbled inside me. How does she know what would happen? Tears burned behind my eyes.

Conn pushed a small round object toward me. I glanced at the rounded stone with the design of a snail, something that remained long after the creature died. The unique and precious object reminded me that life had meaning well past death.

I hugged my youngest brother so tightly he squawked. "Thank you, Conn. Did you find this here, or was it one of your three precious objects you brought from home?"

"One of my treasures. I found it by the stone circle near our house."

"That makes it even more sacred."

His eyes were solemn. "It's yours. To keep."

I swallowed back fresh tears. "Then I shall hold it close to my heart. Perhaps Las and Torr can make us pouches to hold our things. That way, you can keep your other stones with you. Would you like that?"

He nodded again.

I turned to the others. "So, we wait again, Hawlen?"

She nodded. "We wait again."

A few weeks later, we were practicing a new defensive technique. When Las whistled in a particular sequence, we scattered in different directions and hide amongst the bushes. She'd just whistle at random times throughout the day, and we had to scramble, and she'd time us on how quickly we hid.

As we returned from the latest drill, Fiachra said, "I think we've learned this, Las. We really don't need to practice every day, do we?"

Las gave him a scowl. "And the day you don't practice is the day you'll need it."

He rolled his eyes. "This isn't druid learning. It's flying across the lough and hiding in a bush."

Just as he said the last word, a horse whickered. We exchanged a confused glance, and then Las put her hands to her mouth to whistle. We didn't wait for the sound, but darted off into hiding.

Strangers came into view. Ten Milesian warriors and three horses. Then I recognized the one in the front and almost came out from hiding.

Aed held me back and whispered, "What are you doing?"

"That man in the front? I recognize him! He's Áedammair, the Milesian *tiarna* we've met." I hadn't seen him since he'd asked for my hand in marriage.

My brother craned his neck to see but shook his head. "I can't tell if that's him or not. Maybe he just looks familiar. You should wait until Las or Torr says it's clear to come out."

I gritted my teeth but realized the wisdom of his advice. Las gave the traditional formal greeting, then asked, "What is the purpose of your visit here?"

The man in the lead opened his arms wide. "I have come to visit the *bantiarna*, Nuala! I heard she bides here, under a curse. And my purpose is to make her laugh."

I couldn't keep from giggling at his wide grin and Aed shushed me again.

Torr raised his eyebrows. "You've met the *bantiarna*?"

"I have! We've shared several conversations. I even sought to wed her once, but her father turned me down."

Aed turned to me, his eyes wide. "He asked to marry you?"

"Yes, but Father reacted as you might expect. He forbade it and sent Áedammair away the next morning."

Our whispers must have been too loud, as Áedammair peered at our hiding spot. "Is that them in the brush? Nuala, come out! I have gifts."

Pulling my brother out of the shadows, I strode to the clearing, keeping my long neck high. "Greetings, Áedammair. I welcome you to our place."

The *tiarna's* eyebrows rose as I approached and went even higher when I spoke. "I recognize your voice, *bantiarna*. And I have come with gifts of food for you and your brothers. May we share a feast?"

I glanced at Las, and she gave a reluctant nod. Then his men, along with Las and Torr, set up a firepit for their venison and boar meat.

We had a delightful evening, marred with awkward moments when Áedammair or one of his men would mention something we could no longer do as swans. But they shared new songs and stories, from their own people.

I tried to remember the details as much as I could, so I could tell them again, after they left.

As the evening waned and the celebration grew quieter, Áedammair spoke quietly with me. "Is there anything I can do to make your plight easier?"

I shook my head. "Not that I can think of. Unless you know transformation magic to break our curse."

He shook his head with a worried frown. "I know very little magic. I know war, ruling, singing, and hunting. I don't think any of these can help you."

I gazed into his eyes, a sudden idea occurring to me. I remembered the hunter in the roundhouse nearby and his attack on that raven.

"There is something, if you really want to help."

"Oh? Name it, and I will make it so."

I hesitated, realizing that he might not have any influence over the local Milesians. "There's a living man near us, north of the lough. I watched him shoot a raven with his bow."

Áedammair stroked his chin. "Yes, I've heard of some Milesians hunting ravens. It's not our way, but people do sometimes grow desperate."

I shook my head with a frown. "This man didn't look desperate. He had plenty of livestock, but just shot the raven anyway. Is there any way we can stop it? Ravens are sacred to us. And if they start hunting swans, as well…"

He drew up with indignation. "That would not be permitted, not during my reign. I shall ask our Brehon to create a law against such practice, both for ravens and for swans. This is the least I can do for a friend."

A season later, on a stormy autumn day, the Filíd and Stawn arrived at the same time.

Stawn inclined his head to Bé Chuille and gestured that she should proceed first. With a nod of thanks, the High Ollamh brought Porrig forward.

The little Ollamh sat on the ground in front of me. "Gather your siblings together, right in front of me. Yes, yes, like that. Now, remain as still as you can."

Porrig sang. Not a chant, but a true song, with an intricate melody. He had a beautiful voice, high and clear, at odds with his scattered personality.

I didn't recognize the words, though they seemed vaguely familiar. Not like Aoife's strange language, but a glistening, liquid language similar our own.

A deep green glow formed around him, rising into his body. Soon, lightning green sparks crackled everywhere. The ground hummed, rattling my teeth and making my skin itch.

His voice rose and the enchantment of his words melded with the earth's magic. This green-brown force tangled my webbed feet and tendrils worked into my feathers, my bill, until I was trapped within its grasp.

My heart raced and I wanted to escape, to fly away from this frightening power, but I knew I must stay. Fiachra rustled his wings behind me and I shot him a reassuring glance.

The thrum grew until it pounded on my mind. It compressed and pushed, making my skull ache, and I wanted to cry. Then everything went black.

When I awoke, I lifted a hand, but it was still a wing. My heart sank and I looked up at the ollamh.

Porrig stood over me and frowned. "I don't understand. That should have worked, it really should. I gave everything I had." He shook his head. "Stawn, your turn."

I exchanged a glance with each of my brothers, anxious about another attempt, but I was more anxious about being stuck in this form.

Stawn gave no instructions, but I knew better than to move. Hawlen nodded in encouragement and I nodded back.

Stawn cocked his head, speaking with an unusually deep and musical voice. "Our Lady, the Morrigan, was gracious enough to grant me an audience."

The Morrigan, the Goddess of War and Death, She who transformed herself into a raven at will. A guiding force of the Tuatha Dé, a daughter of Danu herself and long since moved on to *Tír na nÓg*. She rarely interfered with our world, and when she did, it often ended in disaster for whomever she dealt with. My skin crawled.

"She's agreed to teach me the magic necessary to help you. However, her instruction will take time."

Time. We have plenty of that.

Bé Chuille folded her hands. "How much time?"

Stawn shrugged. "She did not say, but it won't be quick. The gods run on different timelines than we do. It might be moons. It might be winters. It may be our ability is not enough to break this curse, but we are determined to try. I shall keep you informed of our progress."

He flew into the air and disappeared into the gathering twilight.

Numbed, I had no tears left. Winters. Our last hope may be winters, even decades, away. Even then, it might not be enough.

Conn asked, "Nuala, what did the white raven mean?"

Fiachra swatted Conn in the head with his wing. "It means we're stuck as swans, dolt. Until he can learn how to break the curse. *If* he can learn."

Bé Chuille knelt beside me and touched my wing. I couldn't speak or move. I had no idea what I should do now. How could I protect my brothers for decades as a swan?

I wanted to rage, to throw something, to smash furniture, like Father did when he was upset. Instead, I did nothing.

"Fionnuala. Child, don't despair. We'll continue to work. Porrig might find something new in his research. We haven't given up hope. In the meantime, we shall entertain you, bring you news, food, and companionship. You will never be alone, this I vow." A shimmer spread across the lough with her words. The High Ollamh's vows had power.

Still, I said nothing.

Hawlen hopped over to my side. "Aed, take your sister to get some sleep. All of you, rest. It's been an incredibly trying day, and she is overwrought."

I didn't want guards and entertainment. I wanted to be a young lady, with a young man to love and children around my feet. Tadhg's face came to my mind, with his silly grin as he pushed back his black curls. I wanted to run up a hill in the summer sunlight. I wanted to climb a tree clothed in brilliant autumn colors.

On a sunny afternoon a few days later, Hawlen was teaching me lessons as if we hadn't had our entire lives upended. I stared out at the lough, wishing I was flying rather than learning lessons. A flock of mundane swans had landed on the far side of the lake. I wondered if we could speak to them, if they could even understand us.

Hawlen pecked me on the head, interrupting my thoughts. "Tell me the royal line."

I rolled my eyes. "Ow! Again? You know I know this."

"Again. Rote anchors knowledge, and you must know it instinctually."

Giving him a scowl, I asked, "Why? Why must knowing who the *ard-rí's* second cousin twice removed is be so important?"

"For when you encounter him at court, and you must select the proper greeting. So you don't insult or exalt him beyond his station. So, when it is time to choose the next Tánaiste, you can remember who is descended from the *ard-rí's* great-grandfather. Every one of the Tuatha Dé has his or her place. Ignore that place at your peril, and the peril of your tribe's reputation."

I held up my wings. "As if we're going to be able to do any of that? Like this?"

She clacked her beak. "We must assume the curse will be broken."

I scowled, but she had a point. Giving a deep sigh, I recited the family tree of the *ard-rí* back to the fifth generation. "Satisfied?"

"I am." Hawlen preened her wing for a quick moment. "Now, what is the etiquette during a royal wedding?"

Through a clenched beak, I said, "Weddings are the last thing I want to think about! Can I at least hear a story before we dive back into lessons?"

She cawed several times. "Have you heard the story of your parents' wedding?"

I had, many times. I'd even heard songs from bards, but I've never heard the tale from Hawlen. She hadn't yet been alive then, but the ravens shared something of a group-mind and what one knew, the others could learn. "I don't know if the twins have heard it."

After I gathered my brothers close, Hawlen sang, the familiar tune soothing my soul. A swirling mist formed between us. Within this mist, a pale brown image formed, as if we watched through amber-colored glass.

A great battlefield with many casualties appeared, all tinted brown and gold. Though Hawlen stopped singing, the figures within the mist continued to fight.

"When the Battle of Tailltin ended, the Tuatha Dé had lost to the Milesians. The surface world was ceded to these invading humans, while the Tuatha Dé, the People of the Gods, agreed to move below the hills. They would complete the transition in twenty-five winters. Indeed, this move is not even half-complete today."

Aed curled up next to me, his body warm against mine. The twins cuddled close, as well.

"With many nobles dead and the Dagda, the Good God, wishing to step down from power, a new *ard-rí* needed to be elected. The five sons of the Dagda gathered to choose which among them would be *ard-rí* of the People."

Conn asked, "Why the sons only? Were there no daughters?"

Hawlen ruffled her wings. "Most had married and their husbands would have taken the rule, not them."

The scene changed to the Royal Feast Hall. I recognized the *ard-rí* and my father, and some of the other nobles. Father was vigorous and healthy, a far cry from the old man he was now.

"Bodb Dearg of *Sídhe ar Femuin*, the eldest son of the Dagda, was the first choice. Lir of *Sídhe Fionnachaidh*, your own father, was the second choice. The other choices were Midhir the Proud and Aengus Og.

After much discussion, everyone agreed that Bodb Dearg should become *ard-rí*. Everyone, that is, but your father. Lir was resentful and left the gathering without a word.

I hadn't heard this part of the story and gasped at the grave insult.

"The other *tiarnaí* wished to follow Lir and kill him for his offense, but Bodb Dearg counseled patience. During the moons after the battle, Lir's first wife, Tallin, died of a three-day fever. She'd been much-loved and your father mourned her deeply. After the mourning year, Bodb Dearg sent word to Lir and asked him to return."

Aed cocked his head. "I knew Father was married before mother, but I'd never heard her name."

Hawlen clacked her beak shut, but my brother didn't take the hint. "What was she like? Was she kind or regal? Tall or short? Fair or dark?"

"She looked very similar to your own good mother and was reputed to be very kind. When Lir reluctantly returned to the royal hillfort, he did so in style. Fifty chariots came, filled with warriors and maidens alike.

"The *ard-rí* greeted him as a brother and offered him a wife from his own three foster-daughters."

The image in the mist now showed three lovely young women, each with long, straight hair to her waist. I recognized my mother straight away, though she looked so young. I longed to stroke her silken white-blonde hair just one more time, and my tears fell unchecked.

I glanced at the other two, Aoife Rua and Aillbha. I searched my aunt's face for a hint of her insanity, but couldn't detect a shred of madness.

"Lir said he could not choose one based on beauty, for all three were beautiful. He could not choose one based on temperament, for they were all equally sweet. Bodb Dearg therefore said he should choose the eldest, as she'd be the wisest to help him rule."

The mist shifted into a new scene. People danced and musicians played, all still with that amber cast on the colors. Mother and Father whirled in the center, beaming with radiant joy. My heart swelled with how happy they both seemed.

"Your father was smitten by your mother's grace and good sense, and bards still sing of their love."

The images faded into nothing. Warmth flowed through me at the knowledge that my parents sincerely loved each other. And then that love had died. That warmth turned to bitter ashes in my heart.

Hawlen hopped from her perch. "I think the lessons are over for today. The story of your parents' love is powerful."

In the 5th winter of our curse (445 BCE) 5 years later

After the great Battle of Tailltin, all the People must move below the hills within twenty-five winters, to the palaces they built in *Saol Eile*.

That time had finally come, but we couldn't follow. Not that I'd ever wanted to live beneath the hills, as that idea still filled me with fear and loathing. But we'd be forever separated from all those we loved. Only the Milesians remained, these humans who had almost no magic and such ephemeral lives.

A parade of well-wishing visitors came to our lough. The *ard-rí* and *banríon,* of course, and our father. Tears flowed for days as they said farewell.

Then Tadhg came to say his farewells. His wife, Aillbha, had the grace to walk away to afford me privacy to speak to her husband. Perhaps she felt some lingering guilt over her sister's betrayal or just wanted to be kind. Either way, I was grateful.

My friend gave me a half-smile. "Well, at least you know you'll be alive for nine hundred winters."

I rolled my eyes. "If we aren't killed by roving Milesians or die of disease. That's a fantastic reassurance. Thank you so much for your visit."

He dropped his gaze. "I just meant—"

I held up a wing. "I realize what you meant, Tadhg. You meant to relieve the tension with a jest. Well, it didn't work, did it?"

"I'm sorry, Nuala. I'm so sorry. For everything."

"Are you? Are you really? After all, now you have no guilt for marrying Aillbha. Who would've expected you to remain wed to a swan? No, you go have your life, Tadhg. Enjoy your bride. Delight in your underground palace. I'm certain you'll forget me rather quickly."

He lifted his gaze, his eyes intense. "You're wrong, Nuala. I'll never forget you. That much, at least, I can promise."

"What good will such a promise do me, Tadhg?"

He dropped his gaze again. "I have no idea. I'll think of something."

I couldn't speak to him any more. I turned my back and waddled to Father. "Will you come back, Father? Come to visit us?"

He hugged me tightly. "Of course I will. I'll be part of your life until we once again reunite as Tuatha Dé."

Dervla insisted that we must have guards of the People, and a special council of the humans, our *tiarnaí,* and the White Council had met to consider options. The Milesians had reluctantly agreed to that change. They granted Las and Torr special dispensation to remain above ground.

As the last visitor left from our lough, I stared at their backs. Dust from the chariot wheels kicked up and obscured the details of their bright-colored robes.

Now we were alone once more. Alone in a world where we no longer had any kin.

Chapter Ten

In the 6th winter of our curse (444 BCE) 1 year later

Days became moons. Moons became seasons, and seasons turned the winter wheel as each one passed us by.

On a warm autumn evening, after our afternoon lessons with the ravens, Conn came to me with a question. "Nuala, have you ever tried to talk to them?" He gestured with one wing to the mundane swans swimming at the far end of the lough.

"I thought about it, but what can we say? *Hello, we're really not swans. How are you?*"

He let out a giggle and shook his head. "That's fair. But I want to try. Will you come with me?"

Together, we swam to the flock of six swans. They regarded us with wary eyes as we approached. The largest one stretched their neck and we halted, not wanting to intrude.

Conn stretched his own neck and honked. The leader honked back, but I couldn't interpret the noise into anything meaningful.

I exchanged a look with Conn and he shrugged. "I have no idea what that meant."

The large swan flapped his wings, spraying water on us. I shook my head to get the water from my eyes and spluttered. The wild swans snorted as if laughing at us, turned their backs, and swam away.

I turned to my brother. "I suppose that answers our question?"

"I guess so." He looked so dejected, I put a wing around his shoulders as we swam back. I wondered if he was looking for new friends.

Over the last turn of the seasons, Conn and Fiachra remained cygnets, so it seemed we wouldn't age. I wondered if they would stay so young for the full nine hundred winters. Never older, never adult, never grown. No marriage, children, or grandchildren to anticipate.

We'd never know love. Who of the People would bind their love to a transformed creature? There'd be no physical love as I'd craved with Tadhg.

At the cusp of womanhood, this hurt me hard. The stirrings of lust and passion still surged within me, but I had no way to slake them.

Our days faded into a blur. We worked with the ravens in the morning, to learn more of history, magic and now about the code and conduct of flying creatures. There were courtesies to be maintained within the avian community and we needed to learn those, as was made apparent by the rude dismissal of the other swans.

We spent our afternoons with Las, Torr, practicing defensive and offensive tactics. Messengers from *Saol Eile* came at least once a season with gossip, food, and drink.

The *ard-rí* and Bé Chuille constructed a permanent gate to *Saol Eile*, a *cómhla bhreach*, for easier visits.

Las and Torr were wonderful hunters, but we had no crops or livestock. While we could survive on grasses and reeds that grew around the lough, we still craved the food we were used to. Therefore, we greatly anticipated visits from *Saol Eile* for such treats as fresh bread, cheese, and honey.

One evening, Torr was cleaning the refuse from our evening meal and examined the netting our cheese came in. The tight net had loops at the top for hanging.

He placed several small stones inside and hefted it once or twice to make sure they didn't drop through the holes. "Nuala, can you carry this in your beak?"

"I'm sure I could, but why?"

Aed narrowed his gaze. "That would hurt if we dropped it on someone, wouldn't it?"

Torr grinned. "Even more so if you flung it at them. Your necks have strength and a great deal of flexibility. If you practiced, you might be able to fling the stones with force."

I picked the net up with my beak and flew toward the treeline. With a flick of my neck, I loosed the net toward a tree.

It didn't work so well. My beak caught in the net and the stones just dropped.

We practiced the technique and eventually, Aed managed a good flick. Several birds flew off and chirped angrily at his attack.

Fiachra wanted to try next, but the light was fading. "I promise to bring more nets tomorrow and rig something so it's easier for you to control." Torr mounted his horse and headed toward the gate below the hills.

That summer, the *ard-rí* had directed his people to construct several roundhouses and a pavilion near the shore. One roundhouse for the guards, another for guests, and a third for storage and supplies. The pavilion had movable walls for fierce weather.

The nets Torr returned with worked much better. They had just one handle, a long thin loop that gathered the edges. When we flung it, the loop broke and scattered the net.

It took a great deal of practice, but after several weeks, we could fling the stones wherever we wanted and with a great deal of force.

Torr set up practice dummies on the far side of the lough and we covered them with pockmarks from our efforts.

"I hit another one!" Fiachra crowed.

Conn shook his head. "Those didn't hit very hard."

"Of course they did! See the white marks left behind? That could have broken someone's arm!"

Conn fluttered his wings at his twin. "Could not!"

Fiachra hissed. "Could, too!"

I waded in. "Boys! Enough of that, now! You've both done well today."

Fiachra stuck out his tongue at his brother, so Conn shoved Fiachra into the mud. Fiachra hissed, flew toward him and batted his ears. Or he would have, if Conn stood still. Instead, he snaked his neck under Fiachra's wings to nip at his tail.

Fiachra screeched and fluttered away, a few feathers drifting away. If Conn could smile, I'm certain he'd be wearing a self-satisfied grin.

"Stop it, now! Fiachra, I believe you need another lesson in the proper dignity of a *tiarna*'s son. Where's Crawma?"

His voice was sullen. "I don't know."

"Call for her. She taught you how. Stop sulking."

A noise from Conn made me turn. "And you're no better, Conn. Call Fwallson and tell him you need more instruction. Weapon training is over for the day."

Fiachra honked and said, "As if it would make any difference."

"That is unfair and impolite. Torr has spent a great deal of effort towards making you a better fighter. Will you dismiss his efforts so easily?"

My brother hissed. "We're just freaks. There's no future for us! It's not as if we can go off to war to fight for our people."

"True, we're bound to this place. But what if someone attacks us here? A troop of Milesians might pierce the veil. You never know what might happen, and it's better to be prepared."

I put my wing on Fiachra's shoulder, but he shrugged it off. "Or what, we die? And would that be so horrible?"

It was my turn to hiss. "How dare you! Don't tempt the gods. You know better!"

He bowed his head. I shouldn't blame him for feeling useless, but I mustn't let such a depressive thought fester within him. We had centuries before us, and we must survive in mind and body.

"A life is worth living, no matter what it may hold. We need to hold tight to that ideal like a talisman, no matter what happens."

He nodded, but I wasn't sure he truly heard me. That night, I had dreams of men invading our lough, and got little rest.

Early the next morning, Fiachra went flying with his raven, Crawma. He didn't ask, he didn't tell us where he was going, he just left before anyone else had woken up.

After we figured out what had happened, I paced back and forth, one moment determined to fly out to find him, the next moment worried sick that he was somewhere, hurt, unable to fly back.

Las put a hand over my shoulder. "Crawma will look out for him. If they get in trouble, she'll contact Hawlen."

I shook my head. "No, Hawlen tried to contact them, but couldn't hear anything. What if that hunter with the arrows got Crawma? What if they're trapped in a net or captured?"

I kept pacing, knowing it was up to me to make decisions. But I didn't know what to do.

A caw across the lough caught my attention and my head shot up, peering into the morning mist. Something white came closer, and soon Fiachra dove in, flying fast. He tumbled to the shore, his eyes wide with terror.

I hurried to him, torn between anger and worry. "What happened? Are you hurt?"

His eyes were wide with terror and wet with tears. "They have him! They took Crawma! We have to rescue him!"

Aed placed a wing on Fiachra's head. "Slow down, brother. Who has Crawma? Where?"

"This house, just beyond the trees. Where the smaller river turns. He had a net! I couldn't get him out!"

I exchanged a glance with Aed. That must be the place where the raven was shot. "I know where it is. Las, Torr, we can get there faster than you."

Las shook her head. "Absolutely not. It's already too dangerous. We'll find the place. Fiachra can guide us on the ground."

I started pacing. "I can't just send you off on your own! I need to come with you."

Torr stood next to Las, his arms crossed. "No, Nuala. You must stay here."

I hissed at them both and took flight. Aed launched a heartbeat later, with Fiachra and Conn right behind us.

Conn had grabbed his throwing net. I nodded in approval and shouted at Fiachra, "Show us where!"

With a grim expression, Fiachra darted in front, pumping his wings with furious strength. Despite being the fastest flyer, I struggled to keep up. Aed and Conn fell further behind.

As the tree cover cleared away below us, Fiachra wheeled down and I saw that yes, this was the same farm where the raven had been killed. My heart raced, and I prayed to all the gods that Crawma was safe.

A raven cawed from inside the stable, and I let out a cautious sigh of relief just as Aed and Conn finally caught up.

Fiachra turned to me. "How will we save him?"

I hadn't thought of a plan. Belatedly, I realized that Las and Torr, with their warrior training, would be much better suited to creating a plan of action.

But we couldn't wait for them. "Aed, can you make a fuss? Far enough away that he wouldn't be able to hit you with an arrow, but enough to draw him away?"

My eldest brother nodded. "Sure. I can bother the pigs. They'll set up a huge squeal."

"Excellent. Once the man is outside, Fiachra and I will fly into the roundhouse to rescue Crawma."

Conn asked, "What about me?"

I turned to my brother. "I need you to watch everything and if something goes horribly wrong, you must fetch Las and Torr here to save us."

I expected him to protest that it wasn't heroic, but he just nodded. "That makes sense. Fiachra, do you want to use my net?"

I gave him a hug for being sensible and Aed went to make the pigs angry. Then we waited.

It seemed like forever before the pigs started squealing. A few moments later, the hunter emerged, his arrow already knocked. Aed flew out of range, but the man took aim.

Fiachra poked me. "This is our chance!"

We flew down to the roundhouse, careful to keep out of the hunter's sight. Once inside, our eyes took a moment to adjust to the dim light. There was Crawma, trussed up like a chicken on a spit, but still alive.

We couldn't untie him, and he was a huge bird, but between Fiachra and myself, we lifted him, spit and all, and flew out. A woman's sleepy voice cried out, but I ignored it.

The hunter was taking aim for Aed again, but he dove in circles, avoiding the shots. As we reached the tree cover, Aed darted away, and together we flew toward our lough.

"Crawma," I panted, as he was heavy and flying with him was difficult, "Are you hurt?"

The raven just moaned and fluttered. Fiachra and I pushed harder. He needed healing.

Just as we landed, with Aed and Conn not far behind us, Las rounded on us, her eyes blazing. "How dare you just go off like that? You all could have been killed! Do you have any idea what the *ard-rí* will do to *us* if we fail to protect you?"

I swallowed against an angry retort. "Crawma's hurt. I can't untie him."

Las pursed her lips but knelt beside the raven, loosened the knots, and then sent Torr for ointments.

I sat beside the raven, my wings out. "I'm going to try to heal him, but my magic changed when we became swans. I don't have the same sort of power I used to."

Torr pushed me aside. "We can tend him. You rest. And don't think this is over."

Once a week, we took time off from our training to do fun things. Singing, flying, swimming, just learning how to have fun as swans.

We practiced the complex flight arrangements and the rippled descants endless times. Our goal was to create a performance for our visitors the next time they came.

We filled the glade with music and sometimes laughter. Mostly when someone, often Fiachra, missed a cue or stumbled on a note.

It's not that Fiachra had no skill at song. We all sang sweetly as swans. But Fiachra often acted like a buffoon to get us laughing.

Las cheered as we finished our most recent rehearsal and Torr pumped his arm in the air in approval while he fiddled with the fire.

Las clapped her hands together. "Well done, all! That should impress the whole crowd!"

Torr brought out some steaming morsels. The night grew warm, but the flight had tired me and I craved a warm snack. She had wrapped flatbread around cheese and grilled them on a flat pan, so the cheese melted and bubbled hot. I picked the second one up carefully with my beak and shook it to cool it off.

Aed had no such qualms and hopped around when the melted cheese burned his tongue. "Ow! Ow! Oh, that burns!"

Fiachra laughed, "Silly Aed! You should know better than that."

Aed stopped his jumps and glowered at his little brother. "Stop laughing!"

"How can I stop when you're just so funny!"

My eldest brother growled. "Take that back!"

Torr and Las visibly tried to hide their smiles. Conn shook his cheese bread and bit tenderly into one end. I ducked my head and laughed to myself.

Still, Fiachra had a serious side. I thought back to that day, four summers ago, when he'd resolved that the curse wouldn't keep him to the lough.

On an early, misty morning, Fiachra had woken before any of us. He took wing and flew once all around the lough. Then he'd gotten it into his head that he could just push through the curse-pain, right through to the other side, if only he flew fast enough.

He flapped his wings as fast as he could and darted straight toward the royal hillfort. He'd only gone a few beats of his wings past the tree line when the pain came.

Fiachra said his wings had suddenly felt on fire and he'd glanced to ensure they weren't, in fact, in flames. An invisible force crushed in his bones, as if a massive creature hugged the very life from him.

He laboriously turned around and headed back toward our accursed lough. The pain faded as soon as he came within a few hundred feet of the shore.

None of us ever tried to leave again after Fiachra recounted his ordeal, though I thought about it several times. I just never had the courage to try. Fiachra was the courageous one.

Any of the People might visit us for three days, per the treaty. But time ran differently in the new realm, so what might be three days below ground might be three winters above.

A rustle in the trees caught my attention, and I swallowed the last bit of my cheese bread. The rustle grew into a disturbance, which became a commotion. Then several figures burst from the trees and I recognized the *ard-rí's* entourage.

By now, I knew the trusted guards well, and I waved my wing in their direction. They waved back.

My brothers and I flew up and around the camp to perform our knotwork pattern. We'd rehearsed it many times as our greeting for guests. Also, it might show any strangers that we were intelligent and not for hunting.

After the formal welcomes, the *ard-rí* and *banrion* set up within the guest roundhouse, while the guards and other guests erected tents and set up campfires. It seemed like the whole court came on this visit.

Once she settled in, I eagerly asked Dervla, "Is Father with you?"

"Not yet, child. He should be here in the morning. He had some business to finish."

I hid my disappointment. It was much easier to hide your feelings as a swan. The Peoples' faces were much more expressive. I asked after their own journey.

"Nothing untoward. I do have a gift for you, though. Bide here a moment, while I dig it out."

She entered her roundhouse, but several moments passed before she returned with four strips of elaborately decorated cloth.

I cocked my head. "What are these?"

Dervla held up the strips. "You told me the purpose for your greeting dance. These would be another way that strangers could tell you were magic beings."

Each cloth was woven in rich, jewel-toned colors; ruby red, sapphire blue, emerald green, and amethyst purple. Gold and silver threads entwined in elaborate knots along the length.

We didn't own luxuries any longer. We lived to survive, for the most part. My throat caught at the kind gift. "They're beautiful! Please, may I wear mine now? Can you attach it?"

She tied the red one on with a decorative knot, then stood back to appraise her work. "Yes, that's indeed lovely. Would you like to see?"

Once attached, warmth and security infused me. I felt more peace than I had for many days.

I waddled to the lough shore to peer at the lough surface. The evening was calm, so when I craned my long neck to peer into the reflection, no waves marred the image.

The red ribbon showed stark against my white feathers and I wished I could smile. "Is there something special about the ribbons, *banrion*?"

"Didn't I tell you long ago to call me Dervla? And yes, I wove magic into them. Just some peace of mind. I'm sure it won't go amiss."

Aed didn't seem as enthused. "Only women and girls wear ribbons."

Conn poked at the blue one with his wing tip. "But it's pretty! It sparkles in the sun!"

Aed honked at his little brother.

I touched his ribbon with my wingtip. "They'll look so nice during our performance."

Conn offered his neck to the *banrion* for his purple ribbon.

Aed rolled his eyes. "Fine, I'll wear one. But only because you all are. I wouldn't want to be the odd man out."

Dervla's smile held a trace of self-satisfaction. She clapped her hands when she finished tying on the last ribbon. "So, what's this performance you have for us?"

Fiachra waggled his head, "Oh, no, we mustn't tell! It's a surprise for tomorrow evening. We've practiced for a moon!"

"Ah, very well then, I shall have to wait with the others. That will be my return gift, then."

I was relieved she mentioned that. The ribbons were a gift, and all gifts must be recompensed.

As the visitors settled, they drifted off to sleep after the journey to the lough. I had no energy myself, so we returned to our pavilion. For all my fatigue, I found no rest.

I lay awake for many hours and listened to the odd sounds of so many people. Would tomorrow be the last time the court would visit with so many people?

Each winter, the number of attendees had grown as word went out of our plight. But now, most of them had moved beneath the hills. Would they want to leave their new lives to visit? The journey needed magic and effort to pierce the veil, and not everyone had travel magic.

What if, when we finished with our curse, we couldn't return to our People?

Hawlen and the other ravens had continued to be our boon companions and bondmates, but I worried about them, too. We heard tales of more slaughtered ravens.

Hawlen thought it might have been a reaction to the People still above ground as the treaty came to an end. Now that they'd left, the hunts may have ceased. Either that, or Áedammair had succeeded in passing a law against it. He hadn't visited in a long time.

Porrig visited, each time with a new experimental magic. I snorted at the memory of the funny little Filí. He always came full of grand ideas and new techniques. Some were from the ravens, others were his own invention.

The last time he visited, he was so certain he had an answer to our plight. He worked up a great magic, full of sparks and humming power. The grand result? We turned pink. Pink!

Aed was mortified and sulked for days. I chuckled at the memory. Luckily, the spell faded after ten nights. I still teased him, though, and mentioned a shade of pink in his feathers.

I turned again and tried to find a comfortable position to fall asleep, but my mind still raced.

Bé Chuille returned each anniversary and once with Porrig, but she had no further clues on breaking the curse. Stawn sent word to Hawlen that teaching still progressed.

I railed at the precious time we wasted away as those lessons progressed, but how does one hurry a goddess? Especially one as powerful and mercurial as the Morrigan?

When at last the sky turned from ink black to the deepest midnight blue, I gave up on trying to sleep and waddled out to the shore. By now, I'd memorized every stone, every branch, every tree around our prison.

We'd flown to the top of each tree and explored each nook and cranny below the water's surface. We'd traveled to the edge of our curse-pain in every direction, and found nothing but trees, glades, and a few stray travelers. There were no more hidden treasures to find in this place.

I'd stay chained to this place for another two hundred and ninety-five winters and even then, I'd only be done with one third of my penance.

I shouldn't call it a penance. We'd done nothing wrong. But Aoife believed we did, so we must pay.

I cried beside the lough and my tears made ripples in the black glass surface, distorting my image with the red ribbon around my neck.

Father arrived just as we finished our morning meal. We mobbed him with white feathers and large swan bodies before he laughed and gave us each a bear hug.

Fiachra jumped up and down. "What did you bring us, Father? What's your surprise?"

Father laughed. "My surprise, my son, is right behind me."

Four swan necks craned to see what his great mass hid. There stood all the people we loved from home. Scuida, Maire Mór, and even Nanny Saoirse.

We ran so fast that we left a cloud of white feathers which fell lazily to the ground. Then we hugged each of our dear friends and asked them endless questions. Eventually, even we ran out of energy, and collapsed from an overdose of nostalgia.

Father gave a chuckle. "So, my surprise was worth the wait?"

"Indeed, Father! But, does this mean everyone's moved to the new hillfort?"

His expression turned solemn. "Palace. Underground, we call them palaces. They are gentler structures, not the sturdy fortresses needed for war and weather."

I swallowed, knowing I might never see them. "The new palace, then?"

Father gave a nod. "Yes, all is ready for us. I held off moving the last People, so we could invite everyone here for one big celebration. I'll still visit, mind you. I shan't neglect my children, ever! But it's difficult to cross, so I'll be the only one visiting in the future. Will your poor, tired father be sufficient entertainment?"

For an answer, we all pressed our heads against him. He laughed and petted each of us.

Maire Mór then regaled us with the tale of one of the kitchen maids who'd gotten in a row with a stable lad. I must have drifted off at one point, as they called for the midday meal.

Already? It had just been dawn a few moments ago! But no, the sun rose high in the sky and the day was bright and breezy. My stomach informed me it had been hours since I ate.

With a grumble, I rose and took my portion of the food. The small meal was just a holdover until this evening's feast, but the hot soup and fresh-baked bread smelled delicious. I held bread in my bill and dipped it into the steaming lamb broth.

As I swallowed the hot morsel, I dreamt of a simpler time, when I would sit in the kitchen and watch Maire Mór prepare the evening meal. Chop, slice, skin, knead, she had all the maids working on a different task.

The hustle and bustle of the busy hillfort comforted me then, knowing I lived in such a dynamic place, and I missed it so much.

In my memory, Mother enter the kitchen and put her hand on my shoulder, a comforting, warm weight. Her musical voice asked Maire Mór a question. Then Mother guided me out of the busy kitchen and back to my nursery.

I sighed at the nostalgia and dipped another chunk of flatbread in the cooling broth. It tasted delicious and savory, and just what I needed to settle my stomach.

Scuida asked me something, but I wasn't listening. "I'm sorry Scuida, my mind was far away."

"I said, how is your weapon-work proceeding? Las and Torr appear competent enough."

I let out a mirthless laugh. "They're more than competent. They're brilliant. Torr has had several fantastic ideas about making weapons we can use, so we're not merely defensive."

The older warrior woman nodded and examined the array of odd weaponry near the guard's roundhouse. She raised a brow at the nets.

"They're so we can fling stones, like in a sling. Fiachra is the best at that."

"Hmm. How much flexibility and strength do you have in your wingtips?"

I waggled my right wingtip back and forth. "Some, but the feathers get in the way, and I can't grip anything. I have no thumbs."

She tapped her chin. "I might fashion a small, sharp knife to slip over the tip. You could stab someone easily enough. It can't be too heavy, so it must be thin, but sharp enough to do damage."

"Bronze would be too soft, wouldn't it?"

"I was thinking of blackrock, from a volcano. It can be shaped into a fine edge in the hands of a skilled knapper. My cousin does such work. If not, perhaps a spike made from of bone."

"Thank you, Scuida. We've had no danger except from wild winds here, but you never know when a troupe of Milesians intent on a swan hunt might come through."

Scuida snorted. "I still cannot believe they hunt ravens and swans for food. Sacred animals."

The four of us spent time with the *ard-rí* and *banríon*. We answered questions on our educations, our training, our hobbies.

Conn still collected lovely stones, while Fiachra created stories about our lough and its history. He might have been a bard, had Aoife not cursed us.

I excused myself and went into the treeline to sob, out of sight. My brothers and I had no future, no prospects, nothing to do but survive for hundreds of winters. Where is the joy in that life? A rustle made me spin around and Porrig approached.

I pushed back my grief and the little Druid gave me a wan smile. "It's rather overwhelming, is it not? Well, yes, too many people at once, after not enough for so long. It's enough to make one wish to escape. Indeed it is. Even for me, and I live with these people all season!"

I stayed silent, trying not to cry.

"Duty is a heavy burden, it is indeed. Many people fail to remember that. Duty is one thing that separates us from others. You know your duty better than most, yes?"

He waited for me to agree, but still, I couldn't risk speaking.

"But you also have a duty to your guests, my dear. I feel lonely. Will you do me the honor of accompanying me back to the celebration?"

He was right. With a sigh, I offered my wing, and he placed a pudgy hand upon it. We walked out of the trees and back into the chaos of the gathering.

By the time we returned, it was time for our performance. I found my brothers and we had a quick conference. "Is everyone ready? Any last minute worries?"

Aed shook his head. "We'll be great, Nuala. We've practiced until our very feathers remember the routine. We can do this!"

Fiachra fluttered his wings. "Can we start now?"

"Very well. On the count of three. One… two… three!"

At my mark, we sprang into the sparkling starlit sky. Our routine involved the knotwork flight we greeted visitors with, but it became much more complex.

We hummed a low note at first, just to create a stream of white sparks where we flew. It grew into a living weave. Firelight from below shone on our white bodies, stark against the dark sky. In and out, around and through, we flew.

We sang a sprightly song of rain, flowers, with the promise and hope of spring. We sang of young lambs in the field and chicks in the hen-house. Our songs and flight uplifted my heart and hope to the point I almost, just almost, felt good about life. It's possible that Dervla's ribbons helped my mood, too.

When we completed our production, our friends and family cheered and shouted, stomped their feet, and raised their fists in the air. If I could blush, I'd be bright red with both pleasure and embarrassment. We'd done it!

Once we landed, we headed toward the shore, dead tired after our exertions. I needed a long swim to ease my muscles. They'd been tense in anticipation, and then the exercise had drained all my energy.

A sudden wind snatched me from my path and off to the west edge of the lough. The gale was harsh, wintery, and stronger than usual for the season.

I searched for my brothers and found that the wind had scattered them on other shores, one in each main direction. This wind couldn't be natural.

Hissed words on the breeze confirmed my suspicion. "Sssooo you want to find happinesss, dessspite your cuissse?"

I'd never forget the voice of my stepmother, the voice which had cursed us forever. "Go away, Aoife Rua! You have no power here! I banish you!"

"You cannot banissshhh me! I am bound to you by powerrr!"

I darted around the voice and back to our visitors. Las and Torr must have realized something was wrong, as they hurried toward me.

But before I could reach them, another icy blast shoved me back, wrenching my wings painfully. I cried out, then pulled in my wings, and darted down. I only unfurled them to keep me from hitting the ground. She caught me once, but I evaded her attack the second time. Finally, I landed next to Las and blurted out, "It's Aoife! She's here! Get Bé Chuille!"

Torr spun and pelted back to the High Ollamh, while Las put her arm around me. "Are you hurt?"

"I'm fine, just sore. Find the boys. She may push them out of the lough area and into curse-pain."

"Right!" Las ran along the northwest bank toward Fiachra. A small spit of water dug into the shore, but he'd been clever enough to huddle on the ground.

I spied Aed on the far bank, hugging a tree, but I couldn't see Conn. I wanted to search for him, but that wouldn't be wise.

Instead, I asked Hawlen for help. *Aoife's back. Can you find Conn? Or ask Fwallsan if he's hurt? I don't see him.*

Hawlen sent an affirmative, but nothing else.

Bé Chuille, Porrig, and Dervla ran up, out of breath and in great disarray. Her ceremonial garb was not made for running. "Fionnula! What happened?"

"Aoife Rua is here! She attacked me with a winter wind. I'm unhurt, but I can't find Conn."

The Ollamh's face turned red with anger. "By Danu, she has nerve! To attack now, of all times! It must have taken her all these winters to build up her strength. Well, we shall show her the folly of her actions. Porrig! Useag! Bannin!"

The little Ollamh drew power up through the shore of the lough. A third Ollamh, a round older woman, swirled part of the lough into a water spout.

The fourth, slower than the rest, was a wizened old man. He held glowing coals in a bronze bowl. They sparked as fire exploded up and into the water spout. Bé Chuille called turbulent storm clouds from the sky.

When we were flying earlier, stars shone above. Only the most powerful Ollamhs could summon clouds from nowhere.

My raven hopped toward me and I gripped Hawlen tight as the four elements joined into a roaring cyclone of color and power. Blue, green, red, and white, they rushed in growing spirals. The top of the funnel cast around, as if searching. Searching for Aoife.

Back and forth the funnel whipped. It chased a wisp of cloud or a faint sound. I froze lest it mistake me for prey.

The spout pounced upon a pale spot on the far side of the lough, and I gasped as sparks flew. A ball of lightning shoved the funnel away until it reared back like a startled horse.

The Filíd chanted, nonsense words with a strong rhythm. The whirlwind attacked the growing ball of sparkling light a second time.

Again, the ball pushed it back. Then it darted past the cyclone and headed straight toward me.

Still holding Hawlen, I scuttled behind a tree. Aoife had evaded the Ollamh's magic and I wondered if the *geas* against Aoife's killing was still upon her, now that she was a phantasm.

A faded cry echoed across the lough, mad laughter, and a wispy trail of iridescent white was sucked into the top of the cyclone. Shreds of lightning was sucked away from the ball until only a fist-sized light reached our shore. Then it faded to nothing.

The air popped with a pressure that hurt my ears. A scream cut across my raw nerves and jangled my soul. Everyone covered their ears as the screech cut through bone and into the very center of my being.

Then deadly silence pounded in my head.

The four Filíd lowered their arms and sat down, their faces pale. Acolytes brought them honey-water and flatbread. This was an essential part of any magic work, to ground oneself. Magic takes strength and something as wild and violent as I just witnessed must have drained them all.

Bé Chuille gave me an exhausted nod. "She's gone for now, but I can't banish her forever. You must learn how to combat her yourself."

Panic gripped my heart. "But I don't have power like that! I'm no Ollamh, much less four!"

Porrig said, "But you have something more. You have your brothers."

"They aren't Filíd, either."

The High Ollamh nodded. "No, but they're your strength, your family, and they help complete your soul. You four are forever bound and when you stand as one, nothing can defeat you."

She patted the smaller man on the shoulder. "I shall ask Porrig to return each moon to continue your instruction in defensive magic. He's an adept teacher and enjoys your company. I don't believe Aoife will return quickly. The banishment we crafted would have been painful and took her to a place difficult to escape. Difficult, but not impossible."

I asked Hawlen, "Did you hear from Fwallson? Where's Conn?"

"He took shelter under the ground. He'll be back soon." I grinned at his cleverness.

Aed and Fiachra finally arrived from across the lough, bedraggled and shaken. Then Conn joined us, patches of black dirt staining his white feathers. We touched wingtips for reassurance.

Porrig nodded. "Yes, like that. Can you feel the connection, after we've just raised so much power? It should tingle through your feather tips."

As we exchanged glances, the air crackled. Every bit of my skin tingled, as if tiny ants crawled on each separate feather. I resisted the urge to shake it away. I tasted it, tried to control the flow of power. I drew upon the power and targeted a stone in front of me.

The stone bounced a couple inches away.

Conn's eyes grew wide. "Did we do that, Nuala? Was that us?"

"Porrig, how can we do that? I've never moved anything with my magic. I am a healer, not whatever *that* is."

He smiled. "Just so, just so. Each of us has a special affinity for certain types of magic. You're a healer and your father excels in misdirection. I'm an earth magician. Now, you have new forms, so your magic has also morphed, but with four siblings, you can do amazing things. You're a maker, Aed's a supporter, Conn solves puzzles, and Fiachra adds chaos."

Fiachra straightened his neck. "I'm chaos?"

Aed poked his brother. "Of course, you are. Did you ever doubt it?"

Porrig giggled. "You're reckless, but that lack of fear is necessary for the group to take chances. All magic needs disorder. Your sister has plenty of caution to balance it out."

Bé Chuille nodded. "Porrig has the right of it. You should practice this magic. We can create a program of study. Next time, you shall be more prepared."

I couldn't grasp all of this so quickly, and my mind spun. "But why wait until she attacked?"

The High Ollamh gave me a half-smile. I'd never, in my entire life, seen her look so embarrassed. "To be honest, we thought we had banished her well enough that she'd never return. Tonight proved us wrong."

Chapter Eleven

In the 10th winter of our curse (440 BCE) 4 year later

It took several seasons of practice, but we learned how to use our new magical talents. We did exercises to focus on our strengths. Conn built the strongest magical walls, while I could make deflection spells. Fiachra worked well with sounds, and Aed had a talent for calming magic.

But we couldn't work magic constantly, so we found non-magical hobbies, as well. Fiachra and Aed loved swimming on the lough and trying to communicate with the local swans, but had very little success. They kept trying, though.

Conn preferred exploring the surrounding woods, often coming back with intriguing objects. He'd gone off in the morning, and I kept glancing at the treeline, wishing he was back.

Torr let out a heartfelt curse.

I lifted my head from the garden plot, where I'd just pushed in several garlic bulbs to germinate over the winter. "Torr? Are you hurt?"

"I'm fine, I'm fine. I just need some cloth. Can you fetch me a strip from the rag pile?"

I narrowed my gaze, but waddled over to the pavilion and grabbed one with my beak. When I returned to where Torr was working, I noticed spots of blood on the leather. "Are you sure you're fine?"

He took the strip and wrapped it around his hand, then tied it. "Nothing deep, just a flesh wound."

I poked the piece of leather he'd been cutting. "What's this for?"

He lifted it to show me. "I'm creating braces for Conn to put over his feet and wingtips. These will help him hold the leather-working tools. He won't have much strength, as he has no thumbs, but it will help."

I gave him a sidelong glance. "I hope it works better than the vines."

Torr and Conn had strung up vines tied with shells around our lough. The theory was that they would jangle if someone came near to us. Torr's magic armed them.

He drew himself up. "But they work fantastic!"

"Only once you adjusted them not to go off every time the wind or a squirrel disturbed them. That one night, we were woken seven times. Seven times, Torr!" I chuckled to take the sting out of my words.

Porrig came every moon and drilled us incessantly during his visits. He'd share news of our kin, songs, and stories.

One evening, just as Porrig was finishing a tale, he glanced up, scanning the tree line. We scrambled to hide in safety, but Porrig held up a hand. "The visitor is a friend."

I cocked my head. "How do you know that? Are you expecting someone?"

"No, but I can feel their intent. It's on the edge of my magic, but they mean us no harm, whoever they are."

I filed that intriguing fact away and turned to see who this friend was. His hair had grown longer and his beard thicker, but when I recognized them, I ran to greet him. "Áedammair! It's been so many seasons!"

He bowed his head with a blush and rubbed his chin. "I apologize, *Bantiarna*. I must admit that another woman stole my heart, and my world has been hers ever since."

My heart fell. Since Father had moved below the ground, I had more charge over my life, and if I wasn't a swan, I would have gladly married Áedammair. And while I didn't truly expect him to wait until a nine hundred curse may or may not be broken, I'd still harbored a tiny hope, somewhere in the back of my mind.

I invited him to our fire for stories, but he declined. "No, I cannot stay. But we were traveling nearby and I didn't want to miss the chance to visit you."

He could no longer kiss my hand as he used to, so instead, he touched the tip of my wing. "I wanted to let you know that hunting swans and ravens is now against our law. While I cannot do anything to ease your curse, at least I might help protect you and those you hold dear."

Tears burned behind my eyes and I gave our visiting *tiarna* a bow. "I thank you for that, Áedammair. You are a true friend."

After he left, I suddenly felt so weary, and went to sleep.

In the 12th winter of our curse (438 BCE) 2 year later.

In the pre-dawn darkness, I woke to silence. I wanted to sleep more, but knew that wouldn't be easy. Las had been coughing each morning, loud enough to shatter any morning peace. I went outside to sit beside the water and watch the sunrise.

Sure enough, her hacking cough scattered birds picking at mosquitoes and the flutter of wings woke everyone. My brothers stumbled out of the pavilion, brushing sleep from their eyes with their wingtips.

Something else rustled in the brush. I whispered, "Aed! Conn! Fiachra! In the water. We have company."

We swam to the center of the lough. I didn't bother warning Las, as she would have heard the same thing. She knew her business and with Torr, would handle whatever surprise came.

We saw a man. Then several more followed. I couldn't make out details, but it was a group of four, and a child?

They didn't look like Milesians. In fact, the man looked like…

"Tadhg?" I barely whispered. He couldn't have heard me, but he glanced up just the same. It *was* Tadhg.

He'd changed since I last saw him seven winters ago. Now, he had a red beard and a belly. He held a young girl's hand.

We had no need to hide from my childhood friend and almost-lover, and I flew back to shore.

As I landed, I cocked my head. "Tadhg, is that really you?"

He swallowed and gritted his teeth, but finally nodded. "It's me. Fionnuala. Are you… how are you doing?"

Such an inane question made me snort. I pressed my wingtips into my side, giving him a stern glare. "How do you *think* we are doing, by Danu? Cursed as swans while everyone we loved has moved to *Saol Eile*?"

His mouth hung open. "But you always loved the surface world, Nuala! You never wanted to go below!"

I rolled my eyes. "That doesn't mean I wanted to live here as a swan for nine hundred cursed winters!"

He shrugged. "I guess that shows you, huh?"

"Shows me what?"

"To be careful what you wish for."

I wished I had a real mouth, so I could stick out my tongue for his impertinence. I suddenly wanted very much to hug him. I waddled toward him with my wings open.

Awkwardly, he gathered me in his arms and patted me. It was horribly inadequate, but at least I was in his arms, after a fashion. After several long moments, we held me out at arms-length. "It's good to see you, despite everything."

"And you. Wait, why did it take you so long to visit? Father comes every summer. Couldn't you come with him?"

He dropped his gaze. "No, I couldn't."

I narrowed my eyes. "Why?"

"Because I married, Nuala, remember? My wife was jealous. She knew how much I loved you, and kept me from coming."

I narrowed my gaze. "I find that hard to believe."

He shrugged. "Believe what you will, Nuala. Aillbha was a hard mistress to please, and she had a particular talent at pain magic."

"Hmm. So then how did you come now?"

He stared at his feet. "Aillbha's dead, Nuala."

Our awkwardness grew again. I cast about for a change of subject. "Is that your daughter?"

He gave a sweet smile. "She is."

She was pretty, with white-blonde hair like Mother's, and looked about ten. "What's her name?"

"Finna."

For a moment, I couldn't breathe. The world spun and I sat abruptly. Finna. Did he name her for me? Oh, how Aillbha must have hated that name.

Tadhg beckoned for Finna to come closer, but the child shook her head. "Come, darling. Come meet my friends."

She shook her head again.

Conn tucked his wings in and spoke in a gentle tone. "It's all right, sweet girl. We won't hurt you."

Her eyes grew round, and she backed up a step, to the guard who stood behind her. The guard put her hand on Finna's head. "Go on, child. The swans were People once. Just like you and me. They're good folks and will be kind to you."

With slow steps, she placed one small foot in front of the other until she stood at her father's side.

He grinned as she clutched his hand. "There, that wasn't too hard, was it? I want to introduce you to my old friend, Fionnuala, eldest daughter of *Tiarna* Lir."

Finna bowed and I nodded in formal greeting. "I welcome you both, you and your kin."

After the rest of the greeting, she said, "I thank you." Her tiny voice sounded sweet and light, like a dragonfly skipping across a still pond.

Las brought a bowl of fruit and placed it between us. The girl offered a tub of honey-butter, making my mouth water. I missed honey-butter terribly.

Las gestured to the bench. "You must be tired and hungry after your journey, *Tiarna* Tadhg. Please, join us as we break our fast."

Startled, I asked, "*Tiarna?*"

He glanced sheepishly at Las. "Yes, well, my father died last winter. So yes, I'm now a *tiarna*, though that doesn't mean as much under the hills."

I bowed and fought back the laughter. "*Tiarna*, I welcome you."

"Oh, do leave off, Nuala. No teasing, now."

Another giggle escaped before I could stop it. Fiachra carefully grabbed an apple from the bowl with his beak and dropped it at Finna's feet. "Would you like first portion, as our guest, young *bantiarna?*"

Her eyes grew round again. Nodding, she accepted the fruit and held it in both hands, nibbling like a squirrel.

Torr passed out bread and cider to the guards and my brothers. Torr had baked smaller loaves, as they were easier for us to eat without hands, so I added several to the table.

I turned to our guest. "So, other than your wife's death, why did you come now? And don't give me any guff about difficulties with the veil. Your magic's plenty strong to breach that barrier."

"Actually, I was sent for."

"Sent for? Whatever do you mean?"

I glared at Aed, as if he had betrayed me somehow. He shook his head. "Not me!"

I glared at Fiachra and Conn.

Tadhg held up his hands. "No, none of your brothers."

Las let out a sigh. "I sent for him."

My mind started racing, full of confusion. "Why ever did you do that, Las?"

"It's my cough. I can't seem to shake it. I spoke to Porrig the last time he visited, and he suggested I would heal faster below the hills, out of the winter weather."

I'd tried healing her cough myself, but I no longer had healing talent. Herblore was easier, and I kept a garden of medicinal herbs, but the healing magic itself was weak.

Las was one of my people, and I couldn't protect her and keep her well. I bowed my head as my failure grew heavy on my soul.

Las rounded on me. "No, no, it's not your fault, Nuala! Have you learned nothing? You're not responsible for all that happens in this world, and it's not your place to fix everything, either."

Hawlen stepped in. "I've taught her that since she was a girl. Duty is fine, but there's a point where duty must rest."

I glared at Hawlen. "Since when did you ever teach me that duty must rest?"

Hawlen fluffed her wings with the tip of her beak. "I made it implicit in all my lessons."

I scoured my memory for anything remotely like that, but couldn't think of a single time. "Implicit? You mean invisible!"

"Nevertheless, it was there."

I snorted and let out a sigh of resignation. "So, Las, does this mean you wish to leave us?"

"I don't wish to, but I must, for my health's sake. I won't leave until I train my replacement."

I glanced at Tadhg's guards.

The one who had encouraged Finna to meet us stood, taller than Tadhg and well-muscled. Her long, black hair was braided tightly against her skull. "I am Roisinn. I have requested this duty as a singular honor. Would you be willing to allow me to be your guard and companion, *Bantiarna* Fionnuala?"

I didn't know what to say. Las was leaving us. My dear friend, Las, who'd stood by us, taught us how to survive, sung us songs, and comforted my sorrow on lonely nights.

She was like a mother to me, and I didn't want to lose her. I tossed propriety aside and let out a sob.

"No! No, Las, you can't abandon us. We need you!"

I thought I'd spoken the words aloud and was confused. Yet it wasn't my voice—it was Aed's.

Las gave him a fierce hug. "Aed, I need to recover. Perhaps I can come back when I'm well, and I'll certainly visit."

Aed sat heavily and sulked.

For several long horrible moments, I considered ordering Las to stay, but that would be intolerable and selfish. But our friend and companion had every right to seek a milder climate.

This new woman, Roisinn, stood strong and proud. Too proud? Surely, she couldn't *want* this assignment. She must have a life under the hills. Still, she had confidence in her petition, and had been kind to Finna.

Aed went through an inner turmoil of his own. His eyes shifted from Las to Roisinn, then to Tadhg. Fiachra already gazed at Roisinn with lovesick eyes, so I needn't ask his opinion. Conn dropped his gaze to his bread, his thoughts shrouded.

"Roisinn, you honor us with your offer. May we have a moment to discuss your offer?"

I gathered my brothers and Torr. I had to tug at Aed to get him to move from his sulk. "Torr, did you know about this?"

He nodded. "Las discussed it with me a while ago, but I didn't realize she'd already asked for a replacement."

"Aed, what say you?"

"I don't want to lose Las."

"That's not our decision, Aed. We're talking about accepting Roisinn, not about letting Las go."

Aed sighed. "Fine. I support whatever you decide."

"Fiachra?"

"She has lovely eyes, Nuala. Can she sing?"

I gave him a scowl and turned to Conn. "Have you any ideas?"

He glanced back to the new guard. "I always have ideas, Nuala, you know that. Whether we want her or not, we should give her a trial. If she suits, that's lovely. If she doesn't, she'll realize it as soon as we will. We won't have to ask her to leave."

This was the longest speech I'd heard from him in a long time, and his mature reasoning delighted me.

Aed jumped up. "Then it's decided. May I accept on our behalf?"

"Don't tell me you're smitten, too?"

He laughed. "She's lovely, but no, I've no mind to court any of the People, sister mine. Who would have me, after all?"

I was napping during a chilly afternoon when Conn's voice roused me. I lifted my head, but he must have been outside. Then I heard Roisinn's low, liquid laugh.

While I didn't wish to eavesdrop, I shuffled closer to the wall to hear them on the other side.

Roisin asked, "But you've never left the island?"

Conn sounded more despondent than I'd ever heard before. "No, but I always wanted to. I always dreamt of traveling the world. Now, we can't."

"What about after the curse is over?"

Bitterness marred his words. "Over? Sure, in nine hundred winters."

"Aren't they working on breaking the curse, though?"

"Working, trying, attempting, all that. But after so many failures, I've lost hope. We're stuck in this stupid place for hundreds of years. Then another place for hundreds of years. Then a third. It's like Aoife Rua discovered my worst nightmare and made it true."

"But what do you hope to find around the world that you can't find here?"

They were both silent for a moment, then Conn spoke in a small voice. "I always dreamt that I'd find my love across the ocean."

Roisinn's voice turned gentle. "Do you know where?"

"No. But if I can't travel, I'll never find her."

She let out a sigh. "I wish I could help you travel. I wish I could find a way to help you find your true love. Truly, I do."

"That's kind of you."

They both fell silent, and I felt like an intruder on such a tender moment, so I shuffled back to my bed and went back to sleep.

Before I drifted off, I thought that maybe Conn wouldn't have to travel so far for love.

Torr just finished drilling me with my throwing net, and my wings were sore. It reminded me of when Weaponmistress Scuida would work me past the point of exhaustion, but that was what we needed in order to learn. I sat on the shore, doing the exercises Roisinn had given us to ease aching muscles after exercise, but my mind wandered.

What if, instead of the healing magic I could no longer do well, I could use my magic to defend us? I would have to think about how, but the idea simmered in my mind.

I came up with a half-dozen ideas and discarded each as impractical or unnecessary. Father had already created a veil around the lough to keep unwanted visitors away. But we needed something offensive, in case someone broke through that veil.

I glanced at the net as Torr placed it on a hook. What if I could create a magical net of stones, missiles to throw at someone? Or arrows?

How far could I send a magical arrow? I glanced across the lough, gauging distance, and spied my brother.

Conn was sitting by the far end of the lough with his carving tools, but he was just staring at the bit of leather on the rock.

He looked so despondent, I flew to his side. "Conn? Conn, what's wrong, sweetling?"

"Don't call me that."

I rocked back on my feet. "I won't, Conn. What's troubling you?"

"Nothing. Go away."

Conn didn't say such things. Fiachra, yes. Fiachra was often volatile and prone to excitement. Conn was usually reasonable and quiet.

My instincts prickled, but I'd played this game many times with his brother. I knew how to draw out the real reasons. "I won't go away until you tell me what's wrong."

He sat in sullen silence. I waited.

After several moments, I glanced back toward the pavilion. "Is it Roisinn?"

He shrugged. "Sort of."

I sighed and understood. "Conn, tell me, please. I can help."

"No, you can't. None of us can help. I knew it would happen, and now it's happened, and there's nothing any of us can do about it." His voice grew agitated with each sentence.

"And what's happened?"

He swept the piece of leather off the rock with his wingtip. "I fell in love."

I'd suspected as much. "Conn, let me tell you about love." I tried to remember what Mother had once told me, when I was young.

He held up his wingtips. "No, Nuala. Don't tell me about love. I understand it well enough. I love you, I love our father, I love my brothers.

And yes, romantic love is different. I saw it with you and Tadhg. I love Roisinn. And if you ever tell her, I will deny it completely."

I blinked several times. "I don't think I'd need to tell her."

His face fell into sullenness again. "We both know there's no way any such love could be requited. Even if we transformed back today, I'd still be too young for her. There is nothing that can help me. So, just leave me be."

My mind grasped for something to help. "Maybe we can't fix things, but that's not what love is always about. Sometimes, it's good just to be here for someone else. A shoulder to cry on. Someone who understands you." I pushed away the vision of Tadhg with his full beard.

He blinked back tears and said nothing.

I put my wing around him and hugged him tight. My poor, besotted brother, silent in his grief. I'd never betray his confidence. However, I could be there when he needed me, and I always would be.

Chapter Twelve

In the 70th winter of our curse (380 BCE) 58 years later

Porrig snored. I lay in our pavilion and counted the seconds between his thunderous breaths. His rhythm stayed even, at least, but it sounded like sand against a bronze mirror.

Rain pattered on the wooden roof in counterpoint to Porrig's snores. I prayed to the gods it would lull me into my much-sought slumber.

Finally, dawn rose. I'd gotten some sleep, but not nearly enough. I let out a mighty yawn as I wiped the sleep from my eyes.

The twins rustled their feathers and yawned, too. Thus, the population of Lough Derravaragh woke to another day.

Today, Porrig would try his newest idea, his newly created magical process.

We were all to help him, to hook our magic into his, to bolster the power. We'd practiced for days so the merge would be seamless. I harbored doubts about the value of our contributions, but we had to try.

Since our transformation, our magical strengths were tied with the elements, much like Filíd magic. Instead of healing, I developed an affinity for fire, while the twins were water, and Aed preferred air. Luckily enough, Porrig's magic was tied to earth.

We learned this new magic with both Porrig and the ravens for several winters, but we didn't have their strength.

Remembering my lessons from Hawlen before the curse, I practiced forming bricks for a magical wall, building them fast to guard against attacks. I also worked on shooting a magical arrow, a small dart that glowed blue in the darkness.

Porrig wasn't happy when I suggested practicing such magic. He said magic like that only worked for killing and Aoife Rua had succumbed to such power. Hawlen echoed his worries, but I didn't care.

If I'd practiced this before, I might have been able to stop her curse. So, I practiced in secret and built up a respectable speed from my magic dart, with enough force to pierce a tree-trunk.

I tried other magic, like glamor, but that left a nasty taste in my mouth, as Aoife used it on us.

Yesterday, we'd done a trial run of the ceremony. Porrig set out the ritual space. Then Fiachra and Conn joined their water magic, pulled from the lough. Aed joined in with air, then I added fire. Porrig hooked into our magical mesh and formed a circle.

We poured our power into a central focus, then visualized it as a globe around us. The globe was meant to cut the outside curse magic from our inner selves.

I wandered outside to find that Roisinn already stoking the fire from last night's banked coals. "Good morning, Fionnuala. Did you sleep well?"

"No. Porrig snores."

She chuckled. "I'm glad I can't hear it from our roundhouse. Why doesn't he sleep in the guesthouse?"

I gave a shrug. "He said the affinity is strengthened by proximity, so being close when we sleep helps."

The guard giggled. "Well, I haven't enough magic to tell if that's true or not, but certainly your own power will suffer from a lack of sleep. Perhaps I can fashion a cover for your ears when you sleep."

"I already tuck my head under my wing, but that doesn't help much."

She gave me a sympathetic grin. "We'll figure something else, never fear. Maybe Torr can help. He's handy enough with new inventions."

One twin must have poked another, as a hoot of complaint echoed over the still water just as Aed poked his head out. "Today's the day, Nuala! Perhaps our last day!"

"Perhaps. Is Porrig awake yet?"

Aed glanced back into the pavilion and shook his head. "He's still snoring away. We'd best let him rest. No sense in him being tired for the spell."

Hawlen and the other ravens joined us for our morning meal while we waited for the Ollamh to rouse. The twins were full of nervous energy and I sent them on patrol around the lough.

When they came back still restless, I sent them again. "This time, count the new growths. Daffodils should be in bloom soon. How many are growing around the lough this winter?"

Fiachra grumbled about useless make-work, but they launched. They made a game of it, to see who counted the most flowers.

I knew how many there were, as I counted them each day. I counted each herb in my garden, the vegetables and flowers we grew for food and medicine. This routine was part of my daily litany, designed to keep me from going mad with boredom.

Hawlen sighed. "Ah, to be young again and so filled with energy."

I snorted. "You're younger than I am and I'm only—" I stopped to count. How many winters had I lived? Fifty-eight winters since Las retired. Twelve before that to our curse date. And I'd been twenty then.

That made me ninety winters old. Sweet Danu! Ninety. I still felt twenty. Unlike mine, Hawlen's body wasn't frozen in time. She was aging, as the other ravens did. As we should have, if Aoife hadn't cursed us.

I'd never heard of a raven of nine hundred winters. Even our People rarely lived so long. Most of us retired to *Tír na nÓg* after four hundred winters. The magical bond which held us to our raven teachers granted them life as long as ours, but that bond wasn't meant for such extremes.

Would I lose my teacher? My best friend? My world dimmed and tears of grief burned behind my eyes.

Aed cocked his head. "Nuala? What's wrong?"

"Nothing, nothing. I just realized how old we are. Winters have passed and I never kept track."

His eyes brightened. "I've kept track! We're almost a quarter the way through our time here."

Seventy winters. An entire lifetime for the mayfly Milesians.

Porrig emerged from our pavilion and scratched his bald head. Roisinn handed him a warm mug of broth and he took it with a grin of thanks. After several moments, he burped and smiled. "Well, are you ready? Shall we start soon?"

I glanced at the formal ritual area we'd set up last night. "Is there anything else we need to do?"

Porrig shook his head. "Just your own confidence and power. Hawlen, were you able to contact Stawn for advice?"

My raven bobbed her head. "Stawn seemed ambivalent. He didn't speculate on if it would work, but gave no advice to improve the plan. He said he was still learning from the Morrigan."

Fiachra muttered under his breath. "Seventy winters of instruction from a goddess and you'd think he'd learned something by now."

Aed gasped and I yelled. "Fiachra! Shut your mouth on that talk. You *never* say such things about a goddess. Particularly the Morrigan! What if she heard?"

Chastened, my brother bowed his head and whispered, "I'm sorry. I'm just frustrated."

Conn asked, "But he has a point. Why is it taking so long?"

Porrig came to the rescue. "Magic at that level takes enormous power and discipline. Neither comes easily and takes seasons of meditation, training, and mistakes. Older ravens don't learn as quickly as the young."

Aed poked at the remains of his meal. "Is Stawn bound to someone? I've only seen him alone, never with one of the People."

Hawlen ducked her head. "No, our High Councilor will never bind to anyone. Someone bound cannot be our leader, lest we be subservient to another race." She fluttered her wings, agitated. "Such things are not discussed outside raven society."

Fiachra gasped. "But then he doesn't have the long life of a bondmate! What if he dies before he learns what he needs?"

"Stawn's office grants him longevity."

Porrig cleared his throat. "If we are to begin, we'd best get to our posts."

Butterflies took up residence in my belly and danced with wanton energy. Aed stood confident, while Conn looked green. Fiachra dug at something on his foot.

Porrig sketched out the five-pointed ritual space. Each of us stood at one point. Five gemstones were placed in the star, with an emerald near me, malachite near Aed, sapphire for Conn, and ruby for Fiachra. Porrig had the garnet.

For several weeks, we'd sunk power into these gemstones. Now, they glowed with energy, casting rainbow prisms of light and magic.

I caught my breath at the stunning beauty as Porrig began chanting. We didn't fully understand their meaning, but we'd learned the words by rote.

I recognized a few of the words as similar to our own, such as "gift", "wheel", and "god," but even those words sounded distorted.

We'd asked Porrig the meaning yesterday, but he didn't tell us. "These are old words, to old gods. If something goes wrong, it's better if you can claim innocence of the favor we ask."

I cocked my head. "Old gods? Older than our own? Older than Danu? How is that possible?"

"Yes, well, indeed, who can be older than a god? There are definitely older entities than Danu and many of them. The gods of the Hittites, for example, or of Atlantis. The Egyptians, even some Hellenic elementals predate ours. Danu is a relative newcomer, my dear."

This rocked my soul, my belief in the world around me, and the gods who created it. Danu was a young god? Did she not create the rivers and the earth below us and the sky above us, filled it with twinkling stars?

Father said there was a river named for her in a faraway land. But Porrig seemed so confident in his knowledge, I couldn't argue.

We chanted the strange words and I touched Aed's wingtip with mine. He touched Conn, who touched Fiachra, then Porrig.

As soon as the Porrig touched my wingtip, the circle snapped into creation with a flash-bang of power and pressure. My eyes hurt with the burst of light.

I faltered, but Aed bolstered me with a feather caress of his mind and a glance of reassurance.

Our ravens joined us, forming their own circle within ours, wings outstretched. They also chanted, a rougher counterpoint to our voices.

Now, the circle filled to bursting with power. At Porrig's signal, we fell silent, waiting for the tension to build, for the power to *want* to escape and do our bidding.

Something faltered. I didn't know what, but there was a roughness to the magic, like the edge of a broken branch. I glanced at Porrig, but he didn't seem to notice.

The coarseness grated on my soul, and I couldn't stop thinking of it. It stole my concentration on the magic itself, so I soothed the rough edge with my magic, just a feather touch. Then it felt better and my worry eased.

The ollamh shouted, "*So may it be!*"

Our power swirled in a rainbow tornado away from our ritual area. It stretched into the morning sky and formed daylight stars. These drifted like snowflakes into the trees, onto the lough surface and over us all.

Every bit of strength pulled out of my body, and I collapsed. My brothers, Porrig, and the ravens all did the same.

I woke much later. Torr was holding a cup of warm broth to my bill and entreated me to drink.

My bill. Not my mouth. It didn't work.

But I didn't want broth. I didn't want comfort or food. I didn't want anything that sustained this cursed life.

I pushed Torr away and tried to fly, but my body had no strength for such dramatic gestures.

"Hey, now, Nuala. Come, please drink the broth. You need to heal."

I spat to the side. "Why? The spell failed. We're still swans. We'll always be swans. We'll never escape this evil."

Torr put down the bowl of broth and stood over me, hands on his hips. "And so you should let yourself die, to spite your stepmother? She'll have won. She couldn't kill you, so she cursed you. If you let yourself die, then you give her what she wanted. Do you wish to give her that satisfaction, even after all this time?"

I stared. Torr didn't speak much, as he would rather focus on his inventions, leather craft, and whittling. "Now, drink your broth, and I'll rouse the others."

I let him pour the warm broth down my throat. Despite my despair, it tasted delightful, full of salty warmth.

Roisinn helped Porrig sit up and Torr woke Aed.

I turned to Hawlen. "Wake up, Hawlen. It didn't work."

She didn't move, and my heart began to race. She was warm, and her chest rose, giving me a scrap of hope. "Hawlen? Hawlen, wake up! Aed, can you wake Totawg?"

Aed got no reaction from his friend and teacher, and his voice held a panicked tone. "Totawg! Please, open your eyes."

I stared at the Ollamh. "Porrig? What have we done?"

He cradled his own raven, Kawnan, in his arms. "Hmm. Hmm. Yes, well, they are alive, that's not in doubt. Where there's life, there's hope. Hmm."

I wished I could hold Hawlen that way. Fiachra and Conn wrapped their wings around their own friends.

Porrig had turned pale. "I'll ask the other Filíd and their ravens. I'm afraid our attempt failed."

I snapped. "Really? What was your first clue to *that?*"

Porrig stared at his own bondmate with no expression. A tear streaked down his cheek.

Instant remorse washed over me. "Oh, Sweet Danu, I'm sorry, Porrig. You didn't deserve that."

He blinked several times. "May I take all the ravens with me under the hills? They have the best chance to heal there."

I wanted to say no, to keep Hawlen beside me, to keep her safe. But she wasn't safe, and I helped hurt her.

I silently begged for her to wake up right now and berate me for my foolishness, but she remained silent. A shallow breath fluttered her iridescent black feathers.

With a sob, I nodded and Torr fashioned a litter to carry them. Then he helped Porrig take them to the *còmhla bhreach,* the gate to the other world.

I shouldn't have added my own powers. I had ruined everything. Would I ever see my dearest friend again?

In the 71st winter of our curse (379 BCE) 1 year later

Winter marched interminably on. Porrig visited with news on our ravens, but they still slept. The Council of Ravens cared for them.

Every morning we prayed to the gods to help our bondmates. Each day, we tried to reach them with our minds. Once, I heard a faint echo of Hawlen's voice, but it slipped away.

192

Roisinn tried to tempt us with new music, but we shunned the entertainment. I had done this, and I didn't deserve to enjoy life until I could fix it.

After a visit from the Milesians, Torr tried new fight techniques he'd learned from them. I ignored that, too. None of it would bring us out of our misery and guilt. We all lost weight and our feathers grew drab.

One bright morning, I glared at the sunrise with sullen resentment. A rustle in the trees heralded someone's arrival. We scrambled to the lough as usual.

The rustle resolved into a small traveling group. They were People, but no one I recognized. A young lady, tall and fair, three guards, and a dog.

The People rarely visited the surface world now. The Milesians concocted a silly idea that capturing us meant good luck. In reality, capturing one of the People actually meant horrible luck, for our kin would ensure any captor suffering, perhaps for several of their pitifully short generations.

The fair lady approached, but Roisinn stopped her. "This area is protected, my lady. May I ask who calls?"

Her voice was soft and sweet. "I am Finna, daughter of *Tiarna* Tadhg, and I come to speak with Fionnuala, daughter of *Tiarna* Lir."

Finna? This elegant young lady was the small child I remembered? I felt old and waspish. But I needed to greet her properly, so I swam back to shore.

I spread out my wings, tips up like hands and she placed hers over them in greeting. "I welcome you, Finna, you and your kin. I welcome you into our homes. I welcome you to our bread and our ale. Be safe and sound within our walls."

"I thank you, *Bantiarna* Fionnuala."

Torr offered a bottle of mead for my host-gift, but Finna did not immediately offer one in return.

"What brings you here, after all these winters, fair Finna?"

She grinned and her face lit up. "I bring you a gift from my father. He has fashioned you a magical construction."

My first love, my only love, still thought of me. The cynical ice that had formed around my heart these last few seasons melted slightly. Oddly enough, it even assuaged some of my guilt in harming Hawlen.

Finna dug through her carry-bag and pulled out a package wrapped in blue-dyed leather. Without waiting for me to ask, she unwrapped it to reveal four silver necklaces, so finely made they were like threads.

Fiachra craned his neck over Aed's. "Chains? Why would we need those, Finna?"

She held one up. "These are no ordinary necklaces, my dear Conn."

"I'm Fiachra! He's Conn."

"Oh! My apologies, Fiachra. No, we crafted these necklaces over several winters in my father's smithy. We enchanted each silver chain to find the others. The next step of your curse is to live near the *Sruth na Maoile,* a wild place on the seashore. Should you ever be separated, these chains will help you find each other."

My heart warmed at such a thoughtful, useful gift. Each of us lowered our heads so Finna could place the chains on. They glittered in the morning sun.

As soon as she placed it around my neck, the chain snapped and crackled. Without thinking, I formed a magical brick wall around us. Years of paranoia and training kicked in.

Aed, Conn, and Fiachra added their touch, strengthening the magical wall. The chains flashed with blinding light and I reeled back.

As I shook my head to clear it, a familiar echo tickled the back of my mind. *Hawlen? Hawlen, are you there? Are you awake?*

A sleepy answer came. *I am here.*

Fiachra jumped up and flapped around wildly. "She's awake! She's awake! Crawma's awake!"

Turning to Finna, my mouth dropped open. "Is this part of the chain's magic?"

Her expression turned solemn. "I don't know. Your story has been told many times, and raven healers have all examined your bondmates. Perhaps your reaction recreated something like the bond you have with the ravens? Enough to nudge them awake?"

"I don't know if this was a wild gamble or an accident, but I'm not going to question it!"

Joy danced in my heart again. Hawlen was awake! "Thank you, Finna. Thank you for helping us heal our friends."

I hugged the daughter of my dear love, with all my strength.

Chapter Thirteen

In the 300th winter of our curse (150 BCE) 229 years later

The day of our last day at the lough dawned with bittersweet relief. I didn't want to leave. We'd made so many memories there. Annual visits from our family, lessons we learned, even fears of Aoife Rua, were all indelibly tied to this place.

At the same time, moving to our second spot gave a much-needed sense of progress. Roisinn and Torr left first to prepare a new pavilion. The cliff at *Sruth na Maoile* was inhospitable, but they'd build a shelter from the harshest of the weather.

We crafted packs to carry food for the forty leagues journey. I tried to picture our new home and a shiver ran down my spine. The open sea frightened me after such a sheltered eternity.

When I mapped out our route with Hawlen, she shook her head. "I won't be joining you in the air, Nuala. None of us ravens will."

Aed's eyes grew wide. "But, why not? Aren't you coming north? We can't lose you again!"

"No, no, we'll come north. But we don't have the strength for such a journey. We shall go on our own, in short hops."

Las offered, "I can carry you, if you like."

Hawlen stood tall. "You will do no such thing! We aren't that decrepit yet!"

I stifled a giggle at my raven's pride, but didn't dare say anything more.

The curse-pain tugged, a discomfort that would only be relieved by our arrival at *Sruth na Maoile*. I nodded at Aed, Fiachra, and finally Conn.

Las let out a cheer as we wheeled over the lough and headed northeast. At first, the curse-pain was intensely uncomfortable, like being too full from supper or needing to void wastes. Then it grew until the pain compressed bones and grew intolerable.

Flight was a joy, no matter what the circumstances. To fly beyond our curse-pain was an incredible treat. I soared into the thermals and we dipped and dove through the wispy clouds.

Below me, our island unfolded in green beauty. Tiny farmholds, carved out by the Milesians, dotted the hills. Round houses and stone walls, a village at the river, a field filled with white cows, more variety than we'd seen for three hundred winters.

With giddy excitement, I said, "Do you see those trees? I've never seen ash grow so tall!"

Aed gestured toward a fork in the river. "That's a huge village! I wonder how many people live there."

Fiachra dove toward the ground and came back up with a branch in his beak. We each flew close enough to bite a few berries from it before he dropped it. Their juices were sweet and stained our feathers.

Soaring through the rising winds, we glided further. A fluffy white cloud came up above us and we climbed up into the mystery.

At the lough, we were never able to fly so high. Now, the air was thin and freezing, but we exalted in the freedom to explore.

North and east we flew, ignoring a spray of rain. Rocks and stone circles sped past us on the ground. A massive ritual mound passed below us, high on a great hill. It hulked in the afternoon light.

My wings were tired, but I didn't want to stop. Aed wasn't flagging yet. A glance back at Fiachra and Conn, but I couldn't find them.

"Aed! Aed, wait, where are the twins?"

Did he hear my voice over the wind of our flight, or did he sense my panic? He turned, his eyes growing wide. Our brothers were nowhere to be found.

We searched up, down, around. Then I pointed up with my chin, to a huge bank of clouds, then pumped my wings to reach it.

I cried in the white mists. "Fiachra! Conn!" What had before seemed magical now grew sinister. The clouds hid our brothers, intent on separating us.

A giggle caught my attention and a shadow sped above me. I dropped out of the cloud. "Fiachra, if that's you, come out, now! You scared me half to death!"

Both twins wheeled out of the cloud in an elegant pattern and I sighed in relief.

Aed's eyes glittered. "This is not a game, Fiachra. We're moving to our new home, and if you stray again, you will feel my wrath."

I'd never heard Aed so angry. Fiachra was just acting like Fiachra and Conn had gone along with his tricks.

I said, "Let's just get to *Sruth na Maoile*. Torr and Roisinn are waiting for us."

Several hours later, we wheeled down to the cliff, and I sighed in relief. It wasn't as rugged as I'd feared.

A gentle headland jutted out into the straight, covered in velvet green grass. While there were no trees, Torr stood in a sheltered alcove on the cliff's edge. He'd almost finished an elaborate pavilion, sturdier than the one at the lough. They'd painted it in bright colors and hung lovely decorations.

Torr waved at us as we circled down. When we landed, I worked my wings back and forth. My muscles weren't used to such extended flying, but at least we'd practiced flying and fighting every day.

Even if Aoife never came back, flying was a useful exercise. We made this trip in a few hours, rather than a few days.

As soon as we landed, the pain of the *geas* lifted. I could breathe easier.

Hawlen and the other ravens wouldn't be here for several days. The pavilion wasn't quite finished yet, but we settled into the new space quickly.

Torr had built five chambers. One for each of us and a larger space in the center for gathering.

As we ate our first meal in the new place, Torr explained, "Roisinn's still building the guest quarters, farther down the cliff. We thought about building it here, but thought you might like some privacy. And it's more sheltered from the weather."

"So the winds are indeed fierce?" Aed's voice held a note of worry.

Torr nodded. "Much more than I imagined. The storms might rip a man from the cliff, given the right angle. I want you to promise to always shelter inside when a storm comes in."

What if a gale ripped us past our curse-limit? The pain might rob us of the strength to find our way back. One of us might be lost forever, unable to move to safety, especially in a long storm.

But then I glanced at the silver chains Tadhg gave us. My friend had thought of that already. We would find a windblown swan.

The first night felt so odd. We'd spent so much of our lives at our lough, I barely remembered a time anywhere else.

Around the fire, we told stories of our pre-curse lives. We spoke of life at *Sídhe Fionnachaidh* with Father and Mother with the twins.

Sure, I'd told these stories many times, but we never tired of them. Using the magic Hawlen had taught me, I showed the images of our parents' wedding and sang the song of their legendary love. The familiar tale put us to sleep after a strenuous day.

Thinking of Hawlen, I tried to reach her mind, and a faint echo of her voice tickled my head. I smiled and faded off to sleep.

Three days later, I woke and, as I had been doing each morning, reached for Hawlen's mind. They should be arriving soon. But instead of that faint echo, I heard absolutely nothing.

I bolted out of bed and turned to my brother. "Aed, is Totawg there?"

My brother gave a huge yawn, then cocked his head. "I can't hear him." His eyes grew wide.

A glance at the twins showed me they couldn't hear their friends, either.

I ruffled my wings. "By Danu, where are they? They should be here today."

We fetched Torr, who was already heating up last night's stew for a morning meal. He scratched his close-shaven head. "I can go search."

I paced, my agitation growing. "How could you possibly find them? They might be on any of a dozen paths."

Then my blood chilled. What if Aoife had returned? What if she somehow hurt them?

He grinned. "I'm not without magic myself, Nuala. I should be able to find them."

Torr had magic, of course. He used it to create his inventions. He'd even use it to fashion tools we could use, attached to our wingtips. But I didn't realize he could find things.

"It's part of my construction talent, really. I use magic to build the best path to what I will seek."

But I still didn't like it. "I want to go with you."

He scowled. "What about your curse-pain?"

With a wave of my wing, I dismissed that. "It doesn't matter. Hawlen is more important than my comfort."

Aed chimed in that he was going, too. And, of course, the twins wouldn't stay behind.

We were an odd procession, heading south from the headland, a warrior and four huge swans, all waddling in a row. Occasionally, one of us would take to the air, scout the region, and return with a report.

At first, Torr led us to the southwest, down a path through a forest. I called almost constantly for Hawlen but heard nothing. My panic grew as we traveled.

The curse-pain came as soon as we left the headland, an uncomfortable pressure that pushed in on every muscle, every bone, and got worse as we moved further away. Soon, every step was agony.

But I didn't care about the pain. We needed to find Hawlen.

We climbed a hill and came out to an open space with a cluster of farmhouses, and Torr came to a halt. "There. They're in one of those."

A huge net hung on the side of one house. I tried to call to Hawlen, but only found silence. They must be sleeping, or worse. I should have felt if it Hawlen was killed, but I didn't know for sure.

I turned to Torr, gritting my teeth through my pain and panic. "They must have been captured by Milesians. We don't know how many of them there are. We need a plan."

Without waiting, Fiachra took flight and dove toward the closest house. Someone inside cried out. As he returned, three men ran from the building, each carrying a bow.

We scrambled for shelter amongst the trees, and an arrow whizzed by my ear. "Fiachra! What do you think you were doing?"

"I couldn't wait forever for you to come up with some complex plan. I needed to see."

I sent him a glare from my hiding spot. "Well, that worked wonderfully, didn't it? Now what?"

Torr stepped out from the trees, his arms open. He spoke in the Milesian's language, "We would like to speak to you in peace."

The three men grumbled but one nodded. "Speak your words."

With a few cautious steps forward, Torr said, "We have lost some friends of ours. Four ravens, larger than normal. They were last seen here. Have you seen them?"

While I appreciated Torr not outright accusing the men, I didn't like the chance that they'd deny everything.

Then something stirred in my mind. Hawlen's voice whispered, "help us."

My heart ached to rush the farmhouse and find my friend, but I had to trust Torr. It would do no good to be captured as well.

The closest man, with long, black warrior braids, lifted his bow to his eye. "Come no closer."

Torr cleared his throat. "I mean you no harm. We just want our friends back."

In my mind, I called out to Hawlen, to the gods, to anyone to help us. He pulled back the bowstring, aiming at Torr's chest. "We don't know what you're talking about. Leave our land, now.

A woman emerged from another house, wearing a red kerchief and a scowl. "Who is this man, Tomas? Why haven't you invited him in? I heard someone call out for help."

The men exchanged guilty glances and the woman rolled her eyes and came closer. Tomas lowered his bow. "Come, friend. We have bread and ale. Will you join us?"

Torr glanced back toward us. "Normally, I'd be happy to accept your kind hospitality. But we're searching for friends."

"We? You look alone."

Torr swallowed once before continuing. "I have several swans with me, but they are not normal swans. They were cursed into that form. And we are looking for their bondmates, four ravens. They are in one of those buildings."

I held my breath as the woman's eyes turned wide. Then she turned on the closest man. "Tomas! I told you it was bad luck to take those ravens!"

"But Rian! They walked right into the trap. How can we just give up such an easy catch?"

"These obviously aren't ordinary birds. Now get into here and let them loose. Now! Or I will break our betrothal here and now. I will not marry a man with a fairy-curse on his head. Do you understand me?"

One of the other men rushed into the closest building and emerged, carrying a huge sack. With gritted teeth, he handed the sack to Torr. Pain pounded my head as I prayed all the ravens were still alive.

Once Torr had the bag, we retreated quickly, and after reaching a place far enough away from the farms to be safe, he opened the sack.

All four ravens were there, alive but groggy. They were banged up and bruised, but sustained no permanent damage. I cradled Hawlen in my wings and refused to put him down until we returned to our headland.

Once back, we made sure they were resting comfortably on our own beds, covered in soft blankets. "Hawlen, here, have some fruit. Roisinn picked the berries this morning. Fresh and sweet, just for you."

"You can stop coddling me, Fionnuala. I'm quite capable of eating on my own."

"Of course, you are, my friend. Would you like milk?"

Hawlen ruffled her feathers, but couldn't hide a groan of pain.

"I'll leave you to your meal. Roisinn is teaching Aed and I about the local flowers. Besides, I want to get a start on my garden. Torr has promised to help me dig a large plot."

"You do that, child. I'll just stay here where it's warmer. I'll be along later."

I hadn't even exited the chamber before I heard her whistled snores.

A group of travelers crested the headland on a late autumn afternoon. Golden sunlight made everything glow in sweet splendor, and bits of our visitors' gear glistened in this brilliance.

They didn't look like Milesians, but they weren't one of the People. Their clothes looked exotic, with heavy folds of white cloth so bright, my eyes hurt, vying with purple and red dyes on an intricate border design. A heavy cloak of deep emerald green covered the lead man's shoulders.

Torr and Roisinn greeted the four men, who were pulling heavy carts by hand, while we hid in the pavilion, away from prying eyes.

Soon, Roisinn came to fetch us. "They're traders from Korinthos, an island far to the south, beyond the home of the Milesians."

"There are lands beyond so far away?"

Roisinn pointed at my chest. "You didn't pay attention to your ravens enough. The land of the Milesians is south, and to the east are the Scythians and the Hellenics to the south. There are lands even beyond this, for the Egyptians and Hittites."

I glanced toward the visitors. "What do they want?"

"To trade, of course. They offer several luxuries you may wish to examine. Their fabrics are delightful and the olive oil and wine are promising."

"Olive oil? What's an olive?"

She gestured. "Come see for yourself. Torr has deemed them quite tame."

Aed snorted. "Tame? What are they, horses?"

Fiachra piped up. "I want to see!"

I held him back with a wing. "We shall all go. Were our appearances explained?"

"Yes. Their own legends hold swans as sacred. In fact, their father god once transformed into a swan, so they might even worship you."

She cracked a smile as Fiachra giggled and spread his wings. "All hail Fiachra, God of the... whoever they are!"

I had to laugh. "Well, let's meet these worshipful traders, shall we?"

The leader of the group was a short, muscular man with long, dark curls. He introduced himself as Driteleus of Korinthos.

I held out my wings. "I welcome you, Driteleus, you and your kin. I welcome you into our homes. I welcome you to our bread and our ale. Be safe and sound within our walls." I offered a packet of dried fish, which didn't seem like much, but we couldn't produce much on our own.

The leader offered some treasured wheaten bread as guest-gift and I tried not to drool on it. We grew no grains so bread was a treat.

He and his men bowed in unison. "I thank you for your welcome, *Bantiarna*. I'm told that you and your brothers suffer under a curse. Please know to be transformed into such a magnificent creature is considered a blessing in our lands. I'm here to serve you in any way we may."

He paused, so I nodded for him to continue.

"We have many items for trade, *Bantiarna*. May we present them to you and your brothers? And, of course, to your companions." He gave Roisinn an admiring glance, fairly ignoring Torr.

Roisinn, taller than him by several hands, stood straighter and lifted her chin.

Torr chuckled and walked to the trader. "Please, we've shelter away from the elements. If the weather should change, we don't wish your goods to be damaged."

Driteleus grinned and showed very white teeth. "This land does love interesting weather, I must say."

Our visitor expressed interest in Torr's contraptions, including his wood carvings.

In that moment, I realized why my life had no purpose. As swans, my brothers and I created nothing. We made no food, we created no art. We constructed no shelter, wove no cloth, cured no skins, milked no cows. We only existed and survived day to day.

Even as *bantiarna*, I'd embroidered and trained horses. We learned lore and skills from our friends and our ravens, but to what purpose? Simply to learn? If we did nothing with that knowledge, we were of no use.

Suddenly, I wanted the traders gone. I wanted to feel useless on my own. Despite several surprised exclamations, I launched from the headland and took wing across the straits.

Catching a strong wind, I flew into the gathered clouds until the pressure pain of the curse began. On the horizon, dark clouds roiled. We'd gotten storms every day, now that autumn had arrived. What new drama would the winter bring?

I couldn't do anything about that. I couldn't build a stronger shelter, or do anything to care for ourselves. We must rely on Torr and Roisinn to even pick a simple object up from the ground. I was useless.

The winds grew icy as I flew higher. I heard a cry below me and I spied my eldest brother. "Aed! Go back. I don't need company."

"I'm not going back, Nuala. What's wrong? Why did you leave?"

"It doesn't matter. None of this matters, Aed. Go back and be safe." I dove through a thermal to escape him.

He pumped his wings to catch up. "Nuala, come back! It hurts up here."

I tried to fly higher, above the storm. Angry, frozen drops stung my wings and my eyes clouded. The curse-pain grew.

Aed wasn't below me any longer. Good. I hoped he flew back it to safety. A gust of wind wrenched my left wing. It hurt, but I straightened and regained my balance. Another one wrenched my right wing, and for a moment, I feared Aoife's return.

If the wind blew me into the cliff, would I feel it? But if I were lost, who would take care of the twins? Of Aed? I'd vowed to care for them. I'd promised my dying mother.

I stared at gathering storm clouds, all darkness and fury and suddenly ached to hold my brothers.

I dove back into the storm, past the icy pellets, and searched for our headland. Once out of the clouds, I saw nothing but water. The tether of magic that held me to our place shot an agonized tremor through my bones.

Where was I? Had the wind blown me so far away? I searched my mind for Hawlen but heard nothing.

Then I remembered Tadhg's gift, and I pushed through the magic of the silver chain. But even that magic didn't help. I couldn't think with the pain.

Sweet Danu. What had I done?

The storm yanked me back and forth and my wrenched wings hurt horribly. Hail and sleet sliced at my body. I must find a place to shelter.

There, what's that? A tug from my chain, to the right. I wheeled and tried to fly straight. The tug grew stronger and I closed my eyes to keep out stinging sleet.

A shadow loomed and land came into view. I didn't care if it was our headland or not.

Once on the cliff, I found a hollow to shelter in. I huddled within the meager space, shivering until the storm passed.

After the sun emerged, the sea was oddly beautiful. Strange light shone upon the ocean though the storm clouds still darkened the sky.

As I followed the magic tug of the chain back to my brothers, resting often due to my wings, I vowed never again to abandon my duty, my family, no matter how bad things were. Somehow, I would find purpose even in this life.

When I stumbled back into our pavilion, Hawlen rounded on me. "What do you think you were doing, child? Why did you fly so far?"

I bowed my head, unable to explain the madness that had drawn me away from safety and to the wilds of the storm. "I'm sorry."

"You abandoned everyone! Your brothers, your home, your companions, and what's worse, your duty!"

Every word she said was true. I spent the rest of the evening in miserable self-loathing.

That night, my old nightmares returned, with white feathers smothering me. This time, however, I was able to keep the monsters at bay with magic. I couldn't defeat them, but I could keep them from hurting me.

The next morning dawned cool, and everything sparkled with dew. I breathed in deep and moved my wing muscles, full of aches from yesterday's folly.

The traders had set up tents, as they intended on staying for a few days. Driteleus came out from one and opened his arms wide. "Our delightful hostess is awake! Come, I have many wonders to show you."

He was kind enough not to mention my rude disappearance the day before.

First, he brought out a dozen rolls of fabric. Soft and light as one of my own feathers, I doubted even the *ard-rí* owned such riches. Bleached to a brilliant white, the fine linen felt like a cloud, sumptuous and smooth even against my feathered cheek.

Swans had little use for fabric, but Roisinn clapped with delight. "Will you trade some of this with me? I must make a garment and feel this against my skin all day."

The Greek trader's face broke into a wide grin. "For you, my lovely woman, anything at all."

Next, he brought out several jars full of oval fruits called olives. With his permission, Roisinn picked one up, examining it from all sides. "Are they sweet?"

He shook his head. "Not sweet. Here, let me remove the pit so our hostess can try one." The trader took his belt knife and cut out the black center, handing me the soft part. My brothers finally woke and joined us, each taking a piece.

The salty, sharp flavor reminded me of dulse, a seaweed we added to cheese and bread. According to the traders, oil made from such fruits was rich and tasty on bread. They offered a lovely, decorated *amphora* for storage.

Then, Driteleus brought out wine, pouring cups for each of us. Some were dry, some were sweet, and both were strong and made me pleasantly dizzy.

I enjoyed the traders' stories so much, as they reminded me of evening stories from home. In truth, they traded more than luxury goods. They traded knowledge and stories.

That idea rattled in my brain. Perhaps we could teach others all the knowledge we'd learned over the centuries. Histories, art, and the songs of our ancestors.

But who should we teach? Milesians seemed more ready to kill us than listen to us. Children, perhaps?

We would teach them the tales of the People, that they not be forgotten.

I fidgeted with my wingtips as Roisinn brought up the visitors. After many moons with no more tales of swans or ravens killed, we decided that it was safe to reveal ourselves to the local villagers.

We worked up a plan to offer our services as teachers and storytellers. Torr went into the village and spoke to a few of the fisherfolk, explaining who we were, and asking if their children might come to learn from us.

While some were interested, others were skeptical. That didn't matter, though, as we were eager to meet the first group of three children.

As they crested the hill on the path to our headland, I recognized Torr and his three companions. They looked so small next to him, maybe eight or ten winters at the oldest.

As they approached, I held out my wings. "We welcome you…"

The children giggled all through my formal greeting, and I wanted to smile.

210

As I presented our first lesson, a very basic history of the People, my students stole secret glances at me and pinched themselves. Maybe they needed to make sure they weren't dreaming.

Eventually, they learned to take us as we were, and returned several times each moon to learn our songs and stories.

We told tales of our People, the adventures of the Tuatha Dé Dannan. Songs of battles past, stories of lost loves and great rulers.

They seemed to enjoy the performances and hold us in some strange reverence like gods. Perhaps, to them we were. After all, what other swans told stories?

Many seasons later, they brought their own children to learn the same. And thus, our stories would live forever in the lore of the Milesians. We managed that much from our lives, at least.

Chapter Fourteen

In the 350th winter of our curse (100 BCE) 50 years later

We were eating breakfast on a misty morning, when Hawlen's head popped up. "Stawn is coming."

Those were words I had waited for, what, three hundred and fifty winters? A lifetime. *Stawn is coming.* Had he learned all he needed from The Morrigan? Or did he come with yet more bad news?

I glanced at my raven, suddenly nervous. "When?"

"Today."

That's all she would say, so we waited. The shadows grew long but none of us wanted to start a project. I vacillated between hope and dread.

The twins gamboled in the fog, their dark shapes darted in and out in a game. I was so bone-tired of games, of training, of waiting. And of the bone-chilling wind that seemed to blow continuously on this cliff.

I turned to my raven. "Do you think he might break it?"

Hawlen just stared into the mists.

"Why would he come all this way if he had no solution, right?"

Silence.

"Hawlen, are you all right?"

She shook her head. "I'm sorry, Fionnuala. My mind was leagues away. What did you ask?"

"Nothing, never mind." Voicing my hopes and fears seemed foolish now, after so many winters lost to the curse.

The fog hid sounds and muffled voices. For a horrible moment, I heard Aoife's mad laughter in the mist, and my skin crawled, but it was just Fiachra teasing his brother.

Would Fiachra ever outgrow his silliness? I both hoped he would and prayed he didn't. If Stawn broke the curse, did we have a chance at a normal life?

Would I find a husband, fall in love, and have children? Would the twins stop being eternal children, forever stuck as cygnets? Conn had always been mature, but he was still a child at heart.

Fiachra was both joy and concern every day. I delighted at his antics, and he brought much-needed laughter to our misery. But he often suffered from his own foolishness, and that fear kept me awake on more than one night.

The sun sullenly pushed through the cloud cover and peeked through. Then the wind picked up and raised whitecaps winking in the sunlight. Small coracles were returning from the morning's fishing, to gut and process their catch.

A whoosh of wings caught my attention. I looked into the sky to find a horde of white ravens descending upon our cliff. I'd never seen so many white ravens together in my life.

Stawn was carried in on a simple litter, carried by two Filíd.

If he was so frail he couldn't fly here on his own, he must be too frail to perform magic of the Gods.

Shoving down my worry, I opened my wings to him. "I welcome you, Stawn, you and your kin." My host-gift was a wood carving that Conn had made.

He acknowledged the welcome with a nod of his head and then gestured to one of his Filíd, dressed similar to the Milesians.

I stared at her in panic. A Milesian Filí? Hawlen didn't seem concerned, but Torr's eyes narrowed.

She offered a basket of fruit. "Greetings, *Bantiarna* Fionnuala. The High Councilor has been ill, but wished no further delay in his mission.

He's granted me the distinct honor of becoming my bondmate, so that he may work through me and borrow my strength."

My mind whirled. The High Councilor never bonded, so the ravens would never be subjugated. But he was not only bonded, but to a Milesian. They barely lived a century.

I stared at the Ollamh, taking in her long, blond hair, braided in long strips down her back. She seemed fit, with muscles on her arms and legs, despite her diminutive size.

The Ollamh gave me time to examine her, then bowed. "Allow me to introduce myself. I am Niamh. I have studied Filíd lore for twenty winters and worked with The Morrigan these last ten winters with the High Councilor."

I let out a breath. If she's worked with the Goddess, I had no call to judge her. I returned her bow. "You are welcome, Niamh, and I thank you for your study on our behalf. What may I do to help with your work?"

She smiled and her eyes lit up, making her more beautiful. A shadow cast over her smile and we glanced up to see storm clouds roll in.

The first heavy drops of hail had us scrambling for cover. My brothers and I, along with the ravens and Niamh, squeezed into our pavilion, while the rest huddled in the guards' home and our half-finished guest roundhouses.

Whistling, icy winds battered the pavilion as rain and sleet pounded the roof and walls. I passed out furs for everyone and made sure Stawn was warm and comfortable.

After some discussion, Stawn informed us he needed time to rest after the long journey, so despite my eagerness, two more days passed before we even began preparing for the ritual.

Much as we did with Porrig, Niamh worked with us to charge magical items. But instead of chips of gemstones, she brought True Stones.

They were once Fairy Stones, but had fallen from their original home. One from the Hill of *Uisneach*, the sacred center of the island.

Another from the Hill of *Teamhair*, where *ard-ríthe* were crowned. Another from the hill at *Emhain Macha,* sacred to one of The Morrigan's three faces.

These three stones were placed in a triangle upon our headland and we spent weeks charging them. Each session left us all drained of physical and magical energy. We crawled into bed each night, exhausted.

Finally, Niamh announced that tomorrow would be the ritual. The festival of Samhain, when the veil between the worlds would be at its thinnest. A day of banishing and a day for honoring our ancestors.

We would use this day to call The Morrigan, our own ancestor, our own goddess.

The raging sun set red across the glittering ocean. Yellows and pinks faded into purples and blues. A full moon rose in the east, a pale orange on the horizon, large and baleful.

Soon, the sky teemed with twinkling lights. I saw the paint of the stars above me, splashed across the heavens. A good night for magic.

Stawn roused from his day-long meditation and strode to the center of the triangle. I stood at the stone from *Emhain Macha*, while Aed stood at the stone from *Teamhair.* The twins stood over the stone from *Uisneach.*

Our ravens, weak as they were, each huddled in front of us. Niamh was in the center, with Stawn at her feet.

She raised her arms and sang. Not a chant, like Porrig used, but a wildly descanting song with no words. Her voice sang sweet and clear and soared to the heavens like a bird.

The notes burrowed into my mind and my bones. She sang for hours and called down power from beyond this world. Shimmers of power swept from her across us and out into the night.

The stones radiated warmth and light. They pulsed like a heartbeat, singing an echo of her tones with the deeper, resonant sounds of the bones of the earth.

Sparks danced in patterns around us, spirals within the circle. No, not sparks. Tiny creatures, much like us. I enjoyed their dance for the beauty. Then I saw my mother's face.

I gasped and staggered, only holding my balance by sheer force of will. How was she here? She'd died hundreds of winters ago.

Was this her spirit, come to help break the curse? Why had she never appeared before? She was tiny but perfectly formed. She hovered before my face and kissed me on the bill. Her warm love flowed through me to my feet.

I wanted to grab that warmth and hold it close to my heart. Then she flew off to Aed.

I couldn't hold back my tears. They streamed freely down my face and broke my concentration on the spell.

Niamh had asked nothing of us other than the power already sunk into the stones. I'd never be able to concentrate on magical work after seeing my mother's, what, spirit? Ghost? Projection? I didn't know what she was, but her eyes were my own.

Aed was now crying, and the twins cocked their heads at the tiny light. They'd never seen Mother. How would they recognize her?

No, that wasn't true. They'd seen her in Hawlen's images of our parents' wedding day, the story we'd told so many times. They must recognize her.

I sensed their disbelief in our magical network, woven in through the power of Niamh's magical song. Then it changed to belief and the spell snapped. Something had now completed.

Niamh stopped singing, and her form was enveloped in a pillar of fire. Light shot up from her, caressing the paint of the stars.

With her arms raised and her head back, her mouth stretched open, but no sound emerged. Her muscles tensed in pain. She couldn't stop this surge of power, that was clear.

The energy pulled everything from me. I wanted to block it, to keep It from drawing away my life-force, but I didn't dare. This magic pulled our souls into Stawn and Niamh and then into the sky.

Power rushed like a waterfall, a cascade of crashing white noise. The mad laughter of my stepmother joined the cacophony, and my blood froze. Could Aoife Rua stop the power of a goddess?

The laughter grew stronger as the wind tugged at my feathers. An icy winter wind slammed into us. Aoife Rua, the air phantasm, had returned.

I saw our aunt, a glowing spot of red and purple light, chasing after the miniature form of our mother, chasing her around the circle, almost catching her.

No! She can't stop this now. I wouldn't let her ruin our final hope of breaking the curse. And I wouldn't let her harm my mother's spirit.

With a last shred of power, I pulled upon my magical dart. Blue energy formed into a sharp spear, longer and brighter than I'd ever before created. I searched for where her laughter was coming from, as I had but once chance, and I must strike true.

To the left? No, it whizzed to the other side now. She was moving too fast. How could I hit her?

I needed more power, but I didn't dare pull from Niamh's glowing column of magic. Instead, I cast below me, to the mighty waves of the ocean, that inexorable power that crumbled cliffs and drowned lives.

The frenzied salt water tasted different from the calm water magic of the lough. As I sucked in that raw, tumultuous power, I grew drunk and dizzy.

I created a second spear, just as long and wicked as the first. Mocking laughter came from behind my head.

Drawing again on the sea, I formed a third spear and I aimed one in each direction. Forward, left, and right. Higher than my brothers, higher than the Raven and his bonded Ollamh. Into the insane laughter, I launched my three blue spears, now jagged and crackling with unspent energy.

They flew across the sacred circle and hit the edge in a furious shower of red sparks. Laughter rose, fell, then halted in a painful silence.

Another cry came from the center of the circle. Stawn, his hoarse, aged voice came raw and agonized. He stumbled backward, then collapsed. Niamh cried out and she fell next to him. The pillar of light vanished with a thunder clap.

I lost all strength and fell into a pile, without even the energy left to see if the High Councilor lived. The other Ollamh attended him. Torr bundled me into warm skins, carrying me into our pavilion.

It was all for naught. We were still swans. "It didn't work, Torr. Our last hope didn't work."

My voice cracked and the words didn't sound like my own. Had it been my interference? I couldn't let Aoife attack Mother's spirit, but I ruined our only chance. Despair overwhelmed me, and I cried out in frustration and pain.

The next morning, when Torr tried to wake Stawn and Niamh, both were cold, their bodies empty of life.

My mind grew numb. I'd done this. I'd interfered during their great magic, and caused the death of the High Councilor. My interference ruined the work he'd spent most of his lifetime learning from The Morrigan. I'd killed our last chance to change back to our natural forms.

I fell into a pit of desolation. For the next few weeks, I wouldn't speak to anyone. I cried, I slept, and I ate, alone in my misery

Torr tried everything he could to rouse me. He cooked tempting morsels, but I refused them. I needed to suffer for my meddling. I'd destroyed everything.

Aed poked me. "Nuala, snap out of it, will you?"

I couldn't even tell my brother what I had done. Without me, they might have been normal again. They were better off without me. I was no fit guardian. In fact, I was as bad as Aoife Rua.

Aed pushed something toward me with his foot. Something red, faded and worn. The ribbon that *Banríon* Dervla had gifted us with so many winters ago.

I didn't want to touch it. We hadn't worn them in many seasons. They were so old, they were about to fall apart, and we didn't want them destroyed.

Perhaps the lingering magic would make me feel better, but I didn't want to feel better. I wanted to feel guilty. I *was* guilty. I deserved the pain.

Aed picked the ribbon up with his bill and placed it on me. He couldn't tie it, but he pushed it until it encircled my neck.

There was some vestige of magic in it, since warmth and calm suffused my body. I wanted to shake off the ribbon and disdain the good feeling. But the creeping notion crept in that maybe things weren't so bad, despite my disastrous actions.

Ten days later, just as I returned from my morning fly along the coast, Hawlen got my attention. She seemed shy, for some reason, and that seemed so unlike her, I instantly paid attention.

She glanced at Torr, who nodded, and then my raven, my beloved friend, said, "I must say goodbye to you, Fionnuala. We cannot hold on any longer. I tried, but it's too much. You have been my heart's blood and my dearest friend. I am so proud of you and all you've done. Take care of your brothers, my love."

"Leaving? But, where are you going?"

She shook her head. "I'm not going on a trip. I can't hold on to life any longer. I must seek my peace in *Tír na nÓg*."

"*Tír na nÓg*? But that means that… no!" It felt like someone punched me in the chest.

"Yes, dear heart. Yes."

I sobbed and hugged her tight, trying not to crush her in my wings. "You can't go, my dear friend, my bondmate, my teacher. Please, please don't die!"

"I'm too old, too weak. I'm sorry. All teachers must let go at some point."

Sobs made my voice hoarse. "But ravens live as long as their bondmates! That's the whole point!"

"That is true, but the curse's magic makes you live longer, and I have no such magic. I stretched the bond-magic as long as I could, but Stawn's ritual sapped me of the rest of my strength. I am so sorry, my dearest Fionnuala."

I didn't want her to let go. I saw no reason life should be so capricious. Tears burned my eyes, and when she went still, they burst forth in a flood. I saw nothing around me for the misery.

It hurt so bad, I could never describe it. It hurt worse than when Mother died. Another part of me ripped away, a part I'd never replace.

Hawlen's eyes closed, but a bare whisper of her stayed in my mind.

I cried out in frustration and agony, howling to the sky. Sorrow sliced raw and cut across my nerves and my heart. Roisinn held me in her arms and comforted me, but I didn't feel her.

When Hawlen's mind left my own, all that was left was my despair.

But after my grief finally eased into whimpers, I resolved that my despair would have a purpose. I wouldn't let her teaching be in vain. I wouldn't allow her friendship to become a waste.

I would pass on all the knowledge she'd passed to me. We'd teach the Milesian children to honor the ravens and the stories of the ancient peoples who lived in this land, even if we left nothing else in this world.

Aed's Totawg passed next and we all cried when he didn't wake up one morning. Both Crawma and Fwallsan, who hatched together, died together while we were helping Roisinn make a meal. None of us could do more than mourn our friends for a full moon.

Chapter Fifteen

In the 400th winter of our curse (50 BCE) 50 years later

I tended my new garden most days now. I spent hours digging up rows with my webbed feet or pulling weeds with my bill.

One afternoon, when I pulled up a rotted garlic bulb, I just burst into tears. It was just so frustrating to spend so much time trying to grow something, only to fail.

Conn came up behind me. "Nuala? What happened?"

I shrugged my wings and kicked at the row of garlic shoots. "Nothing. Just leave me alone."

He sat next to me and just shared my company. For a while, that was enough. We stared out at the ocean, sunlight sparkling off the gentle waves.

After a long time of calming silence, he cocked his head and asked, "Tell me what happened."

I let out a sigh and gestured toward the garlic. "It's all rotting in the ground. No matter what I do, I can't even keep a stupid garden right. I'm useless."

He sniffed at the bulbs and poked them with his foot. "Have you tried your magic? Aren't you good with the earth stuff now?"

I let out a snort. "I don't want to touch my magic anymore."

"Why not? I use it all the time with my carvings. It helps me find the shape hidden within the wood."

Staring out to the sea, remembering the last time I'd used magic and how it messed up Stawn's ritual, I spoke in a whisper. "I don't dare try."

"Nuala, you're the one who taught me that we must keep trying. Why would you give up on yourself?"

I turned to him in a temper. "Because! Because everything I touch turns rotten. I can't do anything right! If I had the least amount of ability, we wouldn't be out here stuck on the forsaken edge of the island, living out our lives under a curse! A curse that could have been broken if I hadn't interfered!"

Fiachra came up behind Conn. "What are you talking about?"

I clenched my beak, unwilling to say anything more. Aed now joined us. "What's going on?"

Conn said, "Nuala's blaming herself for the curse. And she said she messed up Stawn's magic. Didn't you talk to the Filí afterward, Aed? Did they say anything about it?"

My eldest brother gave a solemn nod. "I did. They said it was Aoife Rua who ruined it, not Nuala."

Conn turned to me, entreaty in his gaze. "See? It wasn't you. It was our aunt, cursed be her name."

I didn't want to admit they might be right. I wanted to stew in my misery. But they wouldn't leave me alone, and eventually, the day felt a little brighter.

No matter what I may have done wrong in my life, I had a family who loved me, and that was no small thing.

On a quiet spring day, the three children who attended today's stories had just left with their father, Niall Dubh. Niall had trained as a warrior, but appreciated the ancient tales and wanted his children educated. For a Milesian, he was very respectful.

Just as the family disappeared over the hill, another visitor approached. An old, bent man shuffled toward us, using a gnarled stick and dressed in green rags. His head was completely bald.

Fiachra bounced toward him. "Porrig! Porrig, is that really you?"

He held out his hands and grinned. "Whoa, whoa there, young man! Be gentle on these frail bones, now, there's a good lad."

I held out my wings, trying to quell the cacophony. "Everyone, give him space! Porrig, please sit and take a drink. Roisinn, can you please get him some refreshment? We have fresh buttermilk. Aed, fetch the man flatbread with honey. Now, sit here and tell us the news from the other world, Porrig."

We flocked around him, eager for news of our People. After our ravens died, we lost all links to *Saol Eile*. Roisinn didn't have enough magic to cross the veil and Torr grew old and frail, too.

"I'm afraid I have very sad news to relate."

We all grew silent. We heard the howl of the wind around the headland and the far-off cry of gulls.

"Our *ard-rí*, Bodb Dearg, has fallen in battle. I'm afraid he did not recover from his wounds and has gone on to *Tír na nÓg* this fortnight past."

Confused, I asked, "Battle? Whom did he battle in the new land?"

He gave a sad half-smile. "A minor *tiarna* who didn't wish to remain minor. He tried to usurp the *ard-rí*'s crown."

Bodb Dearg had been the *ard-rí* for as long as I'd lived. He made sure we were fed and sheltered when we were cursed. He asked the Filid to break the curse. And now, he'd died and gone on to the next world.

We keened for our benefactor in a sweet song of mourning.

Then Porrig refilled our bowls. "To our *tiarna*! May he live forever in the Otherlands."

The alcohol burned my throat, despite the honey taste. And when our last tears dried, we poured another cup into the earth for his portion.

"And now, we must toast again. The *tiarnaí* elected Tadhg as the new *ard-rí!*" My spirit brightened at this news, and we swallowed the honey wine with renewed spirits.

A week later, as I dug new furrows in my garden, Aed flew in from his daily patrol. "Someone's coming! Everyone in their places."

We scrambled to hiding, either in the pavilion or wherever we could find. This was our normal routine, to keep from being surprised by strangers. Porrig was still visiting, but he was sleeping late that morning.

Roisinn rushed out to meet our visitor with a hug. I peeked from the pavilion and saw it was Driteleus.

The Hellenic trader came every few months, and Roisinn had developed a strong friendship with him. The man might be a head shorter than the warrior woman, but they made each other smile.

A couple of kisses later, and she brought him to the new guest pavilion.

He patted us each on the shoulder. "Well met, my friends, well met! I have new wines for us all to try!"

All work for the day forgotten, we drank and told stories, delighting in our visitor. Porrig and Driteleus descended into a comparison of Hellenic lore with our own legends.

A seasoned storyteller, Driteleus gave us a tale of Tuan mac Cairill, a survivor of the Parthalónians. After he told the first part of the tale, he waited and assessed his audience while letting the tension build. Conn and Fiachra both fidgeted in their seats while I drank more and enjoyed the pleasant warmth of the wine.

Finally, he gave a grin and continued. "Tuan mac Cairill escaped the deadly plague, the lone human to guard the island for many winters. As others came, he transformed into the form of a stag. He became reborn several times. Does anyone remember his next form?"

Fiachra shot one wing up. "A wild boar!"

Driteleus nodded. "Excellent! And after the boar?"

Wiggling in his seat, Fiachra guessed, "A hawk?"

"Indeed, a hawk, a mighty bird of prey. Conn, do you remember what came next?"

Fiachra cried out, "A salmon!"

I narrowed my eyes. He should have let Conn have a chance.

But Conn gave his brother a sly smile. "He was reborn as himself next!"

"Quite right, young man."

It seemed odd, hearing my little brother, the baby I cradled in my arms, referred to as a young man. Even though he was now over four hundred winters.

While Conn was always mature for his age, in my mind, he'd always be ten.

I loved my brothers, all of them. But none of them had gained a great deal of wisdom or maturity over the hundreds of winters they had lived. I suppose I hadn't, either.

What a sobering idea. We might learn as much as we wanted, but would we ever grow wise? Would we ever learn to use that knowledge in the best way? Our People had honored wisdom. Would I forever feel like a child?

We taught the local children stories of the People. In Hawlen's memory, I could do no less. But our isolation seemed desperate at times. Despite his great conversations with Porrig, I almost wish that Driteleus had arrived next season. That way we could savor each visitor as they came, a separate flavor to taste and enjoy, rather than all at once like the glut after a famine.

Roisinn's laughter distracted me from my musing, and she poured more wine. Her gaze locked with Driteleus' and I felt their desire like a tangible thing. I glanced at Conn, and his body was tense.

Roisinn was free to love whomever she wished. I wished I could guard Conn against the pain of seeing the woman he loved bed another.

Would Conn ever be free to find his own love? Would any of us? I still mourned my love of Tadhg. What if we *had* thrown caution to the wind before he married? What if I'd become with child? How might that have changed our fate? Perhaps it would have changed nothing. Still, I'd have known a lover's caress.

I touched one wingtip to my neck and stroked it, pretending it was Tadhg's caress. I closed my eyes, savoring the sensation.

Fiachra's voice cut into my reverie. "Nuala, what are you doing? You look silly."

I dropped my wing and cleared my throat. "Just an itch, Fiachra. Have you had enough to eat?"

He rolled his eyes. "Yes, I've eaten, I've drunk, and now I want to fly! Join me for a patrol?"

I spared one more glance toward Conn before we flew into the sky. Fiachra's voice came thin across the winds. "I'm worried about Conn."

I blinked a few times. "Worried? About what?"

He snorted. "About the moon-eyes he's been giving Roisinn. Haven't you seen? He's completely smitten, the silly fool."

I choked. Fiachra was always so self-involved, I never credited him with noticing things around him.

He let out a snort. "He'll be even worse when she leaves."

"Leaves?"

Fiachra sent me a look of disgust. "Don't you see anything, Nuala? She's leaving with Driteleus."

Roisinn, one of our companions, our guardians, our People, would be leaving. For an outsider, a foreigner!

I had to stop flying and think. I dove back toward the ocean and found a rock jutting out of the water, one the fishermen called *Carraig na Rón*, the Rock of the Seals. Luckily, the winds weren't strong, and I found a good grip. My brother settled beside me on the outcropping.

"Are you certain, Fiachra? They weren't just joking?"

"I'm dead certain. They were talking about meeting his family and what she needed to pack for the journey."

My stomach dropped like a lead weight. Torr was getting old, and he must leave us soon. There'd be no one left. We'd lost our ravens, our family, and now our friends.

I didn't have enough strength to hold us together if we were alone, and I maybe didn't want to. My head swam and my balance faltered. I spread my wings, but a gust caught me and I tumbled into the water.

The wind heralded a squall that fell upon us with quick fury. It whipped me far and away from the Rock of the Seals. Far from Fiachra and the headland. I couldn't get wind under my wings in the icy rain.

Darkness fell fast as black storm clouds blotted out the sun. When I finally regained use of my wings, I wheeled to the ground, scanning the countryside for some distinguishing mark.

The curse-pain pressed in on me, so I must be far from *Sruth na Maoile*. Flying east, the pain increased, so I turned around and flew west. The pain eased, so I knew I was headed in the right direction.

Belatedly, I remembered my silver chain. I pushed magic through mine, to reach out to my brothers. There, to the left and forward. I flew through the remaining squalls, sometimes buffeted by wind. A sudden gust pushed me into the surf, and I spluttered in the icy water. I considered waiting until the storm passed, but I needed to be with my brothers, so I pushed onwards.

When I finally spied our headland, I touched my chain with magic again, but didn't sense my brothers. They must have braved the storm to find me.

At first, I wanted to go find them, but realized the wisdom in staying put. One of us should stay at home I had my chain, so they should find me soon enough.

First, Aed flew in, sodden and exhausted, his eyes red and his feathers drooping. As soon as he landed, he shook so hard, the drops fell inside the pavilion.

Next, Conn straggled in, coasting along the ocean surface. As soon as he landed, he curled up next to me with an exhausted yawn and fell asleep.

For a long time, we waited for Fiachra. The storm raged on, and I despaired for our headstrong brother.

The darkness of the storm faded into true night, but still, he didn't return.

Now, I reconsidered trying to find him. Aed and Conn were here, and we could hone in on their chains if needed.

As I stepped out to go find Fiachra, Aed put out his wing. "No, Nuala. He can find his way back. Trust him."

"He could be hurt, Aed. Or lost."

My brother shook his head. "Then he can get himself unlost. He needs to learn how to come back on his own. If we keep rescuing him, he'll keep getting in trouble."

That sounded wise, but as lightning crashed around us, I stared into the rain, praying my little brother was alive.

Just as the storm waned into a fine mist and dawn crept on the eastern horizon, he wheeled in, flying much too fast, and almost knocked Aed over. Together, they tumbled to a halt.

I wanted to yell at him, to scream about him about how worried I'd been. But I was the one who'd left in the first place, so this was all my fault. In sullen silence, I crawled under my blankets and did my best to sleep.

In the morning, Roisinn announced that she'd leave in three days with Driteleus. With tear-filled eyes, we said our goodbyes, but Conn barely said a word. He watched her retreating form and then kept watching the path she'd disappeared down for hours. Finally, he crawled into bed and cried himself to sleep.

I made certain to stay near him for the next few days. By unspoken accord between Fiachra and myself, we never let him out of sight.

In the 403rd winter of our curse (47 BCE) 3 years later

It was an icy night, and we all huddled in our pavilion for warmth and companionship, including Torr.

Tendrils of freezing wind tried to pry into our home, but the clever construction of overlapping basalt slabs kept it at bay. Occasionally, a drip from above made it through, traveling laboriously into the thick thatch.

Conn played with his carving tools but didn't actually carve anything.

I sifted through my dried herbs and made plans of what to plant next spring.

Fiachra rattled Torr's specially modified cup and practiced throwing bones. Each piece of bone was flat and polished, carved with an Ogham symbol. The symbols represented sounds, but also trees and concepts in the ancient lore.

Fiachra had no particular talent at divination magic, but he made up stories from each combination based. This was a game we'd made up in a fit of abject boredom.

He peered at one cluster in his latest casting. "Hmm. Holly tree, elder, white fir and hazel. 'TRAC.' Then Pine and Gold."

Aed suggested. "Someone tracked a stag through the pine forest during the last gold of the sunset?"

I nodded. "Let's start with that. Who's the tracker?"

Torr suggested one of the Fianna, the tribe of warriors three of our local men had joined.

"Grand. A man of the Fianna, tracking a stag. Is he hunting? Or is there another purpose? Conn, what do you say?"

Conn ignored me and stared at the door as the wind rattled it.

Fiachra chimed in. "He's searching for magic in the form of the white stag."

White animals were sacred, and a white stag was filled with magic and luck, an excellent twist to the tale.

Aed nodded. "But someone else is also tracking it. An old woman."

I cocked my head. "And the old woman is The Morrigan in disguise?"

Conn spoke in a bitter tone. "She tries to seduce him."

I sighed. He must still be pining over Roisinn.

The howling outside rose to a howl. There was an edge to it, a frenzy that hadn't existed before.

I concentrated on increasing our protective wall. We added to the magic each morning after our meal, bolstering the magical wards around our space. I had confidence in our workings, but there was always a chance we'd missed a weak spot.

Cries and sobs circled the surrounding rocks, surely conjured by my own active imagination. I blocked them and returned my attention to our story. "Does she succeed? Does the warrior bed her?"

Torr shook his head. "No, alas, he laughs and tells her to find someone her own age."

Fiachra threw up his wings. "When will these foolish mortals ever learn? Never turn down such a woman. It always ends badly. Besides, who would turn down love?"

I smiled. "Beautiful young people sometimes believe only beautiful young people are worthy of their love, Fiachra."

He shook his head. "Young men are stupid."

He sounded so much like a crabby, old man that I laughed. Of course, we were now over four hundred winters old ourselves, so had a lofty perspective on the matter.

We were all yet innocent of physical love, and we'd likely never have such a chance. Of course, if an old man were to come to seduce me, he'd have to be a god to make it work. Perhaps that Hellenic god who'd turned into a swan for his seductions.

Mad screeches drifted into our pavilion, wending through the space and into our minds. Conn peered up from his tools, and Fiachra glanced between me and Aed, his eyes wide.

At first, I was sure the screams were from Aoife Rua, and my heart leapt into my throat. Then I realized they were human voices. A woman from the village flung open our pavilion door, panting as she gasped out. "They're attacking us! We need help!"

Torr jumped to his feet, weapons already in hand. "Who's attacking? Where?"

Between pants, she said, "The village. A group of warriors. We don't recognize them."

Torr was already halfway out the door when I stopped him with a wing. "Wait, we can't just go out there. We're supposed to be keeping our nature a secret."

The warrior glowered at me. "There are people in trouble. And I don't need to hide mine."

Fiachra was grabbing his throwing net. "These people are our friends, Nuala. We've taught half of them as children! We can't just let them get hurt!"

I swallowed, glancing between Fiachra and Torr. My need to protect my brothers warred with my need to protect the villagers. The warrior ran out, headed for the village. After one final glance at me, Fiachra followed.

Then Conn strapped on his leather wingtip knives and Aed grabbed his stone sling.

With a sigh, I admitted that they had the right idea. The only weapon I had were my magic darts, and it had been ages since I'd used them. But if ever there was a time to use them, it was now.

As we raced through the furious storm, torches flickered in the rain. More screams came from the village, and we hurried down the hill.

The closest roundhouse was already afire, despite the rain. Flames licked greedily at the thatched roof, and a woman inside let out a screech.

I flung the door wide and found two men getting ready to ravish her. I pulled back on my magical arrow, aiming at the man attacking her. The other one turned to see who had entered. His face was almost comical in his confusion as I let loose.

The dart struck him in the chest, and he fell to the floor with a shriek, his shirt covered in blue flames. His companion drew his sword and stalked toward me, a growl escaping his lips.

I let loose another arrow, the magical power cutting through the dim room, piercing him in the neck. He stumbled back, gripping a curtain, and ripped it as he collapsed. The woman scrambled to her feet and rushed out of the roundhouse.

Outside, I found that my brothers and Torr had worked similar results. The invaders were now fleeing, their spluttering torches receding into the distance. As we trudged back to our pavilion, thunder rumbled and the wind howled.

The screams had faded, but now the wind held mad laughter. A chill ran down my spine as I looked up into the roiling clouds and saw a face I recognized.

Aoife Rua had returned.

I shouted out orders. We'd drilled for this. "Form a circle, quickly now! Pull your energy in, slow and steady, just like we practiced."

We touched wingtips with Torr in the middle and I drew on the water energy from the frenetic salt sea below. Mist and rain dried as I pulled the water magic into myself. The earth rumbled and the air rattled with the reaction of my brothers' efforts.

Her mad laughter lessened, but we weren't done yet.

I formed a column of force in the middle of our circle, similar to the pillar of magic Niamh had created. It pulsed green and blue, brown and purple. The column expanded from the center, growing until it engulfed Torr, us, and then the walls of the pavilion itself, then the very cliff we lived upon.

The screams faded, a mere echo of their former strength, but they still echoed in the distance.

Triumphantly, I opened my eyes, ready to disperse our work, when a light flashed before me. Aoife's face, distorted in a rictus of insanity, came so close to mine, I cried out.

Her face grew larger, her mouth opened wide in silent laughter. Her eyes rolled over my brothers and then alighted upon Torr. She gave me a sly glance and returned to stare at our guard and companion.

"No!"

Despite being out of practice, I threw my magic wall up to protect our friend and companion. I shielded him with all we had, an impenetrable shell of blue power.

Aoife twisted her floating image to Fiachra. She sent a destructive blast in his direction. I cried out but had to trust that Fiachra was strong enough to deflect the attack. It hit the wall behind him, which shuddered but stood.

Another scream, this time of frustration, and our stepmother's spirit floated around us, skipping to different places in the circle.

I chanted, putting all the power I'd learned from Porrig, from Stawn, and from Hawlen into my words.

"Liom a bhaint tú as an saol seo, Aoife Rua.
Liom a bhaint tú as an saol seo,
Liom a bhaint tú as an saol seo,
Go riamh dochar a dhéanamh linn arís."

I banish thee, Aoife Rua, to never harm us again.

I hoped with all my heart and all my magic that I could make this true.

With a suddenness that took my breath away, silence descended on us. The howling wind halted, and my stepmother's terrifying shade vanished.

Would she be back?

Chapter Sixteen

In the 404th winter of our curse (46 BCE) 1 year later

Sitting around the campfire on our headland, the wind whipped our feathers and dried my tears. It had been an incongruously sunny day, and I wanted it to be rainy, to match my mood.

Torr had faithfully stood by us for four hundred winters, and I couldn't blame him for wanting to retire beneath the hills. I wanted desperately to beg him to stay. He might even have listened, out of love for us and a lingering sense of duty.

But that wouldn't be right. We couldn't keep Torr here beyond his time.

A warrior from the village, Niall Dubh, had joined us this evening. Torr had trained him to be our guard one he left. I glanced at the young man with black, curly hair. We'd taught his children for several winters, though they'd grown and became warriors or farmers themselves.

While we enjoyed his company, he was still a Milesian, one of the Robogdii tribe. Still, he was well-trained to keep us safe.

When Torr had first announced his departure, I'd balked. "Must you go straight away? We should send you off with a proper feast of thanks for all your work, Torr."

He shrugged. "If you feel you must, I'd welcome one more night with my boon companions. Let us sing the sun down in the west. But I must be past the veil as the stars appear. Will that be sufficient, my *Bantiarna*?"

I didn't qualify as the *bantiarna* any longer. Father would have long since died, I was certain. And if I was a *banríon*, what would I rule over? This gods-forsaken chunk of grassy rock? Then I narrowed my eyes at the headland. "Torr! I have an idea. You can stay here forever, in a way."

He furrowed his brow. "How?"

"We shall name this cliff for you! After all, you built all this to make our life livable. This will be known as Torr Head, and we will honor you here forever."

Fiachra giggled and I shot him a glare. He shrugged. "What? It sounds like he left his head here."

"Hush, Fiachra."

Niall Dubh placed his hands on Torr's shoulders. "I will make certain my people never forget your name. You shall be immortal, friend Torr."

Tears glistened in Torr's eyes. I began a song, an ancient tune of brave men and lost lives. The song told of a battle long since won and lost, so long ago we didn't even recall the names of the warriors.

This was Torr's favorite song, and he joined me, our voices rising in the deepening dusk. A brilliant sunset painted the sky in rays of purple and orange and we sang until our throats grew hoarse.

When he finally left and Niall Dubh settled in the guard's roundhouse, I wept for the last of our People to know us. I wept for the company they'd given us, the love we'd shared, and the stories that would be lost. I cried for everything that had passed in the last four hundred winters and everything that would pass in the next five hundred.

Conn put his wing around my shoulders and crooned me to sleep.

In the 486th winter of our curse (36 CE) 82 years later

It was a bright, beautiful afternoon in the middle of summer, and Niall returned from his hunt with two small children, a boy and a girl. They were dressed in rags, covered in grime, and couldn't have been more than five winters old. They peered at us from behind his legs, darting in and out.

I put on my kindest voice. "Who have we here, Niall?"

He smiled and brought out the boy. "This brave young man is Donnchadh. His sister, somewhere back here," he fumbled until he found the child and brought her forward with a laugh, "she is Cailín."

"Hmm. The Brown Warrior and the Wee Girl. That seems appropriate. Are you certain there're actually children under all that dirt?"

"I think so, but perhaps they've fooled me and it's all some fairy trick." He made a show of wetting one finger and scrubbed at Donnchadh's forehead. The child squirmed and giggled to get away from him.

Fiachra furrowed his brow. "What are we meant to do with them?"

I rolled my eyes. "Teach them, of course. And raise them."

He scowled. "Raise them? We aren't nurses or mothers."

"Why not? It would give us a new challenge. And the first challenge is to get you both clean!"

Conn piped up. "A nice bath in the ocean might be just the trick."

The tide was formidable, so Torr had constructed a bathing pool near the shore when we first arrived, well-sheltered from powerful ocean waves.

For our efforts, we received plenty of screeches and giggles. We surrounded the children to keep them from running off while Niall scrubbed each one, washing away the ground-in dirt. Even their clothes were clean when we finished, though they still hung in ragged strips.

We had plenty of skins, though we didn't sew much into fitted outfits. Torr had never worked out a way for us to use needles. However, Niall fashioned a tunic for each child and a woven belt from flaxen twine. He stood back and crossed his arms, appraising their new look.

I gave a nod of approval. "It will do. Wherever did you find them?"

"Alone in a shack about to fall into kindling. Their parents died of a fever several moons ago and they've been foraging, barely enough to keep them alive. I hoped we might adopt them."

I made a show of looking them up and down, asking them to open their mouths and examining at their teeth. "Hmm. Aed, what do you think?"

"I don't know, sister mine. They shouldn't take up much room, but I'll bet they can eat their weight in fish."

Fiachra cocked his head. "My question is, can they sing? If they can't sing, we can't have them."

I'd never met anyone in this land who didn't sing at least passably well, a tradition our People shared with the Milesians. I cocked my head at the girl. "Well, Cailín? Can you sing for us?"

She skittered behind Niall's legs and hid.

Conn shrugged. "Even if they can sing, will anyone come searching for them? We don't wish to take them from their family."

Niall shook his head. "They said they have no other relatives."

"Very well then. I'll put blankets on the pallets in the guesthouse."

I stared after him with sad eyes. While he had always been quiet, he'd never regained his humor and joy in life after Roisinn left. I'd hoped his love would fade, but I saw no sign. Maybe taking care of these wastrel children would fire his spark once again.

Niall knelt and fixed the children with a stern look. "We're your new family, but we won't force you to stay. We shall feed you, teach you histories and songs, and we will shelter you from the storms. But we also expect you to work. I'll teach you to hunt and forage and, eventually, to fight. A contract is a sacred promise and shouldn't be broken. Do you accept this contract, children?"

I wanted to giggle at the forced solemnity. Niall was not a solemn person by nature, but just now he seemed like the wisest sage. I knew better.

Chapter Seventeen

In the 489th winter of our curse (39 CE) 3 years later

It had been so long since we had children around, and they made us laugh and cry almost every day. While we'd taught children for many seasons, we'd only had them for a few hours each day. Trying to be a mother nearly drove me to distraction.

After they lost their mistrust of us as strangers, both Donnchadh and Cailín scampered about the place. So much that I worried they'd fall off Torr Head and into the sea. The rocks below were unforgiving and would rip their bodies to shreds.

However, they had an innate ability to cling to the rocks like mussels, scrambling up and down sheer faces.

They were much too young for swords, but we taught them to use slings. Both children brought a host of small creatures to eat once we showed them how, and they were so proud to provide. Squirrels, voles, nothing escaped their hunting prowess. Mushrooms, berries, and nuts added to their foraging.

We showed them how to set traps and milk our cow. A moon after they joined us, I explained to Cailín how to churn cream into butter. She was pumping the handle, taller than herself, when the stranger arrived.

Sometimes warriors came to visit Niall and spend the evening exchanging stories and mead. We welcomed his friends with open wings.

But this man wore a long, plain tunic with several bags tied to his belt. He wore no weapon that we could see and approached us with open hands. His pale blond hair was cut short, and his scalp was red with sunburn.

Niall rose from where he and Conn were teaching Donnchadh how to use the leather cutter, and approached the stranger with his hands out, palms up. "Hail, stranger and merry meet. I welcome you, you and your kin. I welcome you into our homes. I welcome you to our bread and our ale. Be safe and sound within our walls."

The man nodded at Niall and then stared at me, seeking me out from behind the butter churn. "I thank you for your kind welcome. I bring a gift for the lady of this place."

He untied a sack from his belt and placed it on the ground. Then, he unwrapped the fabric to reveal a set of bone tied together, with odd grooves and holes carved into them. It reminded me of a precious pipe a bard of the People played. The bard had coaxed ethereal music from the instrument, but it had looked much simpler than this.

Niall offered a loaf of our precious wheaten bread as a host-gift.

I took a hesitant step forward and bowed to our guest. "I second your welcome. May I ask your name, guest? I am Fionnuala. The Milesian warrior is called Niall. My brothers are—"

He cut me off with a raised hand. "I know full well who you are, my fairy *bantiarna*. Tales of your plight cover the land. Most believe you a long-dead legend, but I met a Hellenic trader and his woman who told me the truth. I've been searching for you for a long time."

Searching for us? To what purpose? And who was this man?

He must have seen the confusion on my face. "I am a Gaelic Filí, my *bantiarna*. My name is Mochán of the Auteinii, and I come to offer my services."

Fiachra narrowed his gaze. "Services? What sort of services?"

When he smiled, his blue eyes crinkled. Those eyes were used to smiling. "Why, to be your boon companion, should you allow it, Fiachra.

Or is it Conn? I'm here to learn from you, teach you, keep you company on cold nights, and help your warrior, Niall."

No one had ever come to us, offering to stay. We've asked people to help, but none had ever volunteered. To have sought us out seemed suspicious.

I didn't know why, but something didn't feel right. "How do we know you are who you claim to be?"

Aed gasped. To call a guest a liar was more than rude and could warrant a duel or banishment. Even Fiachra looked shocked into silence.

The man smiled and opened his arms. "You do not, of course. But would you allow me to stay on a trial basis? I'd be happy to help you with chores. Cooking, washing, sewing, perhaps. I'm no great hunter, but I'm a good trapper and fisher, and can keep your bees. I'm at your disposal, my *bantiarna*."

He bowed low and held it, and I felt churlish for having called him a liar. I wanted to take my accusation back but couldn't figure out how to do it with grace. Aed came to my rescue. "Of course, you can stay. We would be honored."

Our new guest settled next the fire. Soon, he was chatting easily with both Conn and Donnchadh, admiring the leather strap they were stamping.

His gift of tied bones turned out to be an instrument, like those pipes I remembered. He demonstrated with lovely, sweet clear tones, and my suspicions fled. The notes soared into the evening sky, and I shut my eyes to enjoy the music with sheer delight.

When he finished, Fiachra asked to examine the instrument.

Mochán held it so we could all see. "I think I can fashion one so you can close the holes with your wingtips, but it wouldn't be as complex. The real problem is that you need lips to blow the air through the pipe. Let me consider this and see what I can modify."

I swallowed down shame at my own distrust. "Honored guest, I apologize for my earlier outburst. We get so few visitors, I'd forgotten my manners."

His smile showed white teeth, emphasizing his tanned skin. "Never fear, *bantiarna*. I was prepared to withstand more than a few suspicions to have the honor to serve you. You see, when I say I've heard of you all my life, that wasn't boasting. I have an ancestor you may remember."

I cocked my head, inviting him to continue.

"I am descended from a Milesian *tiarna* named Áedammair. Do you remember him?"

A grin spread across my face. "I do! He was our friend from the very beginning. He knew us even before our curse. If you're of his family, then we must welcome you here. And please, call me Nuala. Or, if you must, Fionnuala. I am no longer a *bantiarna* of any land." It pained me to speak that truth.

He nodded with a saucy grin. "As you wish, *bantiarna*."

I narrowed my gaze, but he laughed. "Nuala, it is. So, tell me of the two children. Have they been here long?"

I cast a gaze toward Donnchadh. "Just a season. Their parents died of a fever, so we adopted them."

"It would be my pleasure to help with their teaching, if you allow."

I grew suspicious again, though I didn't know why. "What makes you so eager to help us, Mochán? What draws you so?"

He sighed. "To be utterly honest, I grew up with tales of magic and the fairy folk. They fascinated me. The Gaels, who you call the Milesians, have much less magic than the Tuatha Dé Dannan did. We are mundane folk. Our magic is but a pale echo of what your people could do. Alas, I was born too late to have met the gods of old, but I still ached for the magic."

Niall passed him a mug with ale, and he downed half of it before continuing. "I joined Filíd training after my ninth winter. I studied for twenty more and can perform minor enchantments. When I heard of you, though, I realized I had a purpose.

"I vowed to find you and share your lives. Nothing more than that. I can teach you my magic, though I'm certain you know far more than I do. I can teach you of the ways of the modern world, if you should be interested."

"And what do you wish in return?"

"In exchange, I would ask for tales of the ancient world. Does it sound like a fair exchange, Pr… Nuala?" From his wry smile, he made the slip on purpose.

It made sense someone of these people would be curious about ours. He at least had a sense of humor and purpose. There were worse goals in a life. "That sounds perfectly fair. We've been teaching local children tales for many seasons. I imagine they've become somewhat garbled with your short lifespans for memory."

He shook his head. "Not as much as you might think. As an Ollamh, I'm trained to memorize any story precisely as I've heard it, and to relate it word by word. This is an honored tradition. I shall make certain your source tales are as true as may be."

"That would be a great boon, Mochán. I thank you for the offer. Shall we seal the deal with mead? I have a flask in storage for a special occasion. The bees weren't as cooperative last summer."

He reached for his belt and untied another sack. "I brought my own. Sweet mead from the southwest of the island, where the summers are warm, and the bees are busy."

In the 492nd winter of our curse (42 CE) 3 years later

As my brothers sang a lusty song about a drunk sailor, my eyes were drooping from fatigue. I escaped the songs and stories and crept into the pavilion. Another form sat against the wall. "Mochán, is that you?"

"It is indeed, my *bantiarna*. I'm in no mood for celebration tonight. My excesses from last night are telling on me. I'm not as young as I used to be."

Mochán had no gray in his hair, and his protests made me laugh. "Wait until you are five hundred winters old. Then you can complain of the weariness of excess."

He let out a chuckle. "I might do exactly that, Nuala. Just you wait."

At first, I laughed with him. But he was a Gael, and their lifespans were painfully short, and my laughter caught in my throat.

His tone turned tender. "What have I said to sadden you, Nuala?"

"I've seen many friends age and die while I lived, Mochán. It always makes me sad."

He laughed. "Then you're in luck! For I don't plan on letting you down that way."

"But how can that be? You're not Tuatha Dé."

"Not entirely, no. But my grandmother was one of your People. Remember, I've studied Filí magic since childhood. I've learned some life magic. Tell me, how old do I look?"

I studied not only his face, but his hands and his neck. "I am no good judge of the age of Gaels, but I would say no older than thirty winters."

He laughed again, his belly shaking. "Ah, to be so young. I've already counted a hundred winters."

I was shocked into silence. He'd lived longer than any Gael I knew, and yet he was young and vital. Might he live until the end of our curse? It was a hopeless dream, to keep a friend so long.

He placed a hand on my shoulder. "When your curse ends, we can ride off into the night and make a life together. Would that please you?"

It seemed like a cruel trick. To hold out something I'd ached for in lonely nights like a prize. I didn't want to say it out loud in case the dream should be snatched from me.

"Come, my *bantiarna*, you must be weary. Let me sing you to sleep."

He sang a sweet song of a faraway land, where the meadow-sweet grew on the hillside, and it reminded me of my childhood home. I drifted into a peaceful dream.

When I cried out in the night, Mochán remained to comfort me. He hugged me in warm arms until I calmed. "Why do your dreams frighten you so?"

I snuggled into his embrace. "I don't know. Well, yes, I suppose I do. I had nightmares before we were cursed, dreams where I was attacked by something with white feathers. My stepmother used an enormous white bird crafted of magic to cast her curse. White feathers attacked us, and white feathers became us. For many winters, my nightmares have been the truth."

He hugged me tightly. "So, every day you're reminded of your night terrors. Is there any way I can help?"

"Just be here for me when I wake in the night. That's all I ask. I don't wish to wake my brothers, as they may begin the same dreams. But you're solid and safe."

My eyes drooped as I spoke, and sleep crept up on me. I let out a huge yawn.

"I will always be here to comfort you, my *bantiarna*. Never fear that I shall leave. You're my purpose and my destiny."

My fatigue was making me brave, and I asked a question I'd wanted to know for a long time. "Tell me, why do you love us so much?"

"Not everyone. Just you, Nuala. Because you are my favorite color, and I wish my world to be painted in shades of you."

Chapter Eighteen

In the 600th winter of our curse (150 CE) 108 years later

Six hundred winters. Six hundred summers, warm and rainy and six hundred winters, frigid and snowy. Wind and rain, flowers and bees, all had come and gone, lived and died as we tarried here on this lonely headland. Yet we'd made it our home.

Now we had to flee this home and find another. The last third of our curse, the final portion of our swan lives, on *Irrus Domnann*.

I didn't know what to expect from our third home. *Sruth na Maoile*, as harsh as it was, had grown comfortable. Would *Irrus Domnann* be the same?

With no ravens to follow us, we prepared for the flight. Donnchadh and Cailín had long since moved away to their own lives. Niall had passed on, but one of his grandsons, Riordan, stayed with us. It had become a local tradition, for one of that family to be our companion.

Mochán had learned enough of our magic to extend his own mortal life. He still looked young, though he'd now lived over two hundred winters.

I'd grown to love Mochán. Not the love of a brother or a father or a best friend, but of a secret lover. Like the love I still held for Tadhg, deep in my heart, wherever he may be now.

I ached to caress Mochán, to hold him and kiss him, but not until I was myself again. Never until then.

Mochán and Riordan traveled ahead of us to prepare a place, much as Torr and Roisinn had. Wait, no, was it Torr and Las? My memory grew weak with so much time.

They say children live in the present and adults live in the future, while elders live in the past. All four of us were elders now. I thought of the past often and organized my nostalgia with limited success. I'd met so many people, learned so many songs, and told so many stories. How could one person recall them all? I felt weary just thinking about it.

I didn't want to make this journey across the island to a new, scary place, but the curse tugged. The pain increased, pushing us to finish our packing.

At least today was bright, and the view should be incredible. We hadn't sought beyond our cursed tether for so long, I'd forgotten what the rest of the land was like.

I surveyed my brothers with their packs on their backs. "Everyone ready? Nothing forgotten? We can't come back, remember, and it would be unfair to ask our friends to travel so far."

My heart hurt as I remembered our last journey, when our beloved ravens had been captured. How I missed my dear Hawlen. I choked back my tears.

Fiachra rolled his eyes. "I packed two days ago, Nuala. I've left nothing, at least, nothing I want."

Conn checked Fiachra's pack and then mine and Aed's. I checked to make sure his was secure. I couldn't put off the journey any longer, so I took a deep breath. "Well, then, let's fly! Stay in formation until the first rest spot."

My muscles were tense from anticipation and stretching my wings in flight felt wonderful. We glided across the green-clad hills south and east of the *Sruth na Maoile*. I didn't allow myself to glance back toward our empty home.

Below us, quilted greens and browns rushed by. Forests sprang up on hilltops and loughs dipped into rivers.

As we passed a hill covered in white flowers, reminding me of *Sídhe Fionnachaidh*, I had an idea. Could we detour from our path?

While the *ard-rí's* hillfort was far from our path, we'd be traveling close to our childhood home.

When we stopped for our first rest and meal, I asked, "What do you think about trying to visit *Sídhe Fionnachaidh* on our way?"

Aed's head snapped up. "Father's home? Why ever for?"

I gave a shrug. "We'll be so limited once we get to our destination. Why not view as much as we can in the brief freedom we have? We might be able stretch our curse-limit enough to see it one last time.."

Fiachra hopped up and down. "Yes! Yes, let's do that, please! I want to see!"

Aed rolled his eyes. "What a waste of time!"

Conn cocked his head and spoke in a quiet tone. "What do we have but time, brother mine?"

Aed shrugged. "I don't see the point, but if you've a sudden attack of nostalgia, who am I to get in your way?"

Anticipation built in my heart as we took flight. After passing Lough Neagh, we came close to our old home, but all we found was a large mound covered in moss and vines. Where were the roundhouses and the long, grand feast hall?

We landed and poked into the mounds. I found some rotted stakes and the remains of a roundhouse wall. That was all that was left.

I turned, staring at the ruins. Hundreds of the People had called this home. We'd hosted feasts, games, sang songs, and burned our dead. All that had disappeared into crumbling nothing. Six hundred winters of neglect had erased the memories of all we held dear.

My blood chilled and I wished we'd never come. "Let's go, brothers. Our curse calls us."

The trip to *Irrus Domnann* went quickly, and we didn't speak of our childhood home again.

As our curse-pain guided us to our next home, we wheeled down to the jut of land sticking out from the mainland, a green-covered hill near the end and craggy caves beneath.

This location seemed much gentler than *Sruth na Maoile* had.

A spot of bright yellow caught my eyes, down near one of the caves. I wheeled down to investigate, and discovered Riordan's yellow cape, a piece of clothing he was inordinately fond of.

It flapped in the wind next to several piles of building supplies, including logs and bricks. Riordan himself was nowhere to be found, and I saw no trace of Mochán.

The rippling sound of a woman's laughter came from around the corner, and I waddled to investigate. I found the entrance to a large cave set into the hillside, large enough to house twenty men.

Someone, likely Riordan, had built a wattle and daub wall in front, but the door hadn't yet been built. The laughter came from the other side.

She laughed again, but I hesitated to enter. Maybe a local woman lived here? I turned to leave but stumbled on a stone. The pebble clattered down the side of the cliff. Muffled voices from inside started arguing.

In a few moments a half-dressed Riordan emerged from behind the wall. His eyes grew wide and then a grin spread across his face. "Nuala! I didn't realize you were due today. I'm so sorry! Give me just one moment, please."

He held up a finger, then rushed back inside and started whispering.

The woman didn't whisper back. "What do you mean? Why do you care if a swan is here? What in God's name are you talking about, Riordan?"

"I told you yesterday, Mara, don't you remember?"

"I remember you telling fairy tales. Now, where did you hide my leggings?"

"Here, take them. I must get you out of here. They've arrived and must be tired from their journey."

I *was* exhausted, but my curiosity trumped my weariness, and I inched closer. Aed came up behind me. "What's wrong?"

"Shh. Riordan has a woman in there. I think they were sharing pleasures."

He let out a chuckle. "Why does that surprise you? Riordan's had lots of lovers. He's broken many hearts already."

Footsteps approached the wall and I backed away. I didn't want Riordan to think I was spying on him.

Of course, that's what I *had* been doing. Fiachra and Conn came up behind us, having removed their flying packs.

As Riordan emerged fully dressed, his face was flushed red and his hair looked like a rat's nest. The young woman with him, Mara, was dressed in leather leggings and a long tunic. Her red hair had been braided in the back, but bits stuck up, as if she'd been lying on it.

She came to an abrupt stop when she saw us. "These? These swans are why we have to leave? They don't look like they're objecting to us, Riordan. Certainly they aren't dangerous animals."

Riordan cleared his throat several times before he spoke. "Mara of the Auteinii, may I present you to the *Bantiarna* Fionnuala of the Tuatha Dé Dannan, her brother Aed, and the twins, Fiachra and Conn?"

Mara rolled her eyes. "I can take a joke as well as the next woman, Riordan, but this is getting tiresome."

I bowed and cleared my throat. "I welcome you, you and your kin. I welcome you into our home. I welcome you to our bread and our ale. Be safe and sound within our walls."

Mara gaped at me and my brothers. I wanted to smile at her obvious confusion, but kept my expression solemn. Not that my swan face allowed me much expression.

Riordan placed a gentle hand on her shoulder. "As I told you, Mara. They were fairies, many winters ago, until a curse turned them into swans."

She narrowed her eyes, her hands on her hips. "Fairies, you say? Turned into swans? Riordan, what have you been drinking?"

I couldn't suppress a chuckle. "I assure you, my lady, we are as he says. Would you honor us by sharing bread?"

She just stared.

"Fiachra, please fetch my pack. Conn, can you get the honey? Riordan, have you drunk all the mead, or is there some left for our guest? And where's Mochán?"

"Mochán had an errand to run, so we parted ways about a day before I got here. He should be back soon."

Mara abruptly sat on the ground, still staring at me. When Fiachra arrived holding several wheaten loaves of bread in his wings, she turned pale. "All swans? But you sound human."

I gave a shrug. "We lived here before you humans arrived. But our natural shape looks human."

We'd had similar conversations with each new student group, so I was familiar with the cycle of denial and incredulity.

Until then, we must endure the staring and natural fear of the unknown. Mara wouldn't be the first local to go through this cycle.

Six days later, Mochán still hadn't returned. I began to fret and watch the path to the cave whenever I could.

Aed poked me. "Nuala! Come on, you're blocking the path."

I gave him a glare, but kept moving. Our task today was to gather enough hay and wool to create comfortable beds for us and any guests.

Riordan had found a system of four interconnected caves and claimed them for our use. The wall in front of the largest one was to keep the weather out, and once the door was installed, it worked well.

Footsteps on the path made me stick my head out, but it was just Mara, carrying a bundle of sticks for the fire. I moved aside so she could pass, then I climbed back up the path.

Something was wrong, I just knew it in my bones. But no one was walking on the path now. Just a flock of crows picking at insects in the grass.

I hurried back to the cave, where Aed was arranging his sleeping area. As he glanced up, I said, "I'm going to search for Mochán."

"You're what? You can't just go, Nuala. You have no idea where he is."

I shook my head. "I don't care. He needs my help. I can feel it."

He let out a deep sigh. "Wait a moment. I'll go with you."

"Why?"

"He's my friend, too. You don't have a monopoly on him. Besides, if you get in trouble or too tired to fly, I can help."

I had to admit, his logic was sound. We let Riordan know our plan, and got details of where he'd parted ways with Mochán, and flew in that direction.

The curse-pain pressed in on me, but I pushed through. It almost made it difficult to breathe as I flew. But flying was faster than walking, and we quickly came to the crossroads Riordan had described.

Through a gritted beak, Aed asked, "Which way?"

I pointed down the east path. "That way. They came from the north and Riordan headed south."

We took wing again, and flew down this path toward an old forest, filled with underbrush and darkness. Rather than risking a flight through the branches, we waddled along the path as the canopy blocked sunlight.

"I don't like this, Nuala. Why would Mochán have come here?"

"I don't know. Maybe he was supposed to meet someone?"

Something rustled behind us, and I spun, but it was only a squirrel. My nerves were raw. We kept walking down the path.

A moan crept along the ground and I shivered. "Where's that coming from, Aed?"

He nosed through some bushes on the north side, then on the south, and moved further ahead. "Here!"

We shoved the bushes aside and found feet. After a few moments, we discovered the rest of Mochán, his skin hot with wound-fever. A gash on his arm wept pus and looked twice the size of the other.

"Mochán? Can you hear me?"

He moaned again, and his head thrashed back and forth.

I glanced down the path, wishing I could conjure up the village healer, but there was no one but us. For a moment, I considered sending Aed for a healer, but that would take too long.

It had been many, many winters since I'd attempted a healing. My healing magic had faded when I transformed into a swan. Several times over our curse, I'd tried to heal, and never got the results I wanted. But Mochán couldn't wait for anyone else. I'd have to try healing him myself.

Casting my mind back to before the curse, back when I was one of the People, with strong healing magic, I pulled the power up through the ground and into my body.

The magic resisted, kicking and jolting through my muscles. But my desperation would brook no mistakes, and I tamed it into useful power. Just a trickle at first, directly on Mochán's red arm, pouring into the festering wound.

I didn't know how he'd gotten the cut. I didn't need to know. I just needed to pour in my white-blue healing magic, now flowing better, stronger, than at first.

The angry, red edges of skin began to calm into healthy flesh. Mochán's face stopped sweating, and he looked like he was merely sleeping, rather than in the throes of a fever-dream.

But then my magic sputtered and stopped. I tried to begin the flow again and got a couple drops of power before it died again.

With a sob, I dug deep into the earth's well, searching for that vestige of healing magic, that last bit of power, but nothing came. The well was dry, at least for me.

I placed a wingtip on Mochán's cheek, and his skin was cooler, at least. He might even be able to rest normally now. And if he woke, we could walk him to our place.

Now that I was no longer working magic, the curse-pain throbbed through my entire body, making my knees buckle, and I fell next to my friend. Aed curled up next to me, and we all slept, exhausted.

As dawn broke, we each woke, including Mochán. He was incredibly weak, but he had regained his senses, and we led him home.

In the 605th winter of our curse (155 CE) 5 years later

Not as many students willing to brave our cave in our new home. We taught them the stories Hawlen taught me as a child. We sang of Nuada of the Silver Hand and of our battles with the Fomorians. We told of Parthalón and of the Fir Bolg tribes that once lived upon the island. With each new student, we sent ancient knowledge back into the world.

But despite our best efforts, the tales grew garbled. Other than the few Filíd who vowed to keep the stories accurate, most Gaels weren't trained to recall the precise details.

And yet the tales still lived, and that was more important. Memory was a magic that every creature had, to some extent. Memories kept things alive, vibrant, and vital. The memory of a loved one woke them in *Tir na nÓg*. The memory of a place brought it back to living color, though the reality might now lay crumbling, like our childhood home. Memory was a powerful enchantment, even in this world of scarce magic.

As today's class arrived, I sat on our lecture rock. It faced the riverbank, so I could watch for anyone approaching. Aed kept watch in the other direction as I taught, and then we'd switch posts.

Three children came today, all daughters of the local chieftain. He'd been impressed by our knowledge and sent them every other day.

I grinned as the youngest stuck her thumb in her mouth. "Today, I will tell you the story of the Dagda, the father god."

The eldest let out a sigh and rolled her eyes. I cocked my head at her. "Have you already heard this tale, then?"

"It's just more fairy stories. None of this is real."

I gave her a mock scowl. "I assure you, the Dagda is real. As is the Morrigan, Lugh, and Brigid. These are all gods and goddesses of our People."

She jutted her chin out. "Not of *my* people. *My* people are in the real world! *Yours* are all just in tales."

I cocked my head, trying not to chuckle. "And what about the tales makes you think they aren't true?"

"Because they're silly! They talk about magic and gold and madness. The one I heard yesterday was the worst, all about mad *tiarna* Tadhg."

Now my curiosity was piqued. "Please, tell me this tale."

The child crossed her arms with a pout. "*They* say he lives in a palace beneath the hills. And if anyone catches him, then he has to give them his pot of gold!"

I stifled a giggle. "I agree, that's silly. But it's not one of the tales I've told you. Someone else made up that story."

Her tale did make me wonder about the rest of our People. A few brave or foolish Gaels found their way beyond the veil to visit *Saol Eile*, but they seldom came out unscathed.

Sometimes they stayed three nights and three seasons had passed above the ground. Sometimes they returned with a curse or a blessing, such as a disfiguring hump, or incredible musical talent.

The Gaels seemed to have formed superstitions to keep us from cursing them. Bowls of milk or honey left out, bribes to keep us happy. As if we would stoop to skulking around some poor farmer's house for scraps!

Still, I suspect the People would crave such luxuries. I doubted they kept bees below the hills.

Mochán stayed with us as my best friend and my comfort. I snuggled up to him beside the campfire on cold nights as we told stories or played word games.

After the incident in the forest, he convinced me to practice healing magic again, though I remained leery of performing great works.

Conn still used magic to create his carvings, as Torr had taught him. We created a veil around our cave, to keep it from prying eyes unless we invited someone in.

In the harsh winter, strong ocean winds pounded against the cave with unleashed abandon and ice formed within the walls.

We hoarded furs and food against such times. To leave was both dangerous and foolish, so we huddled in a pile for warmth as the wind howled.

Summers, however, were warm and sweet and we reveled in the long days. We dove in and out of the waters of the cove, delighting in our freedom.

In the 676th winter of our curse (226 CE) 71 years later

I wheeled through the bright autumn sky, diving to examine the new village. Just a few houses at first, it had grown into a cluster of ten roundhouses, huddled around a fork in the river. But then someone came outside, and I soared away. I had no wish to be noticed.

On each of my scouting missions, I tried to push past the curse-limit a little more and noticed more of these villages growing across the countryside. At least our caves wouldn't be an attractive settlement for humans.

I returned to our hill, jutting out into the ocean. Dusk was already settling and mists were rising with the cool evening. As I flew above the path, I spied a man walking toward our home, a figure shrouded in the fog.

Wheeling in for a landing, I reached the ground just as Mochán emerged. I didn't have time to make it into hiding, so I took a risk, and greeted our visitor myself. He had a long, red beard and a wild look to his eyes. Despite my nerves, I forced myself to be polite. "We welcome you…"

The visitor's eyes grew wide, and he raised his fingers in the form of a cross, backing away from me.

"Wait, honored guest. We have—"

The big man ran away, and I turned to Mochán with a questioning glance. He gave a shrug, and we retreated to the cave for our supper.

The next night was a wild one, with fierce winds and rain blowing sideways. Despite the howling storm, we heard shouts outside.

I exchanged a glance with Aed, then with Mochán. We were without any other human companion at the moment. Riordan's grandson was our current guard, but he was off visiting his parents.

Mochán and I wrestled the door open and peered out to the hill, but I didn't see anything. Then I saw firelight. Men were carrying torches, marching down our path.

The fire sputtered and danced in the wind and the rain, but they burned strong enough that they didn't go out. Their shouts and screams echoed as they marched up the hill in the blustering wind.

Fear caught in my throat. I turned back into the cave. "Aed, Fiachra, Conn, get prepared to flee. If we must remain in the sky until they leave, we will."

Mochán stepped out to confront the mob, and my fear grew. How could one lone man of two hundred winters withstand this crowd of angry men and women?

Holding Riordan's spear across his chest, Mochán spoke in strident tones. "Halt! What is your purpose here?"

The man in front held a wooden cross in front of him like a weapon. "We come for the devils you're guarding!"

He let out a laugh. "I guard no devils. Go back to your warm, dry homes, my friends."

I recognized the leader from the other day, the man with the long, red beard. His voice was full of hatred. "The devils are here! I spoke with one of them! They took the form of a swan, and they are pure evil! God has commanded that we destroy all the devils!"

Several of the younger men ran around the united front and rushed toward us. I nodded to my brothers, and we took flight into the dusky evening storm. The headland disappeared in the mists below us, and winking torches dissolved into the night.

I didn't want to leave Mochán alone. Visions of him being attacked by the mob ran through my head over and over. So much that I forgot to pay attention to flying, and I faltered. I fell halfway to the ground before I corrected.

Aed came up next to me. "Nuala? What happened?"

I stared down, though I could only see the dancing torches flickering in the wind. "It's just not right to leave Mochán like that. I'm going back."

Without waiting for his response, I dove toward the mob, intent on frightening them away. As I came close, I screamed and rushed past them, my wings wide.

Some of them scattered. Good.

I did another flyby, with more shrieking. I must have seemed like an air phantasm.

Or a devil. Just like they said.

It didn't matter to me, because it was working. More and more people were fleeing the crowd, leaving just a few left to endanger Mochán.

Aed now flew next to me, then Conn and Fiachra. Together, we dove over and over again, scattering the last of the attackers.

Finally, the last man, with the red beard, ran away, and we landed again, utterly exhausted but at the same time, exhilarated that we'd protected ourselves and our friend.

After that, with Mochán's help, we created strong veils around our hill, so none could approach without our knowledge. It was the only way I could sleep at night.

In the 686th winter of our curse (236 CE) 10 years later

I'd created a new garden plot on the hill, bigger than the one in the north. I was pulling weeds with my bill one fair summer day when a warrior party arrived.

We offered bread and milk as proper guest gifts. They sat with us around the fire, exchanging stories.

I peered at one man with a suspicious gaze, as he was no Gael. He looked like one of the People, but so old. His familiarity hovered on the edge of my mind, but I couldn't place him.

Ciaran was telling a story of a harrowing hunt. When the man laughed, a flash of memory gave me his young face. I stripped away the long, white beard and the tanned skin. I erased the sagging wrinkles and recognized Aed Mòr, the son of the late *ard-rí*, Bodb Dearg.

The last time I saw him was at the wedding feast, when Tadhg married Aillbha and my father married Aoife Rua. I swallowed, my throat dry with nostalgia, rage, and memory.

How could he still live above the hills? Didn't he move below, like all the other People? He was traveling the land, fighting with the Fianna, the Gaelic warriors.

I glanced at my brothers, but they didn't seem to recognize him. Maybe Aed Mòr had a child with the Gaels, and I was just seeing a family resemblance.

He laughed again, at something Fergus, his war leader, said. No, it must be him.

I cleared my throat, and everyone stared at me. "We're honored to have such fine warriors visit and sup with us. I would like to offer a toast of thanks. It has been many winters since we entertained one of our own People." I nodded to Aed Mòr.

Aed stared at the man and Conn gasped. Fiachra narrowed his gaze.

The visitor stood and bowed. "I hoped you might recall me, *Bantiarna*. I'm indeed honored you recognized me. I thought it unlikely, given so many winters had passed. I should have had faith you'd know me yet."

Mochán's lips pursed, but Ciaran let out a whoop and clapped. "We have a reunion! More drinks all around. A song is in order. Nuala, could you sing us something of that time? A song your People loved, perhaps?"

Which would be a good representation of the Tuatha Dé? A battle song? A love song? An origin song? I decided on one of the many songs about my parents' love. After my first few hesitant words, everyone fell silent.

Cliach had written this song, so many winters ago. Tears glistened in Aed's eyes after the first line. The twins followed suit, sniffling when I paused.

I worked hard to keep the tears from my voice until the song finished, but my voice grew hoarse and throaty near the end. I drank my mead to clear the pain.

I was relieved to pull back from the center of attention after that, as the mead made me dizzy. Fiachra told a story of a battle with the Fomorians.

I ached to ask Aed Mòr why he'd left our people, but then I asked myself if I mightn't have done the same thing, if I wasn't cursed. I'd always loved the open sky and storms.

Aed Mòr rewarded our performances with one of his own, a tale of the leader of the Fianna, a warrior named Fionn MacCumhall. This man was a great athlete who had magic and wisdom beyond his age. Magic enough for a Gael, at least. He couldn't have the magic of the People.

Tales of his prowess were enough for me to question my cynicism. Maybe that's why Aed Mòr left the People to seek battle and glory like any good warrior, and he found it with this Gael leader.

I sat beside Mochán among these strange warriors. He was a rock, someone I went to for advice and comfort. He put an arm around my shoulders and gave me a squeeze.

He smiled, his white teeth glowing in the firelight. "Are you upset, Nuala? You needn't be. These are honorable men."

"I have no doubt, Mochán. I'm just not used to strangers."

He cocked his head. "But you have new children here every season."

I shrugged. "That's different. They're coming to us for something. useful. Besides, I made a vow to my raven many winters ago to keep her knowledge alive."

I stopped for a moment, catching my breath at grief for Hawlen. "But these men, they have no need of us. When people have no need for magic, they don't understand it. That ignorance can turn to mistrust and then to fear. I've seen what fear does to people."

I recalled that mob who had attacked us 10 winters earlier and shivered. Since that time, I had been distrustful of others.

Usually, such mistrust was misplaced, such as in Mochán's case. There were few people I trusted more, outside my own brothers. On lonely nights, that madman's face taunted me in the flickering firelight. He haunted my dreams, along with my stepmother's laughter.

Aed Mòr's voice cut through my thoughts. "Are you well, Nuala?"

I shook my head. "Just remembering things long past."

"Will it please you for me to take back word of you to our People, Nuala? I would be happy to do so. I visit *Saol Eile* every few winters."

I wished Hawlen was there, so I could send word to her, but I nodded, unable to speak for the tears.

Chapter Nineteen

In the 727th winter of our curse (277 CE) 41 years later

Ciaran had long since left us for marriage with a local woman, a sweet, round girl who cooked wondrous meals. No other warrior had committed themselves to our care in his place, but his sons and grandsons came to check on us.

Storms still frightened me. I knew on a visceral level that Aoife Rua was still out there. While I hadn't heard her mad laughter for many winters, I knew she hadn't yet left this world.

Fiachra got into a series of scrapes with the fishermen along the coast.

First, he'd raided their catch, coming back with several fish in his bill, trying hard to smother the laughter. I told him it wasn't a joke to steal someone's livelihood and made him return them with an apology.

Second, he'd played a prank on Mochán, switching his mead for vinegar. This time, I'd forced him to work for the replacement mead, as honey was difficult to trade for.

This time, just as a winter storm was brewing, he'd torn a farmer's barn door off its hinges.

When the farmer came to complain, I lost my temper. "What were you even thinking, Fiachra? Or should I even ask?"

He paced back and forth, but didn't answer me, just sending me glares every time he turned.

"Why can't you just keep away from them? I swear, you're more trouble than Aed and Conn put together."

More pacing, but no answers.

"Well? What do you have to say for yourself?"

He halted, bursting out with, "I can't stay in here anymore, Nuala. I have to get outside."

"Fiachra, be reasonable. The ice is coming. You can feel it as well as I can."

He shook his feathers. "I don't care. I am so weary of staring at these boring old walls, I could scream. I must leave, if only for a few hours."

Glowering clouds were dark and the horizon misty gray with snow. "No, you can't leave now."

Fiachra begged. "An hour, just an hour."

I threw up my wings. "Fine. I don't care anymore. Go fly for an hour. But if you aren't back before the snow starts and I have to come searching for you…"

He rolled his eyes. "I know, I know. More work for me tomorrow."

I ignored his grumbles as he launched into the mist. As soon as he disappeared from sight, a rough squall blew up.

After a half hour, I grew worried. I didn't sense him in the rain. "Conn, can you feel Fiachra's silver chain?"

Conn cocked his head and closed his eyes. "I can't find him. Wait, no, it's just faint. To the north."

I paced in the main chamber, my mind racing. More of us going out in this storm was a horrible idea, but I couldn't risk letting Fiachra get lost.

Curse him for going out in this. "I'm going to find him. This storm is turning nasty, and he could be hurt. Watch for us, will you? Wake Aed if we're not back in a half hour."

I barely waited for his nod before I flew out of the cave. The arctic shock of the sleet left me gasping.

As the sleet stung my eyes, I squinted and sped toward the north. I quested for Fiachra's chain, but could only sense the steady pounding of wintry rain and the vague discomfort of leaving the curse area. The pain grew as I flew north and I still couldn't find him. "Fiachra! Fiachra, where are you!"

A faint tug drew me toward a stand of pine trees on the shore. A flash of white in the rain, bright white that shouldn't be there.

I dove toward it and found Fiachra huddling under the roots of a fallen tree. "Fiachra, what are you playing at? You're well beyond the curse-limit. Aren't you in pain?"

My brother's voice was full of sullen anger. "Of course I am, but I'm done with it. I don't care if it hurts."

He launched into the air, dipping and wheeling, and I raced to catch up. The squall pounded us, and I had to yell. "Done with it? By Sweet Danu, what do you mean by that?"

He banked left and I followed. "I'm tired of being bound to this place, to any place. If I die, so be it. At least I'll have escaped."

"Fiachra, you're just upset and frustrated. I know how you feel."

He sent me a glare. "You don't! You never did. You were already an adult when we changed. I'm stuck at ten winters old. Forever a child trapped in a cygnet's body! I don't even have the strength you do."

Finally, he settled on a rocky outcropping, and I perched next to him, already exhausted from flying in the rain and battling the curse-pain.

He let out a long sigh before speaking. "For seven hundred and thirty winters, I've been stuck like this, Nuala. Seven hundred and thirty! It's just not fair. It's more than anyone can handle. I'm done."

Before I could answer, he launched again into the storm. Hail the size of walnuts struck my body. "Fiachra! Fiachra, come back now!"

He kept flying until I lost sight of him. I quested and found the faint trace of his chain. I followed, pushing past the pain.

But I couldn't catch him. He had the speed of madness and desperation. How would I make him stop? I cast my mind for a solution, anything to keep him from destroying himself.

Maybe I could heal him. This was like an illness, right? It had been so long since I healed.

I pushed my will through the silver chain link. A faint connection clicked and I pushed harder. I had to fly through the rain after him, not hit any trees, all while working magic. I despaired for it working, but I had to try.

Pushing more and more, the magic touched his mind. A wild maelstrom of anger and frustration, pain and fear. I soothed it, calmed the lunacy, the fear, the pain. I drew the pain into myself and away from Fiachra.

The icy-white folly struck me like a wall, and I fell. Down I tumbled, down to the earth. I hit something soft and then everything went black.

Ravens found me. Not the intelligent, magical creatures I'd known all my life. These were dumb birds with no native magic at all. Still, they found me.

Their beaks pricked my feathers, and I woke in a strange place. Surrounding shapes loomed up with mad screams and laughter. Had Aoife found me once again? Pain throbbed through my body, my head felt ready to split open, and I cried out. I batted at things I sensed but couldn't see.

The black birds picked at me with their beaks and cawed as I hit them. Black wings fluttered with white, and I was drowning in my ancient nightmare.

I screamed, and my throat hurt.

"Shh, Nuala, you're here, you're safe. We're here."

It sounded like Mochán, but the voice came from a raven's beak. Another raven ducked and spoke with Aed's voice. "Nuala, stop hitting us!"

I didn't understand, but I grew tired. My wings drooped and I slept again.

Swirling into an abyss of pain and fear, I found no purchase, no rest for my weary wings or my scarred heart. Cruel, icy winds buffeted me against unyielding sea stacks, breaking my feathers and my bones. White waves crashed on the shore, horses rushing toward the land, trampling my crumpled body.

I cried, oh, how I cried. For comfort, for rest, for just a moment to catch my breath. No rest came, no rescue came, and no heart comforted me.

In the 747th winter of our curse (297 CE) 20 years later

Light burned my eyelids and roused me from terrifying dreams. When I opened my eyes, it pierced through to my soul, and I cried out. Pain throbbed, and I let out a pitiful whimper. Warm arms held me and crooned until I fell back into sleep.

I don't know how many times this happened, but it seemed eternal. Over and over again, I woke from my nightmares, to be comforted and fed, only to fall back into pain and anger.

Through all this, I searched for Fiachra, trying to find him and finding only icy hail, fierce white feathers, or angry, dumb ravens.

Flashes of darkness and light finally faded, and I emerged from the blackness. When I opened my eyes, the light didn't hurt.

Mochán appeared with a bowl of broth, his mouth agape. "Mochán? What happened?"

My friend cried out, "You're back! Oh, Sweet, Blessed Danu, you're back with us again."

He shut his eyes and raised his head as if thanking the gods for answering a prayer.

"What happened? How long was I ill? And where's Fiachra? Did you find him?" I tried moving my wings, but I felt as weak as a babe. I must have been ill a long time.

He sat next to me, his hand on my wing. "Fiachra is fine, my love. How long isn't important. What's important is that you're well again. Aed, fetch the twins. They'll want to welcome their sister back to this world."

This world? Did the mad go elsewhere? A visit to *Tír na nÓg*? I shuddered. If that was what the Afterlife was like, I wanted no part of it.

My friend had new strands of silver glinting in his blond hair. Had he aged so much, nursing me through madness?

Conn walked in, took one look at me, and then turned to a young woman I didn't recognize. "Orlagh, fetch Fiachra. He should be at the apiary."

Apiary? When did we start keeping bees? How long had it *really* been?

My voice sounded rough and faint. "Mochán, tell me the truth." I cleared my throat and tried again. "How long has it been?"

He dropped his gaze. "Over twenty winters, my *bantiarna*."

I shot up, horrified. "Twenty winters! By the Gods, how was I ill so long?"

He gently pushed me back down on the bed. "Your magic healed Fiachra, but you took his madness. He found you and brought you back but being in the storm had taken its toll. You were raving mad for many moons."

He swallowed and placed a hand on my wing before going on. "Then you just weren't here. You woke often enough that we could feed you, but you made no sense. You couldn't even speak words, just sobs and screams. I thought we'd lost you for good." A tear ran down his cheek. "But you're back now."

I gave him a solemn nod. "But I'm back now. I don't know where I may have gone, but it was horrible and confusing. I'm certain Aoife Rua was there, as I heard her laughter."

I shuddered and hoped never to be there again.

In the 898th winter of our curse (448 CE) 151 years later

Our end was near. No, not our deaths, but the end of our curse. Just two more turns of the seasons, and we'd be ourselves again. Even though that might seem like a long time, for us it was but a blink of the eye.

It was difficult to keep us from bursting out into song or prolonged flight in our joy. The biggest feast, the most outrageous gathering, with flower garlands everywhere, something we had waited for all our lives, was on the horizon.

Despite our desperate anticipation, some nights I returned to the madness. My nightmares came stronger than ever before, memories from my madness. Some nights, I screamed everyone awake and couldn't stop except with Mochán's hugs and songs.

One of our favorite pastimes on long, winter nights was making guesses on how the curse would end.

Fiachra said, "Maybe we'll just be really, really old? Decrepit and bent over, having to use canes to walk?"

Conn made a rude noise. "But that wouldn't be fair. We should be as we were at transformation. Young, vital, and able to live our lives at long last."

I cocked my head. "Do you think we'll be able to live a full lifetime? The three or four centuries our People normally live?"

Aed gave a shrug. "Maybe just a Gael lifetime. We live in their world now."

"Yes, but that couldn't have been part of Aoife Rua's original curse, could it?"

Aed rolled his eyes. "I wouldn't put any cruelty past her. She knew we were all moving below the hills. Why not add that aspect?"

I had other thoughts, ones that involved Mochán, but I kept those to myself. He was devoted and we loved each other, but what if only loved me as an enchanted creature of legend? Would he be disenchanted when I wasn't a swan?

As we did on many evenings, especially as the end of the curse grew closer, we examined each of the terms, each word burnt into our memories.

Mochán recited them, one by one.

And when at last your time has done, the bells of the New God shall ring.

And when a tiarna *of the north weds a* banríon *of the south,*
Only then may you return to your true forms once again.

We'd never really figured out what these lines meant for certain, so we kept trying to decipher them. I asked, "Any new ideas on what she meant?"

Mochán pursed his lips. "The bells of the New God. Could she have meant the Christos? His religion is growing strong now. That priest from Rome, Patricius, has run all up and down the countryside, leaving converts in his wake."

I shook my head. "She couldn't have predicted him, though. Besides, he's a minor god. He couldn't even save his only son from dying, from what I hear."

Conn fluttered his wings. "But she didn't specify how big a god, or even which one, just a *new god.* He's new, at least to our island. Maybe that's all the curse needs?"

I shrugged. "Assuming that's true, how do we ring his bell?"

Mochán pointed to the southwest. "On an island not far from here, *Inis Gluaire,* lives a community of his priests. They have a bell, and they ring it every hour."

Aed scowled. "Every hour? Whatever for? Doesn't that annoy everyone?"

The ollamh gave a half-smile. "To remind them to pray."

We all shared a laugh, and Fiachra said, "Remind them? Every hour? How could they forget? In fact, how would they sleep? Sounds like torture, not worship."

"It's quite a relaxing process. Or so my friend Caomhóg tells me."

I wasn't familiar with that name. "Caomhóg? Is he one of their priests, or is he an ollamh?"

Mochán gave a grin. "He's no Filí, I assure you. Yes, he's a priest, though newly sanctified. He joined them a few winters ago. He grew up in my village. The priests farm, raise bees, and help the hungry and sick. They have little magic and their God seems harsh, but they are content, and they help people."

Aed asked, "Is this island with the bell close enough for us to visit, within the curse-limit? We could fly there on the last day."

Mochán furrowed his brow. "No, it's many leagues away. You wouldn't hear the bell from here. I don't know if you would be able to fly that far against the curse-pain. But I'll ask my friend to visit, as he might have a solution. Must the bell be heard from here?"

We all exchanged glances and shrugged.

But I was curious about this new God. "Bring your friend anyhow, Mochán. I should like to meet him."

Conn put a wing on Mochán's arm. "What about the other terms? The *tiarna* of the north and the *banríon* of the south?"

Chapter Twenty

Mochán discovered names of all the unwed *tiarnaí* in the north, as well as any *banríona* who were unmarried. We pored over them, looking for likely matches.

We had so little control over the other aspects of our curse, it felt good to actually do something about it, to try to enact a match.

We had three choices for *tiarnaí*. One, in the far northwest, along the *Dún na nGall* coast. Another was far to the east. But one held land nearby, just north of us at Clogher. And one of the *banríona* was close to us.

I glanced north, toward Clogher. "If we can send a delegation to this *Tiarna* Lairgenn, do you think we could then arrange a meeting with *Banríon* Deoch? We couldn't negotiate a marriage contract, but we could at least arrange a meeting."

Mochán tapped his chin. "I should go, not you. It's too dangerous for you to go out in the world. What if you were hurt?"

I shook my head. "No. It must be us. They might mistrust a human and believe it to be a trick. But four enchanted swans? They'd have to honor our advice as legendary beings. Sometimes fame can have advantages."

"I don't like it. What about your curse-pain?"

I exchanged a glance with Aed and let out a deep sigh. "We can endure it for a while, if it helps to end our curse."

Conn and Fiachra chimed in with their agreement, and Fiachra instantly started planning the trip, full of enthusiasm.

We borrowed a horse and cart from the villagers so we wouldn't have to fly, and one came along for added safety. On the day we set out, my mind whirled with how we should present the idea to the *tiarna*.

After a few hours along a very bumpy trail, my body was already sore and battered, and regretted this whole mad plan.

As we approached the hillfort, anxiety gripped my throat. What if we were walking into danger? I almost launched into the air to fly back, but Aed was on one side of me, with Mochán on the other, and the twins behind me. I drew courage from them all.

We requested an audience with the *tiarna*, interrupting his midday meal. *Tiarna* Lairgenn was a burly man, reminding me of Bodb Dearg.

I swallowed away my worries. "My *tiarna*, I come to you with a proposal for a future bride."

He stopped eating with a chicken leg halfway to his mouth. "A bride, you say? And who would this woman be, who asks a swan to negotiate. Is the woman actually a raven? Or maybe she's a gull? Oh, I know! A puffin. Preening all summer long, with fish in her mouth."

As he howled with laughter at his own joke, I held my temper in check. "I understand there is a *banríon* to the south, by name of Deoch. She's in need of a husband."

He gave another chuckle and washed his mouthful of chicken down with ale, then let out a loud burp. "Is she, now? I've heard of her great wealth. How much is she willing to pay?"

I had to turn to Mochán, who had knowledge of modern customs, to finish the actual negotiations. We hadn't exactly asked Deoch's permission, first. However, we hammered out a decent proposal to present to the *banríon*.

Once we escaped the hillfort, I let out a deep sigh. "I don't like him. I hope that this *banríon* Deoch doesn't destroy us for even suggesting such a match."

But then, our plans were delayed, for when we approached *Banríon* Deoch, we discovered she was traveling, and wouldn't be back for several moons. Defeated, we returned to our home to wait.

About a moon later, on a sunny afternoon, we were teaching five of the children from the nearby village. I sent them scurrying home when a warrior appeared, striding down our path.

He'd pierced our veil, so he must have magic. We five stood, with Mochán in the middle. Our current guard, Clodagh, had gone to the village for supplies, so we were alone.

When the visitor came within shouting distance, Mochán met him. "Hail, friend! What brings you to this place?"

He was tall and blond like Mochán, but much more powerfully built. His shoulders were broad, covered in leather and iron. He wore a long sword across his back and the cold iron pulsed from where he stood.

I shivered. We couldn't stand the touch of iron, though the Gaels loved it. They made weapons and tools from the vile stuff, while ours were bronze.

I whispered, "get ready to fly, brothers."

The man shouted, "My name is Gadhra, and I come to speak with the enchanted ones, if I might. I come in peace. May I be your guest?"

I didn't like it, but we didn't want to turn away a true supplicant. He'd claimed guest-rights, and we were obligated to offer him the protection of our home.

I stepped forward. "I welcome you, you and your kin."

After I finished the rest of the greeting, he glanced around and seeing no walls, let out a hearty laugh. "I accept your welcome, despite your lack of walls to be safe within. But I have brought gifts of wine and song."

Despite my trepidation, we sat around the outdoor fire pit. I didn't wish to invite him below the cliff to our cave, as he made me uncomfortable. I'd grown paranoid in my old age.

Once everyone had food and drink, I turned to our guest. "What brings you to visit us?"

He gave a wide grin. "I come bearing greetings from my mistress, the *Banríon* Deoch. She's the daughter of the *Tiarna* of Munster and has heard of your visit. She offers an invitation to meet her."

I exchanged a glance with Mochán and then Aed. She must have heard about our attempt to see her.

Fiachra eyed the man, who still wore his smile. "What sort of gifts?"

He reached into a sack to his belt. He pulled out four golden torc collars. "These are from the *banríon*."

Intertwining knotwork decorated the edge of each collar with red and white gold, each torc head a delicate carved swan head.

He offered me one and I nodded permission. After placing it around my neck, he did the same for each of my brothers. The strange weight felt heavy on my neck.

As soon as the fourth collar snapped into place, I grew dizzy. I focused on the warrior, but he swayed back and forth. No, *I* was swaying.

Suddenly I collapsed. Every muscle in my body relaxed, and though I strained to move, I couldn't.

From somewhere far away, Mochán shouted. Gadhra's voice, now harsh and demanding, yelled back.

A clash of weapons. Flesh hitting flesh. Someone falling on the ground. I prayed Mochán was unhurt, but my mind couldn't focus on anything. Instead, I drifted into a soft place, warm and comfortable.

Gadhra lifted each of us to a cart in the trees. One by one, he placed us inside and covered us with a piece of leather. Then, nothing but darkness. The jostling of the cart lulled me to sleep.

Voices roused me, more angry words, then wicked laughter. Despite aching pain, I just wanted to sleep. Maybe just a little nap.

Finally, the cart stopped again. I was loath to leave the comfort of its familiar walls, but Gadhra lifted each of us, placing us in a cage.

Soft pillows covered the floor, but the bars were of cold iron. The bars made my skin itch and I cringed away. Touching them would burn. I huddled in the center with my brothers and let out a low, mournful wail.

"Now, now, none of that, my '*bantiarna*.' You'll get used to your new home, I'm certain. *Banríon* Deoch will be out to greet you properly."

When Gadhra left, I struggled to lift my head, fighting against the fatigue. I heard horses, though I only saw stalls. The stink of dung and hay was strong, as well as rotten, soiled hay. That didn't bode well for our own care as captives.

For captives we were. Had we upset her with our visit? But she didn't even know why we'd come. Maybe her actions weren't a direct result of our meddling, and she just desired to possess us. For what purpose? For status? A craving for unique possessions?

I'd known others like that, ruled by their desire for things. Collectors were one thing, but some had an insatiable gluttony for acquiring objects to the detriment of sense.

Finally able to focus a little more, I pushed at the collars with magic, but they were strong. I was weak with their sleep power, but at least the pain of our curse seemed dulled. "Aed, Aed can you wake? Fiachra? Conn? I need your help."

A low moan from Conn answered my prodding. "Where are we?"

"We've been kidnapped and these collars are keeping us sleepy. I need to push against them, but I need your help."

Fiachra yawned and Aed stirred.

"Aed, wake up! I need all of us together."

"Let me sleep, Nuala. Just a little more. Just a little—"

I kicked him and he whined, "Hey!"

"I said, wake up! I need you."

Aed gave a sleepy wave of his wing. "You need nothing, Nuala. You never did. 'Cept Mochán."

"Be quiet and help me work magic."

He pouted and kept silent but kept his eyes open. I drew in magic with a tuneless note. Since I'd been a swan, my magic was attuned to fire. However, I had no fire, so water would have to do.

There wasn't much water nearby, only a trough for the horses with stale, old rainwater, and bits of hay floating on top.

However, beneath the earth, I sensed a trickle. Conn and Fiachra added their water affinity and soon the strength of our magic grew.

Aed rubbed his eyes and concentrated on his air power. I pushed against my collar first, willing it to open, and it just rattled.

Closing my eyes, I drew more from the underground stream. I followed it to its source, a spring two leagues to the north. I pulled from this primal source and a powerful vent of magic flowed.

This time, the collar creaked open. Quickly, Fiachra shoved his wingtips under it, straining to pry it open. Conn added his wingtips, and they cracked it wide enough to get my neck out. I flung it to the side of the cage. It sizzled and popped when it touched the iron bars. I shivered.

My head cleared and the magical flow rushed through me, no longer blocked by the collar. I concentrated on Aed's.

This time, the magic flowed much stronger, and his was easier to break. We'd just popped it off when footsteps approached.

I ducked my head under my wing, so our visitor didn't notice my missing collar. Aed did the same, while Conn shoved a pillow over, so the collars were hidden from view.

The agony of our curse-pain burst upon me. Sweet Danu, but it hurt. I almost wished to put the collar back on, since it had obviously suppressed the pain.

The woman was covered in gold jewelry and velvet, all in rich colors. "Ah, our guests have arrived. How lovely to receive you, my fellow royalty."

Deoch was tall, with blonde hair arranged in elaborate braids, and a gold circlet draped with chains on her head. Her voice was sweet and honeyed, and I almost fell beneath its spell. She carried great magic herself.

Her eyes were quite mad.

"Hmm?" I answered, feigning sleepiness.

"I do apologize for the manner of your arrival. I had to be certain you accepted my invitation, didn't I? You shall be allowed more freedom once we're assured of your loyalty."

Deoch's voice pressed against my mind. I recognized this style of magic. Aoife Rua had used it upon us, so many, many winters ago.

I closed my eyes again, pretending to sleep.

"I shall allow you to rest from your journey. Gadhra will be back to provide a guest-right's portion of food and drink. It would not do to neglect such niceties. Especially after you were so solicitous of my happiness. Imagine, being so kind as to arrange a marriage with that boorish lout."

She left in a flurry of laughter, her jewelry jangling with each step. Aed watched her leave. I waited several moments before I opened my eyes.

My eldest brother shook his head. "That was some powerful woman."

Fiachra snorted. "Are you enchanted by her, Aed? Do you want to run away and be her pet?"

Aed glared over his shoulder. "Of course not. But her power tastes familiar."

"Quickly, we need to break the other collars before Gadhra returns." I pulled the magic again, this time with Aed's full power to bolster mine. We snapped both Conn and Fiachra's quickly, and we hid the collars under the pillows.

Aed's eyes looked strained. "But how are we going to escape the cage? The collars must have been blocking our curse-pain, because now I hurt."

I didn't know if we could do more magic with this agony. And we wouldn't sway Gadhra with logic. Anyone who punched an ollamh wasn't a man of reason or sympathy. But we might still persuade him with magic. Something subtle, that he didn't recognize as a spell.

Conn cocked his head. "Do you think we could sing? We might lull our captor asleep when he opened the cage for food?"

I clapped a wing on his shoulder. "I was just thinking along the same lines, my brother. A wordless song, one he might not suspect. Sing low, so it builds on him. Let's start now to build strength."

We hummed a low, sad tune, a sweet lullaby to relax the worried mind. We arranged ourselves so each of us covered the others' bare necks, in a pile of white, somnolent feathers.

The power built slowly, subtly, almost like a pool of gentle water around us, invisible but strong.

An hour later, our captor returned with a tray of bread, milk, and cheese. He placed it on the ground while he unlocked the cage. "Awake are you, now? That's a lovely tune. I hope you remember it for your hostess. She loves music. Ah, such sweet music."

Gadhra knelt to pick up the tray but hesitated. Then he closed his eyes and sat next to the open cage door. I pushed more somnolent magic through the music, willing him to relax, calm his mind, and rest his eyes.

He stirred once or twice, but after several moments, he snored.

I whispered, "Quickly now and quietly. Conn, you first. Don't jostle him. I wish he'd sat somewhere other than the doorway."

Once Conn and Fiachra were clear, Aed gestured for me to slide past the sleeping guard.

I shook my head. "No, you first. Stop arguing and go!"

Gadhra stirred and I went back to singing. As I left, my wingtip brushed the edge of the cage and fire burned up my arm. "Ouch!"

The guard's eyes flew open just as Aed took flight. "Hey! Get back here!" He grabbed my foot and yanked me back. I beat his head with my wings as the curse-pain flooded me in waves.

My brothers attacked his face with small rocks and sticks, pelting him with the objects. Aed grabbed a wooden bucket and dropped it on him. Gadhra covered his head with a curse.

As soon as he let go of my foot, we took flight. As we soared upwards, into the bright day, reveling in our freedom, everything darkened.

No clouds blocked the sun, but a shadow crept over us like a murmuration of starlings. Laughter danced on the wind, and it whipped at us, slamming me into a tree. I recognized that laughter and my blood chilled.

My brothers wheeled back for me, but I gestured them on. "No, keep going! Don't let her get us all!" But they didn't listen.

"So, you thought to escape so easily?"

I expected Aoife's voice, but instead heard Deoch's. "It took me many years to find a human willing to work with me, but now I can do so much more!"

Branches grabbed at my wings, tangling my feathers in painful twists. They tore my wings and scratched my belly. I struggled and pushed with all my strength, but they held fast.

So close to the end of the curse, and Aoife still found us. It just wasn't fair!

"That's one! And now for your dear, sweet brothers. You'll all look lovely displayed in my feast hall at the spring gathering, trophies worthy of a great *banríon*!"

Another tree reached for Aed, but the swaying branches missed. Not even magical trees were as fast as a swan on the wing.

Fiachra dove and banked, teasing the branches, taunting them into reaching for him, then crashing sideways to break them.

Conn and Aed followed his example, and soon, there weren't enough branches to capture them. They dove toward my wooden cage and barreled into me.

"Oof!"

Fiachra took off again and wheeled back. "Sorry, that's the only way to break it!"

He hit me again, breaking more branches. I was able to wriggle out of the remaining ones. Freed, I wasted no time in flying away. Aoife's mad cries of outrage faded as we pumped our wings back to our home. The curse-pain showed us the way.

By the time we returned to *Irrus Domnann*, we were exhausted, hungry and in no mood for anything but sleep, real sleep. Mochán wasn't there, and I worried he'd gone searching for us, but I had no energy to find him. We bolstered our veil with what little magical strength we had left.

A week later, we'd recovered our full strength from the ordeal. Mochán had gone to visit a friend and would return soon. I spent my days watching the path for him.

Despite having nightmares from the incident, we still treasured each visitor we received, each child we taught, and each new thing we learned. And when I spied our friend coming over the hill, I bowled him over until we were both flailing and laughing.

There may have been a hint of desperation in my own laughter, after the horrid experience with Deoch. I hated being alone now.

Once he'd settled back into his place, Mochán mentioned his friend would arrive the next day to meet us.

I narrowed my gaze. "Please say he doesn't have gold torcs for gifts, Mochán."

My love laughed. "Indeed not! He has no gold. He does, however, bring lovely gifts for you. Wheaten bread, sweet goat's cheese, and fresh honey."

A storm earlier in the season had destroyed our precious apiaries, so my mouth watered in anticipation of this treat.

Fiachra did a celebratory flight around the fire. "What's his name, Mochán? Have we met him before?"

The ollamh shook his head. "No, but I'm sure I've mentioned him. My priest friend, Caomhóg. He lives on *Inis Gluaire*, an island not far from here, the place with the bell."

Fiachra intoned the words of the curse with no inflection, though we'd all memorized it many centuries past.

For three hundred winters, you shall bide, upon this Lough Derravaragh.

For three hundred winters, you shall bide, upon the Sruth na Maoile.

For three hundred winters, you shall bide, upon Irrus Domnann.

And when at last your time has done, the bells of the New God shall ring.

And when a tiarna of the north weds a banríon of the south,

Only then may you return to your true forms once again.

Conn asked, "Will your priest friend be willing to help us on our last day of the curse, with his religious bell?"

"I'm sure he will. Ollamh lore fascinates him, much to the chagrin of his superiors. In fact, he's lost standing with his brothers for his friendship with me and his endless fascination in the old tales. I think you'll like him."

I looked forward to meeting this new man with equal parts trepidation and eagerness.

The next day, when Caomhóg strode up our path, I studied the short, stout, bald man. He wasn't old, but he did roll when he walked, like a goose.

He opened his arms wide as he approached. "Greetings and salutations, my good folk. It is such a pleasure to meet you. I've heard wondrous tales and legends of your lives."

I greeted him formally. "I welcome you, you and your kin. I welcome you into our homes. I welcome you to our bread and our ale. Be safe and sound within our walls."

I presented him with a gift, one of Conn's bone carvings. He accepted it with a bow and exclaimed at its beauty. "Ah, I have no kin left, my dear, but I thank you for your gracious welcome."

He shrugged a pack from his back and presented us with bread, cheese, and a jar of honey.

As we passed these treats around, Conn asked, "Tell me of your god, Caomhóg. What's he like?"

I chided my brother. "Conn, let the man relax before grilling him about his religion. Where are your manners?"

Despite my words, I was curious about Caomhóg's God, and it was a growing religion in today's world, so I wanted the details. Shortly, we'd live in this new world in our proper forms. We needed to understand what this God demanded of his followers.

Caomhóg laughed. "That's quite all right, my dear. I am happy to speak of my Lord. Conn, is it? Conn, my God is benevolent. We like to think he is a good God."

Fiachra asked, "Like the Dagda?"

Our guest tapped his chin. "Hmm. No, not quite like the Dagda. He's more distant than that fine god. He's more like Danu herself. He doesn't interact as much with daily life but created everything around us."

Aed asked, "How can your God—what's his name?—and Danu both be the Creators?"

"We don't know God's true name, but he's known by many. His son, Jesus, was born a man and sacrificed himself for the good of all sinners, but he's also an aspect of his father."

Fiachra cut in, "Wait, he's a god and his son's a god?"

I asked, "So you *do* have many gods? I thought this religion had just one?"

He blinked, as if surprised a woman asked such a question. "Why yes, my dear, we are a monotheistic religion, but our God has several aspects. We call him a Trinity. The Father, the Son, and the Holy Ghost."

Fiachra jumped up. "Like The Morrigan! She has three faces, too. Morrigan, Banbha, and Macha."

Caomhóg shrugged. "Our God differs greatly from The Morrigan. But if you'd like to learn more, we hold services each week with stories of our beliefs. Mochán tells me your curse may soon end?"

I gave a cautious nod. "Assuming the other terms of the curse are met, in two winters."

The priest cocked his head. "And what are the terms of the curse, may I ask?"

I had a flash of danger. Why did he need to know? Did he want to capture us? No, I gazed into his eyes, and he seemed interested. But after our kidnapping, my worry seemed justified.

Mochán answered for us. "First, that they bide for three hundred winters in three successive places. *Irrus Domnann* is their third term. Second, that the bell of the new God rings. Third, that a *tiarna* of the north wed a *banríon* of the south."

He scratched his head. "Well, the time is the easiest one. As for the bell, I'm certain the bell of my church would qualify. Must you be within hearing?"

Fiachra let out a snort. "We don't know. Our stepmother didn't give any explanation."

Caomhóg gave a full-belly laugh. "Indeed not! Well, we may have to relocate for the bell. The last bit, the wedding? That's soon to come. A Donegal *tiarna* is betrothed to a daughter of the Munster *tiarna*."

Aed asked, "Her name isn't Deoch, is it?"

I shuddered and wanted to shrink back into my cave at the mention of her name.

The priest shook his head. "No, no, her name is something with an 'R.' Rian, perhaps? Regardless, they are to be wed next week and the *tiarnaí* are already gathering in Donegal for the feast."

He paused to take a bite of his honey-drenched bread. "That should satisfy the third part. You're more than welcome to attend our church on the final day. We'd welcome you with open arms."

Aed shook his head. "But we are Tuatha Dé Dannan, not Gael."

He gave us a wide smile. "That makes no difference, my child. We're all his children in the eyes of God, though Jesus is his only true son."

I wasn't certain I liked that notion. We were children of gods ourselves. How could we worship the child of another God?

But we shouldn't be rude to our guest. He was pleasant, knowledgeable, and told good stories. He might become a colleague, or even a friend.

It had been a while since we had a true friend other than Mochán. My brothers kept him busy with questions well into the night, but I grew weary and headed to bed. I fell asleep to the sound of his deep, rolling laugh as the firelight flickered into the velvet night sky.

In my dreams, trees snatched me from the sky, holding me still so Aoife's spirit could enter my soul, to steal away my identity.

I must have cried out, for Mochán woke me. "Peace, my love. Peace. I'm here and you're safe."

Chapter Twenty-One

In the 900th winter of our curse (450 CE) 2 years later

One by one, we marked the days on the cave wall. Each day lasted forever, now that we were so close. I fiddled with my garden so much that many of the plants wilted from the surplus of attention.

We busied ourselves with tasks so the time would fly by, but I caught myself checking the sun to judge its progress. Each evening we celebrated as another day gone, another day closer to the curse's end.

With each sunset, I suffered both dread and hope, as I still wasn't certain Mochán would love the real me.

Three days before the end of our curse, our last students arrived for lessons. They knew the end was coming, and brought us lovely spring flowers, but each wore a pout.

Tianna asked, "Will you come visit us once you're human again?"

I didn't correct her calling us human but laid a wing across her shoulders. "If we can. But we'll look different from what we are now. You won't be frightened of us, will you?"

She shook her head so fast her hair whipped her face. "I promise, I won't be afraid! What will you look like?"

For a horrible moment, I couldn't recall anything from before the transformation. My mind froze with vague memories. Panicked, I glanced at Aed.

"My sister has bright reddish-blond hair, freckles and long legs. Something like your older sister."

I'd miss Tianna and the others. We'd taught so many now, hundreds of young minds instructed in the ancient legends.

Hawlen would have been proud. I suppressed a sob at her memory. Perhaps our work made up for my part in Stawn and Niamh's deaths.

At least I tried to atone for my interference, something Aoife Rua had never done.

I took a sip of water to clear it my throat. "Our last lesson today. Is everyone ready? I shall tell of the final battle of Tailtinn, the battle that heralded the end of the Tuatha Dé Dannan in the world above the hills."

I woke before dawn, my wings twitching and my skin itching, more than ready for the curse to be over.

When would it break? As the sun rose? At midday? Or would we have until sunset? As the wind howled outside, I listened for mad laughter. Would she show up and ruin this?

Fiachra stirred and we crept out into the false dawn to stare at the twinkling stars. "What's the first thing you'll do when the curse is broken, Nuala?"

I'd dreamed so often of this day and what might come afterward. Images muddled together with vague hopes and dreams involving Mochán and a darkened room. But I couldn't share these with my little brother, no matter how old he was.

"I want to run. Up and down the hills, on real legs, feeling green grass with my skin, and rolling back down. I miss that so much. What about you, Fiachra?"

"Swim."

I laughed. "Nine hundred winters as a water bird and you want to *swim?*"

He spoke in an even tone. "Swim without being a swan, underwater, using my arms and legs."

"Fair enough. When will it be, do you think?"

He shrugged. "I'm betting on when she set the original curse, so mid-morning."

"I'm thinking not until the bell rings, whenever that may be. Caomhóg said it rang every hour, but it's too far away to hear."

He gave a nod. "If we haven't changed by noon, we should go to the priest's palace."

Conn joined us in the rising dawn. He shook his head. "Caomhóg calls it a monastery. They're monks. We'll just have to push through the curse-limit pain."

Fiachra rolled his eyes. "Whatever they're called, we probably have to be close enough to hear the bell."

I nodded. "Mochán confirmed the wedding took place last week, so the *tiarna* of the north and the *banríon* of the south are married. All we can do is wait now."

Fiachra kicked at the grass. "I hate the waiting."

The first light of dawn broke over the horizon. Rays of peach and lavender spread into the indigo sky, chasing away sparkling stars. Birds heralded dawn's arrival with a bursting song of joy.

We cooked our morning meal in silence, each with our own thoughts and hopes.

Dawn came and went without a change. The hour of our curse came closer and then passed. As noon approached, dark doubt crept into my hope. Nothing happened as the sun reached its zenith.

Fiachra poked at his noon meal. "It's time to fly to the palace."

Conn corrected him. "Monastery."

Snapping at his twin, Fiachra said, "No one cares, Conn. Palace, Monastery, Temple, whatever you call it. It's where they ring the bell."

I chided him, "Fiachra, no need to be rude. Finish your meal, and we'll fly there. It should only take an hour, but we'll have to fly through the pain."

He shoved aside the remnants of his morning meal. "Great. Let's go."

Aed cocked his head at Fiachra. "What's wrong with you, Fiachra?"

"I'm tired of being a swan. I'm tired of sitting around and waiting for something to happen. I want to *do* something and get it over with. If that means I die from pain trying to break it, then so be it!"

Aed shrugged. "He has a point. We won't know if we don't try."

"Very well. Everyone, pack what you wish to keep. We won't come back here. Mochán, will you meet us there?" He'd borrowed a horse from a local farmer, so he mounted the beast and nodded.

We left most of our things behind. I kept some treasured items from Father or Tadhg. We kept our silver chains and the scraps of Dervla's ribbons, even though their magic had long since faded. My most treasured possessions were the carvings Conn had made.

Soon, there was nothing left I wanted.

When I emerged from the cave, Fiachra was hopping from anticipation. "Is everyone ready?"

Conn glanced at the sky. "Are we sure we ought to fly? What if we change while we're in the sky?"

Fiachra rolled his eyes. "There's no bell ringing yet. We'll be fine."

Without another word, Fiachra sprang into the air and flew toward the west, toward the island of *Inis Gluaire*. Conn followed close behind, while Aed and I brought up the rear.

The land grew rockier, with fewer farms and gentle rolling hills and more bare rock. We passed over the small inlet, over green grass, and cultivated gardens. The pain grew horrible, but I pushed through it.

The monks' buildings came into sight. A thin tower surrounded by rounded stone huts, shaped like beehives. Each one was large enough for a man to live in, but not much else.

A few larger ones must be meeting places or a feast hall. They did not appear comfortable, but after my winters in a cave, I wasn't fussy.

As we landed, Caomhóg emerged from one with open arms. "You came! I'm so happy! Come, let me take your burdens from you. I'll show you around our humble home. Is Mochán on his way?" He glanced around, as if he had overlooked the ollamh.

I gritted my teeth against the curse-pain. "He's following on horseback. Today's the day our curse is to end, you see."

"Oh, of course! And you came to hear the bell. We just rang it, so you must wait another hour, I'm afraid. In the meantime, I shall introduce you to some of my brethren."

Aed held his head between his wings. "Can't they ring it again now? It hurts, Nuala!"

"Shh, Aed. Be polite. It's a ritual bell. One doesn't perform rituals casually."

Other monks were poking their heads out of their huts.

An older man with an impressive beard and a fringe of gray hair approached. "Caomhóg? What have you brought upon our community?"

He spoke in a clipped tone as his eyes shifted to each of us, but did not speak to us directly.

"Father Bernardo, please, let me introduce my friends."

The older man's eyes grew wide. "Friends? They're swans!"

"They're *friends*. An evil curse was placed on them, transforming them into swans. They've come to break the curse."

"Curse?" Father Bernardo backed away from us, holding up a wooden icon in the shape of a cross he wore around his neck. Caomhóg wore a similar one. I wanted to examine it, but the man backed away from me.

"As I said, they've been cursed, and we hope to remove the curse. Surely, you can't be against such a divine purpose, Father?"

Father Bernardo backed away, muttering in an odd language, staccato and angular.

Other monks emerged from their homes. Some joined him in his muttering, but a few stood to the side, wearing concerned expressions.

Soon, seven monks arrayed against us in a semi-circle, with only Caomhóg on our side and a few noncommittal monks watching.

The head monk stepped forward and raised both hands into the air, addressing the sky. "Begone, demons! I abjure thee to leave our fair island."

My memory flashed to the man with the wooden cross, back hundreds of winters before, who had encouraged a mob to attack us, calling us devils, and I couldn't suppress a shiver.

Fiachra rolled his eyes. "Oh, no, not that again!"

Caomhóg jumped in front of us. "No! Father, please, I beg of you. They need our help."

"We can't help demons, Brother Caomhóg. If you would join them, then begone yourself from our community."

Caomhóg crossed his arms, refusing to budge. "They aren't demons, Father, they're just like us. A demon cursed them, and it's time for the curse to be over."

The older man halted his incantations and stared at us. "Are they Christians?"

Caomhóg glanced back at us. "No, no they're not. They were born long ago, before Our Lord's lifetime. They've been suffering under this curse for over nine hundred years."

Father Bernardo's eyes widened, and he began shouting his incantations. The other monks joined him.

Caomhóg held up his hands. "Wait! What if they become Christian?"

Everyone grew silent.

Become Christian? To believe in just one God, their dead God, sacrificed on a cross?

I glanced at Aed, but he only shrugged. Then Conn nodded. "If it helps us break the curse, I'm willing. Fiachra?"

Fiachra shrugged. "Absolutely. Let's do so and be done with it."

My own beliefs roiled in my mind, but Conn had a point. We needed to break the curse, and if this was the price, I was willing to pay it.

I turned to Caomhóg. "We agree to become Christian. What must we do?"

The change in the monks was incredible. We transformed from dangerous demons to supplicants, and they fawned over us like baby lambs.

The monks washed, petted, and primped us. They brought us to the fountain for our initiation. I understood that every belief had ritual, but all this ceremony tested my patience. The curse-limit still throbbed, and I wanted them to get it over with.

Caomhóg explained. "First, we must baptize you. It's a washing of regeneration and renewal by the Holy Ghost. We dunk you in water three times. Each time, you declare your devotion and obedience to God the Father Almighty. It isn't a painful process, trust me."

I tried hard to trust him but remembered the fanatic fear in the Father's eyes. It reminded me of Aoife's madness.

Oh, sweet Danu, what if she'd found another host? I glanced at the older man, but he stood calm now. No madness lingered in his gaze. I took a deep breath to calm my panic.

First, Father Bernardo blessed the water then spoke his prayer.

Father, you give us Grace through sacramental signs,

Which tell us o' the wonders of Your unseen power

In Baptism, we use Your gift of water,

Which You have made a rich symbol

Of the Grace You give us in his sacrament.

At the very dawn of creation,

Your Spirit breathed on the waters,

Making them the wellspring of all holiness.

No human possessed by Aoife could have said such words. He confirmed the sacred nature of the earth and the water. Perhaps this new God was not so different from our own gods, after all.

Then, a monk told a story about the children of Abraham crossing the sea. There was a great deal more, but his voice droned on. I tuned out his words and concentrated on blocking my pain.

Most of the monks were young men, unshaven and dressed in brown robes with simple sandals. No women or children, and I thought that strange, as I recalled Mochán speaking of female devotees of the new God.

A whistling wind rose and screamed through the clearing, cold and biting. It whipped the monks' robes and tugged at our feathers. I recognized the mad laughter on the wind at once. Aoife Rua wasn't in the older priest, but she *was* in the wind.

How long had she been waiting for this moment? We hadn't seen her since that horrible fight to be free of the possessed *banríon*.

Mochán galloped up and leapt from the horse's back. He rushed to us, enfolding me in his arms. "Are you hurt?"

I shook my head and hugged him tight.

Caomhóg hollered and pointed into the air. "Do you hear that laughter? That's the demon that cursed them! Banish her! Call upon the Lord God himself to rid the world of her evil once and for all!"

The monks chanted more loudly, shouting their exhortations. They called down the might and power of their God in that ponderous language.

Their magic formed a cone of protection around us. Aoife Rua's spirit circled the barrier, attacking the cone, poking and prodding.

Mochán sang in our own language, calling upon the Morrigan to protect her own, her People. The cone pulsed and glowed brighter. Red sparks now wove into the white.

Aoife Rua's spirit hissed and jumped back. Perhaps no one god could save us, but a partnership of the old gods and the new might work.

Father Bernardo raised his hands and shouted, pointing both hands toward the demon. His manifestation of power formed an arrow of shining green light. He launched this mystical weapon at her, and it struck true.

She screeched and arched her back, her form elongating and bending until she surrounded the cone. The priest formed another arrow and shot again.

I couldn't let him battle her alone. I formed my own magical dart, blue light in contrast to his. I hit Aoife Rua and she screeched again.

A shower of sparks rained down and scattered in the wind. Suddenly, all sound ceased. The monks stopped chanting, the wind stopped blowing, and the laughter ceased.

I glanced around but couldn't hear her mad laughter. Had we banished her at long last? Their God must have true power, even if they don't consider it magic.

The pain returned, but weaker than before. That alone gave me some hope.

Father Bernardo nodded to the other monks. "Resume the ritual."

One monk left as we received our third dunking. Shortly afterward, the bell rung, the mellow tones reverberated through the very earth.

Three times, it chimed. Three times, the sound shook my bones. Three times, the tones echoed across the clearing, resonating in my feet.

My feet. Yes, they were indeed feet, with toes rather than webbing. I wiggled them in delight, dirty as they were. I held out my wings, but now I had legs and arms and fingers. Oh, lovely fingers!

I stretched my arms, curled my hand into a fist and out again. The white feathers had vanished, and I stood in my glorious bare skin. I wanted to caress every part of myself. I touched my head, and I had real hair, still reddish-blond. Tangled and wet, but we'd just been dunked in water several times.

Gasps of horror drew my attention from my transformation. They were hiding their eyes and some ran toward their huts. I looked down and realized I stood naked. Of course, I'd been wearing nothing but my silver chain as a swan. Now, this chain dug tight around my neck, and I yanked it off, breaking the delicate links.

A monk returned from his hut, handing me a brown woolen robe, and I gratefully donned it. Others brought similar garments to my brothers.

Each of them looked just as I remembered. Aed stood lanky and tall, gawky like a colt. Fiachra and Conn were still children, ten winters old.

Conn looked confused, patting his legs and torso as if to verify they were real. Fiachra jumped up and down, whooping with delight.

We each smiled and hugged in one big circle. Caomhóg clapped with delight at the success of the baptism. I figured it was the bell, but I only cared that the curse was finally broken, not how.

We were free at last. After nine hundred winters of servitude, we'd escaped our bindings and were free to be ourselves. No more pain, no more slavery to the curse. More than a transformation, this was a revelation. It was life. It was necessary.

My heart filled with joy and delight. I wanted to run. I wanted to dance. I wanted to sing. I sang a song of sweet, wordless pleasure. Elation colored my voice, and my brothers joined me.

The monks who'd scattered now crept back to listen to our song. Soon, we had an enraptured audience. My brothers and I danced as we sang, holding hands with Mochán and weaving in and out as we had before the transformation, in twining patterns. Some monks joined our dance, including Caomhóg.

Father Bernardo no longer seemed as intimidating. He smiled more like a favorite uncle, now, watching his young relatives indulge their joy of youth.

Chapter Twenty-Two

In the 1st winter of our freedom (450 CE)

That first day exhausted me. Not only did we transform, we danced and ran, sang and shouted. I used muscles I hadn't used in nine hundred winters. I ran up and down the wildflower-laden hills, despite my legs wobbling a bit. Then I tumbled down and couldn't stop laughing.

When I reached the bottom, Mochán held me in his arms. "I can't believe you're actually here. You're more beautiful than I'd imagined, my sweet Nuala." He bowed over my hand and kissed it. I hadn't forgotten how to blush, and my skin tingled.

Fiachra went swimming in the sea. Aed spun around with his arms out, laughing like a madman. Conn traced the exquisite stone carvings on the monk's cross with his fingers, stunned and amazed that he now had the dexterity to recreate such beauty.

The monks held a sumptuous feast that evening, in our honor as new Christians.

I wanted to beg off. While I was grateful to this new God for his help, in my heart, I still believed in the old gods. But I didn't want to insult our hosts with my reservations, and Mochán said I should go, so I went.

Father Bernardo joined us with a huge smile. "And who is this young man? Another supplicant to Our Lord?"

The ollamh turned to Father Bernardo and bowed. "My host, I'm afraid I cannot in good conscience vow myself to your God, as I've already given my sacred word to another. I come with great thanks to him and all his mighty power has wrought for my dear friends."

The Father narrowed his eyes but nodded. "You must join us in our celebration feast. What is your name, young man, and what is your trade?"

"I am Mochán, my host. I am an ollamh."

One monk dropped a wooden mug, the clatter loud in the sudden silence.

Father Bernardo and Mochán stared at each other for several long moments, but then the priest nodded. "Be welcome as a guest to our house, ollamh."

Mochán gave a respectful bow. "Thank you, my host. I am honored by your welcome."

I let out my breath. I hadn't anticipated the clash but was relieved it wasn't worse.

Fiachra handed me a mug. "This bitter ale they make is tasty. Have you tried it yet?"

I stared at my brother. He'd grown three inches since that afternoon. Searching for Conn, I saw he'd also matured. Aed looked broader through the shoulders.

Mochán put a hand on my shoulder. "Nuala? What's wrong? You've gone pale. Sit, have something to eat. You must be overwrought from all the excitement."

My head spun with possibilities. Of course, that was one possibility we'd discussed. It had only been a few hours and Fiachra and Conn had obviously aged several winters.

One hour for every winter? Even if I assumed a full Tuatha Dé Dannan lifespan, that meant only three or four hundred hours. At most, we had a fortnight to live a lifetime.

My blood chilled and I wanted to cry. How could I tell my brothers? Or Mochán? Aoife Rua had managed a last laugh. Curse her and her machinations.

I had to leave. It was beyond rude to burst into tears at a feast held in my honor. I tore myself from Mochán's anxious grasp and escaped into the cool evening air.

I ran to the shore of the lough and gazed into the still waters. My reflection, an image I'd tried for so many winters to recall, gazed back in the moonlight.

I looked older, more like Mother when she died. Not with her face contorted in the agony of childbirth, but before, when she laughed. A face of gladness, a face of youth.

However, mine was no longer the face of a young maiden. I was but twenty winters when Aoife cursed me, and I no longer looked twenty.

Mochán caught up with me. "My *bantiarna*, whatever is the matter? What can I do to help?"

I took several deep breaths before I could answer. "We're aging. Fast. Fiachra and Conn have aged winters in mere hours. At this rate, we won't have much time left."

I couldn't tell if he paled in the scant light, but he closed his eyes for several long moments.

When he opened them, they were full of empathy and sadness. "I think you're right. I noticed but didn't wish to frighten you."

"What can we do, Mochán? We've waited so long for a real life. I can't believe the gods would just snatch it away from us!"

He grasped my hand and gave it a squeeze. Together, we gazed at the water of the lough. "We might ask the gods to help?"

I scowled. "They didn't even have the power to break the curse, or if they did, were unwilling to use it. The Morrigan passed on knowledge to Strawn, but his spells failed."

"What about this new God? Didn't he help break the curse? He might be willing to try."

I shrugged and started pacing along the shore. "I don't honestly know. Destroying Aoife Rua? Yes, I'm sure he helped with that. But the curse broke when the bell tolled, so maybe he didn't help at all."

"Can it hurt to ask?"

I gave him a sad smile. "I suppose it can't hurt to ask either our gods or the Christian God."

"I get the impression that Father Bernardo doesn't care for the competition."

I let out a snort and glanced toward the feast hall. "He's convinced that anything other than his God is a demon."

He hugged me and it was marvelous. The warmth of his body along mine was a tonic, and my head spun. Not in fear or terror, but in love. I didn't want to go organize a prayer or summon a God to beg for help. I wanted to pull Mochán into the sweet grass, caress him all over with my new body, and to feel his upon mine.

Mochán bent his head to kiss me. His lips were so soft against mine, I almost sobbed.

Fiachra rushed out and yelled, "Nuala! Nuala are you out here?"

Abashed, we broke apart. "Over here, Fiachra." In a whisper, I said, "Later, my love."

"Nuala, we're getting older, fast!"

I gripped Mochán's hand, and we exchanged a glance. "I know, sweetling. I know. We've already formed a plan."

Mochán returned to his grove to ask the Filí for help. In the meantime, Caomhóg organized the monks for the same.

As we gathered to enter their religious building, Conn wrinkled his nose. "What are they doing? It stinks."

I peered at the censer Father Bernardo carried around the chapel. "He called it incense. It's not so different from the ritual fire we're used to, Conn. We burned sacred herbs when honoring the gods."

"But ours smell good, like sage and pine and peat. This smells like sweet garbage."

I muffled a chuckle. "Fair enough. They call it frankincense and it's one of their sacred herbs. But you know better than to insult another's beliefs."

The monks chanted and I bowed my head the way Caomhóg did. My robe itched on my new skin, but I resisted the urge to scratch. Aed had no such inhibitions and squirmed beside me on the bench.

I nudged him and he stopped, only to start again when he forgot. I counted myself lucky that Fiachra didn't do the same. He looked more frightened than any of us at the realization that we were aging.

Fiachra had believed he'd live a long, full life. I'd believed the same, but some pessimistic part of my soul knew better than to believe in happily ever after.

We'd never done a thing to warrant such punishment. Aoife had stolen our lives and dangled hope for nine hundred winters. Then, that hope was cruelly snatched away, a curse worthy of Aoife Rua and her twisted, mad paranoia.

I thought of Mother and Father, both now in *Tír na nÓg*. Were they watching the events as they unfolded? Could they offer prayers to the gods? If not, we'd be with them soon. In a fortnight.

A single tear fell, splashing heavy on my clasped hands.

The monks chanted for hours. I didn't understand what they sang, but Caomhóg said they were asking for a miracle, an intervention in the evil curse. They were begging their God to grant us a normal life.

What is a normal life? To marry, to fight wars, to raise children, to feast, to sing? What gave us a satisfied death? To live for a cause? To die for a reason?

We'd done good work across our lives. We'd taught hundreds of children, enriched lives with stories, tales, and histories. We'd kept accounts of the Tuatha Dé Dannan alive so they might continue after we passed. Chronicles of our battles, loves and deaths would stay when we died.

Fiachra and Conn grew into adults in a few days, tall and lean and with broad shoulders. Aed grew a full beard and mustache and was inordinately proud of his new facial hair.

My body filled out with curves. My hips didn't work the way I remembered, so my gait was clumsy.

We were sitting by the lough as the orange moon rose on the horizon, skipping stones across the surface.

Mochán returned that evening, with word from the Filíd Council. "I'm afraid there's nothing they can do."

I gasped. "They're not even going to try?"

He pressed his lips together. "They *did* try. They called to the gods, to those who had passed before, even to the spirits of the ravens. The only answer they received was that it couldn't be changed."

Deflated, I sat on the ground, head in my hands.

"So that's it, then. We've no more options left." My throat burned with unshed tears. I covered my face and sobbed as Mochán knelt beside me.

He hugged my shoulders. "We have one option left, but not for a longer life. A fuller life, perhaps."

I glanced up, my brow furrowed.

He took both his hands in mine, kissing the knuckles. "Come, be with me tonight and every night you're alive, my love. My *bantiarna*. I can't make your life longer, but I can make what you have full of love and pleasure. You've spent thousands of seasons with your brothers and teaching others. May I have your remaining days to myself?"

It's exactly what I wanted, but it meant we were giving up. Sobs burst forth and I couldn't stop them.

"Nuala, please tell me you aren't horrified by the idea? I thought you felt the same?"

Through my tears, I said, "I do, oh, Mochán, I do. I want nothing more. But that's the end of fighting. We've been striving for almost a thousand winters to beat this curse. To admit now that we have no chance…"

He sat beside me. "I know, I know. It seems like we ought to do something. But we are. We're taking what we have and making it beautiful. Can we do that?"

"We can do that. But…" A glimmer of an idea formed in my mind, "but what if we *can* do more? What if we take the magic we've learned and try to heal the curse?"

He furrowed his brow, pulling back. "Heal the curse? But it's already broken, isn't it?"

I waved my hand. "That's not quite what I meant. But in all those years with Porrig, and the magic that Stawn learned from the Morrigan, there must be something in all that which I could use now. I just have to figure out what."

"You know I'll help any way I can."

We exchanged no more words that night. Instead, Mochán showed me a new delight, a new joy in being human. And it was the sweetest night in my thousand winters, a night I would have waited a thousand more to have.

In the morning, I sought out my brothers.

Aed was stuffing fried bread into his mouth. "Did Mochán come back last night?"

I sat next to him, trying hard to keep the tears from my voice. "He comes with no great news. We have perhaps a fortnight left of our lives."

Aed, Fiachra, and Conn exchanged glances. "We figured that out for ourselves."

I gave a nod of approval. "I'm glad to know your observation skills are still strong. Now, I have a plan to fight this. Are you willing to try?"

They exchanged another glance and nodded as one.

I placed my hands on my hips. "We need to start charging stones, the way Porrig did, for a sink for our powers, right? Fiachra, do you remember how he did that? I know he showed you some of the finer points."

Fiachra gave a confused nod. "Sure, but Nuala, I don't want to go back to being a child. I *like* finally being an adult."

I gritted my teeth. "We're just trying to halt the aging, not reverse it. Now, will you help?"

His voice sounded resigned. "I'll help."

"Great. Now, Conn, can you fashion some charms like Stawn used in his rituals?"

We created a ritual space, crafted our talismans, and charged the stones. After five days of intense work, with Mochán and Caomhóg's eager assistance, we'd done everything we could to prepare.

Mochán joined us in the center of the ritual circle, like Porrig had. But while the older Filíd had been full of confidence, Mochán was taking his cues from me.

Caomhóg and several other curious monks watched from a safe distance as we chanted to raise power.

Porrig had drawn power from the earth, so I did the same. Stawn wove that power into a stronger thread, and I copied that, as well.

A blue glow rose from the center of our circle, pulsing and beating like a living heart. The power washed through us in several waves of healing, sweet as honey.

Then the power slipped away, like a rope wet with seawater, slithering out of my grip. I tried to grasp it but couldn't keep hold of the magic.

I cried out and felt someone behind me. A quick Caomhóg and two of his monks joined our circle, taking our hands.

We renewed our chant and the blue glowed more strongly, shining like a beacon.

More monks joined the ritual, making nine of us, a sacred number in many traditions. Our third chant ended with a crystal explosion, blue shards of light shattering out from the center.

In the ensuing silence, I cracked one eye open and glanced around at the others. "Did it work?"

Fiachra rolled his eyes. "If you can't tell, how do you think we can? We'll only know if we don't keep getting older, right?"

I exchanged a glance with Mochán, but he just shrugged. Aed let out a chuckle, but it held a tinge of desperation.

Fiachra jumped up. "Great! I'm off to find a willing lass, then. Maybe more than one. Conn, Aed, come join me? Nuala has hers. Let's make the most of what we may or may not have."

I couldn't tell if I wanted to laugh or cry. After I thanked the monks for helping us, and they went home, I sought out Mochán and buried my frustration in his arms.

Conn and Fiachra would be the easiest to see any aging in. But they didn't seem to grow older over the next few days. I didn't feel any older in Mochán's arms each night and could still run up and down the hills with wild abandon.

A few days later, we decided the ritual had worked. A wave of relief swept over us all, and we toasted to our success.

I didn't see much of my brothers after that, as they went off to live their lives. My brothers found willing girls, and I glimpsed them at times in the nearby village. In fact, Fiachra found several girls. My brothers grew into handsome men.

I gave most of my time to Mochán. At first, it was like being newlywed, though we never actually held a ceremony.

Moons passed, then seasons, and then winters. I finally believed I'd actually halted the curse, that horrific aging once we had stopped being swans.

After a few winters, Mochán and I welcomed twin girls into the world, and I named them Finna and Fainche. They were my delight, and their smiles made everything we'd endured, every century we'd waited, all that much sweeter.

I still taught tales to Gael children. Aed found a woman to love, and they settled on a nearby farm. Fiachra wandered with the Fianna warriors, up and down the coast each summer, finding battle and glory. Conn spent most of his time with the remaining Filíd or cloistered with the Christians, learning new ideas, happier than ever. He even learned to read their writing.

The seasons passed and I was happy.

In the 10th winter of our freedom (460 CE) 10 years later

However, as my girls reached their tenth winter, I felt the cold winter of age upon me. That's when I realized that I had only delayed our fate.

At least I'd bought us some time to enjoy our lives as humans. It may not have been what we wished for, but it was better than what we'd feared.

In another season, my skin grew wrinkled, and my bones ached. My red-blond hair faded to peach and thinned. Soon, my eyes grew rheumy.

I pushed Mochán's hand away from me one night. "How can you stand to hold me now? I'm old and disgusting."

"You are my love, my *bantiarna*, and I shall never shrink from you. I treasure your wrinkles as much as I treasure your freckles. How can you believe otherwise?"

I snorted. "I'm no longer young and beautiful. I'm a crone and ready to die."

He took both my hands and kissed my knuckles. "You're still my beloved and will be until we fade to dust. No matter where you go, I shall find you when I die."

I turned away from him, but he clutched me in his arms. I kissed him, despite my bones aching in the chilly night.

When at last the day came when I couldn't rise from my bed, Mochán carried me to the lough. Caomhóg had erected a shelter for our final days, that we might spend it together, as we'd lived our lives.

Aed came, as did Conn. Fiachra only came back the very last day, when I was barely hanging on to the last shred of life. Each of us looked like a shadow of our former selves, wasted husks of skin and bone, ready to crumble.

With tears in their eyes, Caomhóg, monks, and Filíd alike gathered in a strange vigil, along with our neighbors.

Mochán addressed us all. "And now, we come to bid farewell to these four royal children. Fionnuala, Aed, Fiachra, and Conn, children of Lir and Aobh Bán. Children of the Tuatha Dé Dannan, those who dwelt upon these emerald shores long before we Gaels arrived. We honor them and their efforts to pass on the knowledge of their race. Come, each of you, and offer your gifts."

One by one, our visitors paraded past us. Some gave a kiss, others a prayer. Tianna, one of our last students, offered a spring rose, fresh from the garden, delicate shades of peach and cream.

My voice wavered. "Thank you, sweet child."

She gave me a deep bow. "I'm glad I saw you as a human, *Bantiarna* Fionnuala."

"I'm simply Nuala, my dear. Will you retell our stories and keep us alive?"

She nodded as tears dripped down her cheeks.

When Mochán stepped up, he spoke in a gentle tone. "I bring you my love, now and forever. I shall always remember you, my *bantiarna.* History will never forget you. This I vow."

Though my voice wavered, I sang a poignant song, pouring into my tune the frustrations over lives lost, chances missed, and love gone. My brothers joined and we sang our swan song of terrible sorrow.

My self faded with my love's declaration. Aed's eyes shut and Fiachra coughed. Conn lay still on his pallet.

I grew so cold. I wrapped my arms around my body for warmth, but now I had no arms.

Panicked, I thought I turned into a swan again. My nightmares came back to haunt me. No, I had no wings either. I had nothing. I floated in the air.

I glanced down and stared at my body, wrinkled and ancient, upon the pallet. My brothers, with hair white and faded, even Aed's full, long beard, lay next to me. Mochán wept over my empty body, holding my hand to his heart.

"No, Mochán, don't weep!" But he couldn't hear me.

I thought back to the men I had loved. Tadhg, my first love. Áedammair, who might have been my husband if Father hadn't refused him. And dear Mochán who had shared his joy with me for so many seasons.

I wanted us to be burned, as our mother had been, but the monks didn't believe in that. Instead, they buried us together, at our request, in an even more ancient tradition. Standing vertical, we were placed in a square, each of us facing outward. Throughout eternity, we'd be there for each other. We'd never be parted.

Satisfied, I flew into the sky and my brothers danced as bright sparks beside me. We whirled through the sky and the people below gasped at four shooting stars.

Two more sparks joined us, and my heart leapt to see both Mother and Father. Together, we raced across the glimmering night sky, reunited for eternity. We swooped down to say one last farewell to our friends and continued on to *Tír na nÓg*, the Land of Youth.

When the magical secrets of The Emerald Isle beckon, will she survive answering the call?

Pittsburgh, 1846. Valentia McDowell wishes she could rest. Plagued by nightmares of her grandmother's mysterious brooch lost in Ireland, the well-off woman grows more troubled when a fire ravages her family's business. But as she buries herself in the rebuilding efforts, she can't shake the sense that a powerful inheritance awaits her across the ocean, if she can weather the treacherous journey.

Can Valentia uphold a destiny she doesn't yet understand without losing everyone she loves?

Legacy of Hunger is the sweeping first book in The Druid's Brooch historical fantasy series. If you like compelling female characters, immersive authenticity, and a dash of magic, then you'll love Christy Nicholas's transatlantic quest.

Get **Legacy of Hunger** to trace a family treasure today!

Thank You!

Thank you so much for enjoying The Enchanted Swans. If you've enjoyed the story, please consider leaving a review_so other readers can discover Nuala, Aed, Fiachra, and Conn's adventures!

If you would like to get updates, sneak previews, sales, and FREE CONTENT, please sign up for my newsletter at www.GreenDragonArtist.com/about/newsletter-2/

Other Books by This Author

**See all the books available
through Green Dragon Publishing at
http://www.greendragonartist.com/books**

Historical Note

Dear Readers:

As you close the pages of The Enchanted Swans, the ethereal world of ancient enchantment may leave you wondering—how much of this tale is rooted in reality, and how much is spun from the threads of folklore? Let's untangle the historical web behind this captivating retelling of The Children of Lir.

While the enchanting realm of pre-Celtic Ireland serves as the backdrop for Fionnuala's journey, the specifics of her story diverge from the annals of history. Many of the details of her life before the curse was based on my study of Bronze Age culture, as legend has the Tuatha dé Danann unable to bear iron, and would logically prefer to work with bronze.

Roundhouses were the standard form of housing, built from either stone or wattle and daub, then topped with a conical roof, probably built of thatch. Hillforts might have two or three of these roundhouses, but a royal center, like the one Fionnuala grew up in, might have a dozen or more, some of them large enough to host feasts.

Transportation in the late Bronze Age included two-wheeled chariots, as well as wooden carts pulled by horses or oxen. Horses were used in the start of the Bronze age and then, by about 1000 BCE, they started using carts with wheels. Some of these are described in the ancient lore, as ridden by heroes to battle.

When writing this story, I searched back to get as close to the original tale as I could. However, since I am not conversant in Old Irish, I had to rely on translations into English. And, despite hours of research, I could not find a non-Christian ending. Current scholarship believes the tale to have originated sometime in the 14th century CE, perhaps by someone in north-west Connacht. It's sometimes thought to be an allegory of the Christianization of pagan Ireland. The Children of Lir describes the last of the Tuatha Dé Dannan to live above the land and four children who ran afoul of jealousy and were cursed with evil magic. It is a much-beloved tale of the Irish people, as they equate the children's long servitude with that of their own bondage under the English crown and their eventual emergence from that oppression.

A collection of myths known as the Book of Invasions, or *Lebor Gabála Érenn*, describe the invasion of Ireland by six different immigrant groups: the people of Cessair, the Parthalónians, the Nemedians, the Fir Bolg, the Tuatha Dé Danann, and the Milesians. It describes, among other groups, Bronze Age people who lived on the land before the Milesians (Celts) migrated from northern Spain to Ireland's emerald shores. These people, the Tuatha Dé Dannan, have also been called the Fair Folk, the Gentry, or simply the Fairies.

While archaeological discoveries confirm that people definitely settled in Ireland before the Milesians, who arrived around 500 BCE, we know little of their culture, language, or traditions. Many Neolithic structures were built around 5,000 years ago (around 3,000 BCE), such as the singularly impressive Newgrange. Evidence of roundhouses, ogham stones and other fascinating tidbits survive to the modern age, offering tantalizing glimpses into this pre-historic world.

Since the written word only became fashionable in Ireland with the arrival of Christian monks around 400 CE, much of the oral ancient lore became lost in the mists of time.

One further note on dates. We don't know what dating system the Tuatha Dé Dannan would have used. For the convenience of my readers, I am therefore using the Common Era timeline used by most of the western world today. The story begins in 460 BCE, approximately 2,500 years ago.

Pronunciation Guide

NAMES
Áedammair – AWD-uh-mare
Aed - Ayd
Aed Mór – Ayd Moor
Aillbha – AL-vuh
Aobh Bán – Eve Bawn
Aoife Rua – EE-fuh ROO-uh
Banbha – BAN-vuh
Bé Chuille – BAY Khuill-eh
Bilé – BI-lee
Bodb Dearg – BOH derg
Cailín – Kaw-LEEN
Caomhóg – KEEV-owg
Cliach – KLEE-ikh
Deoch – DEE-uhk
Dian Cécht – DEE-an Keckt
Donnchadh – DUN-chuh
Ériu – EYHR-ooh
Fiachra – FEE-kruh
Fionn MacCumhall – FINN Muh Cool
Fionnuala – Finn-OOL-uh
Fir Bolg – FEAR bol-uhg
Fomhóire – Fom-OR-eh
Illbreach – ILL-brehk
Lasairfhiona – LASS-ar-een-uh
Macha – MAHK-uh Midhir – MID-ear
Mochán – MUH-kawn
Niamh – NEEV Nuada
Parthalón – PAR-tho-lawn
Saoirse – SEER-shuh
Scáthach – SKAT-huk
Scuida – SKWEE-duh
Tadhg – Tyg
Tuatha Dé Dannan – TOO-ah day DAN-in (People of the Goddess Danu, The Fairy Folk)

PLACES

Carraig na Rón – CARE-ig na Rown (Rock of the Seals)
Dun Sgathaich – Doon Skath-ihg
Emhain Macha – EH-vin MAKH-uh (Navan Fort)
Uisneach – ISH-nuhk
Inis Gluaire—IN-ish GLOO-reh
Irrus Domnann – ERR-us DOW-an
Lough Derravaragh – Lock DAR-uh-ver-uh
Saol Eile – Sail ELL-eh (Otherlife/Afterlife)
Sídhe ar Femuin – Shee ar FEHM-ihn
Sídhe Fionnachaidh – Shee FINN-ahk-eethe (Hill of the White Field)
Sruth na Maoile – Srooth nah Mwayl
Tailltin – TALL-chin
Tír na nÓg – Tear nuh NOHG (An otherworld, or Land of the Young)

OTHER

Ard-Rí – Ard-ree (High King)
Banríon – Bahn-REE-ahn (Queen)
Bantiarna – Bahn-tee-AR-nah (Lady or princess)
Filíd – FEE-lee (The Order of the Filíd, plural. Filí is singular)
Geas – Gesh (A curse or compulsion)
Iunula – EE-noo-la (A solid gold mantle worn over the shoulders)
Léine/léinte – LEYN-yuh (A tunic/tunics down to the knee)
Ollamh – OLL-av (An advanced Filíd)
Samhain – SOW-ehn (End of the Harvest Festival/New Year)
Tiarna – tee-AR-nah (King)

Dedication

As I grew up, my mother told me fairy tales. I suppose that's true of many mothers, but her efforts stayed with me all my life. I remember Water Babies and Flower Fairies, Hans Christian Andersen and many others. Tales of Irish swans being transformed were some of my earliest literary memories, and to that memory, I dedicate this book.

Thank you, Mom. Thank you for instilling in me a love of the wonderful, a passion for reading, and the appreciation of stories.

About the Author

Christy Nicholas writes under several pen names, including Rowan Dillon, CN Jackson, and Emeline Rhys. She's an author, artist, and accountant. After she failed to become an airline pilot, she quit her ceaseless pursuit of careers that began with the letter 'A' and decided to concentrate on her writing. Since she has Project Completion Compulsion, she is one of the few authors with no unfinished novels.

Christy has her hands in many crafts, including digital art, beaded jewelry, writing, and photography. In real life, she's a CPA, but having grown up with art all around her (her mother, grandmother, and great-grandmother are/were all artists), it sort of infected her, as it were. She wants to expose the incredible beauty in this world, hidden beneath the everyday grime of familiarity and habit, and share it with others. She uses characters out of time and places infused with magic and myth, writing magical realism stories in both historical fantasy and time travel flavors.

Social Media Links:
Blog: www.GreenDragonArtist.net
Website: www.GreenDragonArtist.com
Facebook: www.facebook.com/greendragonauthor
Instagram: www.instagram.com/greendragonartist9
TikTok: www.tiktok.com/@greendragonauthor

www.ingramcontent.com/pod-product-compliance
Lightning Source LLC
Chambersburg PA
CBHW052155160726
47990CB00015B/1795